Emily Forbes is an award-winning author of Medical Romance for Mills & Boon. She has written over 25 books and has twice been a finalist in the Australian Romantic Book of the Year Award, which she won in 2013 for her novel *Sydney Harbour Hospital: Bella's Wishlist*. You can get in touch with Emily at emilyforbes@internode.on.net, or visit her website at emily-forbesauthor.com.

Annie O'Neil spent most of her childhood with her leg draped over the family rocking chair and a book in her hand. Novels, baking, and writing too much teenage angst poetry ate up most of her youth. Now Annie splits her time between corralling her husband into helping her with their cows, baking, reading, barrel racing (not really!) and spending some very happy hours at her computer, writing.

FALLING FOR HIS BEST FRIEND

BY
EMILY FORBES

REUNITED WITH HER PARISIAN SURGEON

BY
ANNIE O'NEIL

MILLS & BOON

Published in Great Britain 2018
by Mills & Boon, an imprint of HarperCollins*Publishers*
1 London Bridge Street, London, SE1 9GF

Falling for His Best Friend © 2018 Emily Forbes

Reunited with Her Parisian Surgeon © 2018 Annie O'Neil

ISBN: 978-0-263-93335-2

MIX
Paper from
responsible sources
FSC® C007454

This book is produced from independently certified FSC™ paper
to ensure responsible forest management.
For more information visit www.harpercollins.co.uk/green.

Printed and bound in Spain
by CPI, Barcelona

FALLING FOR
HIS BEST FRIEND

BY
EMILY FORBES

MILLS & BOON

For Sheila.

Thank you for being a true champion
of Medical Romance. We couldn't do it without you!

We have had a long association now,
and I have enjoyed it all. I look forward to
many more years, and books, together.

With love and appreciation,

Emily

* * *

Kitty pushed open the door of the Manly Pier Hotel and walked into the pub. After their discussion—Kitty refused to think of it as an argument—Mike had gone out for his regular monthly dinner with his friends from his med school days, and Kitty was relieved that he'd had a prior engagement. She didn't want to continue their discussion all night, but she hadn't wanted to sit at home on her own either. She needed to see a friendly face and she knew she'd find one in the pub that was a favourite among the staff from the North Sydney Hospital and other Manly Beach locals.

The DJ was warming up the crowd. Thursday nights were popular and the place was already busy. She scanned the room.

The crowd was dressed casually but expensively. Kitty hadn't given her outfit a thought. She'd just needed to get out. She looked down at her clothes—jeans, an old T-shirt and canvas trainers. Luckily the dress code for women was never strict but at five feet four inches she felt like an untidy slip of a woman in a room full of glamourous shiny Amazons. She'd pulled her dark hair back into a messy ponytail, not even bothering to brush it, and she doubted any of the make-up she'd sparingly applied that morning was still clinging to her face but it was too late to worry about her looks now. Thankfully her friends and colleagues were unlikely to be done up to the nines. Anything smarter than hospital scrubs was deemed to be making an effort.

There were plenty of familiar faces in the pub and Kitty said hello to several people as she made her way through the room without pausing to chat for too long.

There was one face in particular she was looking for and she didn't want to waste time on other conversations. She wasn't in a particularly sociable mood.

She skimmed over the DJ and looked past him out onto the deck that stretched into the harbour. The Manly ferry was docking at the quay, its lighted windows bright against the twilight sky, and silhouetted against the darkening sky was the person she was looking for.

Joe Harkness.

His broad-shouldered, six-foot frame stood a head above the bevy of women who surrounded him—no surprises there. His short, brown hair was expertly groomed to give him the *I just stepped out of the shower* look and he was laughing at someone's comment. His blue eyes flashed as he laughed and the dimple in his chin only added to his appeal as the women eyed him adoringly. He had a beer in one hand and his other arm slung around the shoulders of one of the women. Again, no surprise. Her life may be a bit of a mess but she could always rely on Joe to be consistent. Happy, charming and gorgeous, he had a constant stream of women moving in and out of his life, there was never a shortage, and Kitty was grateful that he always seemed to have time for her. She didn't want to be one of a string of girlfriends, she wanted to be just what she was—his closest friend.

They'd been friends for almost ten years since meeting on their first day at nursing college. Kitty had been straight out of high school, Joe a couple of years older, having taken a gap year or two before starting university. They'd finished nursing together but had ultimately ended up going in different directions career-wise. She worked in the emergency department at the North Sydney Hospital and Joe had continued his studies and was now an intensive care paramedic. He was based at the ambulance station attached to the hospital, but even if they hadn't ended up in such close proximity Kitty knew they would still have remained friends. In her opinion, everyone needed a Joe in their life. Someone dependable and loyal. He understood her and he never judged her.

Kitty checked out the unfamiliar woman who was under Joe's arm and wondered who she was. A new girlfriend or just a friend? She hoped it was a new girl-friend. She didn't want Joe to have other female friends. Girlfriends never stayed in his life for long and she was happy to tolerate them. She didn't need to worry about them taking her position as his favourite. She knew he was in no hurry to settle down. He'd told her as much often enough, and she selfishly hoped he meant it. His parents had hardly instilled faith in him about the joys of matrimony or the sanctity of marriage and that pleased Kitty. She didn't want to share him, and she worried that a serious relationship might mean he wouldn't have room for her in his life any more. She needed him and she couldn't imagine not having him in her life.

Joe spotted her as she made her way towards him and he smiled and removed his arm from the woman's shoulders as he stepped forward to greet Kitty. Seeing him so casually separate himself from the woman gave her a tiny ping of satisfaction. New girlfriend or not, she was still more important.

'Hey, what are you doing here?' His smile brought out the dimple in his chin even further and his blue eyes sparkled. 'I thought you said you couldn't make it,' he said as he looked over her shoulder. She knew who he was looking for even as he asked, 'Where's Mike?'

'Out.'

'What's going on?'

Kitty heard the concern in his voice and that was enough to get the tears to well up in her dark brown eyes but she wasn't going to explain her circumstances in front of a complete stranger. She shuffled from foot to foot as Joe excused himself from the women around him. He looped his arm over Kitty's shoulder. 'Come on. It looks like you could use a drink.' He shepherded her across the room as he continued to talk, giving her time and space to get her own thoughts together. 'Does Mike know you're here?'

'No.' She shook her head as she replied and dislodged two fat tears that spilled from her eyes and rolled down her cheeks. She wiped them away with the back of her hand but she wasn't fast enough to stop Joe from noticing.

'What happened? He didn't hit you, did he?' Joe was looking at her carefully. She knew she looked like a mess. Her hair was dishevelled, her eyes red-rimmed and her face was pale. She looked like a woman who'd fled without bothering to brush her hair or grab anything but her handbag.

'No! It's nothing like that.' She was appalled that he might think she'd be in an abusive relationship. She knew he'd seen plenty of domestic violence cases in his role as a paramedic. She'd seen more than her fair share presenting to Emergency as well—too many— and they'd convinced her that she would never stay in a physically abusive relationship.

But what about an emotionally abusive one? After the initial honeymoon period in her relationship with Mike she was beginning to wonder if things were changing. And not for the better.

'We had an argument.' She had to admit that was what it was.

'Well, I'm sure it won't be the last one.'

'I think it could be,' she admitted. 'I think we might be over.' It was a scary thought. Kitty didn't like being on her own. In fact, she dreaded it and she knew her fear of being alone often caused her to persevere with relationships for longer than she should, but this disagreement with Mike was likely to be the beginning of the end of their relationship. She knew she couldn't stay with him unless he changed his mind.

Early on in their relationship she'd loved the fact that he'd wanted to be her everything. She'd been adrift, lonely, she'd wanted someone to lean on, to make decisions for her, someone who wanted to be all she needed, but did he only want to love her on his terms? Did he even love her? He must know how big a decision this was for her, how she needed his support. If he really was going to push her on this issue then maybe it was time she stood her ground. Staying with him just because it was better than being alone wasn't a good enough reason any more. Not when there could be so much at stake. If she didn't offer to be a surrogate now, Jess and Cam might never get the baby they wanted.

Kitty wanted to be loved but on her terms.

She needed to move on from this relationship. She was stronger now. She could be on her own.

She could do this.

She wanted to do this.

And if this worked out she wouldn't be alone. She'd be pregnant. You couldn't be less alone when you were physically attached to another human. A baby would fill all the empty, lonely spots in her heart, satisfy her need to be loved and to have someone to love in return. A baby could be the answer to so many prayers and the solution to so many problems.

A baby was just what her family needed.

Joe struggled to keep the smile off his face as he guided Kitty to one end of the bar where the crowd was marginally thinner. Even though he'd never pretended to like the guy, he had tolerated Mike for Kitty's sake, but he wasn't going to pretend that he'd be unhappy to see him gone from her life.

He held up two fingers, indicating his order, and waited for the barman to pour two beers. 'Talk to me,' he said as he handed a drink to Kitty. He couldn't imagine what had brought this about but whatever it was he was grateful.

Kitty took a long sip of her beer. Joe could see her hand shaking. He'd seen her agitated, upset and emotionally fragile before, but lately she'd seemed to be getting back on top of things. Her life, while certainly not without its dramas and tragedies in the past, had been on a fairly even keel for the past few months and he'd thought she was doing well.

'Jess and Cam want to have a baby,' Kitty said.

'Is that possible?' he asked. A couple of years ago Kitty's sister had been diagnosed with uterine cancer and Joe knew she'd undergone chemotherapy, and he thought the surgeon had performed a total hysterectomy.

'Not in the traditional sense,' Kitty confirmed, 'but Jess froze her eggs before her treatment and now they want to have a baby. They need a surrogate.'

'What's that got to do with you and Mike?' He couldn't see how or why this would affect Kitty and

Mike's relationship but as Kitty looked up at him he could see the answer in her eyes. 'You?'

Kitty nodded.

'You want to be their surrogate?' The penny dropped. 'And Mike wasn't happy about the idea?'

'He doesn't want me having another man's baby.'

Joe could understand that. If Kitty was his girlfriend, he might even feel the same way. But he wasn't about to side with Mike. He didn't particularly like the guy, and if Mike was prepared to give Kitty up over this issue then he definitely didn't deserve her.

'He doesn't get that it's not my baby. You know how important Jess is to me. She's all I've got. I don't even know if it's possible to do this but if I can do this for them, I will. He can't stop me.'

'Did he try to?'

'He just told me that if I intend to go ahead with this then he's not going to stick around. I think he expects me to choose him but you know I can't.'

'You've left?'

'Not yet,' she replied. 'We both need some time. I still need to talk to Jess, and I'm hoping Mike might change his mind once he's had a chance to think it over, but if he doesn't then I will make my choice.'

Joe couldn't imagine Mike backing down. He was a surgeon and had the ego to go with his profession. Joe didn't think he was madly in love with Kitty and he imagined Mike would see the surrogacy as an assault to his masculinity. He thought Kitty was going to be disappointed if she expected Mike to change his opinion.

'What can I do?' Joe asked. He would do anything for her. Always had. Always would.

'I need a place to stay,' she told him. 'If I stay at

Mike's it will give him an opportunity to try to talk me out of this. I need a bit of space while I work out how to handle this, and I can't stay with Jess. If she knew what had happened tonight she'd try and talk me out of my decision as well, and I'm doing this for me as much as for her and Cam. Can I stay at your place? On the couch would be fine, I don't want to cramp your style.'

'Of course.' If all she needed from him was a place to stay while she got things sorted then that's what he would give her. And if it meant Kitty went ahead with the idea and Mike ended the relationship Joe wasn't going to pretend he didn't like the sound of that. 'And just for the record, I think it's a fantastic gesture,' he added. He would be as supportive as possible of this exercise.

'Thank you. I knew you'd understand.'

Her brown eyes were still shiny with tears but at least they weren't spilling over her cheeks any more, although she still looked as if she needed a hug. He opened his arms and she stepped into his embrace. He wrapped his arms around her, closed his eyes briefly and inhaled the familiar vanilla scent of her shampoo as he comforted her.

He hated seeing her upset and he would go to just about any lengths to protect her. He had friends, lots of them, but none of his friendships enjoyed the same closeness that he and Kitty shared. Both of them found something in their relationship that they didn't get from anyone else. That sense of being understood without the need for explanation. He wasn't close to his family and avoided serious romantic relationships, but his relationship with Kitty was proof that he was capable of sustaining a meaningful connection.

It proved to him that he wasn't a complete emotional failure. That he could love someone and maintain a long-term relationship, even if it was platonic. He didn't doubt he wasn't cut out for marriage and commitment. He had no evidence that long-term monogamy was for him. His parents certainly hadn't subscribed to that ideology, they'd had five marriages between them, and Joe himself knew he grew bored and irritated if any of his romantic relationships stretched past a few months.

Some of his friends were convinced that he just hadn't met the perfect girl but Joe wasn't sure she existed. Even perfection had a use-by date in his opinion. From what he'd seen, marriages ended in one of three ways—divorce, death or disinterest—and he didn't see the point. But in the absence of other relationships his connection with Kitty became even more important, and he would do whatever was necessary to maintain it. He intended to always be there for her in a way that others hadn't been.

'But if you're going to do this,' he told her, 'then you need a long-term plan. You need to make some decisions about the next few months, not just about tonight.'

'I know,' she sighed, 'but right now, tonight is all I can manage.'

CHAPTER TWO

'HOLY CRAP!'

Kitty was signing notes at the nurses' station in the emergency department when the ED clerk's exclamation interrupted her concentration. She looked up and saw Lisa's eyes fixed on the wall-mounted television screen.

In the centre of the screen was a burning bus.

Orange flames leapt into the air from the rear and thick black smoke billowed around the vehicle and over several cars that had stopped haphazardly around it. In the background, Kitty could see a sandstone pylon and the heavy iron framework of the Harbour Bridge.

The time was fixed in the bottom right hand corner of the screen. Eight thirty-four a.m. Morning rush hour. This was happening in the middle of her city, a few kilometres from her hospital, and the images were being broadcast live from one of the news helicopters.

Kitty's heart was racing. What was going on? Was it a bomb? In the middle of Sydney?

The volume was muted on the television but Kitty could read the words scrolling across the screen under the picture.

Bus goes up in flames.
Harbour Bridge closed.
Morning traffic disrupted.
Use alternative route.

Traffic had come to a standstill but there was no mention of what had caused the bus to catch fire.

Kitty couldn't tear her eyes from the fiery disaster that was unfolding on the screen in front of her as the helicopter camera zoomed in on the chaos. People were out of their cars, doors left hanging open as they ran. Some ran towards the burning bus, others away. Kitty could see a man with a fire extinguisher aimed futilely at the flames as people stumbled from the bus. He was joined by another half-dozen men, all wearing hi-visibility vests and hard hats, and a couple were carrying additional fire extinguishers, but from what Kitty could see the extra hands were having no impact on the fire.

The live feed widened to show the emergency vehicles, the ambulances and fire engines, their red and blue lights absorbed by the thick cloud of black smoke as they weaved their way through the stationary cars on the bridge.

The images from the helicopter cut out and were replaced by a reporter standing on the bridge, a microphone held up to her mouth and the burning bus behind her. How the hell had she got through the traffic and the chaos? Sitting on the ground around her were several people who looked dazed and shocked. Some were coughing and Kitty wondered if they were passengers from the bus.

Lisa grabbed the remote and pressed a button, increasing the volume until they could hear the reporter's commentary.

'...*on the Harbour Bridge, where a city-bound commuter bus has gone up in flames near the northern end. Witnesses say twenty to thirty passengers have been evacuated but there may still be people trapped inside the bus...*'

Kitty didn't want to see the reporter. She wanted the camera to go back to the accident—she was looking for Joe. But the reporter continued to talk.

'*There is no word yet on what caused the fire. Commuters say there was a loud explosion, and you can see behind me that the windows of the bus have all been blown out.*'

The camera panned to the bus, zooming in on the accident, and Kitty searched the scene.

'*The heat is intense, the sky is thick with black smoke and there is a terrible odour in the air. Paramedics are treating victims for smoke inhalation as firefighters try to get the blaze under control.*'

Kitty's eyes flicked from one paramedic to another, from one blue uniform to the next, but she couldn't see Joe. She knew he was working this morning and that crews from the station at the North Sydney Hospital would be some of the closest to the scene. Maybe he was on another call-out? As long as he was safe, she thought—just as she saw a familiar shape at the side of the screen. Smoke was obscuring the image, but she recognised the way he moved.

Joe.

He was running straight at the bus. Her eyes followed his path as he came further into view in the centre of the television screen. There was a man standing in the doorway of the bus, his back to Joe. He was bent over, and he looked like he was struggling with something. Kitty realised he was dragging someone from the bus. And then Joe was there, followed by two other paramedics.

The standing man stepped out of the way as the paramedics threw a blanket over the man who lay in the doorway before lifting him from the bus and putting him on a stretcher.

Kitty could see the other man swaying as he stood next to the bus. Just when he looked as if he was about to collapse Joe caught him and laid him on the ground.

The camera panned out again and the reporter was in the foreground of the shot, blocking Kitty's view. She could see the man lying on the ground but she couldn't see Joe. He wouldn't have gone *into* the bus, would he? Surely not? That would be the firefighters' job. But was he far enough away? What if there was another explosion?

'Firefighters are struggling to douse the flames engulfing a city-bound bus on the Harbour Bridge,' the reporter repeated. *'All lanes on the bridge are closed until the danger is contained. It appears that the bus has now been evacuated with reports that two men, the driver and a passenger, are being treated for burns, but there are no reports of any fatalities at this stage and still no information as to the cause of the fire.'*

There was an increase in activity in the background and finally the camera cut away from the reporter and back to the bus. Kitty could see ambulances, their doors open and lights flashing as the picture showed someone being loaded in through the back doors of one of them.

And there was Joe. Back in view. She couldn't see his face but she didn't need to. He was instantly recognisable. It was more than the width of his shoulders and the shape of his head. It was the way he moved. Purposeful, composed. Unflappable, measured. Despite the chaos of his surroundings he projected calmness. He always seemed to know what he was doing. Not like her. So often she felt completely lost unless he was there to anchor her. Joe had been there for her in the toughest of times, but he'd never seemed to need her in the same way.

He was leaning over one of the victims, but he looked awfully close to the burning bus. Too close. Kitty's heart was still racing. She was trapped in a terrible feeling of helplessness. What if something happened to him?

She tried to push that thought aside as she saw him loading his patient onto the stretcher. She couldn't bear to think of something happening to Joe. He was a constant, solid, reassuring presence, the calm through so many of her storms, and she couldn't imagine her life without him in it. She turned away from the television as Joe disappeared from the screen, willing him to hurry before anything else could go wrong.

He would be on his way to her now. She knew he would be coming to her hospital. She needed to see him, to reassure herself he was OK.

Lisa muted the television as Kitty brought her focus back to the task at hand. The ambulances would be arriving soon. They needed to be ready. The paramedics would be turning around and bringing the injured to the North Sydney Hospital. They might not be the closest but they were on the right side of the bridge, on the same side of the harbour. They would be the most easily accessible emergency department, and they had a burns unit. Time was of the essence, especially for burns victims.

Kitty grabbed aprons and left Lisa to deal with the patients waiting for attention. She would have to explain to them that there was a bigger emergency that had to be dealt with before they could be seen.

Davina, the charge nurse, was assembling her troops and assigning them to teams. Kitty saw Mike arrive, tying his apron over his scrubs. She hadn't seen him since she'd walked out three days ago. Hadn't worked with him, hadn't taken his calls. She'd replied to his messages but that had been all she'd been capable of. She hadn't felt ready for another discussion that would more than likely end in another argument. She needed to have her argument prepared.

She breathed a sigh of relief when she wasn't assigned to Mike's team. She had no idea if that had been deliberate on Davina's part, she didn't think anyone knew about what was going on, but she was grateful. She needed to focus and she didn't need the distraction of worrying about what Mike may or may not be thinking.

'The information I've got is that we have two burns victims coming in. Priority One. Mike, you take the first one, his injuries are more extensive and you've got the most experience. Anna,' she said, nodding at the other doctor, 'your team can take the other. We'll triage any other patients on arrival,' Davina finished as the first ambulance pulled in to the emergency bay.

Kitty pulled on a pair of disposable gloves and craned her neck as the ambulance doors opened, trying to see which paramedics were in attendance.

She couldn't see Joe.

'Young adult male. Unresponsive. Burns to his legs and arms.' She heard the information being disseminated as the patient was wheeled past her but she was already turning away, turning back to the road, on the lookout for the next ambulance.

She waited nervously, hoping the next unit would bring Joe. When her parents had been killed in a car accident, and again when Jess had been diagnosed with cancer and throughout her treatment, Kitty had always been able to rely on him and she couldn't imagine how she would cope if anything happened to him.

She shook her head, clearing her mind as another ambulance pulled in. Anna had her hand on the rear door and she swung it open. Kitty exhaled as Joe emerged from the back. Broad shoulders, long legs, spiky hair. Strong and solid. He reached for the stretcher, pulling it from the ambulance. He bent his head and she could see him talking to his patient. His voice would be calm, reassuring.

Kitty stepped closer as Joe's partner slammed the driver's door and came to help manoeuvre the stretcher.

Joe was filthy. His uniform was covered in black soot and Kitty could smell smoke, diesel fuel and burning rubber. The smell seemed to have permeated the clothes of the paramedics and the victim, but at least Joe appeared to be in one piece.

'Hey! I thought I might find you here,' he said as she fell into step alongside him.

'You're OK?' she asked. When he nodded she glanced over his shoulder. 'How many more are there?'

'Only two seriously injured. The rest are smoke inhalation victims and assorted, non-life-threatening orthopaedic injuries.'

Kitty knew it could have been worse. Joe didn't say anything in front of their patient but Kitty could hear in his voice and she'd seen the scene for herself. Two burns victims, no fatalities and some people suffering from smoke inhalation and a few fractures was a pretty good outcome. It could have been *much* worse. But their patient didn't need to hear that.

'This is Carlos, the bus driver, fifty-three years old, second-degree burns to his hands and arms. Smoke inhalation but airway not compromised.'

Kitty looked down at Carlos. He had a sheet pulled halfway up his chest covering his arms but she could see an ID badge on his shirt pocket and she could just make out the bus company logo. His shirt, like Joe's, was blackened with soot, and he had an oxygen mask covering his nose and mouth but Kitty took that to be a precautionary measure given Joe's summary.

As they pushed the stretcher through the hospital doors and into an exam room, Joe drew back the sheet that had been tented over Carlos's forearms in an attempt to protect him from exposure to bacteria. His hands were bright pink, the skin blistered and hairless, and the burns extended halfway up his forearms. Someone had inserted an IV cannula into his elbow but no fluids had been connected. His transfer had been less than thirty minutes so there had been no urgency.

Kitty grabbed a slide board and prepared to transfer Carlos from the stretcher. She stood next to Joe and waited while Anna and the other paramedic carefully rolled Carlos. She and Joe slid the board under their patient.

'On three.' The transfer went smoothly and Joe and his partner stepped out of the way, removing their stretcher and leaving Kitty and Anna to get to work. With a wink in her direction, Joe was gone.

Kitty didn't waste time. Anna was cutting Carlos's

shirt away as Kitty replaced his oxygen mask and attached monitors. She and Anna worked together well. She was an experienced ED doctor and Kitty liked working with her. She was methodical and didn't miss much.

'Carlos, I'm Dr Lewis. Kitty and I will look after you. Do you have any medical issues we need to be aware of? Any heart problems, diabetes? Anything like that?'

Carlos shook his head.

'I'm just going to take your oxygen mask off to check your airway,' Anna explained softly.

Kitty recorded Carlos's heart rate, blood pressure and respiration rate while Anna did her examination. She replaced the oxygen mask with tubing once Anna was finished, looping it over his ears and sliding the pegs into his nose. She recorded his oxygen levels as Anna kept talking.

'We need to replace your lost fluid and get these burns cleaned up. I'm going to give you something for the pain, OK?'

They worked quickly through their initial assessment, needing to get a handle on the extent of Carlos's injuries. Some, like his burned skin, were obvious but damage to his lungs was less easy to spot and more likely to cause problems, although often not for a day or two. They had to prioritise.

Anna attached a bag of saline to the cannula in Carlos's elbow to replace the fluids he'd lost while Kitty distracted him, asking questions about his family. 'Is there anyone you want us to call?'

'The paramedics called my wife. Someone is bringing her to the hospital, but can you tell me how the boy is?' His voice was raspy and breathless. It sounded painful to talk and Kitty was sure she'd heard correctly. Boy?

She frowned. Was Carlos delirious? Her gaze flicked to the monitors. His temperature was raised but not excessively. 'What boy?'

'The one I pulled from the bus. Did he make it?'

Kitty realised he was talking about the other victim. Their first patient. 'You pulled him out?' The vision she'd watched on the television flashed back in her mind. The man dragging the other body from the bus. The standing man. The one who'd looked as if he'd been about to collapse only Joe had caught him just in time. That had been Carlos. 'Is that when you got burnt?'

Carlos nodded and struggled to talk. To explain. 'When the fire started it was just a bit of smoke. I stopped and told everyone to get off but the boy only got as far as me and said something about his bag. He ran back down the aisle before I could stop him. Then something exploded. The windows of the bus blew out and he got caught in the flames. I couldn't leave him.'

Kitty glanced at Anna, communicating mutely. Carlos would be hailed a hero, which meant the hospital would be swarming with media. They would all want a piece of him.

In silent consultation they agreed to take their time treating him, giving him a chance to catch his breath, and then they'd see if he wanted to make a statement. There were lots of variables and it wasn't Kitty's place to comment on what he should do.

'He was in a bad way. Do you know how he is?' Carlos asked, oblivious to the silent exchange going on between Kitty and Anna. He appeared to be more concerned about the boy than himself.

'He's here,' Kitty told him. 'He was brought in just before you. He's being looked after.'

'So he's alive?'

'As far as I know,' she said. She didn't know what else she could tell Carlos. She didn't have any more information and she wouldn't be able to disclose anything she did know. She was sure that if the boy survived he'd want to thank Carlos personally. She hoped so.

Anna and Kitty worked slowly and meticulously. They washed the burnt skin on Carlos's arms and hands and debrided the blisters, applying antibiotic cream before carefully separating his fingers and wrapping them individually.

'Will your wife be able to manage at home with you?' Kitty asked as she finished wrapping the last finger. 'We will need to keep you here for a few hours, just to keep an eye on you, but then if your readings are all within normal limits you'll be able to go home. You'll need to have some follow-up appointments for your lungs, though, and we will also make you an appointment with the burns unit in a few days. It's here in the hospital. Will someone be able to drive you here?'

'My wife doesn't drive.'

'That's OK,' Kitty replied. 'I'll speak to your employer. They will have to arrange transport for you seeing as this was a workplace accident. Is that OK with you?'

Carlos nodded.

'All right, let's get you comfortable and then I'll pop out and see if your wife is here yet.'

Kitty ducked into the staff kitchen for a break while Carlos had a few minutes with his wife. As all the other accident victims were being taken care of she decided she'd take the chance to top up her caffeine level. As she'd expected, the waiting room was now crowded with reporters all wanting to get an interview with Carlos, but she'd leave that decision to him. She skirted the waiting room and was just adding sugar to her coffee when Mike walked in.

He looked tired and Kitty was worried that things hadn't gone smoothly. He had been treating the boy from the bus, the one Carlos had saved. Kitty hoped it hadn't been in vain. She forgot that she'd barely spoken to him since their argument. At work things were different. She could put her personal issues aside. She'd learnt to compartmentalise her life and, in fact, the hospital often provided an escape. For the most part, no matter how bad things were in her own life, work was a constant reminder that she wasn't the only one suffering. On a couple of occasions she had felt that her life sucked more than her patients', but she always found work to be a good distraction. Right now, her disagreement with Mike was minor compared to their day so far. Things weren't so bad that she couldn't reach out to him.

'How did it go?'

'He's alive but he has burns to about thirty per cent of his body and to his airway. He's been transferred to the burns unit.' He ran his hands through his hair. 'All because he left his laptop behind.' He shook his head. It sounded ridiculous but Kitty guessed the boy hadn't stopped to think about the consequences. Hadn't thought about the risks. And now it was too late. What's done was done. She knew better than most that there was no going back. The past couldn't be changed no matter how much you might wish it.

Mike filled a glass from the water cooler. 'When are you coming home?' he asked over his shoulder.

'That depends,' she said, knowing she wasn't telling

the truth. She didn't think she would be going back. 'Have you changed your mind about my plans?'

'No.'

Which meant he assumed she'd changed *her* mind.

'Well, I haven't either,' she said.

His voice was quiet, his tone not malicious, but he sounded very definite as he said, 'I'm not going to be a cuckold in my own house.'

That was part of the problem. Even though she'd moved in with him after six months and had now been living with him for five, it was still his house. Not theirs. He still held all the cards, still had all the control.

'It's hardly the same thing,' she argued.

'It is to me,' he said as he drained his glass. 'You will be pregnant with another man's baby.'

'But surely you can understand my reasons?'

He was shaking his head. 'I can't imagine what could possibly make you want to do this. Jess has other options.'

'But she's my sister!' That was another part of the problem. He really didn't get her need for family. He didn't get her desperate desire to hold onto what was left of it.

'IVF isn't an option,' Kitty said, even though Mike knew that. Jess had been diagnosed with uterine cancer three years ago and after harvesting and storing her eggs she'd had a total hysterectomy, meaning that the simplest option was not an option. 'That leaves adoption or surrogacy. They're not likely to be approved for adoption given Jess's medical history, and finding someone else to offer to be a surrogate could take months— years even.'

Surrogacy in Australia was heavily legislated. Each state had its own laws and although New South Wales was a bit more lenient than other parts of the country, surrogate mothers couldn't be paid. They could be reimbursed for their medical costs but couldn't benefit financially, which meant that would-be parents needed to find someone who would do it out of the kindness of their hearts. It wasn't like asking someone to mind your pets while you went on a holiday—you were asking someone to lend you their body for forty weeks or more. Asking someone to subject themselves to tests and procedures to fulfil your own dreams. It wasn't easy.

Kitty closed her eyes and pictured Jess holding a baby. Her baby.

She opened her eyes and looked at Mike.

Those was her choices. Mike or her sister's baby.

'You can't be their only solution,' he said.

'Maybe not,' she replied. 'But I am their best one.'

Mike's pager beeped and he pulled it from his waistband to read the message. He glanced up and Kitty knew he was about to leave, but she also knew he'd want the last word. True to form he said, 'If you want to do this you'll have to do it without any help from me.'

He didn't wait for a reply before he turned and left the room.

Kitty stood still for a moment, trying to figure out what had just happened. She thought about what she was doing. What she was giving up. Why was her sister's happiness more important than her own?

Jess's happiness would be shared by Kitty. If she could give her sister an opportunity to have a family then, by association, she would benefit too—she'd be giving herself more family. She did want a family of her own one day but she knew Mike wasn't the man she would do that with. She had to believe her time would come, and meanwhile she'd do what she could. So she would grant Jess's wish. That would bring her happiness too. Being a surrogate meant giving up Mike but it was a sacrifice Kitty was willing to make.

She was still standing in the centre of the room when Joe walked in.

'Is everything OK?' he asked. He'd changed into a clean uniform and washed his face. He looked good in his uniform. The blue suited him, brought out the colour of his eyes, but it was more than that. It was the air of responsibility it gave him. He wore it well. He looked strong, capable and dependable. All the things she knew him to be were accentuated by the uniform. 'Rough day?'

She shook her head. 'No worse than usual. I was just thinking…'

Joe grinned. 'Should I be worried?'

She laughed. She hadn't realised she'd felt like laughing but Joe could always lift her spirits. 'Maybe,' she replied.

'What's going on?'

'You just missed Mike.'

'And?' He hesitated before asking, 'You're not thinking of moving back in?'

Kitty shook her head. 'No. But we had another discussion about the surrogacy. I wasn't prepared for it and I know I didn't handle it all that well, but he's still making it all about him.' Like always, she nearly added but she stopped herself, realising that was unfair. At work Mike was single-minded, putting his patients' needs first. He was focussed and dedicated—maybe all that effort at work made him think he deserved to be at the top of his own list of priorities away from work too, but sometimes she wished she felt as important to him as he felt to himself. 'This isn't about him,' she continued. 'It's not even about me. It's about Jess and Cam. Why can't he see that?'

Joe raised an eyebrow. 'You really want to hear my answer to that question?'

'No, I guess not.' Kitty managed a half-smile. 'But I'm tired of feeling like my opinions don't matter.'

'So what next?'

'I need to talk to Jess and Cam.'

'You're doing this?'

'I am.' She smiled. She'd made a decision and it felt good. She knew it was the right one. She hated being alone but she was willing to sacrifice her relationship with Mike in order to give her sister a baby. Family was more important to her than anything. She'd lost so many members of her family already. First her baby sister had died when Kitty had been just five years old and then, fourteen years later, both her parents had gone too. To offer Jess and Cam the baby they longed for would help to compensate for everything and everyone they'd already lost. 'Provided Jess and Cam agree.'

'I can't imagine they won't.'

'No.' Her smile widened. 'It's perfect. My family needs something good to look forward to, something positive, after everything that has happened.' She needed it too. 'I'll go and see them after work today and then I need to find a new place to live.'

'You know you're welcome to stay with me for as long as you need to.'

'Thanks, but I can't put you out of your bed.' Joe had already spent the past couple of nights on his couch, giving up his bed for Kitty, but that wasn't a long-term solution. 'You said yourself I needed a more permanent plan. I'll figure something out.'

CHAPTER THREE

KITTY STACKED THE empty dinner plates and took them into the kitchen. She had invited herself to Jess and Cam's for dinner and had promised to do the dishes in return, but she wanted to have the discussion she had planned first. Her ultimate agenda was to raise her surrogacy suggestion.

'A little while ago you mentioned that you were thinking about investigating the option of surrogacy using your frozen embryos,' she said to them both as she returned to the table. 'Have you done anything about that?'

'Not officially,' Cam replied. 'We've done some research but it's not a straightforward exercise. We think we'd like to find someone privately who's willing to act as a surrogate but we're not sure how to go about that. If we can't find someone privately we'll have to advertise and that's tricky here, but we can't afford to go overseas to do it. It's not going to be easy.'

'But we have to try,' Jess added.

'I know it's not easy,' Kitty said, looking into her sister's dark eyes. A mirror of her own face looked back at her. There was no mistaking they were sisters. They had the same dark eyes and dark hair, although Jess's was shorter and had grown back with a slight wave in it after the chemotherapy. Jess's face was more oval than Kitty's, whose own face could only be described as round. It made Kitty look young for her years but she was old enough to know what she was doing. She took a deep breath and held Jess's gaze. 'I would like to do it for you.'

'What?'

'I want to be your surrogate.'

'Really?'

'Really.'

'You're serious?'

Kitty nodded and Jess broke into a wide smile. She really was pretty when she smiled, Kitty thought as her sister bounced out of her chair and threw her arms around her. 'I can't believe this! Thank you!'

'Why?' Cam asked.

Cam's reaction took Kitty by surprise. To be honest, she'd thought they'd both be ecstatic but while Jess was obviously delighted and grateful, Cameron was far more reserved.

'That doesn't matter, Cam,' Jess remonstrated. 'All that matters is that Kitty is offering.' Jess was crying now as she continued to hug Kitty. Tears were running down her cheeks and soaking into Kitty's shirt. Kitty was pretty sure they were happy tears.

'I'm not saying I don't appreciate your offer,' Cam said as Jess finally let go of her little sister. 'It's very generous, but it's not as simple as you might think. I expect we'll all have questions, and one of mine is: why?'

In contrast, Jess didn't appear to have any questions. Kitty knew she was far too emotional and too caught up in the idea that she could become a mum to worry about the intricacies and details, but Cam deserved answers.

'You and Jess are my only family,' Kitty explained.

'You're all I've got. If I can give you the baby that Jess desperately wants I get to expand my family. It's a win-win situation.'

'But you can have your own children,' Cam argued. 'You're twenty-seven, this might take up the next two years of your life. Even if this works straight away it's not like you can be pregnant tomorrow. There are meetings, counselling, legalities to sort through. Trust me, we know what's involved, we've looked at everything. It's not straightforward and it will take time. What if you want to have your own baby in the meantime?'

'I'm not at the stage where I want to have a baby.'

'But that might change at any point in the next year or two. And what about Mike? He's older than you, what if he wants children sooner?'

Kitty shook her head. 'I don't think he wants that.' It didn't matter what he wanted, she wasn't going to have babies with Mike anyway. She knew now more than ever that she didn't want him to be the father of her children. He was too intense. Too controlling. She wanted someone fun. She *needed* someone fun. She needed someone to inject that into her life as well as her children's. She knew she had a tendency to get a bit low and she needed laughter and light in her life. That's why she loved being around Joe.

She didn't mention that she'd broken up with Mike. If Jess thought it was because of her decision to offer to be their surrogate Kitty knew she might decline her offer, and she was desperate to do this. Desperate to give Jess the baby she wanted. That bit of news could wait for another day.

'I want to do this.' Kitty would put her life on hold indefinitely in order to give Jess the baby she wanted—

the baby Kitty thought they all needed. 'Can't we at least investigate the idea?'

'Yes.' Jess was quick to agree and Kitty knew then that her offer had been accepted. She knew Cam didn't have the heart to refuse his wife. Kitty knew he would give Jess anything she asked for if it were possible, and this just might be possible. At least they would get to try.

Kitty picked up the pen and signed on the dotted line next to Cam and Jess's signatures. The lawyer witnessed their scrawls and stamped the pages. Signing the surrogacy agreement that had been drawn up was almost the final step in the process. Next their application would be reviewed by the IVF ethics committee and, if approved, she would become a surrogate. Not if, she told herself—when. She had to think positively. There was no reason not to think this wouldn't go ahead.

Over the past two months she had been poked and prodded, examined and tested, but she didn't mind. The tests hadn't raised any red flags and she was told she was a good candidate. She knew the clinic would have preferred it if she had borne children already as it left less room for surprises or problems with the pregnancy and delivery, but it wasn't a requirement in New South Wales, as it was in some other parts of the country, and for that Kitty was grateful. And the tests had given no indication that she wouldn't have a normal pregnancy. She was a healthy twenty-seven-year-old. She was convinced there wouldn't be any problems and fortunately that seemed to be the conclusion after all the tests were completed.

As a single woman in Sydney Kitty could access the medical care she needed as a surrogate. Jess and Cam had agreed to pay any out-of-pocket expenses, which could be quite costly, but they had no complaints. All three of them had attended a medical review at Jess and Cam's fertility clinic and they had all undergone the mandatory counselling sessions, though fortunately they hadn't been sent for independent psychiatric reviews. The lawyer had briefed them on their rights and obligations and had drawn up the agreement, and now they had one last hurdle. Kitty crossed her fingers that the ethics committee would approve their request.

'Kitty Nelson?'

She looked up as the fertility nurse called her name. This was it.

She was going to be a surrogate. The ethics committee had approved their application and now, if everything went according to plan, in nine months' time she would deliver a healthy baby for Jess and Cam, and her, to love.

Jess's eggs had been fertilised and the embryos created. All that was left was the implantation.

Kitty stood up and Jess followed suit. Kitty was surprised to find her legs were shaky. There was a lot of expectation riding on today but she hadn't realised she had felt the pressure. There wasn't much about it she could control, but now that the moment had come she desperately hoped she would turn out to be the perfect host. The perfect surrogate for a perfect baby.

'Are you sure you don't want me to come in with you?' Jess asked.

Kitty could hear the pleading note in her voice but she'd made up her mind and she was going to stand firm on this point.

She reached over and held Jess's hand.

'I don't watch you and Cam making babies, I'm not going to let you watch me getting impregnated.'

Cam was by the window, looking out at the city

streets several floors below, pacing up and down, already looking like an expectant father. Fortunately *he* hadn't asked to watch.

'Cam and I didn't make this baby the traditional way.'

'I know, but it would still be weird to have you in the room.'

'But you're happy for us to be there when the baby is born?'

Kitty nodded. 'Of course!' Although she'd have some ground rules then too—for instance, Cam would have to stay away from the business end, but she would discuss that later. Her first priority was to get pregnant.

'OK,' Jess said as she wrapped Kitty in a hug. 'Good luck.'

Kitty could feel Jess's bones as she hugged her sister back. She was still way too thin. 'It'll be fine.'

'I can't believe that in a matter of minutes you could be pregnant. I'm going to be a mum.'

If everything went to plan, Kitty thought, but she kept quiet. She needed to be in a positive frame of mind. She needed to believe this was going to work. A new life, a new member of the family to love, was just what they all needed. After their baby sister had drowned at the age of two, and then losing their parents in a car accident when Kitty was just nineteen, followed by Jess's shock cancer diagnosis two and a half years ago, they needed something to look forward to.

She kissed Jess's cheek and stepped back. 'See you soon.'

Joe was watching the clock, hoping he didn't get a last-minute call-out before the end of his night shift. It had been busy, but that wasn't uncommon. Saturday nights were always frantic, filled with the usual jobs—drunk and disorderly men getting into fights, drug overdoses, car accidents, car versus pedestrian accidents, heart attacks or indigestion that people mistook for heart attacks... The new crew was due at any moment and if the phones remained quiet for five more minutes he'd get out of there on time. He kept his fingers crossed. If he got out on time he might catch Kitty.

He was missing her company. The week that she'd stayed with him was now months ago but he'd got used to having her around and the months since she'd been gone had dragged. But at least she wasn't back with Mike. She'd moved out of Joe's apartment and in with Jess and Cam. They'd decided that it would be the best place for Kitty to live while they went through the surrogacy application and hopefully a successful pregnancy. That way Jess figured she'd get to be involved every step of the way. They'd assumed that the surrogacy process would be successful. Joe could understand why—what was the point of going ahead with the plan if you thought it was going to fail? But he was worried that they could all be setting themselves up for heartache.

Kitty had had enough heartache in her life.

But he'd barely seen her since she'd moved out. She'd been caught up in the surrogacy plans and even at work their paths hadn't crossed often. Although he was based at the ambulance station adjacent to the North Sydney Hospital, even their shifts hadn't coincided much, and more often than not when he'd brought patients to the ED or called in on a break she hadn't been rostered on.

His shift finished on time and he was able to get across to the ED before Kitty left the hospital. He sighed in relief.

'Hi.' He greeted her as she walked through the exit.

'Joe!' Her smile lit up her face and he found himself beaming back at her. It was good to see her. Really good. 'Have you finished your shift?' she asked.

'Yep. Signed out, all done.'

'Well, your timing is perfect,' she said as she tucked her hand through his elbow and fell into step beside him. 'I need to talk to you and I'm starving. Have you got time for breakfast?'

'Sure.'

They walked the few blocks to their regular café on Manly Beach and grabbed a table with a view over the water. The sun was still low in the sky but after a night cooped up in the hospital Joe knew that Kitty would want to be outside despite the glare.

Joe ordered his usual big breakfast while Kitty chose fresh fruit, yoghurt and muesli. She was restless, her feet jiggled constantly, and she was sitting on the edge of her seat. 'Are you going to be able to sit still long enough to eat?' he asked.

'Not unless I tell you my news first.'

'Go on, then,' Joe said as the waitress brought a coffee for him and a green tea for Kitty.

'I did a pregnancy test yesterday.'

'Already?'

Kitty nodded. 'It's two weeks tomorrow since the procedure.'

He knew that. He'd been keeping tabs on the process. He didn't need to ask what the result was, he could see in her eyes—excitement was written all over her face. He didn't need her to tell him the result but she told him anyway.

'It was positive!'

'You know it could be a false positive this early.' He didn't *think* he wanted to burst her bubble of happiness but his comment was out before he'd had time to censor it. He'd done some research and he knew the fertility clinics advised their patients not to do home tests but to wait for the official blood test. He assumed it was because there were too many occasions when people got false positive results.

'I know.' Kitty nodded. 'But I couldn't resist. I *feel* like it's worked. My boobs are tender...' She pressed on her boobs and Joe had to force himself to avert his eyes. He didn't want to be caught looking. 'And I *had* to know.'

'Who else have you told?'

Kitty frowned, a little crease appearing between her dark brows. 'No one. The official blood test is still a couple of days away so I won't say anything to Jess until then, but I had to tell someone. I wanted to tell you.'

Joe knew he should be pleased, he knew how much this meant to her. He appreciated that she'd shared her news with him but he was surprised to find he was experiencing another unexpected emotion. He could taste it.

The sour taste of jealousy.

He had never actually considered what would happen when Kitty eventually settled down and had babies. He knew it was what she wanted but he hadn't thought about the ramifications, the reality. He hadn't thought about the fact that she would have other priorities in her life, that there would be someone more important than him.

It hurt to realise she was going to have this experience without him. To realise he wasn't going to be part of this experience except in the role of a bystander. This baby wouldn't be hers to keep—but seeing her so excited about it reminded him that eventually that *would* happen and what would that mean for them?

For him?

He pushed down the sense of jealousy—now was not the time or the place to give in to his own emotions— and raised his coffee in a toast, hoping that somehow he would manage to say the right thing.

'Congratulations,' he said as he forced a smile.

Kitty fidgeted in her seat as she forced herself to eat her lunch as she sat across from Cam and Jess. She was on tenterhooks and had been for the past few days, ever since she'd taken the home pregnancy test. She'd thought that by sharing her news with Joe it would settle her excitement to a point where it would be bearable but she still couldn't wait for Jess and Cam to hear the results. It was all anyone wanted.

She was positive the procedure had worked but she hadn't said anything as she really didn't want to get Jess's hopes up. Now, after having to wait for the official test, she started having doubts. What if it hadn't worked? What if the home pregnancy test she'd done *had* given her a false positive? What if all the symptoms she'd been experiencing were just the result of her over-active imagination or wishful thinking? Surely life wouldn't be so cruel?

She placed her elbows on the table as the waitress cleared the remains of their lunch away. She leant forward and her breasts squashed against her forearms. Her boobs were definitely still tender, that had to mean something. She knew false positives were unlikely in those home testing kits. False negatives were far more common—and, besides, she'd also gone off coffee. She'd cut down on her caffeine before the embryonic transfer at the same time as she'd started taking folic acid tablets—she'd wanted to do everything she could to ensure that this worked—but now she couldn't even stand the *taste* of coffee. Something that had been one of her favourite drinks now tasted bitter, making it easy to stay off it.

Her fingers fidgeted and played with the gauze bandage that was wrapped around her left elbow, a constant reminder of what she was waiting for. She'd had the official blood test and she and Jess and Cam were just killing time until they could return to the IVF clinic to hear the results. Kitty was desperate to get back there.

Finally, with ten minutes before they were due back, Cam paid for their meals and they headed for the door.

'All right,' the doctor said as they were ushered into the consulting room and took their seats. 'We were testing for hCG in the blood. Any increase in hCG levels in a surrogate indicates a positive pregnancy but the levels are significant. The higher the better. Higher levels suggest a viable pregnancy. At this point in time, two weeks post-implantation, we expect to see levels above fifty milli-international units per millilitre.' Kitty wished she'd just get on with it. The wait was agonising. 'But we're hoping for numbers closer to five hundred.' There was a sheet of paper sitting on the desk. The doctor glanced down at it and when she looked up she was smiling. 'Your numbers are four hundred and fifty. Congratulations, you are pregnant.'

'Oh, my God, you did it.' Jess jumped up from her chair and hugged Kitty. 'Thank you so much. I can't believe it.' Tears were running down her cheeks as she turned to Cam. 'We're going to have a baby!' she said as she threw her arms around him.

Cam was grinning from ear to ear as he hugged and then kissed his wife before hugging Kitty. Jess was bawling and Kitty could feel her own tears threatening to spill from her eyes. She'd been positive that the embryo transfer had been successful but she hadn't dared to believe it and the relief was almost as great as the excitement.

The doctor let them celebrate the news and when they all managed to get their emotions under control she continued the consult. 'Before I let you go I'll just run through the next steps with you.'

The three of them pulled themselves together long enough to listen to the procedure from here on.

'If everything goes according to plan,' she said, looking at Kitty, 'your hCG levels should double every forty-eight hours. Fast increases in levels are what we are hoping for as that appears to indicate a good pregnancy outcome. I would like to do a follow-up blood test in two days to check those levels. Depending on the results we might then schedule more blood tests but I will also book you in for an ultrasound scan in a fortnight.'

'We'll be able to see our baby that early?' Jess asked.

'Your baby will look like a jelly bean still at that stage but we should be able to see and hear a foetal heartbeat then,' the doctor explained.

Kitty didn't remember much after that, and neither did Jess, she suspected. They were both too excited with the news. They left it to Cam to pay attention to the next round of appointments as they let their minds run wild with the thought of creating a new life. A baby.

'Kitty, incoming ambulance.'

Kitty was tidying an exam room when Davina stuck her head in and called for her attention. 'We've got a twenty-nine-year-old woman with abdominal pain and the doctors are all busy. Can you meet them in the bay?'

Kitty tucked a clean sheet onto the exam bed and carried the dirty linen out with her, tossing it into a linen bag on her way outside. She exited the doors as the ambulance pulled into the bay and Joe climbed out, pulling the stretcher with him.

'Hey,' he greeted Kitty with his megawatt smile. 'Kitty, this is Talia. Acute abdominal pain. BP one-forty over ninety. Heart rate one hundred and ten. Temp thirty-nine degrees. No significant medical history but she's had a positive home pregnancy test. Nausea but no vomiting.'

Talia's eyes were open. She was perspiring and looked a little grey.

'Husband is on his way, following behind,' Joe's partner added.

'Doctors?' Joe mouthed the word silently as they wheeled Talia into the hospital.

Kitty shook her head. 'Busy,' she replied, knowing that Joe was thinking they'd need a consult.

Kitty spied Anna coming out of an exam room as they negotiated the corridor. 'Anna! I need a consult if you're free,' Kitty said before Anna could disappear. She let Joe repeat his summary as they transferred Talia to a bed before Kitty and Anna were able to start their assessment.

Kitty started a file and handed it to Anna while she hooked Talia up to the various monitors. Anna recorded Talia's symptoms, the onset and severity, as well as her activities over the previous twenty-four hours and her menstrual history. By Talia's account, she figured she was eight weeks pregnant.

'We'll need a urine sample if that's possible, Talia,

just to test and confirm the pregnancy. Kitty, can you organise that? I'll duck out and arrange a pelvic ultrasound.'

Kitty nodded and fetched a bed pan but Anna had gone no further than six steps when Talia cried out in pain. She curled into a ball, clutching her stomach and her heart rate escalated rapidly. She was sweating more profusely and her face was now completely white.

'Anna!' Kitty called out.

Talia wasn't the right demographic for gall stones, which left a burst appendix or a ruptured Fallopian tube as the most likely cause of her pain. That or extremely bad gastro.

Anna came back into the room and took one look at their patient. 'Get me a gynae consult and prep a theatre,' she instructed.

Kitty stripped off her gloves and threw them into the bin as Talia was wheeled off to Theatre. She tidied up the exam room again, and after checking in with Davina and finding that the waiting area was empty she took the opportunity to grab a drink and something to eat. Her shift had been busy and she was finding that if she didn't eat something small on a regular basis the morning sickness would rear its head. It wasn't so much morning sickness as nausea whenever she got hungry and she was quickly learning not to pass up the chance to refuel when she was able to.

Joe was in the kitchen, grabbing a coffee.

'Can I make you one?' he asked.

Kitty shook her head. 'No, thanks, I've gone off coffee.' Her body was already rejecting anything that could be considered remotely toxic—alcohol, coffee, strong cheeses, raw fish—and craving healthy options like fresh fruit and vegetables. She'd always tried to eat healthily but she was finding it difficult not to now that she was pregnant, as so many foods made her queasy.

'How did things go with Talia?' Joe asked as he pulled out a chair for Kitty.

'Not great,' Kitty replied. She pulled the lid off a tin of tuna and ate a mouthful before continuing. 'She's in Theatre now. Anna thinks it might have been a ruptured Fallopian tube. I guess she was lucky she was here and not at home.'

Joe thought Kitty looked worried. A crease had appeared between her dark brows and he wondered what was bothering her. She didn't know Talia, and the woman was far from the first ED patient who would have been whisked off to Theatre.

'What's wrong?' he asked.

'I'm just thinking about Talia. There she was all excited about this pregnancy… It was her first, did you know that?'

Joe shook his head. There hadn't been the time or the necessity to go into that detail. It would have been far different if she'd been in labour, but with an unconfirmed pregnancy it was irrelevant to the ambulance crew.

'One minute she's all excited about the news,' Kitty continued, 'and the next, if Anna's diagnosis is correct, she won't be pregnant any more and the best-case scenario is they are able to save her Fallopian tube. Jess and Cam are so excited about my pregnancy, so excited to meet their child, but I can't stop thinking of all the things that could go wrong.'

So that was the problem. Kitty's imagination was

working overtime as usual. She was always of the opinion that if something could go wrong, it would.

'I think I might ask Anna if she can do an ultrasound for me,' she said.

'Why?'

'Just to check things out. It'll make me feel better.'

'You have no reason to think anything is wrong. You've been feeling queasy, you've gone off coffee…' He didn't mention her sore breasts. 'You've got all the right signs.' He knew she had a tendency to worry overly about things and imagine all the things that go awry. 'Have you had another blood test?'

'Yes. My hCG levels are still rising.'

'That's a good sign, right?'

'Yes.'

'When is your scheduled ultrasound?' he asked. He was trying to be the best friend that she expected. He had been consciously trying to stem any negative emotions. Those feelings weren't useful to anyone. But ever since Kitty had confirmed her pregnancy and he'd experienced the unexpected sense of jealousy he had questioned why. And he'd finally figured it out.

Children of his own had never been on his agenda—in his mind if he couldn't commit to a woman he didn't deserve to father children—but with Kitty's announcement he'd had to admit that he actually did want to be a father. He didn't begrudge her the pregnancy, far from it, and it shouldn't matter that she was going to have a baby. That shouldn't impact on his ability to be supportive, and he knew he shouldn't be jealous, but he was finding the reality a little different from the theory. All it did was remind him that someday soon Kitty might be having children of her own, and moving on from their friendship.

But that was *his* issue and he would deal with it, and in the meantime he would make sure he was supportive. Maybe being a surrogate uncle to Kitty's children would suffice.

'Eight days,' she replied.

'I think you should wait until the scan, then. Think of how exciting that is going to be. Don't you want to be able to share that with Jess and Cam? Surely you don't want to take that excitement away from them by having seen it all before?'

She sighed. 'You're right.'

'Good girl. It'll all be fine, you'll see.'

'How come you always know the right thing to say?'

He laughed. 'Maybe to you, because I know you so well.'

'Thanks, Joe.' Kitty stood up and tossed her sandwich wrapper in the bin before hugging him.

He loved the feeling of her arms around him. She was still so tiny and he wondered how long it would be before he'd be able to feel a little baby bump. He didn't imagine it would take long as there was nowhere for the baby to go except out. He wondered too how much the pregnancy would change her. She was worrying now—would she continue to worry progressively more and more throughout the pregnancy, or would she eventually accept that things were going according to plan and relax? Whatever happened, he vowed to be there for her and to help her to cope. He had always been her rock and he didn't want that to change. No matter how he felt.

* * *

Kitty was starting to feel more like her normal self. Her morning sickness was abating and, at twenty-two weeks, she was now feeling like she thought she was supposed to—a glowing, pregnant woman. She hadn't gained much weight yet except for in her breasts, but she felt voluptuous for the first time in her life and it was making her feel very feminine. She knew it was hormonal but she was constantly thinking about sex. She hadn't had sex in six months, nearly seven, and she was beginning to think she might go crazy unless she did something about it.

And it seemed she wasn't the only one. As she sat with Lisa and a couple of other nurses at the Manly Pier Hotel the talk turned, inevitably, to men and the lack of good ones.

Kitty was enjoying the evening. It was good to be out and nice to have the focus off the pregnancy for a little while. At home with Jess and Cam it had become the number one topic of conversation, so she was looking forward to talking about the things she used to discuss with her girlfriends. The pub was busy, the line at the bar a couple of people deep. It was her turn to buy the drinks but she didn't feel like fighting her way through the crowd. Like a knight in shining armour Joe appeared and offered to place their order.

'You and Joe aren't an item?' one of the nurses asked, continuing the conversation as she watched Joe walk to the bar.

'No. Just friends,' Kitty replied.

'With benefits?' Victoria asked.

'No.' Kitty shook her head.

'He's hot.'

He did look good tonight, Kitty thought, although she had to pretend she hadn't noticed. He wore his favourite jeans, and they were her favourites on him too. They hugged his backside, highlighting what she considered to be one of his best features. A white T-shirt hugged his chest. It was a simple outfit but it showcased his body to perfection. He was fit and muscular with just the right amount of confident swagger, she thought as she watched him leaning on the bar. His hair was casually perfect, he looked like he hadn't made a huge amount of effort, as if he got out of bed looking like this—relaxed and gorgeous with a cheeky grin for whichever female he was talking to.

She had to agree with Victoria. Joe *was* hot, but she'd long ago taught herself to ignore it. They were friends, first and foremost, and she was too afraid of ruining the status quo to ever test the boundaries of that friendship. She needed him as a friend and she wasn't going to risk their relationship by blurring the lines.

'Is he single?' Victoria asked as they watched Joe return to their table.

'He's single,' Kitty admitted.

He delivered their drinks with a smile, making the dimple in his chin flash, and Kitty noticed that Victoria couldn't take her eyes off him. He didn't stay, choosing instead to go out to the deck where some of his mates were drinking, and Victoria's gaze followed his path through the crowd.

All the talk about men and, more specifically Joe, had Kitty flustered. She couldn't think about him and sex in the same conversation. She'd trained herself not to and, besides, he'd never even hinted that he'd be willing to cross that line.

But what if he did? What would she do?

She shook her head.

She'd be crazy to even consider it. She wasn't prepared to risk the friendship of a lifetime for a brief encounter between the sheets. Even if her hormones were going crazy, there were others ways to scratch that itch. Kitty drained her water glass and stood up as the DJ played his first track. The pub was full of good-looking young men. Joe was not the only eligible bachelor here, she thought as she dragged Lisa onto the dance floor.

Joe could see Kitty on the dance floor from his vantage point on the deck. She looked particularly beautiful tonight. He knew she was suffering a little from morning sickness but she had a pregnancy glow and by this evening she was obviously feeling, and looking, better. Her hair was thick and glossy and her skin was luminous. She moved well—she was the epitome of someone who danced as if no one was watching, and he took advantage of that fact to watch her.

She was normally slight, but the pregnancy had added some curves to her bust and her hips, he thought as he watched her hips move to the music. She let herself go to the rhythm of the song and Joe let his eyes follow her movements. There was something hypnotic, almost sensual, about her dancing.

He shook his head and turned away. He felt awkward and exposed now—he wasn't used to thinking about Kitty in that sense. Of course he'd noticed little things about her before—the depth of her brown eyes, the curve of her lips, the twin dimples in her cheeks—but he'd never let himself entertain an image of her as a sexual being before. He'd always kept her firmly in the friend zone.

He turned his gaze to Lisa instead as he tried to get the image of Kitty's hips out of his head and watched as the girls were joined by a couple of guys. Strangers—or at least they were strangers to him. Not that who Kitty danced with was any of his business, but Joe felt his hackles rise anyway as his protective, or should that be territorial, instincts came to the fore.

Kitty danced for a few more minutes but when Lisa's boyfriend arrived she excused herself and headed to the bar, closely followed by one of the guys. Joe's protective instincts kicked up another notch. If this guy wanted a chance with Kitty he'd have to go through him first.

Joe pushed his way through the crowd and arrived at Kitty's side just as the guy asked, 'What can I get you?'

'She'll have a water,' Joe answered.

The guy looked from Kitty to Joe. 'I wasn't asking you.'

'And yet I'm answering.' His protective instincts were on high alert now. Kitty didn't need a stranger buying her drinks, and as the guy half-turned away from Joe to face Kitty, obviously not about to listen to Joe, he couldn't resist adding, 'She's pregnant. She'll have a water.'

He saw the guy glance down at Kitty's stomach. There were no visible signs of her pregnancy yet, not unless you knew her. Joe knew that her breasts were bigger and she was a little softer, a little more rounded, more voluptuous, but she was wearing a loose sleeveless top and jeans. All anyone else would notice was the size of her breasts. And Joe didn't want other guys noticing that.

Her skin glowed. She looked beautiful. And cross.

She was glaring at Joe but he pretended not to notice.

The guy looked back at Joe. He looked irritated too but Joe didn't care. 'Are you the father?' he asked.

'No.'

'Then what business is it of yours?'

'It's her brother-in-law's baby,' Joe stated flatly.

The look on the stranger's face was priceless. If Kitty hadn't still been glaring at him Joe would have laughed. The guy looked completely horrified and he disappeared fast. Just as Joe had hoped.

'What are you doing?' Kitty turned on him.

'What are *you* doing?' he countered.

'I was talking. He was cute.' She was watching him walk away. 'And now he thinks I'm a complete crazy.'

'He wasn't *cute*,' Joe said. 'And he looked about eighteen. No wonder he ran.' He couldn't help the smile that broke out on his face but Kitty was still cross.

'Joe, I haven't had sex in almost seven months, my hormones are going wild and I'm about to burst with frustration. I wasn't going to marry the guy. It's just sex.'

Just sex.

Joe saw red. He'd never understood that expression until now. Blackness encroached onto the edges of his vision as a red haze washed over the centre. His scientific background told him that it was probably due to a rush of blood through his body, and he would swear he could feel his blood pressure building. He had a burning desire to punch something.

He didn't want to think about Kitty having sex with strangers. The very idea horrified him.

He was aware of other men looking at her with interest and listening to their conversation. He took a deep breath and tried to clear his vision as he gripped her elbow and steered her out to the relative quiet of the deck before any other strangers offered to help her out.

'I was only talking to him,' she argued again, not prepared to let the discussion drop. 'What's the matter with you?'

'You were talking to him but thinking about sex?' he replied. 'You don't know anything about him.' He knew he sounded like an irrational fool. Kitty was an adult and could make her own decisions, but he really didn't want her thinking about having sex with strangers.

Kitty rolled her eyes. 'If you hadn't scared him off I might have found out more about him. That's how meeting people works, Joe. You meet, you talk, you decide if you like each other.'

'And then you have sex.'

'That was my plan.'

'But you're pregnant.'

'So? You think people don't have sex when they're pregnant?'

He didn't want to think about *her* having sex, pregnant or otherwise. Not with strangers, that was for damn sure.

She was grinning at him now, the little dimples in her cheeks twinkling. He didn't want her to think he was being funny, he was deadly serious. And he wanted her to take him seriously.

He was sorely tempted to offer his services but bit his tongue just in time. There was no way in hell that was a good idea.

She was waiting for his answer. Looking up at him with her big brown eyes, making it difficult to remember just why taking her in his arms and taking her to bed would be so terrible.

'I don't want to talk about you having pregnant sex,' he said as he tried futilely not to imagine what her lips would taste like. Tried not to imagine how her breasts would feel under his fingertips.

'Why not?'

They were standing very close now and the noise from the bar receded into the distance as Kitty continued to look up at him, a challenge in her dark eyes.

Why not what? He couldn't remember what he'd said. He couldn't think straight when she looked at him like that. She was all lips and eyes and breasts and he was a mess.

Their conversation was forgotten as he stared at her lips. He thought about kissing her soundly, showing her what it was like to be kissed by someone who knew her well. Who cared about her. Showing her how much better that was than kissing a complete stranger. Why had he never kissed her before? He couldn't remember.

Everything receded, the noise, the crowd, until there was just the two of them.

He searched for a good reason *not* to kiss her now and couldn't think of one. The urge was overpowering and he didn't know if he could resist.

He bent his head.

She lifted her chin and tilted her head up to him.

CHAPTER FOUR

KITTY'S LIPS WERE PARTED. He could see the tip of her tongue, soft and pink between her teeth. Was she waiting for him to kiss her?

His eyes widened as she licked her lips.

Blood pounded in his veins.

Did she *want* him to kiss her?

How the hell could he know?

Perhaps he was the only one who thought this was a good idea.

No. Scratch that. It was a terrible idea.

He should resist the urge. Although it might be one way to stop her from thinking about sex with strangers... But then where would it leave them?

He was a mess of indecision. He had lost all form of coherent thought and his indecision made him hesitate. In that moment, in that split second when his desire battled with logic, Kitty stepped back.

Her reaction was probably the right one. The best one.

He should also back away before he did something stupid. He'd had several beers and was far from sober. Kissing him was probably the last thing on Kitty's mind. It was highly likely she would have slapped him and he would have deserved it.

He stepped away. That was best. The combination of her hormones and his blood alcohol level may have made them do something they would regret.

He opened his mouth to say something but he was at a loss for words.

Kitty beat him to it. 'I'm tired, I think I might head home,' she said, and she was gone before he could say anything further.

But that was OK. That was good even. That was *definitely* the sensible outcome.

As he watched her go, he tried to gather his thoughts. His brain was fuzzy and it took some time before he could make his legs move.

'Where's Kitty?' Lisa asked as he went back into the pub.

'She's gone home,' he replied. 'She was tired.'

One of the other girls at the table stood up. He recognised her from the hospital, she was one of the nurses. He thought her name was Victoria.

'Would you like to dance?' she asked him. Her voice was quiet and he had to lean in closer to hear her. Had she done that deliberately? She was standing awfully close to him. She was pressed up against his thigh, her hand on his arm, and she was looking at him as if she had no place she needed to be.

Joe didn't dance and he'd had enough to drink. He definitely had somewhere better to be. 'I've got a better idea. Do you want to get out of here?' he said, and was not surprised when she agreed.

Victoria was thin and blonde, the complete opposite of Kitty. She was exactly what he needed to take his mind off what had just happened.

* * *

'Kitty and Anna, incoming patient, three minutes,' Davina said. 'I don't have much information. He's a surfer, picked up by the coastguard, suffering from exposure and dehydration. That's all I've got.'

Kitty grabbed a fresh gown and gloves and made her way to the ambulance bay. Dr Anna Lewis was already there.

The ambulance pulled in, followed by a couple of news vans, and Joe jumped out.

Kitty took a deep breath. She hadn't seen him for several days, not since she'd almost kissed him, but she'd known their paths would cross again. She'd also heard that he'd gone home with Victoria that night. Victoria had made no secret of that fact the next time she and Kitty had had a shift together. What was that all about?

She was still fuming about it. Annoyed with him and annoyed with herself for caring. She didn't normally have an issue about Joe's dalliances or relationships, but something about him and Victoria was bugging her and having to work with Victoria was only making things worse. She knew it was because she'd stupidly thought he'd been about to kiss her at the pub. Until he hadn't. Obviously, that had been the last thing on his mind. He'd probably been about to ask if Victoria was single. Did everyone assume Kitty would just play matchmaker now that she was pregnant? Why didn't anyone imagine that maybe *she* wanted sex? She was pregnant, not dead.

But Kitty had fled the pub after that. She hadn't wanted to give Joe a chance to read what must have been written all over her face. He'd always known what she was thinking and she didn't think she would have managed to hide the fact that she'd thought he'd been about to kiss her—and that she'd desperately wanted him to. What was wrong with her? That would be the surest way to ruin their friendship.

But she still wished he hadn't hooked up with Victoria. That was just rubbing salt into the wound. Victoria was tall and thin and blonde. All the things Kitty wasn't, and Kitty was unusually irritated by the thought of them together.

But there was nothing she could do about it.

Joe pushed the stretcher towards them and Kitty deliberately went to the opposite end, knowing she'd be able to avoid eye contact. She virtually ignored him as he gave them a rundown on the situation while they transferred the patient into an exam room.

Their patient was of Asian appearance, slim with a badly sunburned nose and shoulders. According to Joe he was Japanese. 'This is Toshi. He got into strife in the surf yesterday and spent the night drifting out to sea on his board.' That caught Kitty's attention but she still avoided looking at Joe and instead looked at Toshi. He'd spent a night in the ocean on a surfboard? 'He is dehydrated, tired and sunburnt but otherwise in reasonable shape considering the circumstances. He's had a litre of saline, this is the second litre running through now. His English is better than my Japanese but I think you should call an interpreter.'

Despite his ordeal, Toshi was able to transfer himself from the stretcher to the examination bed, and Joe smiled at Kitty as he wheeled the stretcher from the room. If he'd noticed her less than friendly attitude towards him it didn't appear to bother him. He wouldn't imagine he'd done anything to upset her and, in reality, she *wouldn't* normally have been upset by his behaviour. He was just being regular Joe. It was hardly his fault she was a hormonal mess.

Kitty hung up the bag of saline and attached leads to Toshi's chest and finger to record his vital statistics. Anna connected him to the oxygen as a precaution but Joe's assessment seemed accurate. Toshi seemed physically in quite a good state, although Kitty wasn't sure what a night spent drifting in the Pacific Ocean would do to a person's mental state. She knew she would have been terrified, imagining sharks circling and all sorts of deadly sea creatures just waiting to pounce. It was just the sort of thing that could lead to PTSD, but there wouldn't be much discussion about Toshi's mental health until the interpreter could be contacted.

'Can you organise some food for him?' Anna asked Kitty when she'd finished her physical examination and declared that he was, indeed, in remarkably good shape. 'Something simple to start with, perhaps soup, a salad and some juice?'

'Sure,' Kitty replied.

'And then we'd better see if we can get an interpreter on the phone if one doesn't turn up shortly. He can have half-hourly obs once he's eaten, providing he keeps something down.'

Kitty organised a tray of food and then took her scheduled break while she waited for it to be delivered. The television in the staff kitchen was on the news channel and Kitty recognised the hospital ED entrance in the background of the shot. A reporter stood in the ambulance bay, speaking to the camera. Kitty wondered if this was the same news crew that had followed the ambulance bringing Toshi. She supposed it was an interesting story.

The emergency doors slid open behind the reporter and Joe stepped outside. Kitty increased the volume when she saw the reporter turn to Joe, thrusting the microphone towards him. Joe stopped, and Kitty wondered if he'd been asked to speak to the media. If so, he was a good choice—after all, he had been one of the paramedics who had transferred Toshi to hospital, and the camera loved him. The angles of his face were thrown into sharp relief by the fluorescent overhead lights of the hospital entrance but his skin still managed to look tanned and healthy and his blue eyes were clear and bright.

'I'm speaking now with one of the paramedics who brought the Japanese surfer here to North Sydney Hospital after his harrowing ordeal lost at sea for sixteen hours,' the young reporter said to the camera, before turning to Joe. 'Mr Harkness, what can you tell us about the man's condition? Is he going to be all right?'

The reporter knew his name, so Joe must have been asked to speak and from past experience Kitty knew it was the only way to get them to move on. You had to give them something otherwise they'd be hovering around all night.

'He was very dehydrated and sunburnt but in remarkably good spirits considering his ordeal. He's understandably relieved to be back on dry land,' Joe replied.

He looked fresh and relaxed. No one would guess he was nearing the end of his twelve-hour shift. The dimple in his chin appeared as he smiled at the young news reporter. Kitty just knew the effect his smile would be having on the young woman. She'd be surprised if she could remember her next question.

'How did he come to be on his surfboard in a shipping lane six kilometres off the east coast of Australia?' the reporter asked, and Kitty was sure she could see a blush colouring her throat as Joe looked directly at her.

'As far as we know, he got dragged out to sea in a rip and was unable to paddle back in as the waves were too big.'

'And how did he end up in your ambulance?'

'He was spotted by the crew of a container ship and they were able to pick him up. It was fortunate his surfboard was yellow as they may not have seen him otherwise. The coastguard retrieved him and we met them and transferred him here. He's a very lucky man.'

The reporter asked a couple more questions, but Kitty's mind wandered as she watched Joe. She could tell he'd had enough of being interviewed. He was still being pleasant but the set of his shoulders had changed. He was angled away from the reporter now and although Kitty couldn't see his feet she suspected he had shifted his weight. He'd be getting ready to move. She could read his body language, knew his movements. She had spent so much time with him, watching him, she knew the set of his head, the curve of his cheek, the exact position of the dimple in his chin. She didn't want to be cross with him. She acknowledged that it stemmed from being irritated with herself. It wasn't his fault she was hormonal.

She felt a flutter in her belly as the baby stretched and moved and reminded her of what was important. Family. Friends. Joe was as important to her as anyone. She'd mend the bridges.

She didn't get to choose who Joe spent his time with. That was all up to him and he'd obviously not wanted to kiss her. Thank God when he'd bent his head towards her that night at the pub she hadn't met him halfway—she would have died of embarrassment. As it was, it was bad enough that he'd hooked up with Victoria. Had that been his plan all along for that night?

She remembered he'd asked her not to talk about pregnant sex. Did he think her pregnancy made her unattractive? Undesirable?

Had she just *imagined* that he was going to kiss her? Had she wanted him to?

She knew she had. Did.

But perhaps it was best that she hadn't. She needed him in her life and she couldn't afford to jeopardise their relationship. He was one of the few people she could rely on to have her back. She couldn't risk altering the status quo.

So she'd better stop being in a huff about Victoria. She didn't need to socialise with them as a couple but she should stop ignoring Joe.

Even Jess had noticed that Joe hadn't been around for the past few days. Kitty's birthday was next week and she had always celebrated it with Joe. Jess and Cam had been pressuring her to invite him for dinner. She checked the roster. She wanted to know which nights Victoria was working. She could invite Joe and feign ignorance that Victoria had a shift.

She went out to the ambulance bay, anxious to catch Joe before he left. Suddenly she felt it was important to fix things. To act like an adult.

She waited until the reporter signed off on her segment and the news crew had started packing up their gear before she hurried after him.

'Joe? Can I talk to you?'

'Hey.' He turned around with a smile. He looked pleased to see her. Maybe he hadn't even noticed she'd been avoiding him. He was probably too caught up in Victoria to have time to think about her. She pushed those thoughts aside. She didn't want to think about Victoria any more than she had to, and basked in the warmth of Joe's smile instead. 'How are you?' he asked. 'How's our patient?'

'Hungry.' She smiled back. 'Toshi, I mean,' she clarified.

'That's a good sign.'

'It is,' she agreed. 'I saw your interview.'

'Is that what you came to tell me? Was it terrible?'

She shook her head. 'You know it wasn't. I wanted to ask if you are free for dinner tomorrow night? Cam is going to make a barbecue,' she said, reminding herself she'd have to remember to tell Cam. 'It's an early birthday celebration for me. Would you like to come over?'

'Sounds great.'

'You're welcome to bring Victoria,' she offered, hoping that Joe would already know she had a shift and wouldn't ask her to swap it.

'Thanks, but I don't think we're at that point in our relationship yet.'

'OK.' Kitty did a mental fist pump. That had worked out well—she'd looked gracious while still getting what she wanted. Joe hadn't even thought about checking Victoria's roster. 'See you at seven.'

That was good. He didn't seem out of sorts with her. She didn't want to push him away, to give him a reason to abandon their friendship, abandon her. Everyone left her eventually but she really wanted to keep Joe in her life for as long as possible. She needed him.

Kitty answered Joe's knock on the door. She was wearing a dress he hadn't seen before. She looked good. Pink suited her. She was glowing, making him wonder suddenly if she'd had the sex she'd been seeking out the other night. Had sex put the sparkle in her eyes and the glow on her cheeks?

He didn't want to think about Kitty having sex. Not if it wasn't with him. But that wasn't going to happen, and thinking about it wasn't going to do anyone any good.

'New dress?' he asked as he kissed her cheek and handed her the gifts he'd brought.

'I had to go shopping. I don't fit into my clothes any more,' she said as she led him into the house. His gaze dropped to her hips, which were swaying tantalisingly in front of him. This pregnancy had filled her out, rounding her bottom, in a good way, and Joe felt a corresponding tightness in his groin.

He greeted Jess and Cam and handed Cam a six-pack of beer as he tried to ignore the stirring of lust that threatened to destroy his concentration.

'Good man. I'm living in a teetotaller house these days. I'm trying to be supportive and it's no fun drinking without company,' Cam said as he cracked the tops of a couple of the small bottles and handed one back to Joe. 'Jess isn't drinking either.'

'I'm keeping Kitty company,' she said.

'How many weeks are you now?' Joe asked Kitty. 'Twenty-two?'

'Twenty-four.'

His question had purely been conversational. He knew exactly how many weeks she was.

'We had a scan today,' Jess told him. He thought it was strange that she said 'we'. He knew that genetically the baby was hers and she obviously felt a connection but Kitty was the one who was pregnant. 'Would you like to see the picture?' Jess asked.

'Sure.'

'I'm not sure that Joe is as interested in our baby as we are,' Cam told his wife.

'It's fine,' Joe said, trying to sound enthusiastic.

Jess went to the fridge and removed a small square black and white picture from where it had been held in place by a magnet. She held it out to Joe.

This was OK. He'd seen plenty of ultrasound scans before. It was just a baby. As long as he didn't think that this baby was responsible for the change in Kitty's shape and the subsequent change in his perception of her it was all good. At this stage, it just looked like any baby. With a perfect profile, sucking its thumb.

'Do you know if it's a boy or a girl?' he asked.

Jess shook her head. 'We can't agree. I want to know, but Cam—'

'I want a surprise,' Cam said, finishing Jess's sentence for her as she started coughing. Cam fetched her a glass of water and Jess drank it in fits and starts, between coughs, until she could speak again.

'I want to know because I want to decorate the nursery. If we're only going to do this once I'd like time to be prepared.'

Joe suspected that meant that they *would* find out the sex. In his experience the woman got her way in these things. But who would have the final say? Who would the doctor listen to? Technically, Kitty was the mother. What would she say? He didn't want to ask that question. He decided to stick to a safer topic. 'Only once, you say?'

'I'd be happy with one,' Cam said. 'It's one more than we thought we'd have.'

'I'd like more, but I'm not going to be greedy,' Jess admitted.

'Let's just get this one here safely,' Cam said.

'I know, I'm not going to get ahead of myself but I loved growing up with a sister. I couldn't do this without her,' Jess said as she took the ultrasound picture back from Joe and hugged Kitty, 'and I'd like to think of my own children having the same relationship with a sibling.'

Joe had brothers and sisters, but none of them were full siblings, and he certainly didn't share the bond with any of them like Kitty and Jess had. 'There's no guarantee that they'd get along, you know. I've got five siblings and I don't really get along with any of them.' In fact, he had always thought Kitty was more like a sister than his real ones. Until the past week at least, when he'd started having very unfamilial thoughts about her.

'I find that hard to believe,' Cam said. 'I picked you as one of those blokes that gets on with everyone.'

Joe laughed. 'Maybe that says more about me than them.'

Kitty came to his defence. 'You're not really close in age to any of them and you didn't really grow up together. That makes a difference.'

'I guess what I'm saying is that I grew up virtually as an only child, and in a lot of ways I think I had a happier childhood for it.' His teenage years maybe hadn't been quite so happy, but that was because he'd been old enough to realise that he didn't really fit in with any of his families. But that wasn't because he didn't have siblings—that was because his mum and dad hadn't been able to stay married. To anyone. And that had meant he'd constantly had his boundaries and his living arrangements changed around him, completely out of his control. He hadn't like that and had become rebellious, which had made him difficult to live with. Not just for his parents but probably for some of his brothers and sisters, too. It was circumstances that had made him.

'I didn't know you were one of six,' Jess said.

'Two half-siblings and three step-siblings. In some ways I'm surprised it's not more. My parents divorced when I was four. Mum was Dad's second wife, but they've both been married three times now. That's a lot of families to juggle and a lot of different dynamics. I think I preferred it when I was on my own. In a lot of ways it made life easier.'

Joe didn't think much of a typical family unit but he knew his reservations were due to watching his parents struggle to keep marriages together. Although struggle wasn't the right word—neither of them really seemed to put much effort into making their marriages last. They both seemed to prefer just to give up and move on to the next one. Joe knew that Kitty and Jess had grown up in a stable family unit, at least until tragedy had taken both their parents when Kitty had been nineteen, and he could understand why they expected to have the same stable environment. But in his experience that was virtually impossible. The impossible dream.

'I think we'll just take this one step at a time. One baby at a time,' Cam said as he kissed his wife. 'And see how we manage.'

Joe thought Cam's logic was practical and sensible. There were a lot of unknowns in Cam and Jess's future. The new baby was only one of them.

Dinner was finished—steak and a glass of red wine for Cam and Joe, fish and lime-flavoured sparkling mineral water for Jess and Kitty. Cam cleared the plates and said to Joe, 'Come and join me for a beer while I clean the barbecue.'

Joe followed him over to the grill and took a swig of his beer. 'Do you think this surrogacy thing is a good idea?' he asked as he stood watching Cam work. 'Actually, scratch that. You must.'

Cam didn't answer immediately. 'It's what Jess wanted. I love my wife. I want her to be happy and this is what she wanted. I didn't have the same burning desire to have children. Don't get me wrong, I'm not against the idea, but if it didn't happen for us I was OK with that. But Jess wants kids. I'm doing this for her. That's what love is all about.'

Joe figured he wouldn't know anything about all that but all the same his gaze was drawn to Kitty. He could see her through the window. She was standing by the kettle, pulling mugs off the shelf.

'Speaking of love…' Cam's voice made Joe jump. He dragged his eyes off Kitty and back to Cam, wondering where he was going with this topic, but Cam was scraping the barbecue, seemingly disinterested in who or what Joe was watching. 'Kitty tells me you're seeing someone. Is it serious?'

Joe almost choked. 'God, no. I try to avoid serious relationships.'

'Maybe you just haven't met the perfect girl yet,' Cam

said, echoing the words of so many of Joe's friends, but Joe thought differently.

'No one's perfect,' he said, 'and nothing lasts for ever. I don't see the point in starting something that won't last.'

Even Cam and Jess's relationship, as perfect as it might look from the outside, had its downsides in Joe's opinion. Jess's cancer and inability to get pregnant was far from their idea of perfect. But Joe wasn't about to make an example of Cam's own marriage as his argument.

'What about Kitty?'

'Kitty?'

'Is that so hard to imagine? You and Kitty? You must like her.'

'Of course I like her, she's my best friend.'

He'd been trying to remind himself of that every day since he'd nearly succumbed to temptation and almost kissed her. He continued to tell himself he was glad he'd resisted. That would have been disastrous.

'C'mon, Joe. You don't think Jess and I haven't talked about this? We think you guys would be good together.'

Joe wasn't so sure. As tempted as he had been the other night, he was still convinced that a quick tumble between the sheets would have been a sure way to ruin their friendship. But that hadn't stopped him thinking about it. And opting to take Victoria home that night instead hadn't stopped him thinking about it either. But thinking about it was one thing, acting on it was another thing altogether, and there were dozens of reasons why he would steer clear. Starting with the biggest one—he and Kitty wanted different things out of relationships.

'I'm not the right man for her,' he said. 'Kitty is looking for someone who can commit to her, someone who will promise to never leave her. I don't believe in happily ever after. We'd be a terrible combination.'

'You think?'

Joe nodded. He'd given this a lot of thought over the past couple of weeks, and no matter how much he might wish things had turned out differently he knew he wasn't the right man for Kitty. He was not what Kitty needed. 'Trust me, I'm not the man she needs and I really don't want to ruin a perfectly good friendship.'

Cam laughed. 'There's no such thing as a friendship between a man and a woman. You've heard that saying. Men will always muck it up by wanting sex.'

Cam definitely had a point, but Joe couldn't agree with him. He was desperate to bring this conversation to an end before he admitted to something that had disaster written all over it. 'Wanting and having are two different things, my friend,' he said, 'and it's the having that mucks things up. Better Kitty and I stick to what we do best. It's worked for us so far.'

'OK, mate, whatever you say.' Cam's expression was sceptical as he covered the barbecue and knocked the lids off a couple more beers.

Joe knew he didn't believe him, and he couldn't blame Cam. Even Joe was not convinced, but he knew he couldn't give in to his desires no matter how much he wanted to. He really couldn't risk ruining his relationship with Kitty over his crazy ideas. Surely, given time, he'd get this ridiculous feeling out of his system and life would go on with Kitty being none the wiser.

Twenty-eight weeks. Only twelve to go.

Kitty was no longer thinking of her life in terms of days of the week or even months of the year—everything had been reduced to weeks of her pregnancy and the associated milestones. At twenty-eight weeks she was two-thirds of the way there. The baby was putting on weight, her skin was filling out and she was constantly on the move.

Last week she had volunteered to be a patient at one of the student sonography clinics held at the hospital and she had asked to find out the baby's sex. She was having a girl.

But she had hugged that knowledge to herself. She'd had to share every little piece of this pregnancy with Jess and Cam, and for the most part she'd been happy to do that, but it was nice to have something that was hers alone. She felt a little guilty about keeping the secret, and on occasion she'd had to be careful with her language to ensure she didn't use 'she' in reference to the baby too often. An occasional mention could be passed off as a figure of speech but she had to remember to use 'he' at times too. But in her opinion there was no harm in having this one secret. It wasn't going to hurt anyone.

Cam didn't want to know the baby's sex and Kitty knew it was better to keep her secret than to risk spoiling the surprise for Cam. And not knowing hadn't stopped Jess from starting to decorate the nursery. She had gone for a white palette with pretty pale apple green accents, which she said she could team with pink or navy depending on whether the baby was a boy or a girl.

The baby kicked as if knowing Kitty was thinking about her. She put a hand on her belly and smiled. She was happy. She was doing a good thing for her sister, growing a beautiful baby—and she'd even patched things up with Joe. Things were back on an even keel with him since her birthday dinner. As far as she knew, he was still seeing Victoria but she was trying not to let that bother her. She'd avoided going out with the hospital staff since that night. She used fatigue and the fact that she wasn't drinking as her excuse, but she really didn't want to put herself in a situation where she would have to see Joe and Victoria together. As long as she didn't have to see them together she could pretend it wasn't happening. Ignorance might not be bliss but it was better than the alternative.

And she *was* finding work tiring. Being on her feet for hours on end while carrying around an extra six kilograms was exhausting. She hadn't put on a lot of weight but six kilograms was just the beginning and it felt like a lot on her small frame, meaning she was happy to spend most nights on the couch.

She was due for a break and, unlike her pre-pregnancy days when she'd often skipped or shortened her breaks, now she looked forward to them and made sure she sat down for a few minutes to give her feet and ankles a rest. Her Saturday night shift had been busy and she didn't expect it to get any quieter. She grabbed a sandwich and a piece of fruit from her locker and took it outside.

To her left she spotted Joe, sitting on the retaining wall that separated the garden bed from the ambulance bay. Victoria was standing in front of him, partially obscuring Kitty's view, but she only needed a glimpse to know it was him. Kitty tried to ignore the feelings of jealousy that swamped her. She hated feeling jealous, but she hated seeing Joe with Victoria even more. She was still blaming her hormones even though she knew it was really about the almost-kiss. She was having trouble forgetting that.

She'd been an idiot. She'd nearly ruined their friendship. Of course he'd hesitated. She'd crossed their boundaries. She was relieved that he didn't seem to be holding her faux pas against her, but she couldn't forget it and she couldn't deny that she wanted to know what it would be like to kiss him properly. She'd been dreaming about it. All her searching on the internet had reinforced the idea that her hormones were running wild in this trimester but she couldn't help but think it was more than that. She couldn't get the idea out of her head. She wasn't having fantasies about any other men. Just Joe.

She contemplated going back into the hospital but she really wanted some fresh air. She bit into her apple as she turned right, away from Joe. She didn't think he'd seen her and she certainly didn't want to see the two of them together. It made her feel lonely and diminished her happiness. Jess had Cam and Joe had Victoria, but she had no one.

As if to cheer her up, the baby somersaulted in her womb. She was active tonight, Kitty thought as she put her hand on her stomach. She wasn't alone, not right now, but even the baby was only hers temporarily. This pregnancy was of her choosing, it was what she wanted, but she knew that, ultimately, she wanted to be part of a couple. She wanted to be loved. She wanted a family of her own one day. But for now she needed to focus on the pregnancy and hope that her time would come.

She finished her sandwich and wrapped the apple core in the left-over packaging, then with one final glance in Joe's direction she went back into the hospital. She threw her rubbish in a bin at the triage desk and went to wash her hands, glancing around the waiting area as she dried them. The ED waiting area was empty, the ED quiet; Lisa was the only staff member Kitty could see, which meant that all the other staff were busy in treatment rooms or were taking their breaks. Kitty was walking towards the desk when the entrance doors slid open, admitting a very thin, dishevelled man in a pair of dirty jeans and a grubby T-shirt. Scabs covered his forearms and he was scratching at them agitatedly. He scanned the department as he entered. His eyes were wide, his pupils dilated, and his movements were jerky and frantic. Kitty recognised that look. The familiar look of a methamphetamine user.

His gaze landed on Kitty and he started yelling as he advanced towards her in an unnatural, nervous gait.

'Help me! They're tracking me, they're going to kill me!' His scratching gathered intensity and he had picked off several scabs. His arms were now bleeding.

Kitty was stranded on the wrong side of the desk. The desk was separated from the waiting area by a glass window and access to it was via a pair of doors that needed a security code to open. The desk resembled a bank counter. Lisa was the teller, safely barricaded behind the glass, but Kitty was exposed and vulnerable. She wanted to seek refuge but she was afraid to move, worried that any movement might trigger a reaction in this man. A reaction she wasn't at all keen to witness.

She reached slowly into the pocket of her scrubs and retrieved a pair of surgical gloves, pulling them on carefully as she glanced at Lisa, knowing they needed back-up and knowing Lisa would push the button to call for help.

She reached out a hand, silently begging him to stop, praying that back-up would arrive before he got to her. 'It's all right, no one is going to hurt you here. You're safe.'

He continued to look around but he stopped walking. He'd stopped almost level with the door that Kitty could have escaped through. If he took one more step in her direction he would effectively block her access to safety.

Kitty had to risk it. She knew Lisa could push another button that would open the door and let her in, once Kitty got close enough. She looked at her. Lisa nodded and moved towards the button as Kitty moved towards the door. Towards the man.

'Stay away from me!'

Kitty froze. He'd taken her movement as a threat.

She raised her hands, intending to convey she meant him no harm. Her heart was in her mouth and she could feel every beat echoing through her body. Adrenalin coursed through her, triggering her fight or flight response. She wanted to flee but there was nowhere to go. This man was blocking her escape route, and the only thing between him and her was her pregnant belly.

She couldn't risk it. She had to get out of there. She was terrified, afraid to turn her back, but she had no other option. She was trapped. She couldn't go forward. She could only go back.

Kitty slid back a step, but he took another lurch forward.

'What are you doing?' he yelled at her.

She hesitated. She didn't want to upset him. He was drug fuelled, erratic and unpredictable. Who knew what he was capable of?

Kitty took her eyes off him momentarily, searching to see if help was coming in any form. Surely minutes must have passed since Lisa had pressed the alarm? Where was everyone?

He was watching her. 'Who's there? Is it them?' He turned his head to look over his shoulder and Kitty took another step backwards but she wasn't fast enough. He had turned back to face her, catching her movement.

He advanced towards her, reaching behind his back as he walked. Kitty froze. She was terrified.

He brought his hand forward and Kitty's eyes went wide. He was holding a large knife. Light reflected off the blade, glinting ominously.

Kitty couldn't move. She was so frightened she'd lost voluntary control of her limbs, her muscles stiff and unresponsive.

He lunged at her, and Kitty was surprised by the speed of his movement and the power of his skinny body. She felt a blow to her chest that was hard enough to knock the wind from her lungs. She felt herself falling, and the last thing she remembered was the shine of the overhead fluorescent lights reflecting off the blade of his knife.

CHAPTER FIVE

JOE HAD SEEN Kitty come out of the hospital. Out of the corner of his eye he'd seen her glance his way as he sat with Victoria, and seen her choose not to come and say hello. Things between them had been a little strained for the past few weeks. If he'd had to put a time frame to when it had started he would pick the night at the pub. The night he'd almost kissed her.

Not that she'd said anything. Nothing had been said about it by either of them, and he had to assume he was the only one dwelling on it. That he was the only one who considered it a missed opportunity. He wasn't sure that Kitty had even realised what he'd been so tempted to do. For all he knew, she had been, and still was, oblivious to the whole episode—but it didn't explain how she was behaving.

He'd thought that things might be back to normal when she'd invited him to her birthday dinner but there was still tension between them. He could feel it. And she was definitely avoiding him. She'd made excuses about why she couldn't catch up with him. She'd blamed the pregnancy—she was tired or had appointments—but he wasn't convinced that was the sole reason. He wasn't certain it was to do with the almost-kiss but *something* wasn't right.

Maybe he *should* have kissed her. Maybe that would have brought things to a head and sorted it out once and for all. God knew, he'd spent far too long thinking about the missed opportunity, and he'd thought the best way to get her out of his head was to date someone else but even that wasn't working.

He wished she'd never mentioned wanting sex. He wished she wasn't pregnant and full of raging hormones. Hormones that made her think of random sex with strangers and, in turn, made him think of sex with her. He wished things had stayed the same. But he was having a hard time thinking of her in a platonic sense now. Since she'd talked about wanting sex and his conversation with Cam, all he could think about was 'could it work?' But he knew, realistically, it couldn't. It wouldn't. It would be an unmitigated disaster. He'd mess it up for sure.

But that didn't stop him from dreaming and wishing and imagining. It hadn't stopped him from watching her out of the corner of his eye as she'd sat and eaten and very carefully avoided looking at him.

He knew she'd seen him, and he'd kept an eye on her even as he'd tried to continue his discussion with Victoria. He'd been busy trying to tell her that their relationship wasn't going to work without really explaining why. He couldn't, in good conscience, continue to sleep with her when his head was full of thoughts about making love to someone else. Not even if he knew that was never going to happen. Because the short answer was he couldn't be with Kitty. He'd meant it when he'd told Cam he wasn't the man Kitty needed.

But he'd still kept one eye on her as Victoria had railed at him and called him heartless, and even while she'd accused him of not listening to her or paying attention. He hadn't admitted she was right.

He'd seen Kitty glance their way and choose to head in the opposite direction, and he'd seen her finish eating and disappear back inside the hospital. And, because he'd still been watching the entrance to the ED, he'd noticed a tall, thin man approaching the entrance, too. The man had been dishevelled and talking to himself, and Joe's antennae had pricked.

He'd looked distressed and when Joe saw the guy go into the ED he followed, his suspicions alerted.

The ED doors slid open as they sensed him and Joe stepped inside and found himself in the midst of his worst nightmare.

The ED was virtually empty but despite the lack of people there was noise, chaos and confusion. It was out of proportion considering the emptiness of the space.

Movement to his right caught his eye.

Someone was falling. Fast. He saw their head hit the wall and saw them land in a crumpled heap.

And then he saw that the someone was Kitty.

The guy Joe had followed into the ED was moving towards her and Joe started running before he'd fully taken stock of the situation. All he knew was that he had to get to Kitty.

He sprinted towards her.

Subconsciously he registered that the guy wasn't distressed. He was high.

Joe had seen what methamphetamines could do to people. He'd witnessed the rage it could induce, the psychotic episodes and the physical violence that ensued, and all he could think about was getting to Kitty before this guy did. He didn't stop to think about what he was going to do. He'd seen it take four big men to subdue meth addicts before. He'd been one of those guys holding them down plenty of times so he knew the superhuman strength the drug imparted and there was no way he was going to let this guy harm Kitty. Not more than he already had.

'Hey!' he yelled. He had to distract him. The man turned and Joe reached out, instinctively trying to placate him. It was a ridiculous idea as he was obviously high, but Joe's only thought was to get him away from Kitty. 'What are you doing?'

The guy was still spinning, turning at the sound of Joe's voice. 'Stay away from me.' His rancid breath assailed Joe's senses and his pupils were so dilated that his eyes looked like two dark holes in his face. He lashed out at Joe as he turned. Joe felt a searing pain in his hand and saw the light bouncing off a steel blade.

A knife.

He hadn't anticipated that.

He tried to skid to a stop but his momentum carried him forward, straight into the path of the blade.

Pain burst through his abdomen.

The pain was similar to getting punched in the stomach and Joe had time to think it was strange—he'd always expected knifing pain to be sharp. He pushed the man away from him with a force he hadn't known he had, and as the man stumbled backwards Joe looked down. The pain wasn't excruciating. Maybe he hadn't just been stabbed?

He put his hand over his stomach and it came away

covered in blood. He could feel it now, warm and wet and sticky, soaking into his dark blue uniform.

Ahead of him, over the man's right shoulder, Joe saw four of the hospital security staff arrive, followed by one of the ED doctors. The security guards threw a net over the man, who bucked and thrashed like a wild animal. It took all four guards to hold him down.

As Joe watched the man kicking and screaming under the net, red and blue light bathed the walls of the ED, flashing on and off and making the experience a little surreal as police cars pulled up to the department doors. The police rushed in, tasers in hand and guns holstered, but Joe could see that their holsters were unclipped and ready for whatever happened next. Joe knew they would have been through this process before. They all had. This was nothing new in hospital emergency departments country-wide.

But the police were not the front line this time. The security guards had managed to contain the man. They had his hands pinned behind his back but he continued to resist. Two policeman joined in as they attempted to subdue him, attempted to get him into a position where the doctor could administer a sedative. Six big men and one doctor. All to contain one drug user. And meanwhile Kitty was still lying sprawled against the wall. She hadn't moved and no one had been near her. No one had so much as glanced her way. There was no one spare.

There was only him.

He had to help her.

He took a step towards her but his knees buckled under him, surprising him, and he found himself kneeling on the floor in a pool of his own blood.

He was bent double and it hurt to breathe, but at least

he *was* still breathing. His left hand was pressed against his stomach, just below his ribs, and he could feel his lungs inflate and deflate. His stomach muscles screamed and his right hand throbbed, but he was alive and breathing. Kitty still hadn't moved.

He moved his left hand, placing it on the floor to stabilise himself. He pressed his right elbow into his side and applied pressure to his abdominal wound as he crawled across the floor to Kitty, leaving a trail of blood in his wake.

She was still slumped against the wall. She was pale and her eyes were closed. He could see the small bump of her pregnancy under the blue fabric of her scrubs and he could see the rise and fall of her chest just above the bump. He let out a sigh of relief and some of the tension he'd been holding dissolved with the sigh. She was breathing.

He knelt beside her and reached out, putting his left hand on her shoulder. He winced in pain as the movement stretched his stomach.

'Kitty, can you hear me? Open your eyes.' He shook her shoulder, very gently, and his hand left a bloody print on her top. 'Kitty?' he repeated, and he could hear the desperation in his voice.

There was no response.

'I need some help here,' he called over his shoulder. The sound was loud in his ears, echoing off the walls that were still bathed in blue and red lights from the police cruisers, but there was no reaction. Everyone was busy.

He knew only seconds had passed since he'd stepped inside the ED, even though it felt like an eternity, but Kitty needed help. She needed a doctor.

Joe looked up and saw Anna on the far side of the

department and called her by name. He saw her turn in his direction. He could see as she registered all the blood and hurried over to him.

'Not me,' he said as Anna knelt beside him, assuming he was the one who needed help. 'Check Kitty. She's non-responsive.' He knew he needed medical attention, but in his mind Kitty's need was greater. She was living for two.

'Kitty, can you hear me?'

Joe?

A bright flash of light startled her but as she lifted one hand to block it out it disappeared, only to reappear again a moment later. She felt her eyelids drop and the light went out again.

'Left pupil sluggish.'

'Kitty? Can you hear me? It's Anna Lewis.'

Anna? She was sure she'd heard Joe's voice. What was going on?

'Kitty, open your eyes.'

She opened her eyes and saw the ED doctor squatting in front of her. Why were they both on the floor?

Kitty could hear Anna talking to her and she tried to focus, tried to concentrate on Anna's words. 'You fell and hit your head. We're going to put you on a stretcher and take you to be examined.'

Kitty frowned as she tried to work out what was going on. She felt pressure on her arm, someone was wrapping a blood-pressure cuff around it. She turned her head but the movement made her wince as pain stabbed behind her eyes. She lifted her hand to her head. There was a massive lump at the back of her skull and she had a killer headache.

She closed her eyes as bile rose in her throat. 'I think I'm going to be sick.'

Someone thrust a green bowl towards her, just in time, and Kitty retched into the plastic container.

She lifted her head as she finished vomiting but the pain hadn't eased. If anything, vomiting had made her head throb even more. Out of the corner of one eye she could see someone being restrained by half a dozen men—cops and security guards crowded the ED but she resisted the temptation to turn her head to get a better look, not game to risk more pain. She closed her eyes as the pressure inside her head increased. It felt like her head was on the verge of exploding. The ED was chaotic. Noisy and crowded. People were yelling and moving past quickly. She just wanted some peace and quiet. She just wanted to sleep.

She felt the blood-pressure cuff being loosened around her arm. Heard someone say, 'BP one-sixty over one hundred.'

'Kitty? I need you to open your eyes. I need you to stay awake.' She heard Anna speaking to her. She didn't want to open her eyes. She didn't want to do anything. But she forced one eye open, and then the other. She sensed it was important to do as Anna asked.

Her eyes focussed on a pool of blood on the floor next to her. Where had that come from? Was it hers?

And then she remembered.

The baby!

'Anna?' She pointed to the blood as she struggled to speak. Her tongue felt swollen and her mouth was dry. She struggled to form even a simple word. Her heart pounded in her chest and she could feel the accompanying thump in her brain. 'The baby?'

'Don't worry, it's not your blood,' Anna said.

'Whose…?'

'It's Joe's.'

Another wave of nausea engulfed her and black spots swarmed in front of her eyes as her vision blurred. She resisted the urge to close her eyes and give in. *Joe's?* What had happened? What had happened to Joe? She needed to know how he was. *Where* he was. She looked around the ED but moving her head hurt, and moving her eyes wasn't any better. The nausea intensified and the black spots multiplied and were accompanied now by a ringing in her ears, and as the chaos and noise continued around her she succumbed to the fatigue.

Images flashed through Kitty's brain like drawings in a flip book, but instead of evolving into something recognisable the pictures were jumbled, nonsensical and fleeting. Too fleeting to grab hold of and decipher. There were snippets of conversation, flashes of light and a sensation of falling but nothing that made sense. Her head throbbed and her body ached. She felt battered and bruised but couldn't figure out why.

Her left elbow was sore and when she opened her eyes she could see an IV line snaking its way into her vein.

'Hi. I was wondering when you'd wake up.' Lisa stood at the end of the bed, having moved into the line of Kitty's vision. 'You caused quite a commotion.'

'I did?' Kitty frowned. 'What happened? What am I doing here?'

'You don't remember?'

Kitty shook her head before realising that was a bad idea. 'No,' she said.

'This guy came into the ED, high on methamphetamines, yelling about how "they" were after him. He shoved you. You fell and hit your head and then Joe came in like an avenging angel and—'

'Joe?' Kitty remembered someone saying something about him.

'Yes. He managed to distract the guy, to stop him from assaulting you further, but he was attacked. The guy had a knife.'

A knife! Kitty's heart rate escalated as she remembered the blood. All that blood. It was Joe's. 'Is he all right? Joe? Is he all right?'

'You should have seen him, Kitty. He was amazing. He saved your life.'

Her headache was getting worse. She needed Lisa to stop talking but first she needed an answer. 'Lisa, is Joe OK?'

'He was stabbed,' Lisa said, but she was nodding. 'In the stomach. He had to go into Theatre, but he's out now.'

Kitty breathed out.

'Can you take me to him?' She was exhausted and sore but she had an overwhelming desire to see him.

'I don't think you're allowed to be moved,' Lisa said, just as Anna came into the room.

'You need to rest, Kitty,' she told her, making it clear she'd heard the last part of the conversation.

'I want to see Joe.'

'Joe is going to be fine. You need to rest.'

She didn't think she'd be able to rest, not until she'd seen Joe.

'Jess and Cam are on their way,' Anna continued, 'and the baby needs you to rest. I'm not arguing about this.'

'The baby—'

'Is fine.'

Kitty realised she had instinctively put one hand on her belly. It had become a habit. She held it there, waiting, hoping, needing to feel some movement. 'Are you sure?'

'We did an ultrasound. The baby is fine,' Anna repeated, just as Kitty felt the baby kick. She had a vague recollection of being moved and lifted. Had that been for the scans?

'You need monitoring,' Anna said. 'Your blood pressure is still high and if it doesn't come down I'll need to administer hydralazine, and I am going to arrange a CT scan of your head too. Your baby is fine but I'm sure you want to keep it that way?'

Kitty nodded carefully, agreeing with Anna. But only for her baby's sake.

Joe opened his eyes. The room was dark and it wasn't his room.

Was it morning or night?

He could remember being woken but couldn't remember where he was.

He could hear electronic beeping. Turning his head, he could see monitors beside the bed.

A hospital bed.

He tried to sit up but pain knifed through his abdominals, making him gasp. He clutched his stomach with his right hand and gasped again as pain sliced through his hand as well.

He looked down and saw that his right hand was bandaged, and the memories flooded back. The man. A knife. Kitty!

He tried again to sit up. He needed to find out if Kitty was OK, but the pain in his stomach screamed at him not to move. He lifted the bed sheet with his left hand and saw the dressing on his stomach. He let the sheet fall and rested his head on the pillow.

He should have known better. He'd seen plenty of patients high on drugs and he'd seen first-hand the in-human strength the drug gave them. He should have known better, but he hadn't stopped to think about that this time. All he'd been able to think about was Kitty. All he'd *seen* was Kitty, lying motionless on the floor, with a manic fool headed straight for her.

The clock on the monitor beside his bed said six-thirty and the light around the edge of the window blinds in the room looked like morning, but he had no clue as to what day it was or how long he'd been there.

The call bell was pinned to the left side of his bed. He pressed the button for the nurse.

'Good morning. Back in the land of the living, I see,' the nurse said as she came into the room.

Morning.

That was one question answered.

Joe scanned the nurse's ID badge. *North Sydney Hospital.* The name 'Paula' was typed under her photo. He hadn't moved far. Just upstairs onto a ward.

He frowned. 'How long have I been here?' He held up his bandaged hand. 'And what have they done to me?'

'You were brought to the ward from Recovery last night. You had a deep stab wound to your right abdomen. You had emergency surgery to clean it out and close it up.'

'What about my hand?'

'You've been referred to Dr Clark, she's a hand surgeon, she'll discuss that with you. Now, what can I help you with? Do you need something? More pain relief?'

The nurse picked up the tubing that was feeding pain relief through Joe's arm into his body. He'd seen the monitors but hadn't noticed the IV pump.

'I don't need pain relief but can you find out about a nurse who works here. Kitty Nelson? She was injured in the ED in the same incident as me. Do you know if she's OK?'

'Are you her next of kin?'

'No.' His heart leapt and lodged in his throat. Why was she asking about Kitty's next of kin? 'What happened to her?'

'You know I can't tell you about other patients.'

'Please,' he begged. He had to know if she was all right. He had to know she'd made it.

Paula was older than Joe, closer to forty than thirty, and he doubted his charms would work on her. She'd probably seen and heard it all before. A young nurse would no doubt be more accommodating but he had to try. 'I got into this mess by trying to protect her. I need to know if she's all right.' Paula wore a wedding ring so he tried appealing to her sense of romance, hoping she was happily married to someone who would protect her if necessary.

She looked at him and he smiled. There was no point in pretending he wasn't trying to get her on side.

'OK, I'll see what I can find out.'

It was only when Paula left that he realised he should have asked about the baby too. But, if he was honest, the baby wasn't his concern. Kitty was.

Joe had a constant stream of people in and out of his room for the next ninety minutes. First was the upper limb specialist, who advised him he would need surgery on his hand. The knife had cut through the flexor tendon of his little finger. It could have been worse but even so it would mean six weeks in a hand splint, and surgery had been scheduled for her afternoon list today.

The surgeon had been followed by the police, who wanted a statement from him, but he had no good answer for them about why he'd acted as he had. He'd *reacted*. That was the best explanation he had. He'd reacted without thinking.

Although not totally without thought, but his only consideration had been for Kitty. He'd been taught to assess the danger before diving in but there hadn't been time for that. He'd seen Kitty lying on the floor and reacted, ignoring all his training. His only thought had been Kitty's safety, he hadn't considered his own at all.

Despite the fact that Joe hadn't exactly followed protocols, the police also wanted to know if he would like to press charges. But unless pressing charges meant Kitty's assailant would be forced to undergo rehab Joe didn't see the point, and he didn't want to spend any longer than necessary on filing paperwork. He wanted everyone to get out of his room—unless they were bringing him news of Kitty.

But Paula went one better than news. Five minutes after the police had left she wheeled Kitty into his room.

His heart missed a beat when he saw her in a wheelchair. She had dark circles under her eyes but she was smiling. Maybe things weren't as bad as he'd feared. 'Kitty! Are you OK?'

She nodded slowly. 'I have a concussion, a headache, a bit of dizziness and a few bruises, but otherwise I'm fine,' she said, as Paula put the brakes on the wheelchair and told them she'd be back in ten minutes.

'And the baby?'

'Is fine too,' Kitty said, as she stood and took the two steps to Joe's bedside. She bent over and kissed his cheek. 'I'm doing better than you by the looks of things.'

'I'm OK.' He was much better now that he'd seen her with his own two eyes.

'Lisa said you got stabbed.'

'Slashed, more precisely.' He held up his right hand, downplaying his injuries. 'A cut to my hand and one to my stomach.'

'Lisa also said you saved my life.'

'That's a definite over-exaggeration.'

Kitty wasn't so sure. She preferred to believe Lisa's version of events. The version where Joe had rushed to her side like a knight in shining armour. No one had ever done that for her before. It sounded very romantic but she knew she'd just embarrass him if she made a big deal out of it. It *was* a big deal to her. 'Thank you anyway,' she said, before kissing his cheek again. 'How long will you be in here for?' she asked as she sat carefully on the edge of his bed.

'Hopefully only until tomorrow. I'm having surgery on my hand this afternoon.'

'Surgery?'

'I have to have a tendon repaired, which means six weeks in a splint, but I shouldn't need long in hospital.'

'Does that mean six weeks off work?' Kitty asked. She knew he'd go mad from boredom if he was out of action for that long.

'I'm sure there will be office work or something I can do,' he said. 'Paramedics are always getting injured on the job, there's a constant rotation through the office of ambos on light duties or returning from extended time off. I'm sure they'll find me something. Otherwise I'll go around to Cam and Jess's and help paint the nursery.'

'Left-handed?'

'Sure.'

She smiled. 'Jess won't let you anywhere near her nursery. She's been planning it for ever.' Jess was an interior designer and Kitty knew that her baby's nursery would be the most important project her sister had ever tackled. She had already spent hours obsessing over paint colours, fabrics and furniture to make sure it was perfect. 'You're going to be sidelined for a while, though, aren't you? Showering and dressing will be difficult, let alone cooking.' She'd been a nurse for long enough to know the difficulties Joe would face, being right-handed *and* living alone. 'You might have to get Victoria to give you a hand when you're discharged.'

'Victoria?'

'Yes, haven't the two of you got a thing going on?'

'We hooked up a couple of times if that's what you mean but I wouldn't say we had a thing. I've told her it can't be anything serious and I certainly won't be asking her to help me out.'

Joe *never* had anything serious going on with his women, Kitty knew that. He went through them faster than Kitty could blink but suddenly her day didn't seem quite so dismal.

'What will you do?'

'No idea,' he replied. 'I'll figure something out.'

'I can help if you'd like?'

'What with? I'm not letting you do all the heavy lifting when you're seven months pregnant.'

'Why not? It won't be hard, in fact, it'll be easier than what I have to cope with at work. No aggressive drugged-out patients, for a start. And I won't be allowed back to work until my symptoms have all settled. We can keep each other company while we recover,' she said, as Paula returned to take her back to her room. 'Think about it. I'll come back and see you later after your surgery. You can tell me your answer then.'

'When I'm groggy from the anaesthetic and not thinking straight?'

'Something like that,' she said with a smile, as she kissed him on the cheek and sat back in the wheelchair. 'But don't think this discussion is over.'

Jess got up again to fetch another drink from the water cooler in the corner of the oncologist's waiting room. Cam had offered to fetch it for her as her coughing fit showed no signs of abating, but his wife seemed to be having trouble sitting still.

Cam knew she was on edge. She always went into these appointments expecting the worst, and he always sat there feeling useless and wishing there was something he could do to fix everything. And today was worse than usual due to the added stress over Kitty and the baby after yesterday's assault.

'I'm sure it's going to be fine,' he said, trying to reassure her while knowing that was near impossible. For two years after she'd undergone the hysterectomy for uterine cancer Jess had been having follow-up reviews every three months, but these were now being stretched out to every six months and as far as Cam could work out that was a positive sign. Everything had been fine six months ago, and in his mind there was no reason to think anything would be different this time. But he knew that Jess's mind worked differently from his. 'We'll have the check-up, and then we can go and collect Kitty.'

He was hoping distraction would work as a technique. Kitty was being discharged today and she was waiting for Cam and Jess to collect her after this appointment. Cam hoped that if Jess was thinking about Kitty while they waited to see the specialist perhaps she wouldn't dwell on her own situation. Waiting was always the worst part. The sooner Jess got in to see the doctor the sooner they'd hear good news and the sooner things would be back to normal.

He held her hand and gave it a squeeze. He waited for her to look at him and then he smiled. She smiled back but he could see the effort it cost her and his heart ached. He wished he could relieve all her worries. He loved her and he hated to see her worried or stressed, and he hated feeling so helpless. Not for the first time he wished that he had been the one who had cancer. He would much prefer to have been the one to suffer rather than watching Jess suffer. Her diagnosis had taken a toll on both of them. He didn't imagine that the same wouldn't have been true in the reverse situation but he'd still rather be the one suffering the physical and emotional pain if it meant sparing Jess that burden.

'Jess?' Dr Tennant called them into the consulting room just as Jess started coughing again. She drained the cup of water and refilled it before entering the room as Cam held the door for her. 'How are you feeling?' the oncologist asked as they sat down.

'Tired,' Jess replied, and Cam felt a flicker of concern. Jess hadn't mentioned that to him. 'I've been decorating a nursery,' she continued, and Cam saw that she was smiling and he relaxed. Her fatigue was simply a result of physical activity. 'The surrogacy worked,' Jess said. She'd talked of nothing else at the last oncology appointment. 'We're expecting a baby. My sister is the surrogate.'

'Congratulations! How far along is she?'

'Twenty-eight weeks,' Jess said, before another bout of coughing caught up with her.

Dr Tennant was watching Jess closely and Cam saw her make a note in Jess's file.

'Is that the only reason you're tired?' she queried.

Jess shrugged. 'I'm not sleeping that well. This cough is bugging me.'

Cam's concern spiked again. He knew Jess's cough woke her during the night—it woke them both—but he'd thought she always managed to get back to sleep.

'How long have you had it?'

'I'm not sure. A few weeks?' Jess said, as she looked at Cam for confirmation.

He nodded but then stopped to think. 'Maybe longer,' he suggested. He'd got used to it, they both had, and he couldn't really remember exactly when it had started. With all the excitement over the pregnancy they'd probably both ignored it but the expression on the doctor's face was bothering him. They'd ignored the cough but the doctor looked like she didn't think it was nothing.

'Hop on the scales for me,' Dr Tennant instructed.

'You've lost weight,' she said, as Jess got off the scales and slipped her shoes back on. And Cam felt the first real flicker of alarm building in his chest.

CHAPTER SIX

JESS KNEW SHE'D lost weight recently. She'd tried to increase her portion sizes to counteract it but her appetite hadn't been great and she rarely finished a meal.

'Any other changes?' the doctor continued. 'Headaches? Chest pain? Unusual bleeding? Shortness of breath?'

'Headaches,' she admitted.

'Headaches?' Cam repeated. It was no wonder he sounded surprised. She hadn't said anything to him about the headaches, presumably because she hadn't wanted him to worry.

'Just a few,' she said, trying to wipe out the worry in Cam's eyes, although if she was honest it was more like one, constant, dull headache in the background of her life, which occasionally got worse before settling again.

Dr Tennant popped a stethoscope into her ears and listened to Jess's chest. 'Deep breaths,' she instructed. 'No temperature?' she queried as she packed the stethoscope away.

Jess shook her head.

'Is your cough productive?'

Jess nodded.

'OK. I'd like to send off a sputum sample and I'm also going to send you for a CT scan of your chest.'

'What are you looking for?'

'What do you think it is?' Jess and Cam spoke in unison. Jess was worried now and she slipped her hand into Cam's, needing the security of his touch, even though it wasn't going to affect the oncologist's answer.

'I'm not going to hazard a guess without more information. We'll run some tests and then I'll discuss the results with you when I get them.'

She drew some blood and took a sputum sample before printing out a referral for the CT scan. Jess's hand was shaking as she took the piece of paper.

Cam kept hold of her hand as they left the doctor's office. Jess didn't think she would have made it out of there without his support.

'Do you want to grab something to eat before we collect Kitty?' Cam asked.

Jess shook her head. 'No, I'm not hungry. And please don't say anything to Kitty about the tests,' she said as they took the lift to Kitty's floor. 'She's still recovering from the attack and I don't want her to worry about something that will hopefully be nothing.'

But that didn't stop her palms from sweating and her heart from racing. She tried to keep calm, tried to keep her composure. She didn't want to upset Cam or Kitty, but she was worried. She'd been worried for a while but had been trying to ignore her symptoms by focussing on Kitty's pregnancy, on their baby, but the truth was she *hadn't* been feeling well and had been pretending everything was fine. That was why she'd been edgier than normal today—she knew Cam had noticed—because she'd been expecting bad news. She hadn't got it yet but she certainly hadn't been reassured by anything the oncologist had said. Dr Tennant hadn't needed to spell it out for her. She knew she was on borrowed time.

Kitty stepped out of Cam's car as he pulled to a stop in front of Joe's building. She had spent one night at her sister's house after she'd been discharged from hospital but now she had convinced Joe to let her nurse him. She hovered over him as he gingerly unfolded himself from the back seat. The hospital was only a ten-minute drive from his house but the whole process of discharge appeared to have taken its toll. Kitty could see the little tell-tale lines of pain gathering at the corners of his mouth. She needed to get him upstairs and get some painkillers into him.

She was pleased he had accepted her offer of help. She was pleased, too, that things were over between him and Victoria, although she didn't want to think about the sort of friend that made her—taking pleasure in the fact that Joe had just ended a relationship. But she didn't feel too mean-spirited. Their break-up suited her—now she could have him to herself.

Cam carried Kitty's small overnight bag up the stairs to Joe's third-floor flat as Kitty continued to hover anxiously over Joe. He held his left hand against his stomach, over his wound, and took the stairs slowly but steadily.

'Are you sure you don't want to come and stay at our place, Joe?' Cam asked when they reached his door. 'We don't have any stairs.'

'I appreciate the offer, mate, but after two nights in hospital I'm really looking forward to being in my own bed.'

'Fair enough, but the offer stands. You can take it up at any time if you change your mind.'

'Is Jess OK with me staying here with Joe for a little while?' Kitty asked as they went inside. 'She doesn't feel like I'm abandoning her?'

Cam hesitated before answering and Kitty held her breath. She hoped she wasn't upsetting her sister by opting to look after Joe, but she really wanted to do this.

'She'll miss you,' Cam replied eventually, 'but she understands. Just don't make it permanent, at least not while you're pregnant. She feels more connected to the pregnancy if you're under our roof.'

'I know. I'll be back before you know it. Tell her it won't be for ever,' Kitty said. Nothing in her life seemed to last for ever, so why would this living situation be any different?

'Where do you want me to put your bag?' Cam asked.

'Put it in my room,' Joe replied.

'Leave it out here,' Kitty said at the same time. 'I'll sleep on the couch.'

'You're kidding, aren't you?' Joe remarked.

'Why not? I did before,' Kitty replied.

'This is different now. You're pregnant.'

'All right, I'll leave you to sort that out. I'm going to get home to Jess,' Cam said as he backed out of the flat.

'Thanks for the lift, Cam,' Kitty said. 'Tell Jess I'll pop over to see her tomorrow.'

Cam looked as if he was about to say something in response and Kitty waited, but he seemed to change his mind and just nodded and turned away. Kitty shrugged her shoulders as he closed the door, wondering if she'd imagined the look in his eyes—almost as though he was debating whether or not to say more. He knew where to find her, she supposed, as she turned back to continue her conversation with Joe.

'I think, with your injuries, your bed is the best place for you. You even told Cam you were looking forward to being back in it.'

'And I am. But I thought we'd share.'

'Share?'

'Yeah. It's a king-size, there's plenty of room for both of us.'

Maybe, Kitty thought, *but that was before I started thinking about kissing you. Before my pregnancy hormones made me think about sex twenty-four seven. Before I wanted to tear your clothes off...*

For a moment she wondered how this was going to work. She couldn't imagine sleeping peacefully next to him, not with her rampaging hormones. But he *was* injured—that should dampen his libido—and he hadn't shown any signs of wanting to get down and dirty with her anyway, so she'd just have to rein her hormones in and keep her hands to herself. It could be a long six weeks. But Joe wasn't waiting for her to mentally process the situation. He was still talking.

'...to help.'

'Sorry, what did you say?'

'I appreciate you offering to help me out for the next few weeks but I'm only accepting on the condition that you sleep in my bed. I meant it when I said I wasn't going to let you take the couch. If I thought I'd get any sleep on the sofa *I'd* take it, but there's room for us both in the bed. Although if you think it will be a problem, I can organise a home nurse to come in once a day to give me a hand.'

The new, crazily hormonal, pregnant Kitty knew it

would test her reserves but she *had* offered to help. She'd have to summon up the old Kitty and block out all the crazy daydreams and fantasies.

'Of course we'll manage,' she said as she settled Joe on the couch and busied herself with some housework. She put fresh sheets on the bed and put a load of dirty sheets into the washing machine. She put the kettle on and prepared a simple dinner—omelettes and salad—and pretended everything was completely normal.

Joe was back on the couch after dinner but Kitty's head was aching. Trying to keep busy and avoid sitting down with Joe had its downsides. She'd overdone it when she should have been resting too, and now she was paying the price. It was time for some paracetamol and bed.

She yawned and stretched. 'I think I might call it a night. Will you be able to get yourself undressed if I go to bed now?'

'I'll be fine,' he said. He was wearing tracksuit pants and a T-shirt that he could pull over his head with one hand. They weren't difficult clothes to get out of. In fact, perhaps it wouldn't be a bad idea if he *didn't* get undressed.

Kitty changed into an oversized T-shirt and swallowed a couple of painkillers. If she'd imagined she and Joe would be sharing a bed she would have packed a pair of pyjama bottoms but she didn't currently have any that fitted comfortably. Her expanding waistline made everything too tight. She climbed into bed after first working out what side Joe slept on—there was a charging dock for his phone and a couple of books on the left-hand side of the bed, so Kitty opted for the right side—and pulled the covers up to disguise the fact that she was almost naked.

* * *

She woke to find herself spooning in Joe's arms. His left arm was draped across her, resting on her stomach. He was warm and she was comfortable and she couldn't see the harm in lying there for a few moments while she enjoyed the feel of him. She imagined she could feel his heart beating against her back. She wondered if he was awake. She listened to the sound of his breathing, trying to judge. She was tempted to roll over. Tempted to see what he was wearing.

She could feel his breath on her neck and his stubble was rough on her skin. She liked the feel of it. She was aware of everything. She could even feel each of his fingertips through her shirt where they rested against her belly. It felt good to be lying in his arms. Too good.

She wondered what would happen if she rolled over. They would be lying inches apart. Less.

What would happen? Would he kiss her? Would he back away if she kissed him?

The baby moved, interrupting her train of thought and bringing her back to reality with a sharp and carefully placed kick. She felt the baby push against her belly. Against Joe's hand.

'Was that the baby?'

He was awake.

Suddenly she was more conscious of the position they were in. It had felt comfortable when she'd thought he was asleep, but now she was aware of how intimate it actually was. But it was too late to worry about that now.

She could feel the baby's leg pushing sideways, distending her belly. What would the old Kitty have done in this situation? She summoned up those memories of a simpler time and interlaced her fingers with Joe's.

She moved his hand slightly, holding it over the baby's foot. 'She's doing her morning exercises,' she told him.

Joe could hear the smile in Kitty's voice. He hadn't meant to wake in this position but he wasn't complaining. As always, she fitted just perfectly into his embrace, even if this position was far from their usual.

He'd been awake for several minutes, lying quietly, enjoying the feeling of having Kitty in his arms, trying not to wake her. He had no idea if he'd ever get this chance again.

She smelt fantastic. He closed his eyes and breathed in her familiar vanilla scent. She smelt like she felt—warm and soft and sweet. He wanted to bury himself in her. Inhale her, breathe her in, not let her go.

He'd expected her to wake and move out of his arms immediately. He'd expected her to be flustered, embarrassed, affronted, all manner of things, but he hadn't expected this. This intimacy, this easiness.

Her hips were pressed in against him. Or he was pressed against her. He could feel his erection nestled in the cleft in her buttocks, but as far as he could tell Kitty hadn't noticed. Perhaps she was too distracted by the baby's movements. It was incredible to think that Kitty would be having this experience several times a day. That she had a tiny human growing inside her.

Even though he was doing his best to be supportive, he still wasn't thrilled about the fears for the future that this pregnancy brought up, but he had to admit he was grateful to the baby right now. If it hadn't started moving he suspected Kitty would have been up and out of bed before she'd even woken properly once she realised the position they were in, but half-asleep and still relaxed, she seemed happy to lie there.

He could feel her body heat radiating through her shirt and into his hand and against his chest. She was like a little hot-water bottle. He knew the pregnancy was raising her body temperature. His was raised too, and he knew what was causing that. Heat and desire surged through him.

Waking in this position felt extremely intimate. Intimate and sensual. It made him think about waking like this every morning and how that would feel. He never usually thought into the future like that. He lived in the moment as far as intimacy was concerned, never imagining that his relationships could develop into something permanent. He knew that was one of his major character flaws: an inability to commit.

Lord knew, neither of his parents seemed to be able to manage it. Why would he be any different? But for the first time ever, the idea of waking up every day with a woman in his bed, in his arms, didn't frighten the life out of him.

He knew the reason was because of the woman.

This wasn't about him and his failings—Kitty made him want to try to be a better man. He wanted to try to be the man she needed.

He wondered if that was even possible for him. Could he be that man? What would Kitty think? Could he risk finding out? Should he take a chance?

But before he had time to answer his own question, Kitty had moved away from him.

'Ouch! The baby just kicked my bladder,' she said as she pushed back the covers and climbed out of bed. Cool morning air rushed under the sheets. Kitty had taken her warmth, and his chance, with her, leaving him with a missed opportunity and an ache in his groin.

She disappeared into the bathroom without a backward glance and he wondered if the baby was really causing problems or if Kitty had just needed an excuse to get out of bed.

Kitty wished she'd been brave enough to take a chance. To roll over when she'd wanted to, before the baby's mistimed kick had connected with her bladder and given her no choice but to get out of bed.

Perhaps it was just as well, she thought as she closed the bathroom door. She didn't think she could stand being rejected again. She felt as though she'd only just recovered her equilibrium after their almost-kiss.

She needed time to cool down, to collect her thoughts. She turned on the taps in the shower and stepped under the spray. She imagined she could still feel the imprint of Joe's arm around her, of his hand resting on her belly, before the water washed it away.

She ran her soapy hands over her breasts, imagining how it would feel to have Joe touch her. To have Joe's fingers on her breast, his tongue on her nipple...

God, she was aroused. Her hormones were driving her crazy.

She breathed out, battling to get herself under control. Her imagination wasn't helping.

Perhaps she'd have to rethink her offer to stay and help him. She'd been mad to think she could handle it. But there was no getting out of it this morning. She'd have to manage for at least one day. She needed to get herself together and work out how to control her impulses before they got her into trouble.

She rested her hands on the cool tiles on the wall

and let the water run down between her shoulder blades while she forced her mind to go blank.

She stepped out of the shower, dried herself and pulled her T-shirt back over her head. She had nothing else to put on and didn't think it was wise to come out of the bathroom wrapped only in a towel. She stepped into her underwear. Her clothing wasn't much of a defence against her rampaging desire, but it was all she had.

Joe hadn't moved. He was still lying in bed when she returned from the bathroom. His chest was bare, tanned and smooth. Her pulse quickened and heat flushed her cheeks.

Her gaze flicked down before she could stop herself, following the line of his sternum, down the centre of his abdominals before it stopped at the bed sheet that was pulled up to his hips. She still didn't know if he was naked under the sheet. Surely he couldn't be. He wouldn't have come to bed wearing nothing. More's the pity.

But wondering about Joe's state of undress was not the way to get herself under control. She needed something to keep her mind occupied.

'Do you want to shower?' she asked quickly. 'I'll waterproof your arm for you if you like.'

'Sounds good,' he said as he rolled out of bed. His abdominal muscles rippled as he lifted his head, and Kitty held her breath as the sheet fell away and he swung his legs out of bed to stand up.

Kitty's eyes dropped lower. She couldn't help herself.

He was wearing boxer shorts.

Her disappointment was abated a little by the impressive bulge in his shorts.

She swallowed uncertainly and took a step back. Not

that she was standing too close, but it was instinctive to try to put some space between them. Some physical distance. His semi-nakedness was making her nervous. She wasn't sure exactly how she was going to keep her hormones in check and fight the attraction if they were going to be in such close proximity for the next few weeks.

She got busy fetching a plastic bag and tape to protect the splint on his arm from the shower spray. She really should be protecting *herself.* She couldn't afford to cross the line. Joe's friendship was far too important.

She sat next to him on the bed. So much for keeping her distance—she could feel the heat radiating off him, and she could smell the sleepiness of his body. It was a warm, familiar scent.

His bare knees brushed against hers as she turned to him and pulled the plastic bag over his splint. They'd sat like this plenty of times before, but never in a bedroom. It had never felt this intimate before. She covered his arm carefully, her fingers light on his skin as if she was afraid to touch him, afraid of what that might lead to, and secured it with the tape.

'Can you manage everything else?' she asked, hoping he would say no but half-wishing he'd say yes. Wishing he'd make the first move, take the first step and take the decision away from her. If he made a move she knew she wouldn't resist. She wouldn't have the willpower.

'I can.' He was watching her carefully, his blue eyes dark, making her breath catch in her throat. Was that sleep or desire turning his eyes indigo?

She knew she should get dressed while Joe was in the shower but she couldn't seem to make her legs move.

They were heavy and uncooperative, so she stayed sitting on the bed.

'Kitty? Can you give me a hand?' She heard the shower stop running and heard him call to her.

She went into the bathroom.

Joe had managed to remove the plastic bag that had protected the splint from his arm and was now, very definitely, completely naked. Kitty could feel her blood pounding in her veins. She wasn't sure what she'd expected to find, but she hadn't prepared herself for this. She felt like she knew him so well yet she'd never seen him completely naked before.

Fortunately, or perhaps unfortunately—she wasn't certain yet—he had his back to her. His shoulders were broad and tanned and she could see the outline of his trapezius muscles above his shoulder blades and the ridge of muscle running down either side of his spine. She wanted desperately to run her fingers along his spine, to trace the length of his body, but she had to be content to savour him with her eyes instead. Her gaze trailed down to the cleft between his buttocks. His backside was firm, muscular, nicely rounded. Two perfect globes, slightly paler than the rest of his skin but not much. His buttocks looked smooth and cool, like marble, and her fingers itched to run over his skin, to feel it under her palm.

He was holding a towel in his left hand, obviously unable to wrap it around himself with only one hand. She reached for the towel, resisting the urge to reach for him, and took it from his fingers. From behind she reached around him, wrapping the towel around his waist and tucking one end into the other over his left hip. It seemed such a pity to cover up the view. But then he turned around. Now she was face to face with his naked chest.

This she'd seen before, many times, but somehow today it seemed far more intimidating.

She'd rested her head against that same chest on plenty of occasions. She couldn't count the number of times he'd hugged her, but she couldn't recall him ever hugging her shirtless. She didn't think she'd ever been this close to his bare chest before and she was copping an eyeful—a very attractive eyeful. His chest was still damp and little droplets of moisture glistened on his skin and caught in the fine hair that ran down between the ridge of his abdominals.

The air around them felt positively charged, making it difficult to breathe. Maybe it was just the steaminess of the bathroom. The hot, humid air was heavy and it was an effort to breathe it in. She was feeling a little light-headed. She needed to get him dry and dressed and get out of there.

She stepped back and her eyes dropped lower, down to where the trail of hair disappeared beneath the towel. Her eyes caught on the waterproof dressing above his right hip. The dressing that covered the knife wound. The wound he'd got protecting her. She wondered if he thought it was worth it.

'I would,' he said.

She lifted her eyes and met his gaze. His blue eyes were dark, his gaze unwavering.

'Would what?' she asked.

'I would do it again. To protect you.' His voice was deep, quiet, intense and honest, and his words sent a shiver of anticipation and excitement through her.

She dropped her gaze again, needing to break the spell, and reached out and traced the edges of the dressing with her fingers. His skin was warm. That surprised her. She'd expected it to be cool by now. The warmth of his skin made her fingers feel icy in contrast, and she could see little goose-bumps rising on his stomach, heard him catch his breath.

'Sorry, are my hands cold?'

'No.' His voice was husky now and his eyes an even more intense blue.

Her hand stilled as she looked up at him. Everything about him looked hard and intense—his body, his gaze, his intentions, his need, his desire—and Kitty's heart pounded in her chest. Her breath caught again in her throat.

She didn't know what she should do. Should she reach for him? Tell him how she was feeling? She was so unsure, and her uncertainty made her take a step back just as he stepped forward.

He reached for her. She felt his fingers under her chin and now it was *her* skin that tingled and broke out in tiny goose-bumps.

He whispered her name as he tipped her head up and Kitty closed her eyes, waiting for the kiss she knew was coming this time.

His lips met hers, warm and soft, but his intentions were clear, spelt out in his touch as he pressed his lips against hers. Kitty opened her mouth, desperate to taste him, to feel him, to experience him. She breathed out a sigh as he wrapped his left arm around her, holding her to him. Her hands wound around the back of his neck. His hair was damp—she probably needed to get him dry, but she had other things on her mind.

She could feel his erection, separated from her only by the towel and her underwear. He was hard and long and now all she could think about was how he would feel inside her. She could feel the dampness between her thighs as she imagined him thrusting into her. Uniting them in a way they'd never shared before. Her knees wobbled and she clung to him. In another moment there would be no turning back.

That was good—she didn't *want* to turn back—but he was injured and she didn't want to be the one responsible for pulling his stitches out, opening his wounds.

'Careful,' she whispered. 'You're injured, remember?'

His left hand moved further down her back, cupping her bottom, pulling her hips in hard against him. 'I'm fine,' he replied.

She ran one hand down his chest. She had to agree, he felt pretty fine. His chest was dry now—the water had soaked into her T-shirt, making it cling to her skin. Now that her clothes were damp and she wasn't pressed against his chest, soaking up his warmth, she felt cool. Her nipples jutted against the shirt and as she saw Joe run his gaze over her breasts she felt her nipples tighten in response.

She watched his chest rise as he inhaled. He moved his left arm, bringing his hand to her chest and running his thumb over one nipple, caressing it through the fabric.

Kitty thought she might melt on the spot as a burst of heat raced through her, flaring from her breasts to her groin.

'Oh, God, Joe,' she said as she clung to him, and she could hear the desire and need in her voice.

'Are you sure about this?'

'I've never been surer about anything,' she said, as she took his hand and led him out of the bathroom.

He caught her at the edge of the bed and turned her

to face him. He pulled the towel from his hips and stood in front of her gloriously, superbly naked. Kitty feasted her eyes on him. She took in his broad shoulders, the dark circles of his nipples, the line of dark hair running down from his navel, leading her eyes down to where his erection jutted proudly out from his hips.

He ran his hand around the back of her neck, spanning her spine with his fingers, holding her still as he kissed her neck. Kitty tipped her head back, exposing the soft, tender, sensitive skin of her throat.

He lifted the hem of her T-shirt, keeping her close, before trying to tug the shirt up and off, but it was an impossible task with only one hand. Kitty crossed her arms and whipped the shirt over her head.

'You are beautiful,' he murmured before he bent his head and took one breast in his mouth. Kitty thought she might explode as he sucked her nipple. He ran his hand over her swollen belly and down between her thighs, seeking her warmth, sliding into her wetness.

Joe went to sit down on the edge of the bed and Kitty moved with him, stepping out of her underwear as she did. She stood with her legs apart, straddling his knees, desperate to maintain contact, and granted him access to her innermost secrets.

Her legs buckled as his mouth suckled at her breast again while he reached between her legs, his thumb moving in a tight circle. She rested her hands on his shoulders, supporting her weight. Her legs certainly weren't capable of holding her up as he worked his magic with his fingers. If he could reduce her to a quivering mess with his left hand, what would he be able to do once his right hand was fully functioning again?

She closed her eyes as stars burst behind her eyelids and sparks shot through her groin. She was panting now, unable to take deep breaths as her body was focussed on other sensations. She was close to a climax, she could feel it building, taking control, but she didn't want it like this.

She opened her eyes. 'Wait.'

'What's wrong?' His hand stilled and she could see in his eyes that he was expecting her to call it quits. There was no way she was doing that—she didn't think she could stop now even if she wanted to.

'Nothing,' she said, 'but I want to feel you inside me.'

He smiled, relief and desire reflected in his eyes now. 'You'll have to go on top.'

She had no problem with that. In reply she pushed him gently backwards until he was lying on the bed.

'There are condoms in the drawer,' he told her.

She was about to remind him that she was pregnant and that she didn't need protection but then she thought about all the other reasons to practise safe sex. She supposed she should be grateful that he was being responsible, but she didn't want to think about *why* he had condoms in his bedside drawer. She didn't want to think about all the other women he might have slept with in this bed. It was her turn now and she didn't want to waste a second thinking about anything other than Joe and the pleasure they were about to share.

She reached into the drawer and removed one little packet. She knelt over him and wrapped her hand firmly around his shaft. She slid her hand up and down his length and felt him throb beneath her fingers, felt him tremor under her touch. She watched as he closed his eyes and relaxed on the bed, breathing in and out, slow and deep.

'Kitty, please,' he begged, his voice ragged and breathless.

Her hand slowed but she maintained contact as she tore open the packet with her teeth and sheathed his erection. It was, she imagined, another impossible task to accomplish one-handed. His eyes were open now and he watched her as she lifted herself onto her knees and slowly lowered herself down onto him. She took her time, savouring the moment when they were finally, blissfully joined together.

She placed her hands on either side of his head, supporting her weight as she bent over him. He lifted his head and took her breast into his mouth as she rode him. Their hips moved in perfect harmony, his thrusts keeping time to her rhythm, as if they'd done this dance a hundred times before. His fingers were between her legs, circling the swollen nub that nestled there. Kitty arched her back and spread her legs wider, taking him deeper, wanting all of him, every last piece as waves of pleasure overwhelmed her.

'Now, Joe, now!'

She felt him join her in pleasure and then release, their years of friendship shifting and changing and culminating into something far more powerful, far more thrilling than anything she had experienced before.

She lay beside him, utterly spent, resting her head on his chest, and listened to his breathing as she lay cocooned in his arms. She felt completely relaxed and content, and the feeling surprised her. She had thought there might be some awkwardness but instead she felt like she belonged there. It was a strange but wonderful sensation.

CHAPTER SEVEN

KITTY EMBRACED JESS as she opened the door. She felt thin, but Kitty didn't think anything of it. Jess had always been slim, especially since the chemo, and now her slightness felt even more apparent when contrasted with Kitty's changing shape as she went further into her third trimester of the pregnancy.

'How are you feeling?' Jess asked.

'Exhausted,' Kitty replied as she followed Jess into the house.

'You should have called. You could have come over later.'

She realised Jess thought her tiredness was due to the concussion. Should she tell her it was because she'd spent the better part of the last two hours in bed with Joe, exercising muscles she almost hadn't remembered having?

'No, no, it's fine. I wanted to see you.'

She stuck her head into the baby's nursery, eager to see what Jess had been up to for the past few days. She hadn't thought to look at it yesterday when her head had still been woozy from the concussion and she was surprised to find it almost finished. The bottom half of the walls had been papered in a gorgeous pale green-and-white-striped wallpaper that Kitty hadn't seen before, and mobiles hung from the ceiling above the newly assembled change table and cot. Tucked into one corner in front of a small bookcase and reading lamp was an inviting armchair upholstered in a pale apple green.

'Wow, you've been busy.'

'I had some time on my hands,' Jess said. 'I'm keen to get it finished. It was strange being in the house without you. And without the baby. Working on the nursery made me feel connected to you both, although I can't take credit for much more than the design choices and dressing the cot. I'm keen to meet my baby and I sort of feel that if I get the nursery ready, maybe it will hurry things up. At least *I* feel ready.'

'Don't be in too much of a hurry, I've got a while to go yet!' Kitty wasn't ready for the pregnancy to end yet. The baby wasn't due for another eleven weeks or so, and she wasn't quite ready to give the baby up.

'I know,' Jess replied. 'But I needed something to keep me busy. How is everything going in there?' She asked as she put her hand on Kitty's belly. Kitty was getting used to people touching her stomach without asking. Everyone seemed to think of it as separate from her and didn't seem to think they needed permission. But in this case Kitty didn't mind. Jess *definitely* didn't need permission. After all, the baby was hers.

'Are you positive you're fine after the incident? Both of you?'

Kitty nodded. 'I'm sure. I've got a few bruises and a dull headache still, but the baby is perfectly fine.'

'Your shape has changed,' Jess said as she took her hand off Kitty's tummy. 'That seems to have happened quickly.'

Kitty saw a flash of something on her sister's face but

she didn't have time to work out what it was. Sadness? Regret? Anxiety? Distress?

Kitty remembered Cam's expression of the day before. The similarities between his expression and Jess's now didn't go unnoticed. Maybe staying at Joe's wasn't the right thing to do. She knew Jess wanted—needed—to feel connected to the pregnancy. Maybe she should be here? But Joe needed her too. Kitty was torn. She wasn't used to having so many people relying on her.

'Is everything OK?' she asked. 'Do you want me to move back in? Joe can organise for a home nurse,' she offered but hoped, at the same time, that Jess would refuse her suggestion. How could she tell who needed her more? It made her concussed brain hurt even more just thinking about what to do.

'No, don't be silly,' Jess said as she ushered Kitty out of the room. She was back to her usual no-nonsense organised self as she hustled to the kitchen and flicked on the kettle, and Kitty breathed a sigh of relief as she shrugged off the incident. Perhaps she'd imagined Jess's look of distress. She chose to ignore it for the moment. It was easier to pretend it hadn't happened than to think about having to make a choice. If she had to choose between Joe and Jess she wasn't sure what she'd do at the moment. They were both important to her. They were *the* most important people in her world. The two of them and the baby.

'So, how is Joe?' Jess asked as she poured boiling water into two mugs and dropped bags of green tea into the liquid before letting it steep.

Kitty realised she wanted to tell Jess about what had happened. She was too excited to keep it to herself. She'd finally had sex with Joe, made love to him, and it was every bit as good as she'd been imagining over the past few weeks. Better, even.

'Why are you smiling like that? What's happened?'

Kitty hadn't realised she was smiling.

'I had sex with Joe,' she admitted.

'What! Oh, my God!' Jess dropped the packet of biscuits she was opening but appeared to gather her wits as she picked up the fallen cookies. She was grinning when she looked back up at Kitty. 'It's about time. How was it? I hope it was brilliant.'

'What do you mean, "It's about time"?'

'Cam and I have been hoping the two of you would get together, but we were beginning to think it would never happen.'

'You've talked about this?'

'Of course,' Jess said as she put the untainted biscuits on a plate on the kitchen table. 'We love Joe. The two of you would be perfect together, but we were worried that you were destined to be friends and only friends for ever.'

Kitty *was* worried that she might have ruined their friendship. 'Do you think we can have sex and still be friends?'

'Of course. Cam and I are friends.'

'You're friends *now* but you weren't friends before you started dating.'

'That's true. But you and Joe have so much history. You don't have to worry about all the getting-to-know-you stuff. You already know you like him. Starting from friends is no problem. Not unless you end up making it one.'

Kitty knew Jess was speaking from experience. She

knew what Kitty was like. She knew her tendencies. How she overthought *everything* and always feared the worst. The trouble was, the worst often happened.

'I don't want it to be a problem,' she said as Jess threw out the tea bags and passed her the cup. 'I'd like to think it could work, but what if it doesn't?'

'What would be worse,' Jess asked, 'giving it a go and finding out that it might be the best decision you ever made, or being too worried about what might go wrong that you miss out completely? From where I'm sitting it looks like you've chosen option one already.'

'You forgot option three.'

'Which is?'

'Being brave and then it ends in total disaster anyway.'

'Are you sorry you slept with him?'

How could she be sorry? It was the best sex she'd ever had.

Kitty shook her head. She didn't regret what they'd done but all the doubts were threatening to take the gloss off the experience.

'And he doesn't seem sorry either?' Jess asked.

Kitty shook her head again.

'And are you happy right now?'

She was going to say she wasn't sure, but she closed her eyes and she could see Joe's face. She could feel his hands on her body. His lips on her skin. It had felt right then and the memory felt right now. 'Yes.'

'Then I think you should relax. Don't overthink things, have some fun. So tell me—what was he like?' Jess was smiling.

Kitty sighed, still lost in her memories of last night. 'He was perfect.'

* * *

Joe was lying on the couch when Kitty let herself back in through his front door. He was barefoot and shirtless, and Kitty felt her libido kick into gear as she let her eyes roam over him.

She'd picked up a pizza on her way back and Joe sat up as she put the box on the coffee table. He grimaced as he moved despite the fact that he was holding his left hand over his abdominal wound, and Kitty remembered she hadn't got around to changing his dressing earlier.

'You came back.'

'Of course.' She frowned, not understanding. 'Why wouldn't I?'

'I was worried you might think we'd made a mistake this morning.'

That one simple sentence highlighted just how well he knew her. They'd been friends for so long that she sometimes felt he knew her better than she knew herself. She had been worrying about that. She'd worried that the painkillers had made them reckless, worried they might have ruined their friendship. She *always* thought of reasons why things wouldn't work, rather than thinking of all the reasons they could. 'Have we?'

'No.' He shook his head and pulled her down onto the couch beside him.

'You don't think we might ruin our friendship?'

'I'd like to think we can always be friends.'

'With benefits?' she asked.

Joe smiled at her, the familiar dimple appearing in his chin, and Kitty's stomach somersaulted.

'So I take it you enjoyed it?' he said as he reached out and ran his thumb down her cheek, tracing the line of her jaw, and trailed it across to her lips.

She could feel the heat radiating off him and her heart began to race. 'You know I did.'

His thumb moved back towards her cheek and he slid his fingers around behind her neck, cupping the back of her head. 'I promise we will always be friends. Things don't need to get awkward.'

She didn't think he could make that promise, but she also didn't think she could resist the silent overtures he was making. Sleeping with him once wasn't going to be enough for her.

He pulled her towards him and kissed her soundly, the pizza forgotten in its box on the table.

Kitty wondered if things were being changed for ever by their actions today, but she didn't care. It was a risk she was prepared to take, she thought as she gave herself up to him again.

'Hello, Jess. Cameron. How are you both?' Dr Tennant showed them to the chairs and waited until they both sat down before she started speaking. Jess noticed that the chairs were pushed very close together, as if the oncologist knew that Jess was going to need to be able to reach for Cam—as if she was going to need his support—and she knew what was coming next. 'I'm afraid I don't have good news for you.'

The room felt as though it was spinning, making Jess feel ill. She closed her eyes and reached out for Cam's hand. She felt his fingers wrap around hers and only then was she able to breathe again. She took a deep breath, opened her eyes and waited.

'The cancer has spread to your lungs, and there are some metastases in your brain as well.'

Jess fought back tears. She'd been expecting bad

news, she'd felt it in her bones, which was ridiculous seeing as the doctor was telling her the cancer had spread to her lungs and brain, but she'd known something was wrong and she'd told herself she would be strong. For Cam's sake. But it was hard, almost impossible.

She wasn't strong.

'What do we do?' Cam asked.

'Treatment-wise our options are very limited.'

'What does that mean? Very limited?'

Cam was asking the questions, which was good as Jess couldn't speak. Fear of the future had frozen her tongue. But she didn't need to ask questions. She knew what it meant. She could feel it.

'It's difficult because of where it has spread to.'

'Can you get rid of it? Can you operate?'

The oncologist was shaking her head. 'It's inoperable. The cancer is in both lungs and the brain. What it means is that treatment will focus on relieving Jess's symptoms, but we won't be able to cure it. I'm sorry. The best we can do is try to slow the spread.'

'With what?'

'Chemotherapy or radiotherapy. But any treatment will be palliative only.'

'Buying me time?' Jess found her voice and it caught in her throat as she spoke. 'Is that all you can do?'

The oncologist nodded. 'That's right. I'm very sorry.'

The doctor kept apologising but Jess barely heard her. All she heard was that the cancer had returned and she was on borrowed time.

'How long do I have?'

'With or without treatment?'

'Without.'

'Jess—' Cam started to speak but Jess stopped him.

'No, Cam, please, just listen. There is no cure, no fix and I really don't think I can go through chemo again. I need to know what my options are.' As an expectant mother, she would do whatever it took to ensure she got to hold her child, but she didn't want to be so sick from chemo that she couldn't enjoy the experience. Dr Tennant was telling her that treatment was palliative only. It wasn't going to give her any longer on this earth and therefore she needed to weigh up the positives and the negatives. 'My choice very much depends on what I can expect to gain from treatment. But it is *my* choice.'

She turned back to Dr Tennant. 'How long do I have?' she repeated.

'That's hard to say. The cancer is spreading rapidly. Weeks certainly. Months maybe.'

Weeks.

Kitty was thirty weeks pregnant. Jess couldn't let go now. 'You have to keep me alive for another ten weeks. I have to see my baby.' Her voice broke and she was shaking violently as tears spilled over her lashes onto her cheeks. 'I need to hold my baby. Please. Even just once. Tell me what I have to do.'

'Thoracic radiotherapy is your best option,' the oncologist suggested.

'Radiotherapy?' Cam queried. 'Not chemo?'

'Chemo is an option but not your best one,' the doctor spoke to Jess. 'The dose would be high, which means a higher level of toxicity. That would be OK if you were otherwise well, but you have other symptoms. In your case, radiotherapy will be more appropriate.'

'What about side effects?' Cam asked. Despite the fact that the treatment would be palliative and meant to give Jess relief from pain they both knew there were always side effects.

'The shortness of breath may get worse,' Dr Tennant said, 'and patients often have trouble swallowing, which can make eating difficult obviously. Also, if the radiation is given close to the stomach then you may experience nausea. But studies have shown that the level of comfort provided or the quality of life can be extended by about fifty per cent. I can't give you any guarantees but radiotherapy is your best chance of getting some relief.'

'So maybe some relief but not more time?' Jess said. This list didn't sound that different from the symptoms she was already experiencing. She wondered if it was worth it.

Dr Tennant shook her head. 'No. Time is something I can't give you.'

'I'll need to think about it,' Jess replied. 'Have I got time to do that?'

'Yes. Radiotherapy is not going to change the outcome. All I can offer you is some relief. It's up to you when you need that.'

'What are we going to tell Kitty?' Cam asked as they left the hospital. He had his arm around his wife, supporting her.

'Nothing,' Jess replied. 'Not yet.' She was still shaking even though she wasn't cold, and she knew enough to recognise it as a manifestation of shock. She clung to Cam's hand, needing some of his strength. She wasn't strong enough to face this without him and she prayed he would support her decision about Kitty too.

'We can't keep this a secret.'

Jess realised that, but she needed time to process what she'd just heard and work out how to tell her sister. She had always appreciated the fact that Dr Tennant had never sugar-coated her opinion. She dealt in facts. But now the facts weren't what Jess wanted to hear. Now she realised exactly what the term *harsh reality* meant. Next she had to figure out how to deal with it. 'Please,' she begged. 'I need some time to work out what to say. You know how Kitty gets with bad news. She won't handle it well, and I'm worried about the baby.'

'The baby will be fine. Kitty is thirty weeks along,' Cam argued.

'I know but Kitty still needs to eat, rest and keep her strength up. I need her focussing on the baby, not on me. Just for a little bit longer. Please? And if we tell her now she'll want to move back in to be with me, and I think she should stay with Joe. Their relationship is only new. I don't want this news to jeopardise that for her. She's going to need Joe's support.'

'OK,' Cam agreed, 'but if you decide you're going to start radiotherapy, we're telling Kitty.'

Jess nodded. She'd agree for now to get her way and worry about everything else later.

Kitty put her key in the lock and let herself into Joe's place. She was starving, and something someone in the building was cooking smelt fantastic. She'd just had her first day back at work after the assault, and was looking forward to seeing Joe. They'd spent every night and most of every day together for the past two weeks and she'd missed him today when she'd gone back to work. It was good to be home.

Home.

This wasn't home. It was familiar and she'd spent

plenty of time here, but it wasn't home. But it was starting to feel like it.

Could it be?

No. She shook her head as she closed the door. Joe wasn't the settling-down sort. She knew he didn't believe in serious commitment. He'd always said serious was not for him. She wondered, once again, if they'd made a mistake by sleeping together. Had they complicated their relationship? Was she risking their friendship for what could only be a dalliance? Joe wasn't going to make a long-term commitment. Not to her, not to anyone, and yet that was what she desired more than anything. There was no way she was going to survive if she ruined her relationship with Joe. He was too important. She wondered how they would get through this. Who would leave first?

It didn't bear thinking about.

She dumped her handbag on the chair by the front door as Joe stepped into the foyer. He was smiling at her and she promptly forgot all her concerns. His smile had always made her feel better and now it made her feel special.

'Hey, how was your day?' he asked as he greeted her with a kiss.

She could get used to this, she thought. 'Work was OK, but I missed you,' she replied honestly. Just because she knew they ultimately wanted different things was no reason to pretend she felt differently.

'I missed you too,' he said. His ran his left hand over the curve of her buttock as he nuzzled her neck, kissing the side of her throat.

She leant into him. 'What did you do all day?'

'I rang work to see when I can go back.'

Kitty straightened up and looked Joe in the eye. 'You remember the surgeon said six weeks minimum, don't you? It's only been just over two.'

'Yes, but I thought I'd be able to do some office work. There always seems to be someone on light duties, I figured it's my turn now. I'll go crazy stuck at home alone now that you're back at work.'

Kitty loved the idea that he was missing her, that he was lonely without her. Maybe this relationship *could* work. 'I start maternity leave in four weeks. I'll be around constantly then. You might get sick of me.'

'I don't think so,' he said as he pulled her back towards him and kissed her again. 'But work said they'd find me light duties if the surgeon gives me clearance, so I made an appointment with her for next Tuesday. I thought I'd hitch a lift to work and the hospital with you that morning. I checked your roster and you're on an early.'

'Sure,' Kitty said, just as her stomach rumbled.

Joe put his arm around her shoulder and led her into the apartment. 'And I also made dinner.'

'Dinner? How?' she said as she looked at his splinted arm.

'All right, I admit, I didn't make it but I ordered in. Indian takeaway. It's in the oven, keeping warm.'

'That's *our* dinner I can smell?'

'Yep. Butter chicken, rogan josh, garlic naan and rice.'

Kitty had eaten plenty of curries while she'd been pregnant. She'd found meat was more appetising when it was harder to recognise and she wondered if the baby would grow up with a taste for curry. 'You've been busy.'

Joe broke into a wide smile. 'Yep, but not too busy to avoid thinking about all the things we could do together when you got home.' He stepped behind her and kissed her earlobe as he slid his left hand under her shirt and cupped her breast.

Kitty's knees wobbled and heat pooled low in her belly as her nipple peaked under his fingers. She forgot about work. She forgot about the baby. Forgot about dinner and all her reservations about the future. She was only hungry for one thing now.

CHAPTER EIGHT

THE ED HAD been quiet today and Kitty was grateful. Even though it was almost three weeks since the assault she was still suffering from headaches and fatigue. The headaches weren't bad, just a dull ache behind her eyes at times, but she didn't like to take anything for the discomfort because of the baby. She was still trying to figure out if the fatigue was related to the concussion, the pregnancy or to the fact that she wasn't getting many early nights due to the combination of shift work and Joe's libido. She knew she was as much to blame as he was—she found him irresistible, and getting home to him was the highlight of her day.

She had dropped him at the ambulance station on her way to work this morning and arranged to meet him for lunch after his appointment with the hand surgeon. She'd been counting down the hours and hoping the department didn't experience a sudden influx of emergencies, eager to hear what the specialist had to say about Joe's proposed return to work.

He was getting bored and she hoped for his sake that he would be cleared for light duties but, from a purely selfish point of view, she was worried about how that would impact on her and on their fledgling relationship. In her mind it was the first step towards him getting his independence back, which might also prove to be the first nail in the coffin of their relationship. If he could work maybe he'd figure he could manage without her help. It was only a matter of time before he wouldn't need her as much any more. Maybe only a matter of time until he wouldn't need her at all.

'Kitty, Anna, incoming ambulance, two minutes.'

Her thoughts were interrupted by Davina, which was probably just as well, she figured as she made her way to the triage desk. She didn't want to dwell on the negatives, she needed to learn to be happy in the moment. She was trying but it didn't come naturally to her.

'Two-year-old toddler pulled from a backyard pool,' the charge nurse told her and Anna as they gathered together. 'Resuscitated onsite.'

Kitty went pale. 'I can't do it, Davina,' she said. 'Please, can you find someone else?'

Davina knew her history. Kitty was always the last staff member called to these types of incidents.

'I'm sorry, Kitty. There isn't anyone else. I'll send someone to take over from you as soon as I can. Think of it as a seizure if it helps.'

But Kitty knew that wouldn't work. Treatment was different for a start. And once she'd heard the words 'pulled from a pool' her mind had gone straight to drowning and from there way back to her childhood.

Everyone in the emergency department had their own Achilles heel. Drowning or near-drowning incidents were Kitty's.

Anna handed Kitty a clean apron and put her arm around her shoulders. 'It'll be all right,' she told her. 'Just focus on me, I'll tell you what I need. You can do this.'

Kitty wasn't so sure, but it wasn't in her nature to let her colleagues or their patients down so she nodded and grabbed a fresh pair of gloves as she fought back a rising wave of nausea. She grabbed a blanket from the warming cupboard and followed Anna outside, hoping that the fresh air would clear her mind. Hoping Anna could get her through this.

The ambulance pulled into the bay and Kitty's first reaction was to look for Joe, before she remembered that he was still off work.

The paramedic who climbed out of the ambulance wasn't one Kitty knew. He pulled the stretcher out and spoke rapidly, giving Anna and Kitty the details he had.

'Twenty-six-month-old boy. Pulled from a private pool. Mother isn't sure how long he was immersed for but thinks it was less than ten minutes. Unresponsive. Respiratory and cardiac arrest. CPR was performed on-site. Resuscitated but unstable. Oxygen sats still low, eighty-six percent. Core temperature back up to thirty-six degrees.'

The child had a small oxygen mask over his nose and mouth, an IV line running into his arm and he was covered with a blanket to try to increase his body temperature slowly back to normal. Kitty draped the warmed blanket she carried over his inert body while somehow managing to keep her eyes averted.

'We'll need arterial blood gases and an FBE,' Anna said as they pushed the stretcher into the ED. 'And we'll need to intubate if his pulse ox doesn't improve.'

The little boy was listless, the edges of his lips tinged with blue.

Kitty tried not to look at him but it was impossible as they transferred the child across to the exam couch. She could feel herself starting to shake. Black spots swam before her eyes and she thought she might be about to faint but then nausea swamped her, making her break out in a sweat. She grabbed a bowl from a trolley and vomited into it. She hadn't thrown up since she'd been hospitalised for concussion and before that it had been due to morning sickness, but she'd thrown up more in the past few months than in the rest of her entire life. But this was mental stress, not a physical thing.

'*Davina!*' Anna called out as the paramedics departed with their stretcher. 'I need some help in here.'

Davina came in and took one look at Kitty, who was standing motionless in the centre of the room, holding the plastic bowl in her hands.

'Kitty, go, take a break,' Davina instructed. 'I'll handle this.'

Kitty didn't waste any time getting out of there. She rinsed the bowl in the sluice room and headed for the change rooms. She opened her locker but ignored the salad she'd made for her lunch. She didn't think she could eat. She was still nauseous and shaky. She took her phone from her locker and pushed the button to speed-dial Joe.

'Hi, it's me,' she said when he answered. 'Can you meet me a bit earlier?'

'Sure. When?'

'Now.' She was close to tears. Hearing Joe's voice was almost enough to push her over the edge into hysteria. She needed to see him. She wanted his arms wrapped around her. It was the only thing that would make her feel safe.

'Is everything OK?'

She couldn't talk to him over the phone. She wanted

to see him. Needed to feel him, to hear him tell her everything would be all right. 'I need to see you. Can you meet me in the ambulance bay?'

Kitty was sitting on the wall. She was hunched over, her elbows resting on her knees. She looked tiny. From this angle it was impossible to see her baby bump. She looked small and fragile. Wounded. Joe knew looks could be deceiving but he'd heard the tremor in her voice and he'd known instantly that something was wrong. He just didn't know what.

He could see her shoulders rise and fall—she was taking deep breaths. He reached out with his left hand, putting it on her shoulder. She jumped at his touch. She was shaking and he felt the coldness of her skin through the thin fabric of her scrubs. When she lifted her head, her eyes were dark, haunted, and a tell-tale crease of worry ran between her brows.

'Kitty, what is it? What's happened? Are you hurt?'

He ran his eyes over her but could see nothing.

She stood up, shaking her head, and stepped into his arms.

She fitted perfectly against his chest and he held her tight, as if his life depended on it. As if hers did.

'I'm worried about the baby.'

Joe frowned. He knew Kitty worried more than most people but, even so, something usually acted as a trigger for full-blown anxiety.

'What's going on?' he asked.

'The paramedics just brought in a two-year-old boy. A near-drowning.'

Now things started to make sense. Kitty used to be the middle one of three sisters. Her younger sister, Eliza, had drowned when she was two. Kitty had been almost six years old, and she'd never got over it. Her sister's death had been her first loss.

'It made me think of Eliza.'

'Of course it did,' Joe said as he rubbed her back. 'That's understandable.'

'But it also made me worry about all the other things that can and do go wrong. What if something happens to this baby?' She put her hand protectively over her belly.

'Kitty, you can't worry about unforeseen things.' He knew what she was like and he understood her concerns, but the reality was it wasn't going to be her job to worry about this baby once it was born. That would be Jess and Cam's responsibility. He knew Kitty sometimes forgot this baby wasn't hers to keep but he wasn't about to remind her of that right at this moment. 'I know you've suffered tragedies, but you need to stay positive.' He kept her in his embrace and led her away from the ambulance bay into the sunshine.

'Your body reacts to stress, the baby doesn't need that,' he said, trying to calm her and distract her by playing on her sense of responsibility to her unborn baby. He held her until she stopped shaking. 'Are you going to be OK?' he asked gently.

Her face was pale but he watched as she squared her shoulders and gave him a wan half-smile, nodding. 'Yes,' she answered as she stood up. 'I'll be fine. Thank you for being here.'

'I'll always be here,' he said as he kissed her forehead. As much as he wanted to follow her back into work, he couldn't go with her. He had to trust that she'd be all right. But his words echoed in his head as he watched her go. What exactly was he promising her? Would he always be there for her now? In what capacity? As a friend or a lover?

He didn't do serious commitment, but how could they go back now?

Kitty stretched her legs out in front of her and kicked her shoes off. She'd noticed her feet had started to swell at the end of her shifts and it felt good to have a day when she could put them up.

'What colour would you like?' Jess asked as she held out a selection of nail polishes. Cam had gone to play golf while Kitty visited Jess and they'd decided to spend the afternoon pampering themselves.

'That one,' Kitty said, choosing a pale pink.

'Is Joe working today?' Jess asked as she shook the little bottle before unscrewing the cap.

'Yes. This is his last week in the office. He should get the splint removed next week and he hopes then to be allowed back on the road as a spare.'

'Does that mean he'll be able to manage at home without you?'

'Mmm-hmm.'

'Has he asked you to stay?'

Kitty shook her head. 'No. There's no reason for me to stay once the splint comes off.' He wouldn't need her once the splint was removed, even though she'd be happy to stay. It was ironic really—usually she was eager to be the one leaving before she could be left, but she and Joe were still in the early stages of their relationship and she was happy. She hadn't been really happy in a long time.

'How do you feel about that?' Jess asked. 'Were you hoping he would?'

'Yes.' Kitty answered honestly, avoiding eye contact

with Jess whose head was bent over Kitty's feet as she painted her toenails. Kitty's pregnant bump made that impossible now. 'I was always planning on coming back here to you until the baby was born, and Joe knows that, but it would have been nice for him to ask. It would validate our relationship.'

She'd always planned on moving back in with Jess and Cam once Joe didn't need her help any more but she'd got used to their living—and sleeping—arrangements and she didn't actually want to leave.

'Maybe you should start the discussion,' Jess suggested, but Kitty shook her head.

Joe had said nothing. He'd given no hint as to where he thought their relationship might be heading. She shouldn't have been surprised, she knew he never got serious. It shouldn't upset her. It shouldn't bother her. But it did. Their relationship felt right—perfect even— and she'd never felt like that before, about anyone. But she knew Joe didn't believe in perfect. He didn't believe in happily ever after. He wouldn't commit and she'd just have to accept that and hope that, at the end of the day, they could remain friends.

'Even if you move back here until the baby comes, where would you like to live once the baby is born? You'd be welcome to stay here, of course,' Jess offered as she started to cough.

'Thanks, but I don't think that's a good idea.' Kitty was starting to realise how hard it was going to be to relinquish the baby, and being in the same house would only make it more difficult. She needed to remember the baby wasn't hers, and that would be easier to do if she had some distance. 'You and Cam will need time with your baby by yourselves. Time to adjust to becoming a family.'

Jess was still coughing as Kitty finished speaking, so Kitty went to the kitchen to fetch a glass of water. Jess had had the cough for a while now and Kitty had been meaning to ask her about it but every time she started to, the conversation seemed to get redirected to talk of Joe or the baby or how Kitty was feeling. She'd ask her about it now, she decided as she filled the glass. Silence returned as she carried the drink back into the lounge. Jess had stopped coughing but was hunched over.

'Are you all right?' Kitty asked as she rubbed Jess's back.

Jess looked up. Her eyes were wide with fright and Kitty could hear her fighting to breathe.

'Oh, my God,' Kitty said. 'Is there something stuck in your throat?' she asked, knowing there couldn't be. They hadn't eaten. What was happening?

'Can you sit up?'

Jess shook her head. 'Hurts.'

Was she going blue around the lips? Surely she wouldn't deteriorate that quickly?

Kitty pulled her phone from her pocket and dialled 000.

'I need an ambulance. It's my sister. She can't breathe,' she said when she got through to Dispatch. 'No, there's no airway obstruction. I'm a nurse. Please hurry.'

Kitty put her phone on speaker while they waited, not wanting to be distracted. She boiled the kettle, wondering if warm, moist air would make breathing easier, before hurrying back into the lounge room. She didn't want to leave Jess alone. Her sister was fighting for air.

Kitty placed two fingers on Jess's wrist, feeling for her pulse. Her touch met with rapid beats.

Please hurry. Kitty willed the ambulance to arrive but prepared herself to breathe for her sister.

'The ambulance is almost there.' The dispatcher's voice came through the phone. 'Can you hear the siren?'

'Yes.'

'OK. You can hang up now. Go and open the door for them.'

Kitty waited until the siren was switched off, indicating the ambulance was outside the front before she dared to leave Jess's side to open the door. 'This way,' she directed the paramedics. 'It's my sister. She's in respiratory distress.'

'Is she on any medication?'

'I don't know.' Kitty hated feeling so helpless. So useless. 'She's had treatment for ovarian cancer.'

'Has this happened before?'

'I don't think so.'

She made another phone call, this time to Cam, while the paramedics assessed Jess. She was almost in tears but knew she had to hold it together for a while longer. The paramedics might need more information from her.

The baby kicked in her belly and Kitty had the feeling she was reacting to her distress. Picking up on her emotions. She needed to remain calm. She put her hand protectively over her belly, as if trying to shield the baby from the drama. 'It's all right, little one,' she whispered. 'Your mum will be OK.'

As she made the promise to the baby she realised it was the first time she'd really acknowledged that her sister was the baby's mother. She'd said the words to others but had never said them out loud to herself. She had no idea if Jess would be OK, she had no idea if she was speaking the truth, but knew she was trying to calm herself as much as the unborn child. Jess *had* to be all right. Everyone needed her.

The paramedics had fitted an oxygen mask over Jess's face and were loading her onto a stretcher as Kitty made a second call to Joe. She grabbed her keys, her bag and Jess's handbag as she spoke to Joe. Keeping busy trying to do several things at once meant she didn't have time to fall apart.

She climbed into the front of the ambulance as Jess was loaded into the back and fretted as they negotiated the streets to the hospital.

The ambulance pulled into the bay at North Sydney. It felt surreal to be climbing out of the ambulance and walking into the ED as a family member. Kitty was used to being there as a nurse. She was used to having some control, used to it being her job to remain calm and to comfort, assess and treat patients and victims. She'd been a victim herself once after the assault but her recollection of that day was hazy at best. She had never presented to the ED as a family member before and having no control over the outcome, but all the worry, was hugely stressful.

She was relieved to see Anna and Victoria in the ambulance bay. She was on comfortable terms with Victoria again now that Kitty was the one sleeping with Joe. Victoria didn't seem to be holding any grudges.

She just had time to let them know that Jess was her sister before the paramedics pulled her from the ambulance and began to give Anna the rundown on Jess's condition.

Kitty followed Jess's stretcher into an exam room.

She stood in a corner, out of the way. No one told her to leave and she figured if she was quiet no one would. She watched as Victoria replaced the oxygen tubing before strapping a blood-pressure cuff around Jess's arm and attaching the pulse oximetry monitor to her finger.

'Can you also put the ECG leads on?' Anna asked as she tightened the tourniquet and drew blood from Jess's arm. 'Did Jess have her chemo here?' she enquired. Kitty nodded. 'OK. Can you pull up her file?' Anna asked Victoria.

Victoria finished setting up the ECG and pushed the buttons to record Jess's cardiac rhythm before she went to the computer and pulled up her sister's electronic file. Kitty craned her neck but couldn't read the entries from where she stood.

Anna turned to look at her. 'She has metastases in her lungs?'

'What?' Kitty stepped forward, shaking her head. 'No. There must be another Jess McIntyre. Check the date of birth.'

Victoria read it out—the birthday matched, but the diagnosis didn't. 'No. There has to be a mistake.' Kitty reached for the edge of the barouche, steadying herself.

Anna double-checked the details. 'It's the right file,' she said. 'You didn't know?'

Kitty shook her head. *Secondaries!* The cancer had spread. Why didn't she know?

'We need to get a chest X-ray.'

Anna wasn't wasting time and she and Victoria wheeled Jess out of the room just as Cam arrived. Kitty could see the panic on his face. She expected she looked much the same.

'Where are they taking her?' he wanted to know.

'For an X-ray. Anna thinks she might have a block-age in her lung.' It was obvious to Kitty that Cam was nowhere near as surprised as she'd been by this news. 'You knew she had secondaries?'

Cam nodded.

'How long have you known?' Kitty was struggling with the fact that Jess's cancer had spread and yet no one had told her.

'We only got confirmation three weeks ago.'

'Three weeks! Why haven't you said anything?'

'That was Jess's decision.' Cam ran his fingers through his hair, making it even more dishevelled. 'She thought you had enough to worry about, and then she wanted you and Joe to have some time together where you could just focus on him and you. She knew you'd worry and want to move back in with us. She didn't want that.'

'What's her prognosis?' Kitty was almost afraid to ask. She already knew it wouldn't be good.

Cam's expression was dazed when he looked at her. He was probably in shock and perhaps it was unfair of her to grill him like this right now as he had a lot on his plate, but she had to know. They should never have kept this from her.

'The oncologist is talking weeks, a few months at best.'

Kitty sank onto a chair in the waiting room and wrapped her arms around her pregnant belly. She hadn't thought this day could get any worse. She'd been wrong.

Cam was crying now. Silent tears rolled down his cheeks. 'We're just hoping she'll be around to see the baby.'

'Has she been having treatment?'

Cam shook his head. 'There isn't anything they can do except for palliative options. Radiotherapy was suggested but Jess isn't keen.'

Kitty was stunned. Shocked. This seemed incomprehensible. 'I can't believe you didn't tell me.'

'I'm sorry, Kitty, but Jess insisted. She didn't want you to worry,' he said, just as Anna reappeared.

Kitty took a moment to register her return and another moment to realise Anna didn't know who Cam was. She stood up to introduce them. 'Anna, this is Cam, Jess's husband. Cam, this is Dr Lewis.'

'Is she all right?' Cam's question was abrupt. All sense of the social niceties had gone by the wayside, lost in the concern for his wife.

'She's OK.' *For now.* Kitty imagined Anna's unspoken words. 'She has a pleural effusion. I've called her oncologist and we're going to drain the fluid and hope that eases her breathing.'

'Can I see her?' Cam asked.

Anna nodded. 'Briefly.'

Cam followed Anna, leaving Kitty alone. Even the baby was quiet, which just served to heighten Kitty's sense of isolation. Was the baby asleep or in shock, like the rest of them? Kitty didn't know. She didn't know anything at the moment. She was swamped, drowning in emotion. She was worried for Jess but angry with her too. How could she have chosen not to tell her? *Why* had she chosen to keep this from her? Cam's explanation wasn't good enough. Jess was her sister. Kitty deserved to know.

She sank back down onto one of the plastic chairs,

barely aware of how uncomfortable they were, and she was still sitting there, alone, when Joe arrived.

Kitty burst into tears when he walked through the door.

Joe rushed to her side and gathered her into his arms. 'What's happened?'

She knew he was expecting the worst and she fought back her tears long enough to tell him that the worst hadn't happened. Yet.

Cam came back just as Kitty finished updating Joe. His face was ghostly white.

Kitty stood up. Icy tendrils of alarm wrapped themselves around her heart but Cam reassured her. 'She's OK. They're just about to try and drain the fluid.'

Joe stayed by Kitty's side, offering comfort, waiting until Jess's procedure was complete.

'That went well,' Anna said as she came back to where they waited. 'Jess is sleeping now. You'll be able to see her later.'

They continued to wait. Joe held Kitty's hand but they sat in silence. Kitty was lost in her own thoughts but took strength from Joe's presence. As always, he was there for her in a time of crisis.

Cam went to see Jess when she woke, and he was looking more relaxed when he returned to fetch Kitty. 'She's asking for you,' he said.

Jess was pale but seemed to be breathing more easily when Kitty entered the room. 'How are you feeling?' Jess looked better—she'd lost the blue tinge around her lips—and Kitty needed to know how she was. Any grievances Kitty had would have to wait, now was not the time to air them. 'Are you in a lot of pain?'

'No more than I have been for a while,' Jess replied.

'Cam said you could have radiotherapy. Why haven't you done that?'

'It's not a cure.'

'I know, but it might make you feel more comfortable.'

Jess gave a half-hearted smile. 'I thought I was managing. I wanted to wait until I really needed it. But my oncologist isn't giving me a choice now. She says I have to start treatment. The cough I can handle, but that feeling of not being able to breathe was terrifying. I don't want to go through that again if I can help it.'

'Good. If you can get your pain under control you'll feel better.' Kitty tried to focus on the practicalities, on what could actually be done, rather than the things that were out of their control. It wasn't easy. She topped up Jess's water glass before asking the question she really wanted answered. 'Why didn't you tell me?'

'I was going to,' Jess admitted, 'just not yet. I was trying to protect you and Cam.'

Kitty frowned. 'Cam said you only found out a few weeks ago. How could you protect him if you found out together?'

'The secondaries were only *confirmed* three weeks ago but I'd been feeling off for a while before that.'

'And you didn't mention anything? Not even to Cam?'

Jess shook her head. 'You'd just had the implantation. I didn't want to stress anyone out, especially not you, with my concerns. I didn't want to risk anything going wrong. And I was worried that Cam might change his mind.'

'What—about the surrogacy?'

Jess nodded.

'Oh, Jess,' Kitty said as she clasped her sister's hand, 'I'm sure he wouldn't have. He adores you, he'd do anything for you. So would I.' Kitty wished, not for the first time, that she had someone in her life who adored her like Cam adored his wife.

Maybe she would still find that someone.

She didn't doubt that Joe loved her but only in the same way he always had. He'd not given her any indication that they were anything more than friends with benefits. It would never amount to anything more between them—not when Joe had no intention of committing to anyone. That was still what Kitty was aiming for, it had been what she'd always wanted, but until she was one hundred per cent sure that commitment was absolute, she wasn't going to give her heart away. She wanted to be loved, but it had to be for ever. And Joe didn't do for ever.

'I know,' Jess replied, 'but I thought the ethics committee and the doctors might not approve the surrogacy process if they suspected my health was deteriorating. And I was worried that if Cam thought I wasn't well enough he might change his mind, too. He may have wanted to focus on getting me better instead of on the pregnancy. But I'm not going to get better, so—'

'But you didn't know that at the time!' Kitty protested, interrupting her. 'Maybe if you'd done something earlier?'

'I could only handle one thing at a time, and having a baby was all I could think about. I want Cam to have something of me when I'm gone. I'm not feeling optimistic about this, and I had a feeling, a sixth sense, that things weren't good. The pregnancy gave me something to hold onto, something to look forward to.'

Kitty was crying now. Tears were rolling down her cheeks. She was hearing what Jess was telling her. She was going to lose her, too.

'Do you think I'm being selfish?' Jess asked.

'No. I would have done the same thing.' By offering to be their surrogate Kitty *had* done the exact same thing. Kitty understood all too well Jess's thought process. Family was important to both of them. Jess was only trying to give Cam a family of his own.

'You don't think having a baby will stop Cam from being able to find happiness later on?' Jess asked, leaving the rest of the sentence unspoken. Kitty didn't need to hear the words, *when I'm gone.* 'I am doing the right thing, aren't I?'

'Yes.' Kitty didn't want to make this any harder for Jess by burdening her with guilt. 'Is there anything I can do for you?'

'I don't like to ask, but do you think you could come home now? Just until the baby is born. I don't want to drag you away from Joe and I'll understand if you say no, but I feel like I'm missing out on the pregnancy and it's only a few more weeks. I don't want to miss another moment. I don't know how many more moments I'm going to get. But I'm planning to be around when my baby is born. I want to hold him, or her, in my arms.'

Kitty nodded. 'Of course, I'll come back,' she replied without hesitation. She would do anything for Jess, even if it meant giving up Joe for now. 'And it's a "her".'

'What?'

'You're having a daughter.'

'I am? Really?' Jess broke into a wide smile and Kitty realised then it had been a while since Jess had truly looked happy. How had Kitty not noticed that?

'Yes. Sorry, I know Cam wanted it to be a surprise but I wanted you to know.' Kitty refused to feel guilty about sharing that news. Who knew how long Jess had left? She should know the sex of her baby if that's what she wanted. Jess and Cam had kept the news of Jess's health from her and Kitty refused to be the one keeping secrets. It was up to Jess now to decide whether or not to share this news with Cam. 'I had an ultrasound at one of the student clinics and I asked them to tell me. It's a girl.'

Jess had tears in her eyes. 'Thank you,' she said just as the nurse came in to tell Kitty that Jess needed to rest.

Kitty hugged her sister and left the room. Joe was talking to Cam but he stopped and they both looked at her warily as she approached.

'What are you two discussing?' she asked.

Joe turned to her and Kitty noticed that Cam made himself scarce before Joe spoke. 'I think you should move back in with Jess and Cam,' he said. 'You'll worry if you stay with me. Jess needs you.'

Kitty wondered if Cam and Jess had already spoken about this or if Joe was making unilateral decisions. Regardless, she already knew that she needed to move back in with Jess. Kitty felt terrible that she hadn't noticed that Jess's health had been deteriorating. She'd worried that Jess was too thin and had worried about the cough but had never discussed it. Had she been too caught up in her own life, in her happiness with Joe, to notice? But that wasn't a good enough reason to have neglected her sister. She was family, and moving back to Jess and Cam's was the right thing to do. Kitty hadn't hesitated in agreeing with Jess just minutes earlier when she'd asked her to do exactly that, but hearing Joe suggest it was a little painful. She couldn't help but wonder if he wasn't a little too eager about the idea.

'Do you want to get rid of me?' she asked, only half-teasing.

Joe wrapped his arm around her and pulled her close. 'Not at all. But I know you will regret not spending this time with Jess.' He was right. Jess's time was limited. No one knew how long she had left, although nobody was brave enough to say that out loud. 'I've spoken with Cam and he agrees. It's just up to you.'

'But how will you manage?'

'I'll figure something out. My splint should be off next week and then if I'm back on the road as an extra crew member I won't be around much anyway.'

Was that a warning? Was he preparing her for what came next? She knew his relationships never lasted long. She knew he didn't do commitment. Had he had enough?

This was exactly why she always walked away first. So that she wouldn't have this feeling of betrayal and loss. It was all too much, but she couldn't face dealing with that now. Jess needed her and Kitty wasn't about to let her down. She needed to let Joe go, needed to prioritise what was important, but she couldn't help thinking about the things Joe hadn't said. She couldn't stop thinking of all the things that could go wrong. Not with Jess but between her and Joe. Was this the first step towards the end?

Joe had been trying to do the right thing, sending Kitty back to live with Jess and Cam, but he'd barely seen her for the past four weeks, and there were still three weeks to go until the baby was due. Not that it would change things—Joe knew Kitty would stay with her sister for as long as she could. Until the end.

He knew he was being ridiculous, he understood the situation. Jess was the only family she had left, their time was limited, and he knew how much family meant to Kitty. Still, it hurt that she seemed to have so little time left for him, and he was surprised how keenly he was feeling her absence. He missed her. He had enjoyed the change in their relationship. But he wasn't family and he also knew that if he wanted to be a priority for her he would have to make promises that he wasn't sure he could keep.

And he couldn't do that.

He couldn't give her what she wanted, and he knew that meant he would lose her. Eventually she would choose someone else, a man who could offer her all the things she wanted—love, a future, a family of her own. *Commitment*.

He couldn't be that man.

He would have to let her go.

CHAPTER NINE

'ALL RIGHT, KITTY, you're doing well. I can see the baby's head. You can push with the next contraction.'

Kitty had had no idea childbirth would be this painful, but her labour had progressed quickly for a first-time mum and now it was almost over. She hoped. She was concentrating hard. Thinking about the moment the baby would be put into her arms. It stopped her from thinking about the pain.

'You can do this, Kitty.'

'You're almost there.'

Cam stood on one side of her, Jess sat on the other. Jess wasn't strong enough to stand throughout the delivery but Kitty was relieved that she was going to be able to hold her baby. She'd been determined to make that happen for Jess, and the pain she was experiencing was a small price to pay for her sister's happiness.

Kitty knew that Joe was waiting outside the door. Cam had called him when she'd gone into labour. He'd wanted to know and Kitty was happy for him to be told, but she didn't want him in the delivery room. She needed her energy to focus on the people who were truly invested in this.

'All right, Kitty, push. That's it,' the obstetrician instructed as another contraction gripped her abdomen. She felt as though she was being crushed like a car at the wrecker's yard but she pushed with everything she had. The sooner she delivered this baby the sooner she'd get to rest. 'OK, hold it there.'

Kitty stopped pushing and panted. Jess was talking to her but Kitty couldn't really understand what she was saying. She was tired and sore and all her focus was concentrated below her waist, which didn't leave any room in her head for conversation.

'Nearly there, Kitty. One last time. Push.'

Kitty squeezed Jess and Cam's hands tight and, leaning forward, she pushed hard. She felt the release as she pushed the baby out of her body and she breathed out as she heard the newborn cries.

'Congratulations, everyone,' said the obstetrician, 'you have a healthy baby girl.'

Kitty watched in almost a dream-like trance as the baby was passed to her. The midwife loosened Kitty's gown at the neck so that she could rest on Kitty's chest, skin to skin, and the baby quietened as soon as she felt that contact.

Jess reached out and slid her finger into the palm of the baby's hand and smiled.

'Cameron, are you going to cut the cord?' the midwife asked as she clamped the cord and handed Cam the scissors.

Cam did the honours and the midwife took the baby and swaddled her before handing her to Jess.

They were a family.

A family Kitty had helped them to create. An achievement that should make her proud and happy but there was underlying sadness too. She felt the loss immediately but tried to smile and say all the right things as she watched Jess and Cam cuddle her baby.

No, not her baby. Their daughter. Eliza Kate. The baby was being named for Jess's two sisters—Eliza and Kitty—but she would be Lizzie for short.

Kitty had given them this gift—a family of their own—but she wasn't quite ready to let go. It was much harder than she'd imagined. And she didn't *want* to let go. Of anyone. Not of Lizzie, and not of Jess.

And what about Joe?

Joe had given her space, time to spend with Jess, but she missed him. He'd checked on her, called her, told her he was there for her, but she missed him physically. Her body missed him. She appreciated that he was offering emotional support but she wanted more now. She wanted everything, but she knew he couldn't give her that. She knew their relationship was changing—*had* changed. She'd understood it would have a use-by date, that was how Joe operated. She just didn't know if she was prepared for that. He was her best friend, her lover, but he couldn't—or wouldn't—be her partner, and she knew eventually she'd have to let him go. Or that he would leave.

She wiped a tear from the corner of her eye. She couldn't think about Joe right now. Lizzie and Jess needed her.

Joe was worried about Kitty. He'd visited her in hospital every day since she'd given birth and he knew something wasn't right. Jess had been with Kitty almost every time Joe had visited and despite the fact that Jess was terminally ill and looked tired and frail, she at least looked happy. Kitty did not.

He'd known she would find the first few days post-partum difficult. He knew she would miss being pregnant, would miss being the mother of her baby, and he was worried that, in a way, she would perceive it as yet another loss. He'd seen the sadness in the depths of her dark eyes and he wanted to eradicate it, but he was having difficulty finding the right words. He wanted to be there for her, to offer his unwavering support, as he always had. He wanted to put a smile on her face, to promise her that her future would be bright and happy and everything she dreamed of, but the words kept getting stuck in his throat.

He knocked quietly on the open door of her room, not wanting to disturb her if she was sleeping, but she was awake. She was feeding the baby, watching her as she suckled, and she didn't hear him come into the room. She looked so peaceful. Joe was taken aback. He hadn't thought about what would happen after the baby was born. He'd assumed the baby would be bottle fed, but once he'd got over his surprise he had to admit to himself that he liked to see Kitty mothering the baby.

He stood rooted to the spot as a wave of emotion flooded him. What if that was *his* baby she was holding?

The idea filled him with a longing that was almost painful. For the first time in his life he could picture a future that had more than him, alone in the frame. What if this was his future? Kitty, and a family of their own?

He was still standing stunned and mesmerised in the doorway when Kitty looked up and saw him.

'Hi. You have perfect timing,' she said as she took Lizzie from her breast and pulled her top down. Watching her, Joe felt another pang of longing. Not sexual but visceral. He wanted Kitty. He wanted to make her his.

He didn't want to live without her. *Couldn't* live without her. 'Would you mind holding Lizzie while I have a shower?'

She got out of bed and handed the baby to him without waiting for his answer, completely unaware of the thoughts racing through his head.

He looked down at the tiny bundle that was swaddled in his arms and imagined she was his and Kitty's. He knew then that this was what he wanted. He wanted Kitty to have his babies. He wanted to be part of her entire life. He wanted to feel her swollen, pregnant belly and know that part of him was within her.

'I can't put her straight down after a feed,' Kitty was saying, 'and I need to get ready.'

'Ready for what?' he asked.

'I'm going home today.'

'Home?'

'To Jess and Cam's. I'm going to express milk for Lizzie and it makes sense to all be together. Lizzie has to live with Cam and Jess for at least thirty days before they can apply to transfer her parentage.'

Joe had seen Jess; he wasn't sure that she'd last that long.

'They don't want time together, just the three of them?' he asked, but as soon as the words were out of his mouth he could tell by Kitty's expression that he'd upset her. He knew she thought he was implying she wouldn't be welcome. He started to tell her that wasn't what he'd meant but Kitty was already talking.

'Jess needs me there.' Kitty's voice was tight. She was definitely upset and her eyes were still dark, haunted by pain and loss. 'She won't be able to manage on her own, she's not well enough. I'm not there just to help with Lizzie, I'm going to be Jess's palliative care nurse. Jess wants to spend time with her family and that includes me.'

Joe's heart ached for Kitty and for all the people she had lost and was yet to lose. His heart ached for her future. And for his. For all the things he couldn't give her back. Was she leaving him before he could leave her?

He hadn't seen that coming. He'd assumed they'd be able to sort things out, but it seemed he'd been naïve. He would lose Kitty unless he could show her he could be the man she needed.

He loved her, and he wanted to build a future with her. A future and a family of their own—and he knew there was only one way to make that happen.

Kitty's life had become one long series of appointments. She seemed to spend her days waiting. Waiting for the paediatrician, the obstetrician, the oncologist, and waiting for Jess to have her radiotherapy sessions. But it wasn't helping.

Kitty didn't want to admit it but she was waiting for Jess to die. They all were. Jess was struggling more every day. Struggling with the pain, struggling to breathe, struggling to talk and struggling to eat. She was fading before Kitty's eyes and Kitty didn't think she could bear it. The only time Jess looked at peace was when she was holding her daughter.

Yesterday's appointment had at least been something a bit different. They'd been to court and Lizzie's parentage had been transferred from Kitty to Cam and Jess. Kitty was no longer officially Lizzie's mother. Jess had got her wish—she had her daughter.

But Kitty was scared now about what that meant. She

knew that this was what Jess had been waiting for. Her sister had been barely holding on. All that had kept her going were the milestones she had created to tick off. One—the surrogacy. Two—waiting for Lizzie. Three—waiting to officially become Lizzie's mother. And now she'd achieved all those things. She was a mother. Jess had given Cam his daughter, created a family. And now she could say goodbye.

Kitty's knees buckled as Jess's coffin was lowered into the ground. Joe's arm tightened around her waist, supporting her, offering comfort, but he wasn't sure she was even aware of his presence. She certainly hadn't turned to him for support after Jess had died just over a week ago. Kitty had just locked herself away with Cam and the baby, and Joe was beginning to think she was lost to him for ever. She seemed to have cut Joe out of her life without warning.

Kitty had gone through the entire funeral service without making a sound. She'd cried fat silent tears and had hugged people and nodded in reply to their condolences, but she hadn't spoken a word.

She had looked at Joe when he'd offered to drive her to the cemetery and he'd almost expected her to refuse him, but she'd wordlessly followed him to his car and sat silently beside him for the short trip. Cam and Lizzie were being driven by Cam's parents, who had come down to Sydney from northern New South Wales and Joe was grateful to have Kitty to himself. But what he hadn't expected was the hollow, fragile shell of a woman who sat beside him. She'd lost weight in the past few weeks, and it was more than just the pregnancy weight. Her face had lost some of its usual roundness, her eyes were dark with grief, and her cheeks were hollow and pale. She was a shadow of her normal self.

He had the impression that Kitty was only just holding it together. He kept his arm around her, anchoring her to the ground, anchoring her to him as Cam handed his six-week-old daughter to his mother and stepped forward. He bent down to scoop a handful of dirt from the mound at his feet and Joe watched his lips move as he bade his wife goodbye quietly before he opened his fingers and let the earth fall into the grave.

Cam turned back to his parents and his daughter. He had his family, but Kitty had no one, and Joe's heart ached for her.

Kitty sobbed and turned her face in against Joe's shoulder as the sound of the dirt hitting the coffin echoed in the hole. He didn't know if she was aware she was leaning on him but he wasn't going to abandon her. She had shut him out for the past six weeks, refusing to step out of the house unless it was to accompany Jess somewhere, but, as pathetic as it made him seem, he would still take any opportunity he could get to have her in his arms. He knew she felt alone, and seeing Jess being buried beside her parents and younger sister would only reinforce that. But Kitty had him. She'd always have him and he would be there for her. He knew she would need him again.

The mourners had all begun to make their way, in silence, back to their cars, but Kitty hadn't moved. She was standing still, staring at the ground.

Joe didn't know if she had seen everyone starting to leave. They were all going back to Cam's house for the wake. He didn't know if Kitty intended on going back there but, then again, where else would she go? That was where she was living.

'Kitty?'

'Can you give me a minute?' she said as she pulled away from him.

He let her go. She might have been standing a few inches away from him but emotionally he felt as though there was a chasm separating them. He couldn't remember the last time he'd seen her smile, heard her laugh. He missed her, desperately. The light inside her had dimmed and his heart ached for her and everything, everyone, she'd lost.

He needed her back. He needed to reach out, build a bridge over that chasm and get her back. For her sake and his.

He watched and waited as she went to each of the other graves—her mother's, her father's, her baby sister's. Joe could see fresh flowers at the base of their gravestones and he realised Kitty had already visited the cemetery today. She must have placed the flowers there.

He watched from a distance as she bent and took a flower from each grave. She hadn't asked for his support, but he still waited and watched, feeling as if his heart might break. Kitty had always seemed fragile and he was worried that Jess's death might be the final straw. The thing that would finally break her. He would do anything to protect her but he had never felt so useless. All he could do was to stay close by, to be there if she needed him.

She sank onto the ground, kneeling beside the freshly dug grave and, one by one, she dropped each flower into the hole to land on Jess's coffin.

She sat quietly for a few minutes before eventually standing and coming back to Joe. Her eyes were red-rimmed.

'Shall we go?' he asked as he took a freshly laundered handkerchief from his pocket and handed it to her.

He didn't ask if she was ready to leave. He didn't ask if she was OK. He knew she was neither of those things but she couldn't stay here for ever. Everyone would be expecting her back at Cam's house. She may not want to speak to anyone, and if that was the case Joe would protect her, shield her, make excuses for her, but he knew she would want to be close to Lizzie. It would make her feel connected to Jess.

She nodded and let him take her hand.

He drove her to Cam's house and did all the things that no one else had the energy to manage. He provided endless cups of tea and coffee, spoke to the caterers, topped up people's drinks and tidied away dirty dishes.

Having baby Lizzie there was a good distraction but Joe could see Kitty getting antsy as Cam's mother monopolised the baby. Joe couldn't blame her. Lizzie was her first, and probably only, grandchild, but he knew that Kitty felt a connection that no one else did when it came to the baby.

As Cam and Jess's friends started to leave, Joe managed to persuade Kitty to go for a walk with him. He thought she might need some space, and he needed to talk to her. They didn't get further than the park down the street, but sitting on the park bench in the quiet of twilight gave them a chance to talk without interruption.

'Cam's father told me they're planning on staying in Sydney for a while to give Cam a hand,' he said as he sat beside Kitty. 'What are your plans?' He kept his gaze fixed on a gum tree in the distance, unfocussed and non-confrontational, as he asked his question.

'I can't make plans,' Kitty replied flatly. She sounded upset and confused and he was worried about her. He knew she struggled to cope with situations like this—losing people she loved.

'You're welcome to move back in with me if you like. Let Cam have some time with his family and the baby?'

'I'm his family too,' she replied. 'I'm Lizzie's mother.'

'You're her *aunt*, Kitty.' He knew the paperwork had been signed, officially transferring Lizzie's parentage to Cam and Jess. Kitty was Lizzie's birth mother but she had no claim on her now.

Kitty was shaking her head. 'I can't leave the baby. She's all I have left.'

Joe should have seen this coming. He knew Kitty had a fear of being abandoned herself. She'd lost first her younger sister, then her parents, and now Jess. He knew she saw the baby as a part of her. In a way, the baby *was* a part of her—but not one she got to keep. He couldn't believe no one had seen this coming. Wasn't this the sort of thing that should have been anticipated from the counselling sessions prior to the surrogacy? He could understand how a baby would satisfy Kitty's need to have someone to love, to have someone who wouldn't leave her. Was it any wonder she was having difficulty letting Lizzie go? But Lizzie wasn't the child that would fix all this. Kitty needed to move on. She needed to create a life for herself. A family for herself. She didn't get to keep Jess's.

'I understand you're sad, Kitty, I know you're hurting, but you can't be a substitute for Jess. Cam and Lizzie were *her* life. *Her* family. You need to have your own.'

'I know you think you understand, Joe, but you don't know what it's like to lose everybody. I can't let them go too.'

'I can help you, Kitty. Come home with me.'

'Please don't make this about you, Joe. I can't think about you at the moment.' She stood up from the bench and started walking.

Joe walked with her, in silence. He couldn't let her go alone, but who was he to say she was wrong about him not understanding what it was like. One thing Joe knew he did understand was *her*, but he couldn't stop the feeling that Kitty was removing herself emotionally from him. He'd always been there for her, available to pick up the pieces, but maybe she didn't want that any more.

Maybe she didn't want him.

She was walking away but he wasn't prepared to let her go. He couldn't. She was upset but he couldn't, he *wouldn't*, abandon her. He knew that was her greatest fear and he wasn't about to leave her too. But he knew it wasn't only up to him.

If Kitty chose to walk away there wasn't much he could do.

Kitty missed Joe, but she was trying desperately to hold onto her family, or what she had left of them. She missed him terribly but she couldn't bring herself to abandon Lizzie and Cam. She needed them and she was certain they needed her. They would always be family. In her mind that meant they were there to stay. *Until death do us part.* She'd only been parted from the rest of her family by death. She would hold onto them with everything she had. Even if that meant giving up Joe. He didn't need her. Not like Lizzie did. She needed to stay strong for Lizzie.

Normally she would have relied on Joe to give her that strength, but she didn't want to depend on him now. He wouldn't be there for her for ever. For ever was a long time. Eventually she would have to manage without him, and she should start getting used to it now. Their relationship wasn't serious. It wasn't ever going to last. He would never commit—she knew they wanted different things in life, and she couldn't expect him to hang around. At some point he'd grow bored with her, or see something better. He'd told her that's exactly what his parents did and he was convinced he was cut from the same cloth. Kitty had no reason to doubt him. As long as she'd known him he'd never had a long-term relationship.

Neither had she.

She'd ruined their friendship by sleeping with him, but she couldn't deal with that reality along with Jess's death. She had to put Joe to one side. She'd deal with the consequences later, when she was stronger.

She missed him but she didn't want to see him.

Every time she did she had to fight the urge to run into his arms. Every time she saw him, it felt like her heart was breaking and then she had to start the whole process of getting over him again. She wasn't sure what hurt more—losing Jess or losing Joe—but she had no choice. She knew she had deliberately cut him out of her life, but she figured that eventually the pain would ease. She was hoping so.

This heartache would pass. It had to.

She bent her head to kiss the soft, downy hair on Lizzie's head. She breathed in the baby smell as she rearranged her clothes. She had been breastfeeding Lizzie but the baby had now fallen asleep and Kitty need to put her back in her bassinette. No one knew she was still breastfeeding. She was expressing milk so that Cam could feed his daughter too but Kitty loved the closeness she felt when she was feeding Lizzie and she didn't want to give that up, so she volunteered for the midnight feed when the house was quiet and she and Lizzie could have their moment. She whispered her thoughts to Lizzie at the same time.

She couldn't talk to Jess. Or to Joe. The closest she had to a confidante now was this little baby. Lizzie was only ten weeks old, hardly a substitute for Joe or Jess, but she was the next best thing. This was bonding time for the two of them. She wasn't officially the baby's mother any more, but she was the closest thing to a mother that tiny Lizzie had.

Unless, or until, Cam remarried.

Kitty couldn't stand the idea of Cam replacing Jess, but she knew it was ultimately a possibility. Cam was only young. He had the rest of his life in front of him.

Kitty wiped a tear away. She was crying for everyone she'd lost. Including Joe.

She stood up to wrap Lizzie and tuck her into her bassinette. She didn't want to think about Joe. She didn't have the energy. Cam *might* replace Jess, but Joe would *surely* replace Kitty, and she didn't want to think about how that would make her feel. There was only so much she could handle at the moment, and that didn't include thinking about her relationship with Joe.

She knew she had pushed him away. She'd been scared of losing him but she'd gone and done it anyway, just as Jess had warned her, leaving her more miserable and even lonelier than before.

CHAPTER TEN

KITTY HAD RETURNED to work but she still hadn't moved out of Cam's house. Joe had no idea how long she was planning to stay there. Did she have any intention of leaving? He didn't know, but he knew she was avoiding him. The only time he saw her was when they were at work. She was a shadow of her former self—her wide smile was absent, her dimples gone, her curves shrunk. She'd shut down completely and shut him out.

He'd called around to Cam's house—he refused to think of it as Kitty's even though she still lived there— several times, checking on them both, wanting to make sure they were coping. He'd tried to time it around Kitty's days off, wanting to see her, but every time he'd visited she'd made an excuse and avoided him.

But Joe was refusing to give her up.

She'd made a decision but he wasn't going to sit back and let her throw away their relationship. She was too important to him. Their *future* was too important to him.

So he'd enlisted Cam's help in order to see Kitty. That had been a major exercise in subterfuge. He'd had to anticipate her every rebuttal and plan a response. He had to co-ordinate with Cam to make sure someone was home to look after Lizzie so Kitty didn't have that excuse, and he had to make sure Kitty wasn't either at work or asleep.

He knocked on Cam's front door and invited her to brunch. 'There's something I need to tell you,' he said, hoping her curiosity would outweigh any reluctance.

'Now is not a good time, Joe.'

He could tell from her voice that something had upset her and immediately his protective instincts kicked into gear. If Kitty needed him he planned on being there for her, and this time he wasn't going to let her fob him off.

'Come for a walk with me to the beach then. Talk to me. Tell me what's going on.' Maybe walking would be better than sitting at a café. There would be no one to overhear them and Kitty wouldn't feel as if he was cross-examining her.

She hesitated, and he was preparing his speech to plead his case when she surprised him be agreeing. 'OK.'

He waited while she found her shoes and her keys. He heard her tell Cam she was going for a walk and would be back soon.

'Tell me what's happened,' Joe said as they hit the sand.

'Cam had a letter from the fertility clinic asking him what he wants to do with the remaining frozen embryos.'

Joe hadn't realised there were surplus ones. 'What are his options?'

'He can destroy them, donate them to a couple who need them or he could keep them and use them.'

'What does he want to do?'

As Joe asked the question he realised what the issue could be. Why Kitty was upset. Was Cam's decision not the one Kitty wanted? Joe fought off a wave of panic—was Kitty thinking about offering to be a surrogate again? He knew she'd want to have as much of Jess as possible, which could include another baby, but if she went down this path again she was effectively putting her own life on hold once more and to Joe, that meant his life as well. He loved her but was he prepared to wait for ever?

His heart was in his mouth as he asked, 'What do *you* want, Kitty?'

That was the crux of the matter. What did Kitty want?

A life with him or a life with her sister's children?

She had to choose. He had to offer her a choice, and she had to make it.

Kitty had missed Joe. She'd missed everything about him. His kindness, his smile, his hands on her body, his lips on hers, his ability to listen without judging, his ability to make her feel better. It felt good to be back by his side. To confide in him.

She wanted to slide her hand into his as they walked. She wanted to feel connected to another person, but she wasn't sure if they had that relationship any more. She wasn't sure what they'd done to their friendship. Had they completely destroyed it? Had she?

She shoved her hands into the pockets of her shorts instead and kept pace alongside him on the sand.

He'd asked her what she wanted.

'I want my family back,' she replied honestly, knowing it was an impossible wish.

'Kitty...'

'It's all right,' she said, pre-empting his reply, 'I know it's not possible but it's what I want.'

'And is that why you're still living with Cam?' he

asked. 'Are they your family now? Is that what you want? Jess's family?'

'They are my family too,' she protested. He couldn't begrudge her that. 'Lizzie needs me.'

'I'm not disagreeing with that, but she is not your daughter. She is Cameron's daughter. Your sister's daughter. She is your niece. And you love her, as you should, but you should have daughters of your own. A family of your own. I know you want that.'

But that was the problem. She shook her head. 'It's not going to happen for me. Everyone always leaves me.'

'*I* can make it happen.'

'You?'

'Yes. Me. Where do I fit into your life? Is there room for me? For us?'

'Us? Is there an "us"?'

'Of course there is. Nothing's changed.'

She should be pleased to hear that. She'd been worried that he would cast her aside, move on, but in a sense this was what she'd really feared. That nothing had changed. And she didn't want that. She didn't want to be just friends. She wanted more. She loved him but she wanted her happily ever after, and she wasn't going to get that from Joe.

He stopped walking and turned towards her. His face was serious, his blue eyes earnest. 'You deserve to find your own happiness. With someone who loves you. You deserve a family of your own, a husband and children of your own, and I want to give it to you. You should be with me.'

'What are you saying?' She wasn't sure she understood.

'I promised I would always be there for you. I was

there for you when your parents died, when Jess died…
But I don't just want to be there for you when things go
wrong. I want to be there for you always. I want to be
the one standing beside you in the good times *and* the
bad. I love you, Kitty, and I want to give you a family
of your own. A family with me. Let us build the life we
want together. Marry me.'

'But you don't want to get married.'

'I do.' He reached out and took both her hands in his.
Her racing heart slowed and calmed with his touch. She'd
missed that, and she didn't ever want him to let her go. 'I
was worried I couldn't give you what you needed most—
commitment—but the past few months have shown me
that I want to try. I know you are the woman for me. You
always have been, but the last few months have shown
me just how much better my life is with you in it, how
much happier I am. I've missed you with every piece of
me and I will do everything I can to make this work. I
want to marry you. I only intend to get married once, I
intend to do it right, and with you I know I've got it right.
We can do this. Together. I know I can be the man you
need. I need to know if I am the man you want.'

She loved him, desperately, but she didn't know if
she could do this. 'I'm scared, Joe.'

'Of what?'

'Of losing you.' She'd lost everyone she'd ever loved
and she couldn't bear to lose him too. Her heart couldn't
stand it. She'd lost too many people already.

But you love him. I know you do.

Jess's voice was in her head and Kitty knew what
she'd be saying if she was standing beside her. She could
hear the words.

You have to make a choice. You can love him now

and take a chance or you can send him away and know you're losing him for certain. Make your choice but there's only one choice that might give you the happiness you crave. The happiness you deserve. He's a good man and he loves you.

'I love you.' Joe's voice blended with the voice in her head. Jess and Joe, the two people she loved more than anyone else, were telling her the same thing.

But only one of them was still here.

He continued speaking. 'I've never wanted to make a commitment because I thought I would never find the right person. What I didn't realise was the right person was in front of me all along. That person is you, Kitty. I want to be beside you, I want to spend the rest of my life with you,' he told her. 'My parents were always looking for their next partner, they were never happy with what they had, but I'm always and only looking for you. I can't be truly happy without you and I want to spend the rest of my life showing you how I feel. Being yours. If you'll have me.'

'You won't leave me?'

'Never.'

Kitty was crying now.

'Do you love me?' Joe asked.

Kitty nodded. 'Yes. I do.'

Joe dropped to one knee in the sand, their hands entwined, their fingers interlaced. 'Kitty, I love you with every part of me. I want to share my life with you, for eternity. I promise to love you and adore you and never leave you. I want to make you happy, to make you laugh. I want to share my life with you as more than friends. I want us to be partners, lovers, parents to our children. I want us to be a family. I love you and I want to be your husband. Please, will you be my wife? Will you marry me?'

Kitty had to make a choice. She had to take a chance. If she didn't she would lose everything.

She'd already lost too much.

She would take the chance. She would choose the man she loved.

She had loved him for years and she didn't want to live without him. She needed him, but she wanted him too. He was her best friend, her lover and she wanted him to be her husband. She wanted him to give her a family of her own. She believed him when he promised never to leave her, for he'd always been there for her when she'd needed him. He had *already* proved that he could commit to her. She trusted him—and she loved him.

She tugged on his hands and pulled him to his feet. She wiped a tear from her eye but she knew he'd know the tears were happy ones. He knew her so well. And if he didn't, then the ridiculous smile on her face would surely have shown him how she felt.

'I love you,' she said as she wrapped her arms around his neck and pulled him close, 'and I want to spend the rest of my life with you.'

He bent his head until his lips brushed hers. 'Is that a yes?' he whispered.

Kitty nodded. 'Yes, my love, I will marry you. I promise to love you always, to be your family, your wife and the mother of your children, now and for ever.'

Joe wiped the tear from her cheek and kissed her again and in that kiss she could taste his promises and his love and, finally, she was complete.

* * * * *

REUNITED
WITH HER
PARISIAN SURGEON

BY
ANNIE O'NEIL

MILLS & BOON

This one definitely goes out to our readers.
Without you this book literally could not have been
made. You are the ones who built this hero and
heroine… I hope you enjoy their story.

Annie O xx

CHAPTER ONE

SCENT. SOUND. TASTE. Even the air felt different in Australia; so did the sea water he was ploughing through. But as the days had bled into weeks, then months, Raphael had come to know that travelling halfway round the world hadn't made a blind bit of difference. He was still carrying the same hollowed-out heart, weighted with an anvil's worth of guilt. Leaving Paris hadn't done a damn thing towards relieving the burden.

Volunteering had done nothing. Neither had working in conflict zones. Nor donating blood and platelets. He would have pulled his heart right out of his chest if he'd thought it would help. Working all day and all night hadn't helped. And then there was money. Heaven knew he'd tried to throw enough of *that* at the situation, only to make a bad situation worse.

Jean-Luc didn't want any of his money. Not anymore.

The truth was a simple one. Nothing could change the fact that his best friend's daughter had died on his operating table.

He'd known he was too close to her. He'd known he shouldn't have raised so much as a scalpel when he'd seen who the patient was. The injuries she'd suffered.

But there had been no one more qualified. And Jean-Luc had begged him. Begged him to save his daughter's life.

Raphael thought through each excruciatingly long minute they'd been in surgery for the millionth time.

Clamps. Suction. Closing the massive traumatic aortic rupture only to have another present itself. Clamps. More suction. Stiches. Dozens of them. Hundreds, maybe. He could see his fingers knotting each one in place. Ensuring blood flow returned to her kidneys. Her heart.

Her young body had responded incredibly well to the surgery. A miracle really, considering the massive trauma she'd suffered when the car had slammed into hers. All that had been left to do when he'd been called to the adjacent operating theatre was close her up.

No matter how many times he went through it, he stalled at the critical moment. There'd been two choices. He'd taken one path. He should've chosen the other. His one fatal error had built to that leaden silence when he'd returned to the operating theatre to see his junior lifting his hands up and away from her small, lifeless body.

They'd looked to him to call the time of death.

Raphael swam to the edge of the pool, blinking away the sea water, almost surprised to see that the sun was beginning to set. He pulled himself up and out of the pool in one fluid move, vaguely aware of how the exertion came easily now that he was trying to burn away the memories with lap after lap.

He was tired now. Exhausted, if he was being truly honest. Coming here to Sydney was his last-ditch attempt to find the man he had once been. The man buried beneath a grief he feared would haunt him until his dying day. He was driving himself to swim harder than he ever had before—churning the seaside pool into a boiling froth around him as he hit one side, dove, twisted, and then started again to see how soon he could hit the other—but his burning lungs did nothing to assuage the heaviness of his heart.

Love could.

And forgiveness could do so much more.

In fewer than twenty-four hours he'd see Maggie…

The years since he'd seen her last seemed incalculable. He remembered her vividly. A clear-eyed, open-hearted exchange student from Australia. Apart from Jean-Luc there had been no one in his life who had ever known him so well, who had seen straight through to his soul.

If, when they met again, she could see a glimmer of the man she'd known all those years ago he'd know there was a light at the end of the tunnel.

After toweling off in the disappearing rays of the sun, he tugged on a long-sleeved T-shirt and headed for the exit, already conditioned to look toward the white fence on the right, leading out of the baths towards the coastal path.

Le petit monstre de la mer.

He was still there. The cock-eared mutt that had been following him from his rented accommodation, along the coastal path to the Bronte Baths and back since he'd arrived in Sydney a week ago.

A reject from former tenants?

There were no tags, no chips. Nothing to identify him or his owners.

It shocked him that he'd cared enough to take the dog to a vet the day before.

At least it proved there was still a heart thumping

away in his chest, doing more than was mechanically required.

He huffed out a mirthless laugh.

Or was it just proof that he desperately needed one soul in his life who wasn't judging him? Who still wanted his company?

He winced away the thought. That wasn't fair. After over a decade of virtually no contact, Maggie hadn't merely agreed to meet up with him tomorrow night. She'd found him a job at her paramedic station. She'd gone above and beyond the call of a long-ago friendship.

The memory of her bright green eyes softened the hard set of his jaw.

From what she'd said in her emails, the under-staffed ambulance station sounded like a non-stop grind. Perhaps, at long last, *this* would be the beginning of the healing he'd been seeking, after eighteen months on the run from the pain he'd caused.

He certainly didn't trust himself on a surgical ward. Not yet, anyway. Perhaps never.

"*Allons-y*, Monster." He tipped his head towards the street and the dog quickly met his long-stride pace. "Let's see if we can find you some supper."

CHAPTER TWO

TICK-TOCK. TICK-TOCK.

Why had she brought him to a movie?

Raphael was going to think she hated him. But, no, she was just socially inept. And she wasn't quite ready for him to meet the "real" Maggie.

Maggie's phone buzzed in her backpack, adding to her mortification. She dragged the bag out from under her seat and fished around until she found it. Working in the emergency services meant checking your phone every time it beeped or buzzed, whether or not you were sitting next to your teenage crush from the most perfect year you'd ever had.

A year in Paris.

Raphael Bouchon.

Match. Made. In. Heaven.

Not that there'd been any romance. Just a one-sided crush that had come to an abrupt end when she'd boarded the plane back to Australia.

She pushed the button on her phone to read the message.

Dags, Dad needs more of those hyper-socks next time you come.

She speed-typed back.

They're compression socks, you dill.

Her expression softened. Her brothers were doing their best in the face of their father's ever-changing blood pressure. They were mechanics, not medics.

She glanced across at Raphael. *I could've been a surgeon, like you.*

An unexpected sting of tears hit her at the back of her throat so she refocused on her phone.

See you in a couple of weeks with a fresh supply. Maggie xx

She jammed the phone back into her backpack and suppressed the inevitable sigh of frustration. Moving to Sydney was more of a hassle than it was worth sometimes. But staying in Broken Hill forever? Uh-uh. *Not* an option.

She dropped her pack beneath her chair and readjusted in her stadium-style seat, only to succeed in doing what she'd been trying to avoid all night—grazing her thigh along Raphael's.

"Desolé." Raphael put his hand where his knee had just knocked Maggie's and gave it an apologetic pat.

She stared at his hand. Long, gorgeous, surgeon's fingers. Strong. Assured. Not the type of fingers that caressed the likes of her lowly paramedic's knees.

Wait a minute.

Had it been a caress? If it had been then this whole high school reunion thing was swiftly turning into a dream come true. If not…

She glanced across at him and saw he wasn't even looking at her. His bright blue eyes were glued to the flickering screen twenty or so rows ahead of them. Fair enough, considering they were at a movie, but…

"*Non, c'est*—it's all right."

Maggie fumbled her way through an unnecessary response, all the while crossing her legs, tucking her toes behind her calf to weave her legs together and make herself as small as possible. If they didn't touch again, and she could somehow drill it into her pea-sized brain that Raphael wasn't fabricating excuses to touch her, then maybe—just maybe—she'd stop feeling as if she'd just regressed back to her sixteen-year-old, in-love-with-Raphael self.

Ha! Fat chance of *that* happening.

Tall, dark and broodingly handsome, Raphael Bouchon would have to head back to France without so much as a *C'est la vie!* if she were ever going to give up the ghost of a dream that there had once been something between them to build upon.

The second she'd laid eyes on him tonight Maggie's body had been swept straight back to the giddy sensations she'd felt as a teen.

Two hours in, she was still feeling the effects. Despite the typically warm, late-summer Australian evening, all the delicate hairs on her arms were standing straight up. The hundredth wave of goose pimples was rippling along her spine, keeping time with the swoosh and wash of waves upon the shores of Botany Bay. Off in the distance, the magical lights of Sydney's famed harbor-front were glowing and twinkling, mimicking the warm sensation of fireflies dancing around her belly.

The outdoor cinema in Sydney's Botanical Gardens

was the perfect atmosphere for romance. Perfect, that was, if Raphael had been showing the slightest bit of interest in her.

It would've helped if she didn't feel like a Class A fraud. Yammering on about living the high life in Sydney as they'd walked through the gardens toward the cinema instead of being honest had been a bad move. How could she tell him, after he'd achieved so much, that her "high life" entailed a pokey flat that needed an epic cleaning session, a virtually round-the-clock work schedule and quarterly trips to the Outback to tackle the piles of laundry her brothers had left undone.

Hardly the life of a glamorous city girl.

She was such a fraud!

Not to mention all of the appalling "Franglais" that had been falling out of her mouth since she and Raphael had met at the entrance to the gardens. Every single stern word she'd had with herself on the bus journey there had all but disappeared from her head. Including the reminder that this was *not* a date. Just an old friend showing another old friend around town.

Nothing. More.

The second she'd laid eyes on him…

Total implosion of all her platonic intentions.

Whether it was because thirty-year-old Raphael was even better looking than seventeen-year-old Raphael, or whether it was the fact that looking just a little…*haunted* added yet another layer of intriguing magnetism to the man, she wasn't sure. Either way, Raphael had the same powerful effect on her that he'd had the first time they'd met at her host family's home all those years ago.

Jean-Luc. A twist of guilt because she hadn't kept in touch with him either cinched her heart.

She'd had a lot on her plate when she'd come home. She wasn't Super Girl. She couldn't do everything.

She readjusted in her seat and gave herself a little shake. *Just watch the movie and act normal!*

About three seconds passed before she unwove her legs and twisted them the other way round. She'd seen *Casablanca* a thousand times—could quote it line for line and had planned to do so tonight, back when she'd had just the one ticket...

Maggie dropped her eyelids and attempted another sidelong glimpse at the man she'd known as a boy.

His expression was intense and focused, though the rest of the audience was chuckling at one of Humphrey Bogart's dry comments. Smiling was not Raphael's thing.

Not anymore, anyway.

Back in Paris it had been an entirely different story. At least when they'd been together. His laugh had brightened everything, every day. It had made life appear in Technicolor.

Not that his surprise reconnection on social media had come in the form of an emotional email declaring his undying love for her—a love that demanded to be sated in the form of his flying halfway across the world to fulfil a lifelong dream of making sweet, magical love to her.

Quite the opposite, in fact.

His email had been polite. To the point. Bereft of what her father called "frilly girlie add-ons". Silly her for thinking that vital little details like why he'd decided to get in touch and move to Sydney after years of successfully pursuing an emergency medicine surgical career without so much as a *bonjour* were "facts."

Picking a movie as their first meeting hadn't exactly

been a prime choice in eliciting more information either. It had just seemed a simpler way of easing back into a friendship she wasn't entirely sure existed anymore.

Back in Paris he might not have had romantic feelings for her, but there had been no doubting that their friendship had been as tight as they came.

Her eyes shifted in Raphael's direction. Seeing the sorrow, or something a lot like it, etched into his features had near enough stopped Maggie's heart from beating when they'd met up earlier that evening. Not that he was the only one who had changed…

She shivered, remembering the day she'd flown home from France as vividly as if it were yesterday. Seeing her brothers at the arrivals gate instead of her mum…their expressions as sorrowful as she had ever known them…

Leaving France had felt physically painful, but arriving home…

Arriving home had been devastating.

How could she not have known her mother was so ill?

She dug her fingernails into her palms and blew a tight breath between her lips.

It wasn't anyone's fault. It was just…life.

Her breath lodged in her throat as Raphael's gaze shifted from the massive outdoor cinema screen to Maggie's arms.

He leaned in closer, his voice soft as he asked, *"T'as froid?"*

"Cold? Me? No. This is Australia! Sydney, anyway," Maggie corrected, her nervous laugh jangling in her ears as she rubbed her hands briskly along her arms. Just about the most ridiculous way to prove she was actually quite warm enough, thank you very much.

Being in lust did that to a girl.

That, and haphazardly wading her way through a state of complete and utter mental mayhem.

Sitting next to Raphael Bouchon was like being torn in two. Half of her heart was beating with huge, oxygen-filled thumps of exhilaration, while the other half was pounding like the hoofbeats of a racehorse hell-bent on being anywhere but here.

Raphael shifted in his chair and pulled his linen jacket off the back of his seat, brushing his knee against hers as he did. Accidentally. Of course. That was the only way things like that happened to her.

Just like Raphael "deciding on a change" and moving to Australia to become a paramedic. At her local station.

Sure she'd offered to help him, completely convinced it would never actually happen. And yet here they were, thigh to thigh, sitting in the middle of the Botanical Gardens, watching a movie under another balmy summer night's sky.

Raphael held his linen jacket up to her with an *It's yours if you want it* expression on his face. He was so earnest. And kind. Not to mention knee-wobblingly gorgeous.

"Megarooni gorge", as her friend Kelly would say. Kelly would've been slipping into that jacket and climbing onto Raphael's lap in the blink of an eye. Kelly had confidence.

Maggie…? Not so much. Just the thought of climbing onto Raphael's lap reduced her insides to a jittery mass of unfulfillable expectation.

So she waved off his kind gesture, mouthing, *No, thank you*, all the while rubbing her hands together and blowing on them as she did.

Nutter. What are you doing?

"Please," Raphael whispered, and his French accent danced along the back of her neck as he shifted the silk lining of the coat over her shoulders. "I insist."

"Merci." She braved the tiniest soupçon of French as she pulled the jacket and Raphael's spicy man-scent closer round her. She mentally thunked herself on the forehead. *Why* was she acting like such a dill?

As if the answer wasn't sitting right next to her on the open-air theater's bleacher seating, looking like a medical journal centerfold.

Raphael Bouchon, *Casablanca* and the glass of champagne he had insisted upon buying her while they were waiting for the film to start were all adding up to one thing: the most embarrassing exchange student reunion ever. Besides, it wasn't like a first date, when—

Whoa!

It's not a date. This is not a date. You are showing an obviously bereaved, gorgeous friend from high school around Sydney. That's. It. The fact that his arrival coincided with a non-refundable ticket to the Starlight Cinema and the most romantic film ever is sheer coincidence. And practical. Waste not, want not. And that includes Raphael.

At least that was what she'd keep telling herself.

Along with the reminder that this movie ended with a friendship. Nothing more.

She looked down to her fingers when she realized she was totting up the number of short-lived boyfriends who hadn't made the grade over the years. Expecting anything different when everyone had been held up to The Raphael Standard was hardly a surprise. Inaccessible. Unattainable. Dangerously desirable.

And here she was. Platonically sitting next to the man

himself. Not flirting. Not reveling in the protective comfort of his jacket around her shoulders. Not trying to divine any hidden meaning behind the chivalrous gesture no one had ever shown her before. Nor was she sneaking the occasional sidelong glimpse of his full Gallic lips. The cornflower-blue eyes that defied nature. The slightly over-long chestnut hair that all but screamed for someone to run their fingers through it. Someone like her.

And yet…

The mischievous glint in his eyes that she remembered so vividly from high school hadn't shown up once tonight. And even though he'd only just turned thirty, the salt and pepper look had made significant inroads into his dark brown hair. The little crinkles beside his eyes that she might have ascribed to smiling only appeared when his eyebrows drew close together and his entire visage took on a faraway look, as if he wasn't quite sure how he'd found himself almost twenty thousand kilometers away from home.

It didn't take a mind-reader to figure out that his relocation halfway around the world was a way to put a buffer between himself and some dark memories. This was *not* a man looking for a carefree year with a Down Under lover.

Not that she would've been on his list of possible paramours. She wasn't anywhere close to Raphael's league. The fact that she was sitting next to him at all was a "bloody blinder of a miracle" as her Aussie rules footie-playing brothers would say, midway through giving her a roughhouse knuckle duster.

Sigh…

Maggie feigned another quick rearrangement of her hair from one shoulder to the other, trying to divine whether Raphael was genuinely enjoying the al fresco film experience. Or *cinema en plein air*, as he had reminded her in his chocolate-rich voice as her rusty French returned in dribs and drabs. There hadn't been much call for it over the years.

She swung her eyes low and to the left. Yup. Still gorgeous.

As opposed to her.

She was a poorly coordinated, fashion-challenged dork in contrast to Raphael's effortlessly elegant appearance. Not that he'd said anything of the sort when he'd first caught sight of her at their prearranged rendezvous point. *Rendezvous?* Get her! Far from it. He'd even complimented her on her butterfly print vintage skirt and the "land girl" knotted top she'd dragged out of the back of her closet. Not because it was the prettiest outfit she owned, but because it was the only thing that was ironed apart from her row of fastidiously maintained uniforms.

Appearances weren't everything. She was proof of that. Freckle-faced redheads were every bit as competent as the next person. Well…maybe not literally, seeing as the person sitting next to her was a surgeon and she was "just" a paramedic. Anyway, her hair was more fiery auburn than carrot-orange. On a good day.

When they'd first met, in the corridors of the Parisian Lycée, she'd shaken off her small-town-girl persona and found the butterfly she'd always thought had been living in her heart. Well…a nerdy butterfly. Raphael had been every bit as nerdy as she back then. Or so she'd thought. But he'd called it…academically minded. He had been the best friend of her host's brother and she'd fallen head over heels in love with him.

Her mother had been right when she'd cheekily told

her daughter to keep her eye on the "Nerd Talent." Now, at thirty years old, Raphael was little short of movie-star-gorgeous. His tall, reedy body had filled out so that he was six-foot-something of toned man magnificence. His chestnut hair looked rakishly windswept and interesting. He looked like a costume drama hero who'd just jumped off his horse after a long ride along the clifftops in search of his heroine.

Whether his cheekbones were *über*-pronounced because of the weight he claimed to have lost on his travels or because his genes were plain old superior was unclear. Either way, he was completely out-of-this-world beautiful.

Even the five o'clock shadow that she thought looked ridiculous on most other blokes added a rugged edge to a man who clearly felt at ease in the most sophisticated cities in Europe. Although she would bet her last dollar he'd do just fine in the Outback too. His body confidence spoke of a man who could change a car tire with one hand and chop wood with the other.

Not that she'd been imagining either scenario. Much.

Those blue eyes of his still had those crazy long black lashes…but shadows crossed his clear azure irises more often than not…

As if feeling the heat in her gaze, Raphael looked away from the flickering screen, giving her a quick glance and a gentle smile as she accidentally swooshed her out-of-control hair against his arm. The most outlandish hair in Oz, she called it. If she wanted it curly it went straight. Straight? It went into coils. Why she didn't just chop it all off, as her brothers regularly suggested, was beyond her.

Again she stared at the half-moons her nails had

pressed into her hands. After her mum passed it had seemed as if her hair was the one thing she had left in her life that was genuinely feminine. So she'd vowed to keep it—no matter how thick and wild it became.

"So!" Raphael turned to her, with that soft, barely there smile of his that never quite made it to a full-blown grin playing upon his lips. "Did you have anything else in mind?"

Maggie threw a panicked look over her shoulder.

Like holding hands underneath the starlit sky?

Gazing adoringly into one another's eyes in between soul-quenching kisses?

She glanced at the screen and to her horror realized the credits were running. Sitting beside him and not making a complete fool of herself had been hard enough, but— *Oh, crikey.* She hoped he didn't expect her to conduct an actual conversation in French. It had been hard enough when she was in her teens, but now that she hadn't spoken a word in over thirteen years…

All of her tingly, flirty feelings began to dissolve in an ever-growing pool of insecurity.

"Sheesh. Sorry, mate… Raphael. Sorry, sorry…"

She stumbled over a few more apologies. Years of being "one of the guys" at work and growing up as the tomboy kid sister in a house full of blokey blokes had rendered her more delicate turns of phrase—if she had ever had them—utterly obsolete.

She puffed up her cheeks and blew out a big breath, trying to figure out what would be best. A meat pie and a pint?

She took in a few more blinks' worth of Raphael, patiently waiting for her to get a grip, and dismissed the idea. French people didn't go out for meat pies and pints! Why had her brain chosen this exact moment to block out everything she could remember about France?

Oysters? Caviar? More champagne?

Crêpes! French people loved them. Sydneysiders did, too.

There was a mobile crêpe caravan she'd visited a couple of times when she was in between patients. She grabbed her backpack and began pawing around for her mobile to try and find out where it might be parked up tonight.

What was it called? Suzettes? Flo's Flaming Pancakes?

"Actually…" Raphael put his hand on Maggie's forearm to stop her frantic excavation. "As I am starting work tomorrow morning, perhaps we'll take a rain check?"

Maggie nodded along as he continued speaking. Something about heartfelt thanks for her help in getting him the job. The stacks of paperwork she'd breezed through on his behalf.

In truth, it was far easier to stand and smile while she let herself be swept away with the rhythm and musical cadence of each word coming out of Raphael's mouth than to actually pay attention to what he was saying. Each word presented itself as a beautiful little stand-alone poem—distinctly unlike the slang-heavy lingo she'd brought with her from her small-town upbringing.

That year in Paris had been her mother's last gift to her. A glimpse of what the rest of the world had to offer.

She'd found out, all right. In spades.

A glimpse of Raphael's world, more like. And she wasn't just talking about trips to a museum.

For her there was only one Raphael and he was standing right here, speaking perfectly fluent English, his mouth caressing each vowel and cherishing each consonant so that when his throat collaborated with his tongue and the words hit the ether each word was like an individually wrapped sweet.

A bon mot.

She smiled to herself. Of course the French had a phrase for it. In a country that old they had a beautiful phrase for everything. Including the exquisite pain of unrequited love.

La douleur exquise. And, wow, was she feeling that right about now. Why had she been so *useful* when he'd written to her a couple of months ago from…? Where was it? Vietnam? Or was it Mozambique? Both?

Regardless, his email hadn't suggested he was intent on coming to Australia. Just "considering a change."

Typical Maggie. She'd just picked up the reins and run with it. Filling out forms. Offering to get the right information to the right people on the right date at the right time.

"Best little helper this side of the equator," as her mother had always said.

And now that he was here…

Total. Stage. Fright.

She'd been an idiot to think—

Nothing. You're friends. Just like Ingrid Bergman and Humphrey Bogart.

"Yeah, you're right. Early to bed sounds good. In fact…" she glanced at her watch "…time's a-tickin'. Best get cracking!"

An image of Raphael tangled up in her sheets flashed across her mind's eye as the rest of her barely functioning brain played a quick game of catch-up.

"Wait a minute. Did you say you were coming to work *tomorrow*?"

"*Oui*. Didn't I tell you?" His brows cinched together in concern.

Again the nervous laughter burbled up, scratching and becoming distorted as it passed through her tight throat. "Well, yeah, I knew you were coming. My boss told us about it the other day. But I didn't—" She stopped herself.

She'd thought she'd have more time to prepare. To become more immune to the emotional ramifications of working with the one man she'd imagined having a future with. In Paris. On a surgical ward. In a marital bed. *Together.*

"Maggie, if you do not want me working at your station…"

Raphael pulled out the vowels in her name, making it sound as if she were some sort of exotic bird or a beautiful length of stretchy caramel.

Quit staring at the gorgeous man and respond, Mags.

"No. That's not it at all. I'm totally on board with it. You'll be amazing. Everyone will love you. I must've gotten muddled. It'll be nice for you. To hit the ground running, I mean."

"Absolutement." Raphael nodded. "I am completely ready to be a true Australian."

Maggie couldn't help herself. She sniggered. Then laughed. Then outright guffawed. "Raphael, I don't think you could be a 'true Australian' even if you paddled backwards on a surfboard, dropped snags down your throat and chased them up with a slab of stubbies, all with a school of sharks circling round you. You're just too…" She held her hands open in front of him, as if it was completely obvious.

"Oui?" Raphael looked straight down that Gallic nose of his, giving her a supercilious look.

Had she taken the mick a bit too hard and fast?

"What is it that I am too much of, Maggie?"

"Um…well… *French*." She gave an apologetic shrug. "You know… You're just too French to be Australian."

The warm evening air grew thick. Whether it was an impending rainstorm or the tightening of the invisible tension that had snapped taut between them, she wasn't sure. Her body ached to step in closer. To put her hands on his chest.

"I suppose I will have to rely on you to help me," he said.

Whether he meant it or not was hard to tell.

"No wuckers, Raph," she joked, giving him a jesty poke in the ribs with her elbow, trying to defuse the tension. "I'll give you training lessons on Aussie slang and you can help me with my…um…"

Her vocabulary deserted her as her eyes met and locked with Raphael's.

"Francais?"

It would be so easy to kiss you right now.

"Maggie?"

Oh, God. She was staring. Those eyes of his…

But, again, the bright blue was shadowed with something dark.

What's happened to you since we last met?

Something about the slight tension in his shoulders told her not to push. He had his reasons for giving up his surgical career and zig-zagging around the world, only to land here in Oz. The last thing she was going to do was dig. Everyone had their "cupboard of woes," her mother had often said. And no one had the right to open them up and air them.

Just chill, Mags.

He'd spill his guts when he felt good and ready. Listening to people's "gut-spills" was one of her specialties. But when it came to spilling her own guts…there was no way she was going to unleash *that* pack of writhing serpents on anyone.

When they reached the aisle and began walking side by side the backs of their hands lightly brushed. Another rush of goose pimples shimmied up her arms, ultimately swirling and falling like a warm glitter mist in her tummy.

She was really going to have to train her body to calm the heck down if she was going to be his shoulder to cry on. Not that he looked even close to crying. Far from it.

Had she stuck her foot in it with the whole "you're too French" thing?

"For what it's worth," she said, "I really enjoy working on the ambos, and the fact you have extra language skills is great. Work is different every day. And it was an amazing way for me to get my bearings when I moved to Sydney."

"I'm not sure I'll be at the wheel. I haven't qualified for driving yet. All I know is I'm going to be working on an MIC Ambulance."

Luckily Raphael missed her wide-eyed *No! That's what I do!* response as he scanned the area, then turned towards the main bus stop outside the Botanical Gardens as if he'd been doing it every day of his life. He'd been born and bred in one of the world's most sophisticated cities—acclimatizing to another must be a piece of cake.

"I was actually surprised by how easy it was to get my working papers. Something about a shortage of Mobile Intensive Care paramedics?"

"Yeah, that's right." Maggie nodded, her brain more at ease in work mode. "They've really been struggling over in Victoria. Well, everywhere, I think. The most skilled mobile intensive care paramedics seem to be running off to the Middle East, where the pay is better. Well, not all of them. And it's not because working here is horrible or anything… I mean it's actually pretty great, when you consider the range of services we provide to the community—and of course to the whole of New South Wales when they need it. Like when there are forest fires. Or big crashes out in the back of beyond."

She was rambling now. And in serious danger of sending Raphael packing.

He was one of the only people in her life who had known her before her mum had passed. There was something about that link that felt precious. Like a tiny priceless jewel she'd do everything in her power to protect.

Maggie looked up, her eyes widening as Raphael's expression softened into an inquisitive smile. The trees behind him were laced with fairy lights and the buzz and whoosh of the city faded into a gentle murmur as her eyes met with his.

A flash of pure, undiluted longing flooded her chest so powerfully that she had to pull in a deep breath to stave off the dizzying effect of being the sole object of those beautiful blue eyes of his. The ache twisting in her lungs tightened into a yearning for something deeper. How mad would the world have to become for him to feel the same way?

Slowly he reached out his hands and placed them on

her shoulders. The heat from his fingers seared straight through her light top, sending out a spray of response along her collarbone that gathered in sensual tingles along the soft curves of her breasts. He tipped his chin to one side as he parted his lips.

Was Raphael Bouchon, man of her dreams, going to kiss her?

"I think this is where I catch my bus." Raphael pointed up to the sign above them. "I am afraid I will need my jacket back if we are going to part ways here. Will you be all right?"

"Of course!" she answered, too loudly, tugging off his jacket and checking her volume as she continued. "I'm the one who should be asking *you* that, anyway. Where was it you got a place again?"

It was the one thing she hadn't helped with. Finding him a place. He'd told her it was already sorted, but that didn't stop a case of The Guilts from settling in.

She should've offered him a bed…well, a sofa…while he sorted something out. Played tour guide. Called estate agents. Cleared the ever-accruing mess off of her countertops and made him dinner.

Not invited him to a movie and then scarpered.

But that level of support would have been slipping straight into the mode she was still trying to release herself from with her family.

The girl who did all the chores no one else wanted to do.

Besides, her home was her castle and there wasn't a chance on God's green earth that she would be inviting him round—or anyone, for that matter. She'd had almost seven years of looking after her brothers and father—

enough housekeeping, laundry and "When's the tucker gunna hit the table, Daggie?" to last a lifetime.

"It's a place I found on the internet, near Bondi Beach. I thought it sounded..." he paused for effect "...Australian."

Maggie laughed good-naturedly and leant forward to punch him on the arm. At the same time he leant down to kiss her on the cheek. Their lips collided and skidded off of each other's—but not before Maggie caught the most perfect essence of what it would be like to *actually* kiss him.

Pure magic.

Raphael caught the sides of her arms with his hands, as if to steady them both, and this time when their eyes met there was something new shining straight at her. That glint. The shiny spark in Raphael's almond-shaped eyes that erased every single thought from her harried brain except for one: *I could spend the rest of my life with you.*

The fear that followed in its wake chilled her to the bone.

An hour later Maggie held a staring contest with herself in her poorly lit bathroom mirror. Red-haired, freckle-faced, and every bit as unsure whether she was a country mouse or a city mouse as she had been thirteen years ago.

Closing her eyes, she traced her fingers along her lips, trying to relive the brush of Raphael's mouth against hers. It came easily. Too easily. Especially when she had been in love with him for almost half her life.

Her eyes flickered open and there in the mirror was the same ol' Maggie. The one who would never live in

Paris. The one barely making a go of it in the big smoke. The girl born and raised and most likely to return to a town so far from Sydney it had its own time zone. In other words, she could dream all she wanted, but a future with Raphael Bouchon was never going to be a reality.

CHAPTER THREE

RAPHAEL TUGGED HIS fingers through hair that probably could have done with a bit of a trim. He chided himself for not putting in a bit more effort. For not trying to look as if he cared as much as he genuinely did.

Seeing Maggie yesterday had done what he'd hoped. It had re-awoken a part of him he'd feared had died alongside Amalie that day in the operating theatre.

When their lips had accidentally brushed last night there'd been a spark.

He was sure of it.

Enough so that he sorely regretted not kissing her all those years ago. But Jean-Luc's mother's warning had been a stark one. *"Hands off!"*, she'd said, and so he had obeyed.

If he hadn't been relying so heavily on Jean-Luc's family for that vital sense of stability his parents had been unable to provide he would've gladly risked his pride and seen if Maggie had felt the same way.

For an instant last night he'd been certain of it.

This morning… Not so much.

Not that Maggie was taking a blind bit of notice of his *does-she-doesn't-she?* conundrum.

Listening to her now, reeling off the contents of the

ambulance they'd be working on, was like being in the middle of an auctioneer's rapid-fire pitch.

From the moment she'd arrived at the station she'd barely been able to look him in the eye. More proof, if he needed it, that he hadn't meant to her what she'd meant to him. After all, who took someone to a movie when they hadn't seen each other in over thirteen years?

Someone with a life. Someone who'd moved on.

"Raphael?" She clapped a hand on the back door of the ambulance to gain his attention. "Are you getting this?"

He nodded, not having the heart to tell her he'd actually spent the long flight over memorizing the equipment breakdowns and layouts he'd been sent along with the confirmation of his posting.

"And over here we've got your pneumocath, advanced drugs, syringe pumps and cold intravenous fluids. It's not so much a problem this time of year. The hypothermia. What with it being summer. But…" She screwed up her face and asked, "Is hypothermia a problem in Paris?"

She quickly flicked her green eyes towards him, then whisked them back to the supply bins as if looking at him for longer than three seconds would give her a rash.

"Well, you've got snow, so I suppose so," she answered for him. Then, almost sheepishly, she turned back to him and said, "*Neige*, right?"

He nodded, parting his lips to say he was actually ready to head out if she was, but she had already turned back toward the ambulance and was reeling off yet another list of equipment specific to the MICA vehicles.

"Hey, Mags. Looks like the A-Team is being broken up."

Maggie stopped mid-flow, her green eyes brightening as a beach-blond forty-something man came round the corner of their ambulance with a timorous woman who only just prevented herself from running into him when he abruptly stopped.

"All good things must come to an end I guess, Stevo." Maggie heaved a sigh of genuine remorse, then shot a guilty look at Raphael with an apologetic smile following in its wake.

"Raphael, this is my partner—my *former* ambo partner—Steve Laughlin."

"Crikey, Mags. It's only been ten minutes. And no lines have been drawn in the sand yet. No offence, newbie!"

He turned to the young woman behind him and gave her a solid clap on the shoulder that nearly buckled her knees before turning back to Raphael.

"Nice to meetcha, mate." Steve put his hand out for a solid shake. "You've got yourself one of Bondi Junction's finest here, so consider yourself lucky. I'm counting on you to look after her. She can be a bit of a klutz—"

"I'm more than capable of looking after myself, thank you very much!" Maggie cut in.

"Yeah, yeah. *Help me, help me!*" Steve elbowed Raphael in the ribs and laughed. "You know what I'm saying, mate? All these girls *really* want is a big strong bloke to look after 'em. Get a load of these pecs, Casey. This is what happens when your partner doesn't carry her fair share of the equipment bags."

He flexed his arm into Popeye muscles and grinned as his new charge instantly flushed with mortification.

"Yes, Steve. Nothing to do with the hours you spend at the gym instead of helping your wife with the dishes," Maggie answered drily, clearly immune to Steve's *über-*

macho version of charm. "And, for the record, I think I can live *without* a big strong Tarzan swinging in to rescue me, knowing that there's a fully qualified surgeon sitting in your old seat. Twice as many patients in half the time, I'm betting."

She gave Raphael a quick *Am I right, or what?* smile.

Raphael winced. Bragging rights over his surgical skills was something he'd rather not be a party to.

"Ah, well, then." Steve gave Raphael a knowing look, completely missing his discomfort. "If you're not busy curing everyone in Sydney over the next couple of hours, perhaps you'll be able to shake a bit more fun into our girl, here. Tell her there's a bit more to life than work, will ya? When we heard you were a Frenchie we all started laying bets on how long it'd take for you to get her out on the town after her shift. She's got a thing about France, you know?"

He rocked back on his heels, crossed his arms over what looked like the beginnings of a beer belly and gave him a solid once-over.

"You're a better looking bloke than I am, so maybe you're in with a bit of a chance."

"Hardly!" The word leapt out of Maggie's throat, lancing the light-hearted tone of Steve's comments in two.

"Easy, there, Mags." Steve rolled his eyes and gave her a half-hug. "I'm just messing with you. Give the bloke a chance, all right? We're just worried about you. All work and no play…"

"Yeah. I get it, Steve. Don't you have some work you should be getting on with?"

Raphael stayed back from the group, preferring silence to watching the increasing flush heating up Maggie's cheeks.

He stepped forward for a handshake when Steve did a quick introduction of his new junior partner, Casey, before heading for their own ambulance. As soon as they'd left Maggie poured her obvious irritation into filling up all the supply bins in their ambulance.

The idea of spending time with him outside of working hours obviously didn't appeal. Had he said something last night to offend her? Perhaps taking a rain check on a post-film drink had been bad form if it wasn't her usual *mode opératoire* to go out.

Raphael swallowed against rising frustration. Hitting the wrong note seemed to be his specialty of late. Making the wrong move. Insisting upon operating on a little girl he was far too close to, only to have to break the news to his best friend that his young daughter had just died on the operating table because of *his* mistake.

Jean-Luc would never forgive him. Not in this lifetime anyway.

He tried to crush the memory of what Jean-Luc had said to him to the recesses of his mind. A near impossible task as he revisited the cruel words each and every night while trying to fall into a restless sleep.

"You just take! All you do is *take*!"

The medical report had told a different story, had said that Amalie would have died anyway. Her injuries had been too severe. The loss of blood too great. But Raphael knew the truth. *He* was the one who had made the decision that had ultimately led to the little girl's death.

He returned his gaze to Maggie, who had shifted back into her efficient self and was doing a swirly *ta-da!* gesture with her arms in front of the ambulance.

"Clocked that? Are we good? Am I going too fast? Too slow? Should I just stop talking altogether?"

Her eyes widened and he saw that his worries about Maggie not wanting to work with him had been ridiculous. Those green cat's eyes of hers were alight with hints of hope and concern, making it abundantly clear that her nervous energy wasn't anti-Raphael. It was worry that he might not be interested. It was hope that he shared her passion for the job she loved. And, if he wasn't mistaken, there was an underlying pride at what she did for her community.

"All right, Frenchie? How're ya settlin' in, mate?"

Raphael turned at the sound of the male voice, not missing the pained expression taking hold of Maggie's face as her eyes lit on the paramedic behind him.

A tall black-haired man—big—was holding out a hand. "Marcus Harrison. Fellow paramedic. Friends call me Cyclops. I'll give you three guesses why."

Raphael threw a quick look to Maggie, who shrugged, rolling her eyes rolling as if to say, *Indulge him. It'll be over in a minute.*

When he turned back he was face to face with an eyeball.

"It's glass. Get it? I've only got one eye. Been that way since I was a nipper. Too much rugby, and one day…" Marcus pinched his fingers in front of his eye then made a flying object gesture.

Behind him Raphael could hear Maggie muttering something about *putting it away, already.*

Totally unfazed by Maggie's disgust, Marcus popped his eye back into the empty socket and doubled up in a fit of self-induced laughter. "Oh, mate. You should see your face. Priceless."

"Are you finished?" Maggie asked, her tone crisp, but not without affection.

"Yeah, but…" Marcus bent in half again, another hit of hilarity shaking him from head to toe.

"Marcus, I'm *trying* to show our new colleague the truck."

"What? He'll be all right." Marcus waved off her concerns. "You were a surgeon or something back there in Paris, right?"

Raphael nodded, knowing that a flinch had accompanied the reminder.

"Leave the poor man alone. He's got enough on his plate without you showing off your wares and quizzing him about his credentials."

Marcus strutted in a circle in front of Maggie. "Darlin', let me assure you, you can look at my wares *any* day of the week."

Again Maggie rolled her eyes. This clearly wasn't Marcus's first flirt session. Nor Maggie's first refusal. Clearly having three older brothers had toughened her up.

Marcus crossed to her, leaned in, gave her a loud smack of a kiss on the cheek, then gave Raphael a good-natured thump on the back as he passed, heading towards the tea room whistling a pop tune.

"He seems…"

Raphael searched for a good word, but Maggie beat him to it.

"A right idiot. Except—" she held up her index finger "—when it comes to work. He is a first-class paramedic. Claims he always wanted to be a paratrooper, but the eye thing made that dream die real quick—so he became another kind of para. Paramedic," she added, in case he hadn't caught the shortened term. Something the Australians seemed to do a lot of.

"And you two are...?" Raphael moved a finger between Maggie and the space Marcus had just occupied. "Were you a couple?"

He caught himself holding his breath as he waited for an answer. Was he hoping she would say no?

"Pah!" Maggie barked, her eyes almost tearing up as she laughed at the suggestion. "You have *got* to be kidding me!"

Just as quickly she recovered, throwing an anxious look towards the tea room.

"I mean, he's a lovely bloke, and will definitely make someone incredibly happy, but he's not..." Her eyes flicked to his so quickly there was no time to catch her expression. "He's a really good bloke. I'm lucky to know him. He's taught me loads."

Loyalty.

That was the warmth he heard in her voice. And it was a reminder of why he'd come to Sydney. She was loyal. She hadn't even questioned why he was here. Just helped in every way she could.

He swallowed. She didn't know the whole story.

He turned at the sound of Maggie snapping her fingers together before displaying a clear plastic bag of kit as if she were a game show hostess.

"Right. Back to work. So, we call these nifty little numbers the Advanced Airway Management Sets—or AAMS if you're in a hurry."

"*Très bien.* It all looks very familiar." He nodded, aware that his attention was divided.

Again and again his eyes were drawn to the fabric of Maggie's dark blue overalls tightening against her curves as she leant into the truck to replace the kit and then, by turns, pointed out the defibrillator, the suction kit, the spinal collars, spine board, inflatable splints, drugs, sphygmomanometers, pulse oximeters and on and on.

In her regulation jumpsuit she looked like an action heroine who donned a form-fitting uniform before bravely—and successfully—battling intergalactic creatures for the greater good of the universe.

Her fiery hair had been pulled into submission with a thick fishtail plait. Her green eyes shone brightly against surprisingly creamy skin. Ample use of sunblock, he supposed. An essential in Sydney's virtually non-stop "holiday" weather.

Instantly his thoughts blackened. As if he'd come here for some R&R after a year and a half of trying to put some good back into the world.

"All you do is take."

There was no coming back from the death of a man's only child.

He scrubbed his hand along his neck, still hearing the heavy church bells ringing out their somber tones on the day they had laid Amalie to rest. Amalie's funeral was the last time he'd seen Jean-Luc and the rest of the Couttards.

It was the first time they had fought. The last time they had had any contact.

"You took from my parents and now you've taken my daughter. No more!"

He opened his eyes to see Maggie waving a hand in front of his face. "Hello? All right in there? Time to jump in. We've been called out. Twenty-five-year-old mother, imminent birth. We're about seven minutes out. Wheels up, mate!"

* * *

Five minutes into the ride, Maggie's internal conversation was still running on a loop.

Mate?

What was it with her and calling Raphael *mate*? Almost as bad as Cyclops and Stevo calling him Frenchie.

Grr… Instead of bringing out that Parisian butterfly she knew lay dormant somewhere within her, Raphael's appearance was turbo-charging the country girl she'd tried to leave behind in Broken Hill.

Then again, maybe he didn't care what she did one way or the other. It was difficult to gauge exactly what was behind that near-neutral expression of his. Chances were pretty high that *he* hadn't stayed up half the night reliving their near-miss kiss. How mortifying. She hoped her feelings weren't as transparent as she feared.

Pretending to check for oncoming traffic, she gave Raphael a quick glance.

Still gorgeous. Still impossible to read.

But it went deeper than that. He didn't seem *present*. And that was something he had always been—*here*, engaged.

Could a person change so much that they lost the essence of who they were?

She swallowed the lump of contrition rising in her throat. *She* had. She'd changed a lot since her bright-eyed and bushy-tailed days.

She glanced across again, unsurprised to find his expression stoically unchanged. Not that she could see his eyes beneath the aviator glasses he'd slipped on once they'd strapped in for the blue lights ride.

"You sure you're all right?" She moved her elbow

as if to prod him. The gesture was pointless as she was strapped into her seatbelt.

A curt nod was her response.

"This isn't the first run you've had since you left France, is it?"

"No." His gaze remained steadfastly glued on the road ahead of them.

Okay. Guess we're not feeling very chatty today.

Not fair, Maggie. The man's got a lot on his plate today. New country. New language. New job. Old friend...

An old friend she was having to get to know all over again.

The old Raphael would've been laughing and joking right this very second—teasing her about her driving, or about the fact that she couldn't help making her own sound effect along with the sirens and each switch she flicked. He'd maybe even have started quizzing her about why her career had gone to the blue lights instead of the blue robes of the surgical ward.

Not a freaking peep.

When she'd told him to jump into the ambulance they'd done one of those comedic dances, with one person trying to get past the other, that had ended up looking like really bad country jigging. It should have, at the very least, elicited a smile.

Not from Raphael.

Not a whisper as to what was going on with him. Why he was here. Why he had downgraded himself.

The only thing she could guess was that the man was trying to put as much space as he could between himself and some intensely painful memories.

"You know, if you want to talk or anything…"

He glanced across, his brows tugged together. "About the job? No, no. I'm fine."

"Or about other things…" She pulled the ambulance around a tight corner, grimly satisfied to see his expression change from neutral to impressed, if only for a nanosecond.

Why wouldn't he talk to her? They'd once told each other *everything*.

Everything except the fact that she was a born and bred country girl doing her best to believe it wasn't above her station to dream of life as a surgeon in Paris.

Come to think of it, neither of them had talked about their home lives much. Just the futures they'd imagined for themselves. Her host family's beautiful Parisian home had been the base for most of their adventures. And the rest of their time had been spent exploring. With a whole lot of studying on thick picnic rugs in the shadow of the Eiffel Tower thrown in for good measure. After they'd hit the books they would roll over onto their backs, gaze up at the huge steel structure and talk about their dreams for the future.

Raphael had achieved his goals in spades. Resident surgeon in a busy Parisian A&E department. Addressing conferences around the world on emergency medicine. But then there had been an the about-face, eighteen months ago, and he had gone to work in refugee camps and free clinics in developing countries only to turn up now in Sydney.

Mysteries aside, Raphael's life was a far cry from being a jobbing paramedic in one of Sydney's beach neighborhoods with no chance of climbing up the ladder.

Cut yourself some slack.

She had returned from France only to be told her

mother had died while she was flying home. A girl didn't recover from that sort of loss quickly. And then there were the add-on factors: the shock of discovering her mother had known she was ill when she'd handed Maggie the ticket to Paris, the expectation of her grieving father and brothers that Maggie would step into the role her mother had filled—the role her mother had made her promise she would never, ever take.

Cramming her dream of moving back to France and becoming a surgeon into the back of a cupboard, she had cooked and cleaned and washed an endless stream of socks for her family while they got on with the business of living their lives…

It had taken her years to break out of that role. And she had finally done it. She was living life on her own terms. Sort of. Not really… Four weeks of her year were still dedicated to sock-washing, floor-scrubbing and casserole-making, but it was a step. Who knew? Maybe one day she would be the world's first ninety-year-old junior surgeon.

She glanced across at Raphael, saw his jaw tight again as they wove their way through the morning traffic. It wasn't her driving that drew his muscles taut against his lean features. There was something raw in his behavior.

If it was ghosts he was trying to outrun, he looked as though he'd lost the battle. It was as if they had taken up residence without notice, casting shadows over his blue eyes.

If only she could help bring out the bright light she knew could shine from those eyes of his.

A little voice in her head told her she'd never succeed. *You don't have the power to make anyone happy. That can only happen from within.*

"So…" Her voice echoed in the silent ambulance as she tried to launch into the work banter she and Steve had always engaged in. "When's the last time you delivered a baby outside a hospital?"

"Is there not a midwife attending?"

Raphael's tone didn't carry alarm, just curiosity. As if he were performing a mental checklist.

"There's been a call made, but it's usually luck of the draw as to who gets there first. We'd be fighting rush-hour traffic to get to the Women's Hospital, so I don't think we'll have time to load her up and take her there. They said the birth was imminent when they rang. That the mum is already wanting to bear down."

Raphael nodded, processing.

She doubted it was the actual delivery of a child that was cinching his brows together.

Maybe…

No guessing. You do not get to guess what has been going on in his life. He will tell you when he is good and ready.

She shot him another quick look, relieved to see that the crease had disappeared from his forehead.

Work would get him on track. It was what pulled *her* out of the dumps whenever she was down. It was what had finally pushed her up and out of Broken Hill.

That twelve-hour drive to Sydney had felt epically long. Mostly because she had known she'd never wanted to go back and that it would be the first of many round trips. They weren't as frequent now…

Instead of saying anything in response, Raphael looked out of the window as they whipped past apartment block after apartment block on their way to the Christian housing charity that had put in the call.

Unable to bear the silence, she tried again. "The mother is Congolese, I think. Democratic Republic of Congo. A recent refugee. My Lingala's pretty shoddy. How's yours?"

The hint of a smile bloomed, then faded on his lips.

"Was there any more information about the mother? Medically?" he qualified.

"Nope." Maggie deftly pulled the ambulance over to the roadside. "We'll just have to ask her ourselves."

A few moments later the pair of them, a gurney, and the two birthing kits Maggie had thrown on top were skidding to a halt in front of a group of men standing outside a door in the housing facility's central courtyard.

"She's in here." One of the lay sisters gestured to an open door beyond the wall of men.

Like the Red Sea in the biblical tale, the men parted at the sight of Maggie and Raphael, letting them pass through, a respectful, somber air replacing the feverish buzz of what had no doubt been a *will-they-won't-they-make-it?* discussion.

Abandoning the gurney out in the courtyard, Maggie grabbed the birthing kits, but stepped to the side so that Raphael could enter the room first. The distant mood she had sensed in him had entirely evaporated.

Inside, curtains drawn, a crowd of women in long skirts and brightly patterned tops shifted so they could see the beautiful woman on a bed that had either been pulled into the sitting room for the birth or was there because of constant over-crowding. Either way, the woman's intense groans and her expression showed she was more than ready to push.

She was pushing.

"I'll do the hygiene drapes if you're all right to begin the examination," Maggie told Raphael.

"Good. *Bien*."

Out of the corner of her eye she watched as he unzipped one of the kit bags, quickly finding the necessary items to wash and sterilize his hands and arms in the small, adjacent kitchen, re-entering as he snapped on a pair of examination gloves. His movements were quick. Efficient. They spoke of a man who was in his element despite the dimly lit apartment and the crowd of onlookers.

But there didn't seem to be any warmth emanating from him. And that surprised her. It wasn't as though he was being mean, but... *C'mon! The woman's about to have a baby.* A little bedside manner would be a good thing to use around now!

The women, as if by mutual consent, all pressed back against the wall, necks craning as Raphael made his way to the expectant mother's side.

"You are happy with an audience?" Raphael asked the woman in his accented English, and the first proper smile to hit his lips all morning made a welcome appearance.

Finally! So it *is* there. Just hard to tap into.

The expectant mother nodded. *"Bien sûr. Voici ma famille."* She groaned through another contraction.

"Ah!" Raphael gently parted her legs and lifted the paper blanket Maggie had put in place across the woman's lap. *"Vous parlez Français? Très bien."* He turned to Maggie. "You are all right to translate on your own?"

Maggie grinned. Trust Raphael to have his first patient in Oz be a fluent French-speaker.

A seamless flow of information zigzagged from the

mother to Raphael to Maggie and back again—including the woman's name, which was Divine.

Maggie smiled when she heard that. What a great name! As if the woman's mother had predestined her daughter to be beautiful and feminine. Maggie was all right as far as names went, but Daggie—as her own family insisted on calling her—made her feel about as pretty as if she were called Manky Sea Sponge.

"Can you believe it?" Raphael was looking up at her, his brow furrowed in that all-work-no-play look she was still trying to get used to.

"Divine? Yeah." She offered the mother another smile. "It's a beautiful name."

"This is Divine's fourth pregnancy."

Ah. That was the vital bit of information he had actually been alluding to. She'd heard. Registered. Moved back to the pretty name. Was he going to be like this all the time?

Three pregnancies without any problems meant this one would likely be a cinch.

Maggie shifted her features into a face she hoped said, *Wow! Impressive!* Not, *Four children before you've turned thirty? No, thank you.*

Her mother had been down that path, and look at all the good it had done her. A life of cooking and cleaning in the Outback before being hit by an A-Grade cancer cluster bomb. Pancreatic. Lymph. Stomach. At least it had been swift—though that hadn't made it any less of a shock.

"First time for a home birth?" Maggie asked, to stop herself from exploring any further her instinctual response to a life of full-time parenting. She'd been down that dark alley plenty of times, and this was definitely not the time or place for a return journey.

"*Non…*" Divine bore down, her breath coming in practiced huffs. "I have never had one of my children in hospital."

"Just as well," said Raphael neutrally, in French, "because you are crowning. I can see your baby's head now."

Cheers erupted from the women around, and to Maggie's complete surprise a chorus of joyous singing began.

Raphael indicated that Maggie should kneel down beside him as he kept pressure on the woman's perineum to prevent any uncontrolled movements while first the forehead and then the chin and finally the child's entire head became visible.

Finding herself caught up in the party-like atmosphere, Maggie beamed up at Divine, congratulating her on her ability to get through the intense moment without any tears or painkillers, and out of the corner of her eye watched Raphael check for the umbilical cord and its location.

"Are you up for one more big push?" Raphael asked over the ever-increasing roar of song. "We just need to get those shoulders out." His voice was gentle, but it conveyed how strong the determined push Divine gave would have to be.

Divine tipped her head back, then threw it forward, her voice joining in extraordinary harmony with the women around her as she bellowed and sang her way through a super-powered push.

Raphael held the baby's head in one hand, turning it towards the mother's thigh, and gently pressed down with the other to encourage the top shoulder to be deliv-

ered as Divine bore down for the one final push that…
oh, yes…yes…would bring her new son into the world.

"*Felicitations*, Divine. You have a beautiful little boy."

Maggie was shocked to hear Raphael's strangely vacant tone. Why wasn't he as lifted and carried away by
the raucous atmosphere as she was? No matter how often
she tried to be blasé about moments like these—it was
impossible. And to play a role in this miracle of a child
coming into the world surrounded by song…

She might not want one herself just yet, but it was
just so…so *happy*. One of those truly magical moments
a paramedic could have. It brought a tear to her eye
every single time.

She swiped away her tears as swiftly, expertly, Raphael suctioned the baby's mouth and nose, giving Maggie a satisfied nod to tell her that the amniotic fluid was
a healthy color. Maggie handed him a fresh towel to vig-
orously and thoroughly dry the baby, then waited with
another dry towel to swaddle the infant before gently
placing him on his mother's chest.

The cooing and murmurs of delight that followed
wafted and floated around them, and Raphael delivered
the placenta at the very moment the midwife opened the
door with a cry of, "G'day ladies, I'm finally here—no
thanks to the traffic. Shall we get to it?"

Laughter, cheers and yet more singing broke out as
the midwife's expression changed to one of delighted
wonder when the little boy took his first proper wail.

A few more minutes of cleaning up took place while
the rest of the women began handing round plates of
food.

Raphael and Maggie turned to go, but stopped upon
hearing Divine calling for them. Raphael went over to

the side of the bed where the little boy was, and after a bit of insistence finally accepted the child into his arms.

Again those shadows shifted and darkened his eyes. It heartened Maggie to see that the shadows weren't so dark as to mask his genuine pleasure at seeing the child was healthy and well, but there was *something* there. Something that colored even the happiest of experiences.

"What is your name?" the woman asked in her heavily accented English. "I am so grateful for your help. For my son, I must know your name."

Maggie shot him a quick look. It wasn't unknown for people to name their children after a person who had helped them in a significant way. She couldn't contain a grin. Barely twenty-four hours into his new life and already he'd brought a child into the world who might bear his name. What a way to make an impression!

One look told her he wasn't nearly as delighted by the prospect as Maggie was.

"Raphael," he said finally.

The answer was reluctant, and his posture followed suit when Divine's eyes lit up at the sound of his name. He gave an almost imperceptible shake of his head, silently communicating that under no circumstances did he want his name to go to the child.

As clearly as Maggie had read the message, so too did the new mother. She gave Raphael's arm a grateful squeeze, then stretched her arms out to him so she could hold her son close again.

"Thank you, Raphael," she said. *"Merci."*

He nodded his acceptance for the gratitude, but remained silent.

"You were amazing. You looked like you deliver babies

every day of the year," Maggie couldn't help saying, feeling a puff of pride that her friend had handled the birth with such ease.

She, too, received a silent nod of thanks.

"I think," Divine continued, her eyes brightening again, skidding from Raphael to Maggie and then across to the group of women who were with them in the room, "I will call my son…"

Everyone leaned forward to hear the name of this precious new life, born into an entirely new world, his whole life stretching out in front of him with a perfectly clean slate…

"Walter."

"Walter?" Maggie clapped her hand over her mouth.

A sea of heads nodded in unison, as if it were the perfect choice. Maggie bit down on the inside of her cheek. Hard. She glanced to the side to see Raphael nodding too, as if it were the ideal name for the tiny infant.

Maybe the name wasn't funny in France, but Maggie was straining not to break down in a full fit of giggles.

Walter!

"Shall we go?" Raphael was impatient now, shifting his run bag from hand to hand as if the incident had unbalanced him.

Maybe it was being stationary that had him so fidgety. He had that faraway look in his eyes again. The unsettled one that needed the immediacy of work to dull its jagged edges.

"Sure." Maggie picked up the other run bag full of supplies, relieved to hear her radio crackling with another call-out.

As she took down her notes she tried to shrug off the disquiet that had formed between herself and Raphael.

This was a *que sera sera* situation if ever there were one.

Whatever would be would be.

Shouldering her own run bag, she received pats of thanks on her shoulder as she passed through the group of men outside with a grim smile, furious with herself—and Raphael, if she were being totally honest—that her joy had been so thoroughly diluted.

Moments like these were her daily gold dust! Unexpected names for children. A singing birth support group. Plates full of exotic sweets being passed around as if it were Christmas Day itself. What other job gave a person access to the most intimate, personal moments in someone else's life? Sure, the bulk of them were horrible—but some, like this one, were pure sunshine.

From the look of his glowering expression, Raphael didn't really seem to "do" sunshine moments. He'd moved to the wrong country, if that was the case. Aussies were optimists. And she'd thought he was one as well.

There had been countless times when they had rolled around on the green grass at the base of the Eiffel Tower in absolute stitches. Imitating a teacher. Trying to outwit each other. Wondering what Jean-Luc was getting up to with his latest girlfriend. Or Raphael finding it hilariously funny that her favorite place in Paris was so clichéd.

She'd insisted it wasn't clichéd—it was essential. She hadn't come to Paris to hang out in burger joints or milk bars, like she could at home. She wanted all her memories to resemble the pages of the tour books she'd read before coming over.

Perhaps this—Raphael's new curmudgeonly persona— was evidence that she was the butt of another one of life's cruel jokes. The man of her dreams had come back into her life, only to be dangled in front of her like a carrot she could never catch. A carrot she wasn't entirely sure she *wanted* to catch.

"You sure you're all right?" she finally asked as they began restocking their run bags.

He shot her a look. One demanding an explanation.

"You did a great job in there. I mean, *obviously*. It's not like you're underqualified or anything…"

"But…?" He scraped a tooth across his lower lip and held it there—as if in anticipation of drawing blood if she said the wrong thing.

"It's nothing, really." She broke eye contact to reorganize the immaculately laid out supply tubs.

"Maggie, if there's something I'm not doing properly you need to tell me. Before we get any more calls." He tapped the face of his watch as if she were holding him back from a super-important meeting. On purpose.

Maggie's lips thinned. Someone had stolen Raphael and replaced him with a robot. She was becoming more certain of that by the minute.

She turned and faced him. "Your medical skills are not in question. Surprise, surprise—you're perfect." *In more ways than one.* "It's just… I thought your bedside manner would be a bit more… I don't know… *French*."

He tipped his chin to the side. "What exactly does *that* mean?"

Nice. Warm. Kind. Compassionate. Letting a woman name her child Raphael instead of Walter.

"Just…you know…a bit more Casanova than clinician."

"He was Italian."

She turned away and rolled her eyes. This was going to be a *long* shift.

Mercifully, the radio crackled, and again she tipped her head to the side to press her ear closer to the speaker on the clipped-on unit at her shoulder.

"We've got a slip and fall about ten blocks away, and then another call after." She picked up her pace to get to the ambulance, forcing herself not to register Raphael's implacable expression.

Whatever. She'd done her bit. Helped him get a job. Taken him out for a so-so night on the town. He was a big boy.

A grown man who looked as if he was truly hurting inside.

The radio crackled again. There was a third call for them to do a hospital transport as soon as they'd dealt with their first two calls. *Good.* No time to worry about feelings. They got in the way of everything. They reminded her of all the dreams she'd let go of in an instant.

An unexpected film of tears fogged her eyes as she opened up the back of the ambulance to put her gear in. She grabbed Raphael's bag without looking and said she'd meet him up in the cab as the sting of emotion tore at her throat. How she longed to share her hopes and dreams with someone. And not just any someone. Raphael.

But he was no longer the bright-eyed optimist she'd known back then. They each bore invisible scars from the harsh realities life had thrown at them and would have to find a new way to relate to one another.

"You ready?" she asked unnecessarily as Raphael

buckled up beside her after closing his door with a solid *thunk*.

"Always," he said, his eyes intently focused on the road as she pulled out into traffic.

Are you going to be this stoically bereft of charm forever? Or just when you're with me?

"All right, then."

Maggie tried to shake her head clear of the nagging thought that there was something edgy behind his response. As if he'd missed a step somewhere along the way and it had had devastating consequences. But until she knew what was really wrong, it wasn't fair to judge.

She flicked on the blue lights and siren.

"Let's get this show on the road."

CHAPTER FOUR

Stroke. Stroke. Stroke.

Raphael's arms were a blur the instant he surfaced from his dive into the seawater pool.

She'd been fine when he'd left to attend the next surgery.

As fine as someone could be when their proximal descending aorta had been near enough sheared off the heart and stitched back on again. But he had fixed it. He'd repaired the tear.

He went through the steps of the surgery again.

Traumatic aortic rupture. The tear had been sited near the subclavian artery branch, adjacent to the aorta. Sudden deceleration saw far too many injuries of this type present themselves. Surgery worked sometimes. And that time it had. He had been sure it had.

High blood pressure in the upper body. Very low below the waist. Standard stuff. Renal failure. Internal bleeding in the abdominal cavity. The accident hadn't been kind to the little girl, but he'd gone about repairing each and every tear and shear as if his own life depended upon it.

Again the water foamed and churned around Raphael as he hit the far end of the pool, dove under, circled round, then kicked off to get to the other side, oblivious to the families playing in the sea water around him.

He'd gone through the injuries in order of importance. He'd focused on her heart first. A partial aortic tear. The possibility of a pseudoaneurysm had lurked. He'd been relieved—elated, almost—to see the outermost layer of the partially torn blood vessel was still intact. This meant her small body stood a better chance of avoiding severe blood loss.

Other thoughts had lurked in the back of his mind as he'd worked his way through the cardiovascular surgery. The possibility of paraplegia. Renal failure if the sluggish blood pressure in her lower limbs was indicating what he thought it was. Renewed aortal tears if a moderate blood pressure wasn't maintained. The ever-present threat of anesthesia taking the child's life.

But if he hadn't called the anesthetist and begun surgery she would have died within minutes of being brought into the hospital.

Two hours in, he'd been certain Amalie's cardiac functions were normal. Or as normal as they could be before he began repairing the blood vessels sheared from her kidney. Stitch by meticulous stitch he had restored blood flow to her kidneys. Renal function would return to normal once she'd had a chance to recover. It would be a long road, but she was a survivor.

He remembered telling himself that when the call had come for another surgery.

All that had been left to do was close her up. Something any junior doctor could be relied on to do.

He'd had to make a choice. There hadn't been any other qualified surgeons available to help. He'd simply had to make a choice.

He gasped for air when he hit the far side of the pool and then began again.

He should have known that even so much as a hint of high blood pressure would exacerbate the tears he'd so diligently stitched back together. That she would go into cardiac arrest. That the junior surgical staff wouldn't be able to massage her poor, damaged heart back to life.

All this while he had been saving a life in the next room. *That* patient had lived. Had told him he was a hero.

Jean-Luc had called him something else. Lots of things he simply couldn't shake.

A murderer. Careless. Reckless.

Raphael knew grief made people say things they didn't really mean, but later, when he'd shown up at the funeral, Jean-Luc had known exactly what he was saying and the damage it would do to their friendship. Making it as irreparable as the injuries Amalie had been unable to survive.

"All you do is take!"

No matter how hard he pushed, how powerfully the blood roared between his ears, Raphael still couldn't drown out the memories.

Coming to Australia had been a mistake.

The Arctic, Brazil, the moon… Nowhere was far enough to outrun the burden of guilt chasing him down like a pack of savage wolves.

He'd thought seeing Maggie again would be the salve he needed. A reminder of the man he had once hoped to become.

She was trying. God knew she was trying her best to elicit a bit of good-natured fun from him as they went from patient to patient, but he just didn't seem to be able to do it. The whole idea of getting someone to the hospital and leaving their care to someone else echoed the situation with Amalie and knocked his response time out of sync. As if his timing was permanently a beat or two behind what it had once been, diminishing his ability to relate to people in real time.

In the refugee camps in Mozambique he had convinced himself it didn't matter. The mass of humanity there had been so overwhelming, their need for care so urgent, that patient had blurred into patient as the weeks had turned into months without his seeming to have noticed.

So he'd moved to Vietnam. The free clinic there— funded by a wealthy French businessman—had been built specifically to allow physicians more time to establish a doctor-patient relationship. There he'd been allowed to have the follow-through he hadn't been able to provide in the A&E. And he'd tried. Tried to make connections. Tried to open his heart.

It had been like tapping blood from a stone in the end. No dice.

He'd told himself it was the language barrier...conveniently forgetting the fact that many of his patients spoke French in some form or another.

He just didn't seem to have it in him to connect anymore.

Not with the beautiful newborn he'd held in his arms. Not with the grandmother who had slipped in the shower and seemed to have bruised her ego more than her hip. Or the drug addict who had, after refusing treatment twice, finally begged them to take him to rehab, give him a chance to start again.

Another chance. That was all *he* wanted. Another chance to prove that he was a good man beneath this ever-darkening cloak of grief he didn't seem to be able to shake. Another chance to look into Maggie's eyes and feel worthy.

He swam until his lungs burned with exertion and then pushed himself up and out of the seaside pool. Without turning back or looking down he began his long-legged stride, with the cock-eared mutt faithfully matching his pace.

What the little monster saw in him he'd never know…

Before he turned down the walkway leading to his rental cottage he stopped and stared at the dog.

"Qu'est-ce que tu veux, eh?"

What is it you want from me?

He stared at the scrubby-looking mutt. No collar. A little ribby beneath the multi-colored wire-haired coat, but not starving. Definitely not a pure breed. A slightly crooked gait, as if he might have had a broken leg at some point, or endured some form of trauma he'd never properly healed from. He would carry traces of that injury forever.

Raphael knew the feeling.

"Life's not fair—is it, *mon petit monstre*?"

The dog shook his head at him, maintaining eye contact the entire time.

The corners of Raphael's mouth tugged downwards in one of those rueful smiles he'd used to see his father give when Raphael had presented him with his latest set of exam results.

"Eh, ça va," his father would say, disguising any pride he might have felt with chastisement. "You'll do better next time, won't you, boy?"

His mother had never looked once—too busy "catching up" with her friends over yet another bottle of red wine.

And his marks had always been perfect.

Raphael opened the low wooden gate and let the dog into the small garden. Everyone deserved a break.

Leaving the dog outside, he went into the kitchen and pulled a takeaway container out of the refrigerator— some grilled chicken he'd bought a couple of days earlier but never got around to finishing.

Back outside on the small veranda he unceremoniously sat down on the steps leading into the garden, where the little monster waited with a patient expression on his little furry face.

"Asseyez-toi. Ici," he said gruffly, handing the dog a piece of chicken once he'd obeyed the command to sit beside him.

A few moments passed in companionable silence until he felt as if something had begun to thaw within him. Perhaps one day Jean-Luc would see he had done the best he could. Would know a surgeon's life was full of critical choices and that at the time… *No.* He'd had to make a choice and he'd made the wrong one. *He* was the one who would have to own the mistake. Jean-Luc had enough to bear without adding forgiveness to the mix.

Raphael reached out and gave the dog's head a rub. *"Alors, mon ami.* How about I teach you some French?"

CHAPTER FIVE

MAGGIE HELD THE mobile phone at arm's length and stared at it in disbelief. Had her brothers gone completely mental? Why would she want to drive twelve hours to make a birthday cake…for *herself*? The least they could do was crack a couple of eggs into a bowl and throw in some sugar and flour.

"Aw, c'mon Daggie," her older brother cajoled.

Maggie flinched at the childhood nickname and took a deep breath as he continued.

"You know Daddo would love it. He hasn't had your choccy cake in I don't know how long."

Maggie did. About five years, eleven months and a handful of days ago. The day she'd turned twenty-four, called enough enough and packed her meagre stash of belongings into the rusted-out ute her brothers had refused to drive.

She'd upgraded her car in the years since, but she wasn't so sure how much progress she'd made on achieving her dreams.

"I'll think about it."

"Dad's not getting any younger, Mags," her brother said, his voice completely sober this time.

"I know. I didn't say I wasn't coming, I just said I couldn't believe you're putting in recipe requests."

Maggie swallowed away a thousand other things she could have said. Facts she could throw back at him. Like the simple reality that Sydney didn't exactly have a fortress wall around it, forbidding them from visiting *her*. They had cars. The ability to book a train. There were flights. Daily.

Who said *she* was the one who always had to rearrange her life to accommodate them? To go back to a place that held so many bad memories?

Her mother's voice rang in her ears, clear as a bell. *"They love Broken Hill, Maggie-moo. Let them. You're my little wandering star. Now, go shine and make the world a brighter place."*

The ache that never seemed to have lessened since her mother had passed tightened in Maggie's chest as her brother continued his campaign for her to make sure she included her birthday in her next trip. There'd be a barbie. And a bonus: the washing machine was broken so she wouldn't even have to worry about catching up on laundry.

Out of the corner of her eye she saw her old ambo partner Steve approach the bulletin board she'd parked herself in front of but had yet to examine.

"I gotta go, Nate. Work."

Her eyes darted across to the new staff rota. Maybe now Raphael had had a bit of acclimatizing he'd be all right with another partner.

"You better mean it, Dags. The thinking about it," Nate said, his voice carrying a bit more warning than it usually did when he made his "time to come home" calls.

"Yeah."

She clicked on the red handset symbol on her phone and felt the weight in her chest sink to her gut. No matter how many times she'd been home since she'd moved to Sydney fear still built in her chest as strongly as it had when she'd boarded the plane at Charles de Gaulle airport.

She'd buckled into her seat thinking she would have time. Time to tell her mum how much she loved her. How she had, at last, found her place in the world.

She'd disembarked to be told she had to find herself a black dress for her mother's funeral.

She'd been three hours late.

One hundred and eighty minutes short of telling her mother she loved her.

"Looks like you and I are busted up forever, Mags."

"What do you mean?" Maggie followed the line Steve was drawing along his neck before he flicked his thumb toward the new staff rota.

"No more you-and-me squad, from the looks of things. Tough luck. For Casey, at least. You've got yourself a cracking good partner. Not as good as me, of course..." Steve shrugged, shaking his head along with her as she finally connected the dots.

Maggie and Raphael were to be permanent partners.

She stared at the roster in horror. She hadn't protested—much—when she and Raphael had been posted together for the first couple of rounds of shifts, but now it seemed the chief wanted him to be her permanent partner.

Her boss was plain cruel. Hadn't he *seen* how hard she was finding it, working with a man who seemed to elicit every emotion she'd ever hidden from? Lust. Hurt. Complete and total unrequited love.

To name but a few.

Was she still attracted to him?

More than ever.

Was he an incredible doctor?

Hands down the best she'd ever worked with.

Did she want to be stuck in an ambulance with him for the rest of her working days, only for him to discover she hadn't even come close to applying for medical school, let alone got in?

Not a chance in hell.

Whenever Raphael looked at her she felt as if she was being X-rayed. As if he was trying to figure out what had changed. What was different.

She could answer that easily enough. She wasn't the person she'd let him believe she was when they'd been in Paris. And when she'd come home her whole world had changed.

For that one blissful year she hadn't mentioned her Outback upbringing. Not once. She hadn't exactly lied. There had been no fictional sophisticated past she'd had to scramble to remember. But she hadn't exactly been forthcoming about the way she'd really been raised.

Not that she was embarrassed about it. She loved her family. Even if they *were* a bunch of lunkheads. It was just… They were so…*content*. And she'd always dreamed of life being so much *more*. Sometimes she envied how plain old-fashioned happy they were.

Pffft. Well. Stuck in an ambulance together for pretty much three entire days at a time, Raphael was bound to figure out she was a small-town girl whose dreams hadn't really got her all that far.

Already her cheeks burnt with embarrassment at what she would have to admit to.

Years ago she had dreamt of working with Raphael.

Scalpel by scalpel, suture by suture, as they approached each and every surgery with the same tenacity and *joie de vivre* they'd seemed to elicit in each other. Countless hours they'd spent talking about it—discussing which classes they'd need to take to get into pre-med programs, quizzing each other on the different disciplines they'd like to study.

Hand on heart, they had even jinxed each other after simultaneously shouting out, "Trauma surgeon!"

Jinxed was right. For her, at least.

That day as they'd sat near the Eiffel Tower—at her insistence, of course—she and Raphael had crossed their hearts and made up a silly handshake to confirm that they would each do everything in their power to work together as surgeons one day.

She'd truly believed all her dreams would come true. But when she'd returned home it was as if she'd never had them in the first place.

She'd remembered getting almost dizzy as they'd tipped their heads back and tried to see all the way up to the top of the Eiffel Tower, making a promise that in ten years' time they would come back and compare notes. Then again in twenty.

Little had he known she was hoping they'd also be seeing each other every day in between.

Little had he known how the bubble of perfection she'd woven into her heart had shattered into a thousand irreparable pieces when she'd flown home the following day.

She watched now as her old partner made his way to his ambo, prepping it for the day's jobs.

She sternly reminded herself that being a paramedic *wasn't* second best. She loved it. Much more than she'd anticipated. It was a way of reaching people who often had no one else in their lives. She'd seen it countless times—particularly with the elderly. She loved knowing how a simple chat, a moment of human connection, was often all they were after. And she was more than happy to be the person to bring a smile to their face.

Besides, she was good at it. The human touch part. After she'd finally moved to Sydney she'd considered going to pre-med night classes, but life had got busy and she was always knackered at the end of her intense shifts.

At the end of the day, *she'd* given up on her hopes and dreams and Raphael hadn't.

He was the most driven person she had ever met. Lycée. Pre-Med. Med School. Surgical Intern. Surgical Resident. He'd hit every one of his goals as if his life had depended upon it.

There wasn't a chance in the universe he'd ever want to be with someone who had given up at the first hurdle. Even if it was the biggest hurdle she'd ever had to leap. This whole "slumming it" thing on a paramedic crew was obviously a blip on his timeline. Something he would look back on and wonder, *Why did I do that?*

"Maggie?"

The sound of Raphael's voice threw Maggie's tummy into its usual tailspin of swirls and loops. "I'll meet you at the truck in five," she called across to him, heading to the station chief's office.

Masking how she felt about Raphael was getting harder and harder. Not only had it thrown her long-dormant feelings into full-on active volcano mode, but his brooding presence was also starting to impact her ability to treat her patients with one hundred percent focus.

That was a line she was completely unwilling to

cross. And she wouldn't leave her boss's office until he understood her, loud and clear.

"Everything all right?" Maggie smiled across at Raphael as she clicked open her door, but the note of anxiety in her tone was echoed in her green eyes.

He nodded. He was the one who should really be asking *her* how she was doing. As if he didn't already know.

She jumped out of the ambulance and closed the door with a solid clunk.

"I think he hates me."

The words were still ringing in his ears nine hours into their shift. He'd overheard Maggie speaking to the station chief before they'd started work this morning. This was their third round of three days on, four off, and it looked as if she'd had enough of him. Perhaps coming to her favorite food truck was her way of letting him down gently. Sugaring the pill before letting him know that things simply weren't working out.

He hung his head and gave the back of his neck a rough scrub. This wasn't right. Just letting things fall apart. He had tried to make things right with Jean-Luc but it had been too soon. Too fresh. He saw that now. But he had the ability to change the here and now.

"Stay with my little girl."

He shrugged his shoulders up and down, then climbed out of the ambulance. He had to rid himself of the toxic emotions that had been feeding on each other, multiplying instead of diminishing. It was an unhealthy pattern and it needed to be broken.

The thought of losing Maggie was the spur he needed. He knew he wasn't a barrel of laughs to work with, but *hate*? He didn't *hate* her.

He admired her.

More than that.

He lifted his eyes up to the heavens for inspiration.

He was *grateful* to her. Grateful to this woman who'd unquestioningly helped him when he'd written to her from Vietnam. She hadn't asked a single question. She'd simply helped. And when he'd arrived she hadn't pressed, not having the remotest clue why he had changed from the laughing, trivia-obsessed pre-med student she'd met all those years ago to this darker version of the man he'd hoped to become.

She wasn't the only one who'd stopped writing when they'd said goodbye all those years ago in Paris. But she was the one who had kept her heart open. The one he'd come to when his own heart had been worn raw with effort to atone for a mistake he could never change.

The simple truth was that Maggie Louis was the only person left on earth who treated him with respect.

A vinegary twist of guilt tightened in his gut. Not telling Maggie about his past—what he'd done that awful day at the hospital—was akin to lying to the one person who deserved his honesty more than most.

A shot of energy surged through him and gripped his heart.

He couldn't lose her. Not now.

He hadn't travelled around the world only to let her slip through his fingers. He'd lost Jean-Luc's precious friendship. And Jean-Luc's parents'. Not that the Couttards had spelled it out for him, but he knew there was no coming back from the loss of a beloved child and grandchild.

Well, he was damned if he was going to let Maggie slip away. Not this soon. Not without letting her see the real him.

She needed to know about the Raphael who'd grown up in a wealthy neighborhood—not in a beautifully appointed home like Jean-Luc's, as he'd let her believe, but a few blocks away on an estate for low-income families. She needed to be told about the teenaged Raphael who had fallen head over heels for her but only offered friendship after Jean-Luc's family had cautioned him to keep things platonic.

Maggie deserved to understand why he'd honored the request. How Jean-Luc's family had all but raised him, virtually adopting him after his own parents had passed away the summer he'd finished Lycée. He couldn't have compromised that level of support. Support he'd known he'd need if he were ever to come good on his dream of becoming a doctor.

The near-impoverished upbringing...the less than loving parents. They were things he'd been able to put behind him. And now he had to find a way to learn from the experience of Amalie's surgery and put that behind him, too.

Maggie needed to know he'd become the man he'd promised her he would become one day. But now he'd lost track of that man. And he'd sought out the one person he thought could help find him again.

He closed the ambulance door behind him with a renewed sense of purpose. He would tell Maggie everything. And when the slate was clean he'd live with the ramifications.

She would either accept him or say goodbye. But he would not let her believe he hated her. Or let her "dump him" over a gourmet sandwich across the street from the beach. Not until she knew the truth anyway. After that, the decision was solely hers.

Raphael rounded the ambulance to where Maggie stood, glanced across at the brightly colored food truck, then back to Maggie. "So, this is the best food in Sydney?"

Start small. Aim high. Earn this. Earn the place in her heart.

She nodded. "I think so, but I suspect your standards may be a bit higher."

"I'm always open to trying new things."

Her eyebrows shot up, then cinched together. "Well... I like it, anyway. Hopefully you will, too."

Lead. Balloon.

He was going to have to ramp up his conversation skills.

"Do you remember that last day we were in Paris?"

Her brow furrowed. Okay. It was a bit of a non sequitur, but he could see it so clearly.

"At the Eiffel Tower?"

She gave an embarrassed laugh. "I made you go there loads, didn't I? You must've thought I was a right nutter."

"Remember it was raining?"

She'd been twirling round one of the lampposts as if she was in a musical. It was the most free-spirited he'd ever seen her. There had been a fraction of a second when the ache to pull her into his arms and kiss her had been almost overwhelming, but he'd made a promise to the Couttards. That friends-only promise had been one of the hardest he'd ever had to keep.

"Yeah, well, that was a long time ago. So..." She sucked in a big breath and pasted on a smile. "Now it's all sunshine and tucker trucks! Who would've thought it, eh? From Paris to...uh... Tuckerville."

He arched a perplexed eyebrow.

"Tucker truck? Not heard of that? Food. Food is tucker. So..." She tipped her head toward the truck and gave a shy grin. *"La cuisine...c'est superb!"*

She exaggerated her French accent—a habit, he noted, that she fell back on when she was unsure of herself. The ache returned. The desire to kiss her. Hold her. Be the man she wanted to swing round lampposts and sing in front of.

He had to tell her. Tell her everything.

Together they took another step forward in the admittedly impressive queue, and after a moment she asked, "Don't you have food trucks in France?"

He nodded. More with each passing year if memory served. Food might top most French people's list of Important Things About Being Alive, but it hadn't been anywhere on *his* radar during those last six months he'd been in Paris. Food had become merely something he had to consume in order to stay alive.

Maggie took in a big breath and popped on that nervous smile of hers again. "I probably should've brought you here the first day we worked together, but—" She stopped herself short.

He knew what she was going to say...what she *should* say. *I would've brought you here earlier if you hadn't had such an enormous thundercloud hanging over your head since you arrived.* Or, as a more straightforward Australian would've said, *If you hadn't been so bloody rude after all the hospitality and kindness I've showed you.*

"They say good things come to those who wait."

His eyes drifted to the menu hung alongside the service windows of the silver caravan. He'd have to meet those catlike green eyes of Maggie's soon. Answer her questions. Tell her the truth.

"Well, I know it's just my opinion, but Betty's Big Baps is totally worth the wait." She grinned as she said the name. Then giggled. "I just love saying the name of this place. I don't know if I love the name more, or the sandwiches."

He tried to return her smile—the first genuine one he'd seen on her all shift.

Maggie didn't miss the fact that the smile didn't make it to his eyes.

She turned away and feigned interest in a couple of surfers joining the queue. They were laughing, regaling one another with stories of the waves they'd caught. Light. Free.

The two words caught his attention. He hadn't felt either one in eighteen long months.

Driven. Determined. Committed. Those words worked.

Driven to do penance for his mistake? Determined to do—what? Go over and over a surgery he couldn't re-do until the details eventually began to blur? Committed to staying out of Jean-Luc's path to avoid any more painful confrontations?

That was a coward's way out.

And he was no coward.

As his gaze returned to Maggie he was suddenly struck by the delicacy of her features. The smattering of freckles across her button nose. The gentle angles of her high cheekbones. The delicate swoop and dip at the apex of her upper lip. One that was begging to be traced with a finger. With a tongue. She was a beautiful woman. And he hated it that he was the reason behind the uncertainty in her gaze when their eyes finally met.

It's not brain surgery. Start a conversation.

He nodded at the ten or so people in front of them. "What if we get a call?"

Nice one. Très bien. *You really have mastered the art of embarking on a meaningful* tête-à-tête, *Raphael.*

"No worries on that front," she replied. "The station chief has promised us half an hour off before sending any more calls our way since we've been flat out all day. It's worth the wait. Honest. You won't have tasted anything like it before. *C'est magnifique!"*

A soft smile softened the usual hard set of his mouth. Maggie had been dappling her conversation with French with increasing frequency, but she was still twisting her forays into his native tongue into a comedic parody. As if she didn't quite trust herself to just...*speak.* She'd been practically fluent when she'd left. Had all the confidence she'd gained over the course of her year in France disappeared?

The thought detonated another black hole in his chest.

He knew how easily confidence could take a knock.

When he'd walked out of that surgical room he'd been one hundred percent certain Amalie would make a full recovery. He had told himself that hanging around just to make sure was an instinct he wouldn't have had if she'd been a stranger. Walking away was what he would've done with any other patient.

But ten minutes later it was as if he'd entered a different time and space continuum. He should have stayed. The instinct hadn't been a case of emotional involvement. It had been a surgeon's decision—and he'd gone against it.

His team of junior surgeons had tried their best to resuscitate her. He'd come as soon as he'd heard the Code Blue had been called. And it had still been too late.

As a group, the surgical team had looked up to the digital clock and they'd all waited for him to call the time of death. Then they had each followed suit, as per protocol. The same protocol that had dictated he had been too close to the patient to be her surgeon.

Hearing the collective confirmation that Jean-Luc's only daughter had in fact died in his care had been akin to receiving an axe-blow to his heart.

A part of him had died that day too. And the quest to find it again—that vital spark that had made him courageous enough to believe he could perform surgery on the most critically injured people and give them another shot at life—had brought him here. To Maggie.

A gentle sniggering at his side brought him back to the present.

"I still can't believe you let that poor child start going through life being called Walter." Maggie was shaking her head in disbelief.

"Sorry?"

"The baby from our first call-out? The other week?" Maggie prompted. "He was adorable. Absolutely gorgeous, with chubby little cheeks and a little round belly. He would've been even more adorable if he'd had your name. *Walter?* You really think he's going to be down with the kids with a name like that?"

"Raphael isn't exactly a guarantee of a gilded life."

Maggie sucked in a sharp breath, rolled her eyes to the cloudless sky then swore softly under her breath. Not something he'd ever heard her do.

"*Desolé.* I'm sorry, Maggie." He tugged his fingers

through his hair. "I seem to be hitting all the wrong notes lately."

She gave him a sharp *no kidding?* look, her features instantly melting with a wash of remorse. "Don't worry. We all have off days."

Days. Months. Years, almost.

Everyone in Paris had eventually drawn back. Not that he blamed them. Until he made things right with Jean-Luc and his family he was no good to anyone. He'd gone to their homes to try and explain, to apologize, each time knowing whatever he'd say wouldn't be enough. Could never be enough.

All you do is take!

There was truth in those words. He'd taken their love. Their hospitality. Their kindness.

Their daughter and grandchild.

Every single time he'd raised his hand to the door to knock, he'd turned and walked away.

"What'll it be, mate? Big Bap? Little Bap? Cardboard box?"

Without his having noticed, they'd reached the front of the queue.

Maggie was tipping her head toward the rotund sandwich vendor. "You're up, Raphael. I'm having the Pie-Eyed Pastrami. What'll you have? My shout."

His heart softened at the hopeful expression playing across her features. He owed her kindness. The kindness he seemed to be able to show the little mutt who still followed him faithfully from the seaside pool and back every night. But extending it to a *person*... Too risky. Too painful.

"Raphael? Your order?" Maggie gently nudged his arm.

"Yes, of course. Um…cheese. A plain cheese sandwich with be fine."

"We don't do plain old cheese, mate." The counter clerk looked at him as if he'd grown an extra head, then changed his disbelief into a suggestion. "We've got a Buttie Brie Blinder. Would that float your boat? It's got horseradish and some properly ponging brie in it. I can stick some beetroot in there for you if you like. Adds sort of a vinegar twist. A real ripper."

Raphael blinked up at the vendor, not entirely sure how to respond.

"Smelly cheese," Maggie prompted, her brows cinching together. "You know… Brie. Just like at home, in France. You always said cheese wasn't any good unless you could smell it a block away." She laughed at a sudden memory. "That's how you taught me which cheese was which. The smell-o-meter."

He looked at her, almost confused as to who she was referring to. Had he *ever* spoken with her about cheese in such a light-hearted way?

"He'll have the Blinder," Maggie told the perplexed-looking vendor, and then, after collecting their drinks, steered Raphael over toward an empty picnic table under the shade of a large tree a few meters from the van. She handed him a cold bottle of water. "Here. You don't seem entirely with it. Probably dehydrated. You've got to remember to keep drinking water. It's really easy to dehydrate here. Even in the winter."

"You shouldn't be working with me."

The words were out before Raphael could stop them. And they had the opposite effect to what he'd been hoping for.

Maggie's body language instantly shifted from open

to closed. A woman protecting what was left of her dignity in the wake of an excruciating dressing-down. She pushed aside the packet of crisps she'd bought unopened, and began toying with the lid of her water bottle.

"Um… Raphael. I've actually already spoken to the chief. You're obviously in a different league to me, so it shouldn't be too hard to get you transferred to a different station or working with a different partner. It's pretty obvious you and I aren't exactly a match—"

"Non."

Her eyes widened as he held his palms up between them.

Fix this. Now.

"No, no, Maggie—that isn't it at all."

"Look, there's no need to try and cover up the fact that things have not exactly been relaxed between us." She looked away for a moment, swallowing the emotion rising in her throat. "I know we were friends back in the day, but things change. People change."

He had to stop this before it went too far.

"Maggie, it's *me* who is not worthy to work with *you*."

"What are you talking about?" Her green eyes widened again, this time in disbelief. "You're a qualified surgeon. You've worked around the world. All I've done is my paramedic training and then managed to move from a small town to a big one."

He shook his head and lifted a hand to stop her. "Please, don't do that."

"Do what?"

"Put yourself down. You are…" He reached across the table and took Maggie's hands in his before she could withdraw them. "You are, hands down, one of the kindest, most qualified medical personnel I have ever met."

She huffed out a disbelieving laugh. One entirely bereft of humor. "If you're going for flattery to let me down easily, please don't bother. Look." She threw a look over her shoulder. "The sandwiches will be ready in a minute. We've not eaten all day, so let's just get our blood sugar back to normal, get through the rest of our shift and then I'll ask the chief again for one of us to be transferred. They need people everywhere in Sydney, and with someone of your caliber it shouldn't be a problem. Easy-peasy."

She looked as miserable as he felt. And that was when it hit him. She cared for him. And not just as a friend.

Hard hitting waves of emotion bashed against his chest, one after the other. Disbelief. Concern. Regret. And then, like the smallest ray of sunlight penetrating a sheet of pure darkness…hope.

Hope that if Maggie could still see something good in him there might be a way for him to redeem himself.

He moved the crisps and their drinks to the side and reached across the table, tipping Maggie's chin up with a finger so that her gaze met his. The sheen of tears glazing her eyes didn't come as a surprise. But his response to them did.

He had nothing to offer Maggie right now and she needed to know why.

"I killed a child, Maggie. I don't know who I am anymore. I think I came to you so I could remember who I once was. To see if I could be that man again."

CHAPTER SIX

MAGGIE STARED AT the foil-wrapped sandwiches the vendor had deposited on their table, swiping at the tears spilling freely onto her cheeks. The ability to breathe had been snatched from her. She forced herself to meet Raphael's gaze, knowing it hadn't left her since he'd dropped his bombshell. She didn't recognize her own voice when she finally spoke.

"A child? What do you mean?"

Raphael tipped his head into his hands for a moment, and when he raised it again those dark shadows all but obliterated the blue in his eyes.

"Her name was Amalie," he began, his voice hollow with grief. "She was my best friend's daughter."

"You mean Jean-Luc?" Disbelief was icing her veins. "But… I don't understand. You would never do anything like that. *Never.*"

"She was in an automobile accident," Raphael conceded.

Maggie felt the pounding of her heart descend from her throat to her chest as he continued in that same, painfully toneless expression.

"It was a motorway pile-up. One of those multi-car incidents that happen when everyone's in a hurry and a thick fog descends. One minute everyone was driving at the national speed limit and the next—" He made a fist and rammed it into his other hand.

The gesture was so finite that Maggie flinched against the suggested screech of tires and clashing of metal on metal as one car ran into another.

"Were you in the car?"

Raphael shook his head. "*Non*. It was Jean-Luc's wife, Marianne, and their daughter Amalie who was three."

Maggie's curiosity flared. This was the first time she'd heard him mention Jean-Luc, though she'd tried raising the topic a couple of times. Pressing for details would have meant explaining that she'd dropped the ball too, so she hadn't pursued it.

She'd stayed with Jean-Luc's family for her student exchange year and they had been unbelievably kind and generous. Over the year she had wanted to write to them so many times, to tell them how grateful she was for that incredible year in Paris, but apart from the quick thank-you note she'd forced herself to write she had ceased all contact.

She should tell him. She would. But this was *his* time.

"What happened?"

"Marianne suffered superficial injuries and a couple of broken ribs, but was fine. Thank heaven. But Amalie—she suffered massive internal trauma when another vehicle hit theirs from the side."

Maggie's fingers flew to cover her mouth. "I am so sorry."

Raphael's brows cinched together as he huffed out a frustrated sigh. "Don't be. Not for me, anyway."

"What are you talking about?"

"We were all going to go for supper after Jean-Luc

and I had finished work. You know he's become an amazing lawyer?"

His sad smile was in direct contrast to the pride in his voice that his friend had done so well.

"I don't see why this means I can't feel sorry for the loss you suffered. You two were so close. Amalie must've been like a—"

He shook his head. He didn't want her to say the words. *Like a daughter.*

Had he wanted children? Lost one of his own?

"Going out was my idea. We'd moved to different areas so didn't see each other socially as much. Nothing fancy. A walk along the Seine... Amalie always enjoyed watching the boats, so we had picked a little restaurant on Ile Saint Louis."

Something flickered in his eyes. Was it the same memory that had popped into Maggie's mind? Of that bright spring day when he'd taken her for some of the famed ice cream on the little island in the middle of the Seine? She'd somehow managed to get ice cream on her cheek, and he had leant forward and swiped it off with his thumb. His eyes had linked to hers for one moment longer than she would have expected of a friend...

Maggie forced the thought away. This wasn't about her. Nor was the blame for that car accident something Raphael should shoulder. She could see where he was coming from. The number of times she'd asked herself whether or not her mother might have had just a few more months if she'd been the one at home caring for her...

She pressed her thumbs to her eyes and did her best to squish the thoughts away. She watched Raphael tease at the aluminum wrapper holding his sandwich hostage.

He looked about as interested in having lunch as she was. *Not very.*

She ducked her head and tried to catch his eye. "You know, people organize going out for supper all the time. That hardly makes you culpable. Road traffic accidents are just that. Accidents."

Raphael continued as if he hadn't heard her.

"Jean-Luc's wife and Amalie had been out of the city for the day and, as they were running late, had decided to drive in. Normally they would've taken the Métro." His voice grew hollow. "And then the accident happened."

"How did you find out?"

He looked her square in the eye. "The casualties were brought to our hospital. When Jean-Luc arrived I said he must stay with his wife in the recovery ward while they waited on news of Amalie. He was so frightened. I've never seen a man more terrified in my—" His voice caught in his throat.

Maggie dug her fingernails into her palms, forcing herself not to reach out for him. Every pore in her body ached to console him. To tell him it would be all right. But he didn't want comfort. She would have had to be blind not to see the torture that had become all but ingrained in his cell structure.

"He knew the protocol. He knew I was too close to Amalie to be her doctor. But he begged me to look after his little girl. To do everything I could. There were only junior surgeons available, and she had suffered severe internal trauma as well as massive blood loss by the time she reached the hospital."

"So…you were following his wishes." Maggie gave a

little shake of the head. "I don't understand why you're torturing yourself."

He widened his eyes in disbelief, opened his palms wide and slammed them down on the table, sending shudders through their untouched meals. "I should have said no. I was too close."

"So why didn't you?"

The look he shot her told her he had asked himself the same thing again and again.

"We were short-staffed. Most of the other doctors on duty that day were less experienced—fresh out of medical school—and casualties from the accident were flooding in, one after the other. The senior surgeon on staff told me to find someone else, if I could, but there was no one I trusted with that precious life. My best friend's child."

The anguish in his voice was palpable, and despite the heat of the day Maggie wrapped her arms around herself to fend off the wave of shivers trickling down her spine.

"Had you been specifically told not to operate on her? Before you took Amalie into surgery, I mean?" Maggie wasn't sure why she'd asked the question, but getting everything in order seemed essential if she was to understand why Raphael was blaming himself for something that had patently been an awful accident.

He shook his head. No. He hadn't.

"I was a surgeon. A good one, I thought. I had vowed to do my very best—promised my dearest friend I would save his child—and when it came down to it I failed. I failed as a friend. I failed as a doctor. I failed a child. It is *my* fault his little girl died and I will carry the weight of that burden until the end of my days."

"And that's why you came here?"

He shook his head, not entirely understanding.

"To try and unload the burden…with distance?" she clarified.

He tipped his head back and forth.

"No. It's not so simple. I just—"

This was the moment he'd been over again and again. Doing the checklist. Ensuring he'd done everything he could to stabilize Amalie.

"My instinct was to stay, to see the surgery through right to the end, but there was another patient in the next room. They needed me to operate straight away. All that was left to do with Amalie was close up. An easy enough job for the junior surgeons."

"But…?"

"She went into cardiac arrest."

From the look on Maggie's face he knew he didn't need to spell out the lengths his team had gone to in their vain attempt to keep her alive.

"If I'd made the decision to stay in the room instead of rushing off to the next surgery she might have lived."

"*Might* have?"

"I'll never know."

He rattled through Amalie's injuries in detail. The surgical procedures he'd followed. The gut instinct that had told him to stay. The pragmatic override that had pulled him from the room.

"And the other patient? What happened with them?"

"They lived." He corrected himself. "*She*. She lived."

She'd even sent him flowers, with a note expressing her gratitude.

"So…" Maggie pressed her fingertips to her lips for

a moment. "Africa? Vietnam? What was that for? Were you atoning, or something?"

Raphael considered Maggie for a moment before answering. He should tell her what Jean-Luc had said and the cutting effect his words had had.

All you do is take!

He'd felt... He'd actually felt *orphaned* after the Couttards had made it clear they weren't ready to see him and Jean-Luc had dismissed him with a flick of the hand. More so than when his actual parents had died. That was how precious his friendship had been. Jean-Luc and his parents had been his family.

"Go," Jean-Luc had said. "Go show what a big man you are somewhere else. You obviously know what is best. Who deserves your magic surgeon's hands. Your time. It must be so precious, your time. Please..." He'd stepped in close and said the last words so quietly Raphael had had to lean in to hear him. "Don't let me take one minute more of it."

And then he'd shut the door. Hadn't taken his calls. Raphael had no idea if he'd read the letters he'd written or torn them to shreds still in their envelopes.

"Things were difficult between me and Jean-Luc. His parents, too."

"What?" Maggie laughed. "They didn't banish you from France, did they?"

The black look that swept across his features suggested she wasn't far off the mark.

Raphael cleared his throat. "I needed to prove to myself I could still do it. Make a difference as a doctor."

"And did you?"

He shrugged. He'd been so emotionally absent he

knew he hadn't made a difference on any sort of personal level, but as a doctor...yes. Yes, he had.

"So why are you here?"

He gave her his best Gallic shrug.

He wasn't ready to explain that it was Maggie he had sought. That she was the one person he believed would give him the most honest perspective on the type of man she thought he was. Mortal or monster.

He heard her muttering something under her breath.

"A quelque chose malheur est bon."

She remembered. It was a saying equivalent to *Every cloud has a silver lining*. Or, the more French interpretation, *Unhappiness is, at the very least, good for something*.

He'd used to say it when, inevitably, it had rained on one of their outings and they were forced to seek refuge under a small awning or in a tiny alcove. He'd always wondered if she'd ever cottoned on to the underlying meaning... Though it had rained, it had meant he could be closer to her.

"So." He clapped his hands together, the sound sharp against the white noise of the late-afternoon activity surrounding them. "I understand why you wouldn't want to work with me anymore. If you need to transfer me out, please... I completely understand."

"You have got to be absolutely joking me." Maggie shook her head back and forth.

This was a lot of information to take on board, but it certainly answered the bulk of her questions.

Raphael had been through the wringer. He'd changed, all right. But he was truly trying to make himself a better man than he had been before this tragedy. He was living with an unanswerable question and it had obviously been hell.

Would the child have lived if he had made a different decision?

As little as she knew about surgery, she knew enough about the traumatic injuries Amalie had suffered to imagine the answer would be no. And he'd returned to medicine. That wasn't something a man who doubted his skills would do. There *had* to be something more. Something he hadn't yet come to terms with.

"It's okay." Raphael's accent thickened. "I wouldn't want to work with me either, after knowing the truth. I am sorry I wasn't more honest before I came—"

"No." Maggie stopped him with a hand gesture. "Are you *mad*? Now that I know what you've been through there isn't a chance in the universe I'd let you work with someone else."

He bridled and it pleased her to see there was still fire in his spirit. He wasn't beaten. Just lost.

"Cool your jets." She took a deep breath and put her hands up so she could take a moment to put her thoughts in order. "I'm not keeping you pinned to my side because I think you're a bad doctor. Or a liar. Or a disappointment. Or whatever other words you attack yourself with. I want to work with you because what you need more than anything after what you've been through is a friend."

A quizzical look passed across his features. "Why would you want to work with me after this? Trust me? You said at the beginning of this that people change. I am proof of this, Maggie. I have changed."

"Raphael Bouchon." She fixed him with a stern expression, hoping he was reading affection in her expression rather than someone passing judgment. "I know it's been a long time seen we've seen each other, but a man can't change *that* much. That young man I met in Paris was the most honest, honorable, kind person I had ever met. And, though an awful lot of water has passed under the bridge since then, I still believe that's true. You're still that young man. But with maybe just a bit more of a distinguished air."

She pointed to her temples trying to indicate that she liked the salt and pepper look working its way through his rich chestnut hair.

"No, Maggie. You are kind, but…" Raphael opened his water bottle and took a long draught before continuing. "I thought when I saw you I would see the old me again. That I would find him somewhere buried in here." He made a fist and thumped it on his chest as he shook his head. "Now that I'm here, I see that you're just the same. But I don't think that seventeen-year-old Raphael you met all those years ago exists anymore. I'm not fun to be with. I can't see any point in looking forward to the future the way I once did. I don't even see the point of dreaming about the future. I failed my friend. I have the blood of a child on my hands. My best friend's child."

She shook her head—no, no, *no*—as a powerful rush of energy charged through her bloodstream.

If Raphael believed in their friendship enough to tell her about his darkest moments, she would show him just how strong her love for him was. Unrequited or otherwise.

If he needed a friend, he had one. If he needed a shoulder to cry on, she had two. If he wanted to believe in the possibility of love again…

She swallowed. That might be pushing things.

Baby steps.

She sucked in a deep breath of air and parted her lips. It was time to be as brave as Raphael.

"That's where you're wrong."

Wide blue eyes registered incredulity at her statement. "Maggie! I was *there*. I failed as a surgeon. I was the one who let Jean-Luc down. Let all the Couttards down."

"First things first."

She gave the picnic table a solid tap with her index finger, then wove her fingers together in front of her heart.

"I am very sorry for your loss. It must've been horrible for you. But you surely must see it was an impossible situation. And who's to say another surgeon might have made a different call? However cruel and personal it must feel, these things are random. It wasn't like you willed the fog to appear on that motorway or anything. And secondly—" she held up a hand so he would let her finish "—how exactly did you let Jean-Luc down? He asked you to do your best. To look after his little girl. I can't imagine you did anything other than try and save her."

Raphael looked at her, his features wreathed in disbelief. "Amalie *died*, Maggie."

She sat back and eyed him silently for a moment before taking another drink of her water.

Her heart ached for him. He was seeing the world through a distorted lens. One that showed him branded as a failure for not being omniscient. In that respect, yes, he *had* been too close to the patient. But in terms of deciding he didn't cut it as a surgeon...he'd just made it all up.

And then it hit her. All of the insecure dark thoughts

she'd been having about Raphael not liking her, or thinking she was a loser, had also been a complete fiction. She'd seen what scared her most instead of stepping outside of herself and facing facts. It was something Raphael needed to do, too.

In that instant Maggie knew she would do everything in her power to help Raphael take off the blinkers that seemed unrelenting in their mission only to let him see the dark side.

The thought stopped her cold.

Had *she* worn the same blinkers with her father? Her brothers? Instead of being sexist, demanding, nineteen-fifties throwbacks, on a mission to keep her in a pinny, had they actually been as blindsided by her mum's death as she had?

They hadn't been in tears, or lost in faraway thoughts or anything. It had seemed on the surface that everything was business as usual. But men were good at disguising things. Raphael being a perfect case in point.

But there was something else that was torturing him. Something beyond the failed surgery that he had yet to set right.

There were things *she* needed to set right as well.

When she'd come home to find her mother had been ill the entire time she'd been away, only to die while Maggie was flying home, Maggie's world had been turned upside down. At the time it had felt as though she'd been drowning in the past she had only just begun to escape. Blinded with grief and frustration, she'd blamed her brothers and her father for pushing her into the vacant role their mother had left behind. Carer. Cook. Cleaner. The very roles her mother had made her promise she would never take on.

But could it be that instead of being pushed she had willingly stepped into the spot her mother had once filled in their lives? That she had naturally found herself filling that void because she was the girl and that was what girls—*women*—did? Instead of it being a weak decision, perhaps she had been the only one strong enough to make sure their lives somehow returned to normal in the wake of their collective grief.

A strengthening weave of resolve unfurled within her. Raphael needed to believe he had been the only one strong enough to step into an impossible situation. If he could see that—know it in his heart—he would finally be able to forgive himself. He would finally be able to believe that, no matter who had operated on that poor little girl, her fate had already been decided when their car had been struck by another.

And if she wanted Raphael to believe that about himself she would have to take the same risk—and see her own life from another perspective.

"Maggie, please." Raphael raked his hands through his hair. "Put me out of my misery."

She looked at him as if seeing him for the first time. She'd been miles away. About a twelve-hour drive, in fact.

Maggie tipped her head to the side and wove her fingers together under her chin. "After this shift is over we've got four days off, right?"

He nodded.

"How would you feel about making it a bit longer?"

Maggie held her breath, waiting for his answer. Taking him home to meet her family was akin to unzipping her chest and handing him her heart. And then throwing some warts on top of the whole mess for good measure.

Raphael didn't look too pleased about the invitation.

"This isn't about you wanting me to be transferred to a different paramedic station, is it?"

"No! Crikey! No, not all."

"So we're good on that front?"

"Yeah! Of course. Now that I understand why you've been such a downer— I mean…"

To her relief, Raphael gave a self-deprecating laugh and held up his hands. "I *have* been a downer. But…" again that Gallic shrug "…now you know I have my reasons."

"I know. And it's a pretty big reason." She played with the edge of the aluminum wrapping on her sandwich and then, feeling a sudden hit of hunger, went ahead and unwrapped it. "Now that I know what's been going on in that head of yours…" she pointed her finger between the pair of them "…you and me? We're solid."

Maggie took an enormous bite of her sandwich and then grinned at him, a daub of sauce teasing at the crest of her upper lip before she swiped it away with her tongue.

He didn't deserve her. The open-hearted way in which Maggie had absorbed the worst thing he'd ever done in his life and simply…*accepted* it, forgiven him for the transgression and moved on.

It was humbling.

Maggie munched on a few crisps, then took a gulp of water. "So, back to me. Have you had your fill of being a tourist in Sydney?"

Raphael shrugged. The only reason he'd come to Australia was to see Maggie. So saying yes was an honest enough answer. And honesty was the only way forward. He saw that now.

"I think you and I need to go on a road trip. Get you out beyond the black stump."

Her tone was decisive. As if hearing his story had given her a new course of action. More to the point, her entire demeanor had changed…as if they were actually friends again.

"Black stump?"

"City limits," she explained, a soft flush coloring her cheeks. "If you say yes, there's a whole lot more Aussie slang waiting for you outside of Sydney. If you're feeling brave enough, that is."

Something in him softened. She was trying. He'd been making this whole reunion thing tough. More than tough. And yet she was still trying.

"Are you sure this isn't some attempt to take me out to the desert with a flint and a bottle of water to see if I make it out alive? A survival of the Aussie-est?"

She shrugged and smiled. "We-e-ell…" She drew out the word. "Nah. Of course not. Look. I have to go out there. Family."

He lifted his eyebrows. She hadn't mentioned her family. Not once.

"A reunion?"

She shook her head. "No. But let's just say you're going to see a whole side of me you never knew existed if you say yes."

"Sounds intriguing." Was she trying to ease his guilt? Prove he wasn't alone?

Her features darkened.

"It's not a reunion, but… You've been incredibly honest with me and I appreciate it." She pressed her hands to the center of her chest. "From the very bottom of my heart. It proves to me our friendship meant as much to you as it did to me."

Raphael locked eyes with her. "It did. It still does."

He watched as she sucked in a tight breath, then made the decision to speak.

"I don't think you are responsible for Amalie's death."

He scrubbed his hands along his legs. "Maggie, you weren't there—"

"No. I know. But I know *you*. You made the best decision you could at the time. I've been watching you work and you have it. That ability to make a split-second decision about a patient that is going to be for their benefit. No matter what you think of yourself now, I know without a shadow of a doubt that you simply do not have it in you to let another human's life pass through your hands if it doesn't have to."

The words struck so deep Raphael knew they would be embossed on his heart forever. But Maggie didn't owe him this: an easy out. She didn't owe him anything.

"*Tu es trop gentile*, Maggie. I am so grateful to you for not…for not thinking the absolute worst of me."

"How could I?"

There were countless answers for that one. He began totting them up before answering, then stopped himself. Holding back from Maggie had only meant making himself his own worst enemy. Could this be the first step in forgiving himself? Finding a way to claw himself out of the black hole he'd all but swan-dived in to?

He met her clear green eyes and saw nothing but compassion in them. Empathy. Her unfiltered gaze was the oasis of peace he'd been seeking all these months.

"I'm glad I came." He reached across and took her hand in his, stroking his thumb along the back of it.

"Me, too." She gave him a shy smile, thought for a minute, then winced. "But I do think…perhaps…you need to decide if your heart is really in the paramedic world."

"What?" He feigned affront. "You don't think I've been doing a good job?"

She gave a melodramatic sigh. For his benefit entirely.

"Quite the opposite. And you know that." She tugged her hand out of his and poked him in the arm. "But it's not where your *heart* is. A blind man could suss that one out. And although running around the world and showing off your medical prowess is an amazing thing to do, I don't think that's what you're doing. You're more… It's more like you're living life on the run. Waiting for that one medical save that will put you back to the place you were before that night. From where I'm sitting, what you're feeling is grief, not guilt. And you're not letting yourself be good old-fashioned sad. Maybe you should do that, instead of all this globetrotting."

She put on a dramatic television presenter's voice. "*'Dr. Raphael Bouchon has been spotted in yet another country. Paraguay this time. Or was it Brazil? Will he keep interested parties guessing as to his whereabouts for years to come? Or will he suck it up, go back to France, and have a weep and a talk with Jean-Luc? Will he finally make peace with his dearest friend?'* Apart from me, of course." She smirked.

Despite himself, he smiled.

"This isn't—" He stopped himself. It *was* running. All of it. He hadn't even fully unpacked his suitcase and he'd been in Australia over a month. Even "his" dog wasn't his. Just a stray he'd called Monster who helped him eat his leftovers.

He shrugged, accepting her comments as fair, and finally picked up his sandwich. "Are you saying you don't like the idea of me living as an outlaw in your fair city?"

She laughed and when their eyes met he knew she liked the idea of something, all right. But he was guessing it wasn't the outlaw thing.

A sting of regret that he hadn't kissed her all those years ago resurfaced.

An even bigger hit of remorse could so easily follow in its wake if he didn't get his act together and start to actively live his life. With purpose. With passion. With *love*.

Maggie put her sandwich down and took a sip of water.

"So, if you can scrape the bottom of your soul and put your darkest moments on display, why don't you take a break from beating yourself up about it and come out and see a bit of mine? The soul stuff I mean. The black parts."

"Just because I've done something awful it doesn't mean you—"

"Uh-uh!" She held up a hand. "I'm not done yet. I think this trip will be good for you. Maybe help you see life isn't always the way you think it is."

"You're talking in riddles."

"Yeah, well… I didn't exactly think I'd ever be telling you any of this."

"Any of what?"

She shook her head. "It's a show and tell sort of thing. You have to be there to understand."

Her eyes shifted up to the tree above them and glassed over. She shrugged her shoulder upward to swipe at the single tear snaking down her cheek and took another bite of sandwich. A poor disguise for an obvious rush of emotion.

When she'd finished chewing she swallowed, waved a hand as if erasing a whiteboard, and said, "Forget about all the 'feelings' stuff. It's a road trip—plain and simple. You are under no pressure to say yes. But at the very least, after we get past the Blue Mountains, you'll see first-hand that there is a whole lot of nothing in between the coasts of this fair isle. Besides, I need someone to keep me awake. It's a long drive."

There was something else. Something she wasn't saying. But he didn't press. He'd wanted a change and Maggie was delivering.

Maggie.

A life-affirming electrical current shot through him and the first undiluted desire simply to say yes to life took hold of his heart.

Maggie was the difference. He'd just told her about the worst moment in his life and already he felt…not lighter, exactly, but less alone. If Maggie could believe that one single shred of the man she'd met still existed…

"What?" Maggie's features scrunched up as she tried to interpret his expression. "You haven't gone soft on me, have you? Not up for a bit of rough and tumble out in the Woop Woop?"

"Quoi?"

"The Outback," she explained with a laugh. "The middle of nowhere."

He crossed his arms, narrowing his eyes in a dubious squint.

"Is this some sort of Australian ritual? Bringing a poor, defenseless Frenchman to the Outback to see if he can make his way back to civilization as a means of proving himself?"

"Something like that." The hint of a mysterious smile teased at the corner of her lips. "Or it could just be to prove you can survive a couple of days with my brothers. Believe me—if you can make it forty-eight hours straight with the Louis brothers, you can survive anything."

A warmth hit Raphael's heart, and with it came a sudden hunger. Nothing to do with being invited to meet the family of the girl he'd always wondered *What if?* about, he told himself drily.

He began unwrapping his sandwich, abruptly stopped and locked eyes with her.

"One question."

The change in his own voice surprised him. It reminded him of the man he'd used to be before the harshness of grief had turned him irritable. It was the voice of a man who *cared*.

"Can I bring my dog?"

Maggie's eyed widened and stayed wide as her radio crackled to life and a rapid-fire stream of instructions rattled through. "Code Twenty-one," she whispered, her green eyes locked on his as she continued listening.

Can I bring my dog?

What was *that* all about? It wasn't like Monster was actually *his*. Or that he needed a buffer between him and Maggie. She was…she was *Maggie*. The sunny-faced, flame-haired girl—

Who was pressing herself up and away from the picnic table, grabbing her half-eaten sandwich and making a "wheels up" spin with her finger as she continued to take down the details of their call-out.

It was at that moment that he truly saw her for who

she was. Maggie wasn't the lanky, shy, still-growing-into-her-skin teen he'd met thirteen years ago, who'd tied an invisible ribbon round his heart.

She was a woman.

And a beautiful one at that.

He'd been so preoccupied with shaking off the ghosts chasing him around the world that he hadn't stop to breathe her in. This past year he had felt as if he'd only just been holding on to the back of a runaway train, and now Maggie had leapt on and hit the brakes. Showed him there was more than one way to handle the grieving process he knew he had to go through.

"We've got a broken arm, a possible neck fracture, and a few more injuries."

"All for one patient?" He grabbed his own sandwich and drink, following her at a jog.

"No. Cheerleading pyramid gone wrong."

"Cheerleading?"

"Cheerleading. Or not, as the case may be," she added soberly, before jumping into the ambulance.

When they arrived at the high school they pulled into the car park at the same time as another ambulance. Maggie's mate Stevo and his new partner Casey. Raphael rolled down his window as a man ran between the pair of vehicles, waving his arms and identifying himself as the headmaster.

After a quick conference with the headmaster they drove the ambulances round to the school's large playing field to find a huge group of people gathered in several circles.

"I'll grab the tib-fib compound," Stevo called, heading for a group already opening up to let him and his pale-faced junior through. Those injuries had the potential to be pretty gory. Raphael felt for Casey.

"She looks horrified, poor thing." Maggie made a sympathetic noise, then grabbed a run bag and a spine board. "Oh, well. There's only one way to learn and that's by confronting the tough stuff. Can you grab a couple of extra collars and a pile of blankets? It looks like you and I are over here."

Maggie tipped her head at the pair of girls in cheerleading outfits running toward them.

Confronting the tough stuff.

Precisely what *he* needed to do.

"Over here!" One of the cheerleaders arced her arm and pointed toward a nearby group. "She says she can't feel her legs!"

Raphael shouldered his run bag and set off in a jog alongside Maggie, hoping the situation wasn't as grim as it sounded. At the very least, the patient was alert. Speaking. From what he'd heard, cheerleading injuries could be catastrophic, with all the gymnastics involved.

Words whirled round him—"flyer", "base holders weren't there", "on her head"—as they approached the circle around a sixteen or seventeen-year-old girl. A hush fell upon the crowd.

"Hello, love." Maggie dropped down to her knees behind the girl and immediately stabilized her head by bracing her elbows on the ground and holding her temples steady. She shot Raphael a quick look, then shifted her gaze to the girl's legs. They were lying at peculiar angles and, whilst alert, the girl had an entirely mystified expression playing across her face.

"Looks like someone took cheerleading to some new

heights—oops. No, no. Stay still, darlin'. We want to make sure we don't move anything we're not supposed to."

Maggie gave Raphael a nod and he ran a series of quick checks for additional injuries, keeping a sharp eye on the patient as he moved the teen's legs into place. No response.

"Have you seen anything your end? Spinal injuries? Brain?" He asked his questions in French, and a swift murmur of approbation followed from the teenagers behind him. If they knew he'd spoken in French to keep potentially bleak news from them, they wouldn't be saying such nice things.

Maggie shook her head. "Protocol says we should use the stiff neck braces for precautionary immobilization, but I think they're too much for her." Maggie held her hand alongside the girl's neck, as if measuring it.

"I think the vacuum mattress would be best. It will keep her entire body stabilized without any unnecessary jarring—particularly if she has a pelvic fracture."

Maggie's eyes flashed to his.

"We won't be able to see any internal bleeding, so the best we can do is stabilize her as much as possible."

Raphael's mind had ticked over to automatic pilot—which didn't second-guess his every decision. And it felt good. It felt like being a trauma doctor again.

Maggie tugged a couple of blankets off the pile Raphael had placed on the ground and started rolling them into boomerang shapes. "I'll use these to stabilize for now, while you do the rest of the checks."

After examining the girl for any immediate evidence of neck wounds or the potential for underlying hematomas, Raphael ran to get the mattress.

When he returned he saw Maggie checking the girl's

vitals again. "Have you looked for signs of neurogenic shock?"

Maggie shook her head. "I've only just started. I've done a quick pulse check—doesn't seem too low. Or high, for that matter." She smiled down at her young charge. "All right, there, love? Seems as though your ticker's all right." Then, in a lower voice she continued. "Amazing…good. Not bradychardic in the slightest."

"What does that mean?" the girl asked.

"It means your body seems to be doing its best to help you recover." Maggie brushed her fingers along the girl's cheek, then rattled through a few stats with Raphael.

In between all the medical speak with Raphael, Maggie continued to keep up a steady flow of fact-gathering in the guise of casual chit-chat with their patient. This was her forte. He could see that now.

Being calm, warm and conversational kept the patient relaxed, the atmosphere less stressed, and significantly reduced the patient's potential for panic. His quest to be as exacting as he could had all but turned him into an automaton. A patient's worst nightmare.

He smiled as Maggie continued.

What was her name?

Jodi.

How long had she been a cheerleader?

Four years, and this was to have been her last as she was planning on becoming a veterinarian.

Any favorite animals?

Dogs. Definitely dogs.

Maggie shot him a quick look, so he threw in a comment about dogs being wonderful.

What pyramid routine had they been practicing?

The Eiffel Tower.

A pair of amused green eyes met his.

"Well, isn't that a coincidence?" Maggie put her hand directly above Jodi's eyeline. "Can you move your eyes toward the handsome chap over there on your left?" Maggie used her finger above the girl's face as a guideline.

Raphael smiled. That was a clever way to check her responses.

Wait a minute… *Handsome?*

"He's a genuine Frenchman, and—would you believe it?—the very same man who took me all bright-eyed and bushy-tailed around Paris. The first day we met he took me to see the Eiffel Tower."

Maggie's eyes flicked up to Raphael's and for a microscopic instant they caught and locked. Something in him flared hot and bright as he saw Maggie in full, glorious high-definition. The flame-colored hair. The beautiful green eyes. The milky white skin, flawless save a tiny scar at the corner of one of her eyes.

How had he not noticed that before? Had someone hurt her? Another swell of emotion built in him. A feeling of fierce protectiveness. If anyone had hurt Maggie he'd—

"Raphael?"

He cleared his throat and looked up at the sea of expectant faces. This was definitely *not* the time for flirting or thumping his chest like a he-man.

Had Maggie been flirting or just being nice?

"Um, Raph?" There were questions in Maggie's eyes, and not all of them were about work.

"*Alors*…shall we get Jodi onto the spine board?"

Raphael moved the board to Jodi's right, ensuring the vacuum mattress was in place, and on his count they rolled her onto the board and secured her with the series of straps attached to the mattress.

"How's your breathing, Jodi?" Raphael asked.

The teen stared at him, wide-eyed. "Say that again."

"How's your breathing?"

He shot an alarmed look in Maggie's direction. Breathing problems indicated much more serious injuries that might require intubation, the need for a positive-pressure bag-valve-mask device—though there were issues that went along with that as well. Distorting the airway could impair breathing, then circulation...

He was surprised to hear Maggie giggling.

"I think her breathing's just fine, Raphael. It's your accent. She likes it."

"And his name, too." Jodi's voice was positively dreamy and her expression fully doe-eyed.

"Oops! Easy, love—let's keep you looking straight up. Even if it's just *my* old mug you're looking at."

Maggie quickly pushed the blankets back into place, realigning Jodi's head to a neutral anatomical position. She widened her middle and index fingers between the girl's chin and suprasternal notch to get a measurement.

"Maybe we'd better slip an extra-small soft collar on her for the journey. Especially..." Maggie dropped a teasing wink at Raphael "...as you're the one who's going to be sitting in the back of the ambulance with our girl, here."

Raphael laughed and together, with the quick efficiency that usually came from years of working together, they inflated the mattress, lifted Jodi onto the wheeled gurney and loaded her into the ambulance for their ride to the hospital.

* * *

A few hours and several patients later they were sitting in companionable silence at the front of the ambulance as they headed back to the station.

Raphael's thoughts returned to Maggie's invitation.

"Did you mean it?" His voice sounded more intense than he'd anticipated. Pulling back the emotion, he clarified, "About the road trip?"

Maggie threw him a quick look, the bulk of her attention on the rush hour traffic she was battling. "Yeah, I suppose…"

"That doesn't sound as if you've entirely made up your mind. If it was a charity invitation—"

"No, no." She batted a hand between them. "That wasn't it at all. It's just that it's a long way. *Aussie* long. I thought it might be part of your How-to-be-an-Australian training, but if you don't plan on sticking around it might be too much bother."

He dropped his head and looked at his hands.

Why was he here?

To see Maggie.

Why did he want to see Maggie?

To find out if a human heart still pounded in his chest.

What happened when he was with Maggie?

Blood charged through his veins.

"Sounds good. I'd like to do it."

She threw him a quick glance. "All right, then. Well, in that case, the invitation is still open—but it comes with a warning."

"Are there venomous snakes where we are going?"

She laughed. "Loads. But they're everywhere in Australia. The warning is much bigger. My brothers can't cook for toffee. Chances are you're going to have to eat whatever I manage to rustle up—and let's just say most of the takeaways near my flat would go out of business if I moved."

"Didn't your mother cook?"

His mother's cooking was one of his better memories of his home life, but from the chill that instantly descended between them, it was obviously not the right question to ask Maggie.

"She did." Maggie's voice sounded hollow. "Best cook in town."

"Did?"

"She passed a while back."

"I'm sorry to hear that."

She made a small noise, her gaze fastidiously trained on the cars in front of them, each battling for those few precious centimeters taking them that much closer to home.

Home.

Such a simple word, but one laden with the power of a nuclear bomb.

He didn't know where home *was* anymore. He'd rented expensive modern apartments in Paris. A total contrast to the cramped, low-rent housing he had grown up in with his parents. A tent in Africa. A tiny beach house here in Sydney.

Nothing seemed to fit.

The thought twisted and tightened in his gut.

Would anything? Anywhere? Would yet another trip finally give him some answers?

He looked out of the window as they crawled past one of Sydney's most famous beaches. It was mid-week but the shore was packed with families, couples, surfers, sun-worshippers. The sky was a beautiful, crisp blue. The air was tinged with a lightly salted tang. It was heaven on earth, and yet he still felt as though being a part of it all remained out of reach. Impossibly so.

He looked across to Maggie, startled to see her swipe at the film of tears blurring her clear green eyes. The moment was over so quickly he wondered if he'd imagined it. And in its place was her bright, ready smile as the radio crackled to life with a call-out to an asthma attack.

She flicked on the blue lights.

"Let's hit one more before we call it quits, shall we?"

CHAPTER SEVEN

Don't forget the socks, Dags.

MAGGIE GROWLED A response at the text message, half tempted to throw her phone out the car window. But she knew she'd go to the store. Buy the socks. Take the washing powder. Make the meat pies. Enough to put in the freezer for later.

She could already see herself rolling up her sleeves and cleaning up the three months' worth of detritus that had no doubt accrued in the Louis household.

It was what she did. It was what *they* did. Annoying as they were, at least she *had* a family. It was a lot more than Raphael had.

Losing the Couttards had genuinely seemed to set him adrift.

Not that she'd gone over the reasons he'd chosen to seek her out a thousand times, or anything, but...had he come to fill a void? One that Jean-Luc and his parents had filled when they were teens?

Losing Jean-Luc as a friend must have been devastating for him.

When she'd lost her mother she had felt as if the world

had disappeared from beneath her feet. But that was cancer. Just one of life's cruel turns.

Losing a friend…losing a child.

The thought gave her chills. Raphael's loss was a vivid reminder that, even if they *did* drive her bonkers, her father and brothers had been there for her all along. The proverbial wind beneath her wings.

She glared at her phone for a minute, then felt her features soften as she punched in a reply.

I've already put holes in the big toes. Just the way you like 'em. x PS Don't call me Dags. I'm bringing a friend. Who has manners.

Another message pinged straight back. Something about bringing extra "talent" into town for the brothers' pleasure which she chose to ignore. There was no chance she'd bring a *female* friend out to meet that lot of larrikins. Kelly had once begged her and she'd flat-out refused.

Besides, if she explained to her brothers that her "friend" was actually the man she was trying to convince herself she wasn't head over heels in love with, her phone might blow up with their responses.

And it wasn't as if it was reciprocated. If Raphael had actually come to Oz because he was in love with her it would've come out by now.

So it was Just Friends, then. And that was the way the biscuit was bashed.

The instant Maggie laid eyes on Raphael the next morning her tummy went all fluttery butterfly park, and she knew the talking-to she'd given herself about the whole Just Friends thing had been entirely unsuccessful.

He was already out on the street, lit by a single lamp-post in the pre-dawn gloaming, his hair scruffy, blue eyes still a bit sleepy, his trousers hanging on his slim hips, a soft navy blue chambray shirt making the most of his shoulders and trim build—well, it *looked* soft. Not to mention the just-about-as-adorable-as-they-came dog by his side.

Raphael with a hang-dog pooch? That image all but nailed Raphael's place in her affections for evermore.

If he hadn't spied her—unleashing one of those bright smiles of his that had the power to make the world a better place—she would've spent a few minutes banging her head against the steering wheel. Doomed! That was what she was. Doomed to be a spinster forever. Lost to an unrequited love that would never blossom in a million years.

What had she been thinking? A fourteen-hour road trip with the most gorgeous man in the universe and his dog? If she came out of this with one single shred of dignity left intact it would be an out-and-out miracle. Particularly once he met her family.

Oh, *cuh-rikey*. This was a Class A brain failure.

She dropped her head to her steering wheel anyway, little flashes of ominous foreboding appearing in her mind's eye. One of her brothers' huge workman's hands crushing Raphael's beautiful surgeon's hands in a friendly *How-ya-going? Don't-you-dare-mess-with-my-sister* handshake. Their unrelenting passion for burnt snags on a barbie. The coolbox filled with a fresh slab of tinnies "just in case" it was a scorcher. It was *always* a scorcher.

Raphael would catch the first flight out of Broken Hill. If there even was one that day.

Was it too late to talk him out of it?

"*Salut, Maggie. Ça va?*"

The man had a voice like melted chocolate. What was she meant to say?

Why, yes, Raphael. I would be perfectly well—if inviting the only man I've ever loved to my crazy Outback family home were not the type of thing to send a girl stark raving mad. Which it is.

"Maggie?"

"*Oui, ça va.*"

Sigh. Swirl. Flip. Loop-the-loop. A pop song clicked on in her head… If she could turn back time, indeed.

Raphael walked round to her car door and handed her a coffee through the open window. "*Un café* for my chauffeur…"

Before she could thank him, he passed her a beautiful eggshell-blue box with a cream ribbon around it.

"And a little something special for you."

An image of opening it and finding a diamond ring flicked into her head, instantly unleashing a ridiculously huge explosion of tingles. Maybe fairy tales *did* come true…

"You didn't have to do this—"

"Of course I did." He waved away her protest. "I couldn't have you driving all the way across the state without some of Sydney's finest croissants."

His lips twisted into the inevitable Gallic *they're-not-French-but-they'll-do* twist, then melted into a smile.

"Yeah!" She rubbed her tummy in a show of gratitude, her heart sinking straight through to the foot well of the car.

Idiot.

Diamond ring.

Croissants. Of *course* the box had croissants in it.

Ah, well. Being a well-fed spinster was better than being one with a grumbling tummy.

She popped the box and the coffee into the central console between their seats and climbed out of the car.

"So this is Monster?" Maggie nodded down to the scruff-muffin who hadn't left Raphael's side.

The dog looked up at the pair of them, as if he knew he was the topic under discussion.

"Oui." Raphael hooked his fingers onto his hips and looked down at him with a warm smile. "He seems to have adopted me."

"Smart dog," Maggie said before she could think better of it.

Nice one, Mags. Why not just out-and-out tell the man you're completely in love with him?

Oh, mercy.

Was she?

Was the Pope Catholic? The sky blue? The earth beneath her as red as the blood pumping through her heart?

Yes. *Yes.* Near enough.

She hid her grimace of embarrassment as best she could as Raphael turned to her, his expression suddenly shadowed with sadness.

"Perhaps he is a little foolish. Pinning his hopes on a man who doesn't know if he is coming or going is never a wise investment."

Thunk. There went her heart. Plummeting straight down to the very center of the earth.

Her eyes lit on the harness in his hand. "Looks like you've made a bit of an investment in him."

"This?" Raphael held up the safety restraint and smiled at it. "Yes. Perhaps it is me being hopeful."

"Hopeful is good." *Hopeful means you might stay.*
"Oui."

Raphael nodded, and their eyes connected so completely that Maggie was sure he could read her thoughts.

"Hopeful is good."

"Guess we'd better hit the road, then." Her voice came out more as a croak then a chirp. "You'll want to make the most of the time you two have together."

She scurried to the rear passenger door and opened it up so Raphael could secure Monster to the buckles and harness, all the while thinking, *Nice cover.* Way to show the man it would be a dream come true if he stuck around. Stayed a while.

And by "a while" she meant forever...

Raphael was marveling at how different the landscape was already. Fewer than a handful of hours outside of Sydney, they were working their way through the Blue Mountains. The vistas were utterly breathtaking. Unlike anything he'd seen before. And the atmosphere in the car was nice. A bit of chat. A bit of silence. Repeat.

"Maggie, this may seem like a silly question, but with a trip this long...in France we would fly or take a train. Why do you drive?"

"What?" Maggie shrugged away his question. "You never drove anywhere in France?"

"Of course—but not almost twelve hundred kilometers for a short visit."

Maggie tipped her head to the side and considered her response.

He smiled. She'd done that as a teen as well. Usually the questions had been about algebra or advanced chemistry. Those two thick fire-red plaits she'd always worn had shifted across her shoulders as she'd tipped her chin up to the left, her green eyes following suit until she gave her answer.

"I suppose… Oh, I don't know… It gives me a sense of being in control of my destiny."

"Driving for over a thousand kilometers?" He laughed. "So *that's* the answer to taking charge of your destiny. *Bof…*" He let out a low whistle. "If only I'd known."

If only it was that simple. He would've driven ten…a hundred thousand kilometers if it would have changed things.

A thought struck him. He couldn't change the past. But he could change the future.

He reached his arm back between the seats and gave Monster a scratch behind the ears. The dog nestled into his hand. Trusting. Believing there was a future.

He looked across to Maggie, her eyes firmly on the road. He had a dog and a friend. A dear friend who… who maybe held the promise of something more?

"Holding the steering wheel of destiny is a personal thing." Maggie tip-tapped her fingers along the steering wheel, as if divining good advice. "Everybody's got their own thing, right? The thing that lets them soar. Perhaps you just haven't found yours yet. Besides…" she laughed "…it's not as if driving from Sydney to Broken Hill a dozen times has landed me a gold-plated mansion by the sea and the love of my life or anything!" She gave another horsey laugh, then quickly swallowed it.

"Is that what the goal is? A gold-plated mansion?"

She huffed out another laugh and gave him a look as if he'd just turned into a stranger. "Yeah. That'd be about right. You read me like a book."

Raphael turned in his seat and looked at her. She was obviously being sarcastic. Of course she had zero designs on a gold-plated mansion, but…the love of her life? Something told him she meant *that* part. She was ready for love.

He was tempted to say something—crack a feeble joke and tell her that if a slightly the worse for wear heart was what she was after, his was all hers—when Maggie picked up the conversation again.

"Buses, trains, airplanes…they're just…you can't *do* anything if they're running late, you know? If you're driving then you get to be in charge. Pick your speed. Choose the route. Stop. Start. Do what you like, when you like, so you can get where you need to go exactly when you want to."

"Is that why you like driving the ambulance?"

"A little bit." She tipped her head back and forth, letting the idea settle, then smiled broadly. "A lot, actually. Even more so than my 'civilian' car, because I've got the lights, the siren. If they invented one that would let me drive above the traffic I'd be the happiest girl in Sydney."

She looked just like a little girl as she imagined the scenario. Which made him wonder if the answer wasn't, in fact, a simple one. "Does your desire to be mistress of your own time spring from always being late for things as a child?"

"No." She shook her head emphatically. "But I was late for something once…"

Maggie's sentence trailed off into nothing and the vibe coming from her distinctly said, *Time to back off,* mon ami.

He understood that feeling well enough, so he settled back into his seat and scanned the views spreading out beyond them—a rich palate of rusty cliff-sides, greens and blues still alight with the golden glow of the morning sun.

"If the rest of the journey is anything like this, I completely understand you wanting to be the master of your own destiny."

"It's pretty beautiful, isn't it?" Maggie said proudly.

"I didn't realize there were so many wineries near to the city."

Maggie nodded, much more relaxed now they'd shifted conversation topic. Playing tour guide suited her, and it was enjoyable to see her visible pride about all that her nation had to offer.

"We could've gone through the Hunter Valley, but that would've added a couple hundred kilometers to the trip. Really we could travel for weeks—months, even—and not get across to Perth. Australia's awash with wineries. Maybe not as many as France, but Aussies definitely like their wine." She laughed at a sudden memory. "Do you remember when you took me to that one cafe?"

They'd been to a lot of cafés and bistros, but a picture sprang to mind of a little corner café they had visited early on in her trip. It had been the French cliché. Cast-iron tables—a bit wobbly, with green tops. Rattan-framed bistro chairs with a blue and cream weave. A sun-bleached red awning beneath which the ubiquitous rude waiting staff jostled between the tightly packed tables. He'd been showing off. Acting the sophisticate for his New World charge.

Falling in love.

"Do you mean the café where we were served wine by that waiter who thought he was a model?"

"Exactly." Maggie laughed again, her green eyes

sparking at the memory. "I was too embarrassed to tell you, but I'd never had wine before. Only stolen a few sips of my brothers' beer. I loved those little glasses so much…you know, the bistro glasses…but I didn't have a clue if I was doing anything right. I was amazed it was even legal!"

She sighed, and from the expression on her face he imagined even more memories were flooding in.

"Want to hear a confession?"

"Definitely. Yes." She shot him one of those bright smiles of hers that always seemed to land in the center of his heart.

"It was my first time, too."

She turned to him, features wide with astonishment. "*No.* I don't believe that for a second. Compared to me, you were so suave and sophisticated."

"Were?" he teased. He'd never felt suave or sophisticated for a single day of his life.

"Are," she parried solidly. "Believe me, when you see where I've come from you will see for a fact that you are, hands down, the most sophisticated person I know."

"Maggie Louis," he reprimanded her playfully. "You are being ridiculous. I am just a kid who was lucky enough to be born in a beautiful city. I wanted to show it off to you."

"You did that all right…" Her voice drifted off. "But I don't agree with you about the 'lucky kid' thing. You knew everything about Paris. I never felt for a single moment that I wasn't with the perfect person."

Her eyes flicked across to him and then quickly returned to the road, her upper teeth taking purchase on her lower lip as if she'd admitted more than she'd wanted to.

"I had a wonderful time showing you Paris."

He meant it to his very marrow. Going home to two parents more interested in the next bottle of spirits or who would win the inevitable fight over who'd spent the last of the welfare check had been a lot less fun than seeing Maggie's eyes light up when he showed her the nooks and crannies of Paris he'd discovered on the endless walks he'd taken to avoid going home.

"The truth is…" Maggie began slowly, then continued in a rush as if she'd dared herself to finish. "I think I was always a bit in love with you."

The instant she'd said it a thousand memories fell into place. The gentle looks. The soft smiles. Those moments when their hands or fingers had brushed and it had felt as though time itself had decided to stand still.

It was blatantly obvious that Maggie couldn't take it back fast enough. Words began tumbling out to erase what she'd said.

Of course only in a schoolgirl kind of way…a teenage crush…ridiculous…nothing to worry about. He mustn't think he was trapped in the car with her…she wasn't a stalker or anything."

"Maggie! *Arrêts.* It's okay. We were kids. Besides, even if I'd wanted to I couldn't have done anything about it."

Her lids lowered to half-mast and she shot him a look.

"Jean-Luc," he said as a means of explanation.

Tell her! Tell her you felt the same way!

She lifted a finger and rolled it round. *Keep on talking,* it said. Clearly just saying Jean-Luc's name wasn't enough.

He sucked in a deep breath. Talking about Jean-Luc

in any capacity was tough. Going back to the "good old days" was the hardest. Because they seemed the furthest out of reach.

"He told me he'd give me a black eye if I even so much as *thought* of kissing you."

"He did?"

Raphael nodded. "He did."

"And you listened to him?" Maggie gave him a quick glance.

"Let's just say Jean-Luc was acting at his mother's behest."

"Um…" Maggie's voice sounded dubious. "Since when do teenage boys listen to their mother? I grew up with three brothers, remember?"

"If one of your brothers had threatened someone who had designs on you with a black eye, would the boy have listened?"

Maggie obviously didn't need long to work that one out.

"Most likely—but that's small town stuff. Jean-Luc was your best friend. And he already *had* a girlfriend. Surely he would've just ignored his mother and told you to go for it?"

"Is that what you would have liked?"

"Raphael." Maggie threw him a stern look. "This is already immensely embarrassing. I'm not going to beg you to explain to me why you never kissed me."

There were a thousand reasons why. How did he explain to her that the Couttards had been his second family? That they had provided the structure and the balance—and sometimes the square meals—he had needed throughout his teens.

It had been out of loyalty. Maggie would understand that. And yet every part of him wished he had taken the risk.

"I know it sounds a bit pathetic, but think about it. Would *you* have disobeyed Madame Couttard?"

Maggie's features stayed static as she considered the question. "No. Definitely not. She was lovely, but she was a stern woman. I remember every time I asked why they ate so late she would fix me with an astonished expression, pop her hands on her hips and say. *'Je n'aime pas manger avec les poules, Margaret!'*"

"Exactly." Raphael tapped the dashboard soundly. "She saw being your host mother as akin to being your *own* mother. Looking out for you. Caring for you. Making sure errant teenage French boys didn't get any wayward ideas. The only change she wanted in you when she returned you to your own mother was speaking better French."

Maggie nodded and made an undefinable noise. "Yeah, well…my French certainly improved, all right."

She pushed a button on the display panel and turned on the radio.

Topic. Closed.

A brick wall to bang his head on would be useful about now.

Ça me soûle!

He scrubbed a hand through his hair and looked out of the window. Well, that had been about the quickest way to go from awkward to awful. The perfect tone to set for a road trip lasting over a thousand kilometres. *Très bien.*

Just say something to make her feel better about you not kissing her when you should have.

"It was a long time ago."

Nice. Exactly what she wanted to hear. That her feelings were silly and adolescent.

"Yeah. It *was* a long time ago." She nodded, cheeks flaming with embarrassment. "Would you—? Would you just…just forget I said anything? All right?"

She was gripping the steering wheel so hard her hands were trembling. Her eyes were glued to the curve of the mountainous roads ahead of them as if her life depended on it.

With every pore of his body Raphael ached for things to be different.

And that was precisely the moment when Raphael knew why he'd come to Australia.

Not to find himself. Not to make peace with his past. It was to find Maggie. To see if he could put a name to that elusive *something* that floated around in his heart whenever he thought of her.

She'd named it first. It was love.

Maggie held up her ice cream cone and tipped it towards Raphael's wattleseed flavored scoop for a "cheers" bump.

"So this is the world's best ice cream?"

"Don't look so dubious. This town may not look like much, but when you're about five hundred kilometers from civilization it's the height of sophistication."

Maggie took a satisfyingly cold lick of her saltbush and caramel cone. Ice cream fixed everything. Even incredibly awkward atmospheres in a car after you'd confessed to the man of your dreams that you've loved him since you were a teen and he's told you that someone's mom told him not to kiss you.

What she *should* be taking away from the whole mortifying scenario was the fact that Raphael had, for at least a nanosecond on the universe's timeline, *wanted* to kiss her. Not be sulking about having great French and no mother to show it off to. It wasn't as if she could change anything now.

Besides, if the *chaussure* had been on the other foot and *her* mother had laid down a similar order...

No pashing on the French exchange student, love. We've got to return that boy to his mother the way we found him.

Pffft.

She would have obeyed, too. Small town kids knew that parents talked. Nothing was a secret.

Except that her mother had already been dying of cancer the day Maggie had boarded a plane for Europe.

Raphael "clinked" her ice cream cone again. "You're right. This is excellent. I have to confess, finding a gelateria in a petrol station is not something I thought would happen today."

He was handing her an olive branch. Trying to get rid of the weirdness as well. So it looked as if they'd be friends forever.

If it was good enough for Ingrid Bergman and Humphrey Bogart...

Maggie gave him a *Strange things happen in Oz* shrug and a grin. "There are loads of Italians who settled in Australia, so the country definitely does good ice cream—wherever you are."

"As good as France?" Raphael arched a prideful brow.

Ruddy French. Not *everything* was better over there!

"I would bet you any amount of money in the universe they don't have wattleseed ice cream in Paris."

Raphael laughed. "You are probably right about that."

He took a lick and made *mmm* noises as he swirled the entire tip of the cone between his parted lips.

Maggie tried not to stare. *Too much.*

"It's good. Tastes a bit like coffee. Would you like to try?"

"Yes, please." She leaned forward and took a lick, vividly aware of Raphael's eyes upon her. Was there something…*different* about the way he was watching her? Something softer?

The man was now aware that she'd been in love with him forever and a day…

Or maybe she had dirt on her face.

Whatever it was, his gaze was making her flush.

"Mmm. That's good. Want to try mine?"

Maggie held up her cone, felt her eyes going into some sort of crazy blinking fit as once again—almost in slow motion—his lips parted before surrounding the top of her cone and taking a small taste.

Her breath caught in her throat as she imagined the cold ice cream hitting his warm tongue, melting and swirling in his mouth. Hot darts of desire shot across her more intimate regions as he made that delicious noise again. He looked up at her through dark lashes with those beautiful blue eyes of his, and in that instant she felt as though her skin was on fire.

He wasn't even *touching* her and she was on fire.

Gulp.

She still loved him.

No, she didn't.

She *lusted* after him.

Loving someone meant knowing them, and she was about as far from knowing what made Raphael tick these days as she was from knowing how to fly a jumbo jet.

Road trips were fun only if you weren't dying of humiliation at the same time. This was obviously a mistake.

Even if Raphael *was* still gazing at her with that beautiful soft smile on his lips.

She started when he reached forward and tucked a wayward strand of hair behind her ear, his fingers softly grazing the side of her neck as they passed. It was all she could do not to groan with pleasure.

What would she do when they finally kissed?

You're not going to kiss!

Madame Couttard had made sure of that.

Pah!

If they kissed then she'd be completely in love with him—which was stupid because they were heading for Broken Hill and her mad-as-a-sack-of-frogs family.

When they arrived Raphael would find out who she was and what sort of place she came from. A universe away from his own background. The whole charade of being someone she wasn't would come to an abrupt end, her heart would break into a million tiny pieces and then they could all get on with their lives. Which would be a good thing.

Except right here, right now, Raphael was licking a little bit of wattleseed off of his lip and was inches away. If she moved her ice cream cone a tiny bit to the right and went up on tiptoe…

"Maggie? Is that your phone ringing?"

The hum and rush of desire dropped from Maggie's internal soundtrack and was replaced by the very clear chirruping of her ringtone.

Mortified that she'd been staring at Raphael all goofy-eyed and lovestruck, she turned away and pulled her phone from her small bag. It was Cyclops.

"What's up, mate? I'm out in the Woop Woop."

"Yeah, I know."

Cyclops' voice was in full business mode. *Uh-oh*.

"There's been a car crash reported between Cobar and Wilcannia. Coupla lorries and some secondary vehicles. Quite a few, from the sounds of it."

She listened intently as he detailed the location.

"You anywhere near there?"

Maggie closed her eyes and pictured the road. "We're about ten kilometers east, give or take. Is anyone else on the way?"

"Yeah. They're sending a chopper out from the Blues, but it'll take at least an hour to get it crewed up and in the air. The fire crews in Cobar are all out on other jobs, but I'm coming in a chaser air ambulance. Probably two hours out. The coppers are on their way. I think they're trying to send a fire crew in with some Jaws of Life, but they'll all be volunteers. Not sure how up on first aid they'll be. It sounds serious. Any chance you can get to them and help until we arrive? Got any gear on you? Is Frenchie with you?"

"Yes, yes and yes." She looked at Raphael and gave him a tight nod. "I've got a small run bag in the boot, but not much else. Hang on a second, Cyclops."

She took the phone away from her ear, tugged a couple of notes out of her pocket and handed them to Raphael.

"Do you mind grabbing a few extra bottles of water from the guys in the shop? Loads, in fact. And as much paper toweling as you can get. Tell them it's for a medical emergency. Car crash up the road."

Raphael's features tightened instantly, and the all too familiar clouding of the bright blue in his eyes shifted into place.

This was difficult terrain for him, given his recent history, but it was an emergency. And it was what Australian paramedics did. They mucked in when there was no one else.

He was gone before she had a chance to ask if he was up to it.

Good.

Maybe working on the ambos was helping take the edge off the guilt he felt.

You couldn't save everyone, she thought as she signed off with Cyclops, grabbed her medical kit from the boot and threw it in the back alongside a perplexed-looking Monster.

But you sure could try.

CHAPTER EIGHT

RAPHAEL SAW THE smoke before the vehicles came into view. These weren't his first crash victims since he'd left Paris, but it was the first time he'd been on-site at a multi-vehicle accident. Adding scent and sound to a scene he'd imagined again and again might be torture. Or it might be the first step in putting the past right.

A couple of kilometers down the road cars were already starting to tail back on the wide highway.

"I don't suppose you have a spare set of blue lights in your car?" Raphael asked rhetorically.

Maggie shook her head. "No. But I do have a red and blue top in my bag on the back seat, if Monster hasn't turned it into a bed. Do you mind digging through my things to find it? Hopefully it's not too near my undies." She shot him an apologetic smile.

He shook his head and smiled. Trust Maggie to problem-solve her way out of a situation other people would duck out of at the first hurdle.

"Here it is." He held out a red shirt with blue polka dots.

"Right. Your job is to hold that thing out of the window."

"What for?"

She yanked the car brusquely out of the slowing traffic and onto the hard shoulder. "Tell Monster to cover his ears. You're the lights. I'm the siren."

Clamping her lips together with a determined expression, Maggie pressed on the horn of her car with one hand and gunned the car down the hard shoulder with the other.

It was impossible not to be impressed.

He ventured a guess. "Older brothers?"

"Got it in one." She flashed him a smile. "As I said, there wasn't much to do in Broken Hill as a girl."

When they were close enough to start picking out details, Raphael's gut told him the next few hours were going to be grim.

"You ready for this?" Maggie's tone suggested she didn't really care if he was or he wasn't. Either way, he'd be rolling up his sleeves and getting to work.

"Of course. You can count on me."

He meant it, too. Medically, of course. But also to support Maggie. The last thing he wanted was for her to have to worry about if he'd be all right on the accident scene.

"Why don't you have a dig around the medical kit and familiarize yourself with what we have? From the sound of things, we'll have to make it last for about an hour. Criticals first." She gave him an apologetic smile. "Sorry. I forget you're hardly a stranger to trauma. Talking it through before I arrive always helps me calm down."

"*Bien.* Talk away."

He secured the blue and red top between the window and the window frame, keeping half an ear on Maggie's ideas for the best tactical approach as he pulled her medical kit onto his lap and had a quick run through it. Rather than the handful of plasters and couple of bandages he had been expecting, it was a proper first responder bag, full of wound dressings, burn gels, eye gels, thermal blankets, Epi-pens—the lot.

"I like your version of a 'small' kit."

"Things happen out in the Woop Woop." Her eyes remained glued to the road. "There's also a couple of picnic rugs in the back. No doubt some of the other drivers will have them as well. Blankets are going to be our stretchers, our braces...just about everything until the choppers arrive."

Raphael nodded. Though it wasn't as good as having an ambulance's worth of gear, for some of these people the difference between no equipment and this soft bag could be critical.

Maggie slowed as they approached the jack-knifed road train. Its accordioned cab was enough to produce shivers. The trailers lay sprawled across the highway amidst a tangle of combis, caravans and utility vehicles—or utes, as the Australians called them.

When they pulled up at the apex of the crash Maggie was pure business.

A police car was already on the scene and she quickly identified herself and Raphael, offering to start setting up a triage area on the side of the road farthest away from the smoking vehicles.

"That'd be great." The officer introduced her to a nearby female in uniform and pointed them toward a spot they'd already pre-identified as being appropriate for triage. He lifted his chin towards Raphael. "You're a doctor?"

He nodded.

"Good. Come with me."

After rolling down the windows of the car and pouring Monster a bowl of water, he shouldered the medical bag and jogged along after the policeman to the other side of the road train.

"We need as many people as possible. There's a motorcyclist who landed under a ute when he was skidding to a halt. Bloody miracle he's still alive. Don't think he's conscious, though. Hasn't said a word."

They rounded the corner. About ten people in crouching positions surrounded a mid-sized car still smoking from a recently doused engine fire.

"Quel desastre!"

The officer shot him a sideways glance. "You're not from around here, are ya?"

"France."

He let out a low whistle. "Well, this is a far cry from France, mate. Prepare to get sweaty. If we lift this ute on a three count are you good to pull him out?"

The officer had a couple of people shifting the vehicle, including the ashen-faced male driver who looked close to fainting. Raphael made a quick mental note to find him later and check for symptoms of shock or whiplash, then knelt down to see where the motorcyclist was. His lips thinned when he saw just how much of the vehicle's undercarriage was resting on his chest. He slipped two fingers beneath the man's helmet to check for a pulse. Thready. But it was there.

"Okay." He looked up at the officer, feeling his adrenaline kick in. "Whenever you are ready."

The three count came fast.

"Now—*lift!*"

Amidst the groans and grunts of exertion Raphael

channeled his strength into a swift and fluid move, pull-ing the motorcyclist out and away from the undercar-riage of the ute.

Leaving the biker's helmet on, he flicked the visor up, unsurprised to see the man was unconscious, a blue tinge appearing on his lips. Raphael dropped his gaze to his chest, taking in the depth, rate and symmetry of his chest as he struggled to breathe. The shallow, jag-ged breaths suggested a pneumothorax or flail chest.

It was difficult to tell what had happened without tak-ing off his leathers. But taking off the leathers would come with its own set of complications. In a worst-case scenario the motorcycle gear might be the only thing holding together compound fractures and preventing massive blood loss. But palpating the man's chest with them on was pointless.

His brain kicked up to high gear.

"Can I get a couple extra pairs of hands, please?"

Protocol in France dictated leaving the helmet on, so he did. On his instructions, a pair of bystanders rolled the man onto a thermal blanket from Maggie's medi-cal kit and, with their help, he carried him away from the site to the triage area Maggie had magicked out of nothing.

Most of the color coding seemed to come in the form of pieces of colorful fabrics secured to the white road reflectors on the edge of the hard shoulder.

Maggie appeared by his side. "What've you got?"

"Possible pneumothorax. Do you have any fourteen-gauge needles in there?" He nodded to the run bag. "His lung will need decompressing. It'll keep him stable—"

"For up to four hours," Maggie finished for him.

"When you've done that are you happy to attend the patients still in their vehicles?"

Raphael nodded, taking a fraction of a second longer than he needed to search her eyes for any doubt in his ability. But, no. She was already pawing through the medical kit for the equipment he'd need for decompression.

Faith. Loyalty.

Two of Maggie's standout qualities. A shot of pride surged through him. Maggie believed in him. She trusted him in spite of everything she knew about him. It meant more to him than he'd expected. All he wanted to do now was make sure he kept it. Earned it. Sustained her belief in him as a doctor. As a man.

With the help of one of the women who'd carried the man over he quickly rolled thick supports to place on either side of the motorcyclist.

Once satisfied the patient was supported, he unzipped his leather jacket and inserted the fourteen-gauge needle, his head tipped to the man's lips as he waited for the return of steady breathing.

Beat. Beat. And breathing returned.

"Is he going to be all right?" The woman who had helped carry him over was still kneeling on the other side of the motorcyclist.

"He should be." Raphael did a quick scan of the man's abdominal area. No blood. No obvious sign of other injuries. A miracle, really.

"Will you be all right to watch him?"

The woman nodded, yes, still wide-eyed from seeing the quick-fix release of air from the man's chest cavity.

With a renewed sense of determination Raphael set

out again with the police officer, who seemed to have a good handle on all the people involved in the accident.

The rest of the afternoon passed in a blur of serious traumatic injuries and quick fixes.

Supplies were severely limited, forcing him to come up with an innovative way of stabilizing one particularly bad compound fracture.

"Ooooooh…*maaaaaaate*! That really, *really*—"

Raphael blanked out the stream of blue language coming out of the middle-aged man's mouth.

He was lucky to be alive. He was lucky the volunteer fire crew had been able to cut him out of his car.

Raphael's features tightened as he tried to stem the flow of blood with the pile of assorted clothing and towels other drivers had been bringing to him.

This man would be lucky to keep his leg. Keeping the area clean, blood loss to a minimum and the rest of his organs functioning properly was paramount.

"Incoming!"

Calls signaling the arrival of the first helicopter began to ring out. Raphael used himself as a cover for the man, steeling himself for the screams of pain he knew would follow as he continued to keep pressure on the open wound.

"What you got here, mate?"

A uniformed doctor appeared by his side, with another doctor running behind with a stretcher.

"Compound tib-fib. Possible comminute fracture—but that's just from what I can see."

"Right." The heli-medics gave him a short nod and turned their focus to the patient. "We're gonna get you into town, cobber…take a look at that leg. Hope you're all right with— Whoops! He's losing consciousness. Let's get him on the chopper. On three."

Raphael helped with the transfer and, satisfied the man was in good hands, felt clear to move onto the next patient.

Steadily, swiftly, he worked his way through each of the patients who were unable to leave their vehicles— or hadn't done so yet.

The generosity of spirit amongst the drivers who were uninjured amazed him. Each time he brought a new patient to the triage area there were more sets of helping hands.

"Easy. You don't want to put any weight on it if you can help it." Raphael was helping a teenaged boy hobble towards the lower-grade triage area in the hope of getting some ice.

"Do you think I crushed it? I've got a footie match tomorrow. Do you think I'll be able to play?"

Before Raphael could answer a couple of men ran and scooped the lad into an actual armchair.

"We gotcha, mate."

They caught the surprise in Raphael's gaze.

"We've got a lorry-load of furniture we were moving to a charity store. Figured it would come in handy for you lot."

"What else you got in there?" the teen asked. "Is there a couch or a bed? I'm going to need to elevate and ice this baby if I'm going to play tomorrow."

Raphael couldn't help but laugh. "I don't think you will be playing tomorrow. Even if you ice it."

He knelt on the ground and lifted the boy's ankle up onto his knee, noting as he did so the sharp wince the boy tried to hide.

A quick examination and Raphael was close to certain the lad had suffered a pilon fracture. It would compromise his footie career for a while—if not forever—but without an X-ray there was no point in diminishing the boy's clear fighting spirit.

He rose to his feet as the other "furniture man" appeared with a footstool.

"Here you are, mate. Best we can do. The sofas are going for the ladies."

Raphael jogged over to the edge of the triage area where people who had portable ice boxes—including several huge ones—had made ice, tea towels—whatever they had to hand—available.

He brought a tea towel full of ice over to the boy.

"Who have we got here?" Maggie appeared from behind the chair with a notebook and pen in her hands.

"Charlie Broughton."

Raphael grinned as he watched the boy turn into a young man before his eyes, ratcheting up his flirt factor. Gone were the winces and groans of pain, and in their place was a broad smile and an extended hand.

"And you are...?"

Maggie gave him a quick smirk. "The woman who's going to get you a lift into the city. What do we have here? Sprain?"

Raphael shook his head. "He will need X-rays, definitely, but his injury is not critical."

"What? *Mate*..." Charlie looked at him, aghast. "The footie team is going to be absolutely furious if I'm not on the field—"

"The footie team is going to have to learn to do without you for a match," Maggie cut in as she leaned over and took a peek beneath Charlie's icepack. "Even if it is a sprain, there's no chance you're playing tomorrow."

"Well…" Charlie managed to make the word sound flirtatious. "Yes, ma'am." He gave her a wink and another smile.

Maggie laughed good-naturedly and started taking his details.

Raphael took a moment to grab some water and take in the scene.

People were handing round water and food. Their own small but increasingly useful first aid kits. A young girl had even "adopted" Monster to make sure he didn't overheat in the vehicle.

With rapidly dwindling resources, Raphael was being forced to rely on the spirit that had compelled him to choose medicine in the first place. Compassion. Skill. Dedication to helping people through their most vulnerable moments.

He felt like a doctor again.

And there was one person he had to thank for that.

A freckle-faced, green-eyed, redhead whose attention was now solidly with the newly arrived air ambulance teams and helicopter crews from Sydney.

She was pointing out the triage areas, handing across her notes as well as giving verbal hand-overs for each and every patient and details of the medicine they'd been given. Florence Nightingale had nothing on his girl.

His girl?

Mid-flow, Maggie looked across the crowds of people gathered on the roadside, met his gaze solidly…and smiled.

"Here." Raphael held out a cold bottle of water to Maggie as they walked back to her car. "I hope you have been taking your own words of wisdom to heart and staying hydrated."

"Oh, brilliant. And *cold*!" She pressed the bottle to her throat and gave a sigh of relief. "I always forget how much hotter it is out past the Blues."

She shifted the bottle to one sunburnt cheek and then the other, only to realize Raphael had been watching her the entire time. She swigged down a few grateful gulps. When she lowered the bottle from her lips there was something in his gaze she hadn't seen before.

Curiosity.

And not a brother-sister, friend-friend curiosity either.

A rush of goose pimples rippled across her entire body.

"That was pretty intense. Are you all right after all that?" Though it was a dodge away from what she was really thinking, the question had been playing in the back of her mind all day. She might as well use it as a cover for the fact that all she wanted to do was jump the man and snog him senseless.

He nodded with an assurance that put her at ease. She'd seen a change in him today. Glimpses of the "old" Raphael. Assured, confident. And more than that. There had been genuine compassion in the care he'd provided for those people today. Not that frightening hollow look in his eyes.

Today he had been *present*. Today he had been the man she'd always imagined he would become.

She balanced the water bottle on the car bonnet and rubbed her hands along her arms. "Whoo! You'd think I had a bit of heatstroke from my body's reaction to that water."

She tried to laugh, but when her eyes caught with Raphael's again it died in her throat.

"Do you think you might? You were pushing it today."

Raphael took a step towards her that caught her by surprise. So much so that she stumble-stepped backwards, only to bump into the car.

"Do you feel dizzy?"

Again, Raphael closed the distance between them, his eyes searching hers for answers. Or for dilated pupils. Which he would definitely see. And that wasn't just because the sun was beginning to set behind him.

"Maggie," he persisted, "are you feeling unwell?"

Dizzy. Weak-kneed. And a bit dreamy-eyed.

"No." She tried to shake her head, but couldn't.

Raphael reached up and cupped her face between his hands, searching her features for symptoms. She knew he'd feel heat in her cheeks. An acceleration in her heartrate. Her breath had become shallow, her lungs impossible to fill, because everything in that instant was... *Raphael.*

And then he was kissing her. Softly at first. Tentatively. As if asking for permission to continue.

He didn't need to ask twice.

Her lips parted as his kisses gained confidence. And when she felt the initial sweep of his tongue along her lower lip a soft whimper of pure longing hummed from her chest. As the kisses deepened their breath intermingled to exhilarating effect, as if they were at long last joined as one.

One of Raphael's hands dropped to Maggie's waist, firmly tugging her closer to him as he wove the fingers of his other hand into the thick fistful of hair at the base of her neck.

For thirteen years she'd wondered what it would be like to kiss him... It was even better than she could ever have imagined.

The kisses...his touch. Everything about him was sensual. Erotic in its simplicity of purpose. The culmination of a day's intense work was pared down to these perfectly intoxicating expressions of desire and pent-up longing.

At last she knew in her heart that he felt it too.

The kisses came in so many variations it was impossible to keep track. Some were so passionate she thought her heart wouldn't be able to keep up and others were so exquisitely tender she could hardly breathe.

The world had long since blurred around them, but traffic was beginning to make its way away from the crash site.

Snail's pace? Lightning speed?

She didn't have a clue. All that mattered was Raphael. The sweet taste of his lips. The tang of salt on his skin. The rough bristles of growth upon his cheeks shifting past her fingertips as she swept her hands into a loose cinch behind his neck.

She was half tempted to sling a leg up onto one of his hips when a sharp wolf whistle broke through the thick heat of the afternoon air.

They pulled apart, surprised to find themselves the object of an entire fire crew's attention. More wolf whistles began to ring out from passing cars, along with cheers and cries of, "Good on ya, mate!" and "Nice one, cobber!"

Maggie didn't know whether to shrivel up and die of embarrassment or laugh and scream, *Finally!*

Feigning a demureness she knew she didn't possess, she sought her cue from Raphael.

But instead of withdrawing in horror, Raphael rested his hands on Maggie's hips—protectively, almost—and smiled, tipping his chin toward the firemen and drivers before returning his gaze to her. And that bright twinkle in his blue eyes was alight for the first time in... It had been a while. And a long time coming.

"Do you mind? The attention?" he asked, his gentle accent adding an extra level of sensuality to the question.

She shook her head—no. It was a lot better than being the center of attention because she was the only one who knew how to get grease stains out of work overalls. Better by a mile.

She squinted at the setting sun, the brilliant wash of colour doing its magic behind him. Though she would have happily stayed on the roadside, woven into Raphael's arms, absorbing the full impact of just how incredible it was—how incredible *he* was—practical Maggie kicked into gear.

"We'd probably better hit the road. We're going to be driving all night from the looks of things."

"It's too far, Maggie. Especially having worked flatout today. *Non.* Is there not a town nearby where we can stay?"

"What? You mean like in a motel or something?"

OMG! One room or two? One room or two?

Raphael pulled back and examined her, his fingers hooked on her hips with a sense of familiarity that unleashed another thrill of expectation in her heart.

One room. Definitely one room.

That was what his eyes were saying...what his hands were saying. The lips just about to meet hers—

"Maggie!" The police officer who had been coordinating the accident scene—Scott Roland—was jogging towards them, waving something vaguely familiar-looking in his hand. "Don't forget your knickers!"

Flames of embarrassment streaked across Maggie's cheeks.

Why, why, *why* had she used her superhero panties as triage color tags?

Scott slowed to a halt in front of them, eyeing the pair of them with a smirk. "I'm not interrupting anything private, am I?"

"Hardly!"

Maggie scooted out of Raphael's loose hold on her hips and reached out to grab her knickers.

"Not so fast, little lady." Scott's features broadened into an ear-to-ear grin. "I think the press might be interested in hearing about the real-life superhero of today's accident."

"I don't think so. *You're* the real hero and no one's interested in your undershorts!" Maggie ground out, trying again—unsuccessfully—to nab the brightly colored bits of cotton that no one was meant to know about apart from her.

So what if she wore superhero knickers to give herself a little private motivation as she worked her way through the inevitable piles of debris and gunk that had built up at the Louis household in her absence? Her secret little charwoman's outfit. Fit for no eyes other than her own!

"Let's see…" Scott was relishing her discomfort. "What do we have here…?"

From perfect moment to perfectly mortifying…

This was the cringe-worthy material nightmares were made of.

If she could just grab them before Raphael—

"I particularly like these ones, Maggie," Scott said,

holding up her favorite pair—the Wonder Woman knickers—for one and all to see.

"Stop it!"

"What? Or what about these? Don't you want the world to know you've got Cat Woman panties? I wouldn't mind a glimpse of you in these, if you don't mind me saying."

He put his fingers at either end of the black knickers with sassy cat's eyes on them—one for each buttock—and tipped them back and forth like a cat about to pounce.

"*I* do."

Raphael reached out, took the knickers, handed them back to Maggie and then pulled her close to him, snugly wrapping an arm around her shoulders.

If swooning was still a thing she would be doing it. And then crawling beneath her car and crying fat, hot tears that said, *Why, oh, why can't I be the cool one? Just once!*

"I'm guessing these are Bat Girl?" Scott pulled one final pair out of his back pocket.

Raphael held out his hand for the panties and made a *put 'em here* gesture as Scott held them out: black, with a bright gold bat embossed on the behind.

Unfazed, Scott gave him a wink. "I suppose you've got the matching Superman boxers, then, big boy?"

Raphael tipped his hand back and forth in a move that said, *Maybe I do, maybe I don't. Superheroes don't tell.*

If Maggie hadn't thought she was in love before, her affections were cast in stone now.

"Right!" Maggie pulled the car into a huge dusty rectangle that served as a car park. "This is us, I guess."

Her state of mind was the same as Raphael's: one part *Why are we still wearing clothes?* to one part *Are we really ready for the next step?*

The hour-long ride to the motel had seen the sun set and their expectations of what was to come rise.

Now that they were here…

In unison, they looked up at the large neon sign blinking in front of them. With its blood-red lettering and handful of blown-out letters, the level of invitation to come on in and stay the night was questionable.

Big Pe e's Road use & ottleshop

Monster made a noise expressing his doubts from the back seat.

"Do you think they have room service?" Raphael asked.

Maggie laughed, then echoed Raphael's dry tone. "If you're after a hunk of cheese stuck between two bits of bread and an ice-cold stubbie I think you might be all right."

"That's more than I grew up with most days." He shrugged nonchalantly, before remembering Maggie still didn't know that side of his upbringing.

She squinted at him, hands still braced on the steering wheel as if she hadn't entirely decided whether or not she was going to let go. "What are you talking about? Compared to me, you had a *lovely* upbringing."

Something instinctive and fierce rose up in Raphael. From what he could remember, *her* upbringing had been similar to Jean-Luc's. "What do you mean, compared to you?"

Maggie rolled her eyes. "No, no… Nothing bad. Just…no fancy Parisian neighborhood with all the trimmings." She tipped her head toward the back seat. "Shall we give Monster a bit of a stroll?"

Raphael agreed, grateful for the chance to stretch his legs and enjoy the cooler night air.

After a few moments of strolling around Raphael tried again, adding as much of a light-hearted tone to his voice as he could. "What was so bad about your upbringing? If I should have brought my sword to your home, you could have warned me."

Maggie laughed and shook her head. "Honestly, it was nothing like that. My family are goofballs, but they're all very loving. It was more…what the town *wasn't*."

"What do you mean?"

She huffed out a laugh. "Suffice it to say Broken Hill doesn't really throw a patch on Paris. Trust me. You're in for a bit of a shocker tomorrow."

He sucked in a breath. Was she ready for the real Raphael? Warts and all?

He reached across to her and took one of her hands in his, tracing along the lines written into her palm. Before things went any further—and he knew in his heart he wanted them to progress—he owed her this much.

"If you think back," he began softly, his eyes trained on hers, "you never actually came to my house."

Maggie's lips parted in protest, but just as quickly she screwed them into a little moue and thought. "It never really occurred to me…"

Her fingers covered her mouth and she drummed them along her lips for a minute—lips he would do anything to be kissing again.

"We did everything at the Couttard's or around Paris, didn't we?"

He nodded.

"Why was that?" She looked utterly baffled.

"My parents were both…how do you say?…fond of a drink. Or eleven. Do you understand?"

Maggie's eyes widened. "It's not strictly a saying, but I get your drift."

She wasn't judging—just listening. She'd been that way when they'd met. He should have trusted her with this information back then.

The fog cleared in his head. How pointless it had all been! To disguise part of himself from her. Maggie's affection for him wasn't attached to wealth or status or—he looked round the dusty car park outside the motel—to Paris. Paris hadn't been a factor. She'd simply cared for *him*.

"They didn't hurt you, did they?"

Raphael shook his head, no. They hadn't been that bad. Most of the time. The odd cuff to the ear. An arm gripped too tightly. Impossible to fulfill their expectations because they simply weren't happy people.

"They weren't horrible—just poor. And not terribly motivated." He shrugged again. It eased his heart to realize he'd let go of that anger long ago.

"So…how did you and Jean-Luc—?"

"Become friends?" Raphael finished for her. "We met at school. My parents had a small apartment—subsidized housing—in the same neighborhood where the Couttards lived, and at school we were seated in alphabetical order."

"Bouchon and Couttard," Maggie murmured, as if

saying the names helped her picture the scene. "And they basically…what? Adopted you?"

Raphael gave a soft smile. The Couttards had opened their hearts and their home to him as if they were his own parents.

"Without the formalities, I suppose you could say they did. Jean-Luc didn't have any brothers or sisters and, as you may remember, both his parents were lawyers so they worked a lot. It was one of the reasons Madame Couttard accepted foreign exchange students."

"Someone for Jean-Luc to hang out with?"

"Yes—precisely. And they had always wanted a large family. The year you came, you had the fortune—or misfortune, depending upon how you look at it—of being lumped in with me. If you remember, that was the year Jean-Luc discovered girls?"

Maggie laughed at the memory. "It was impossible to keep track of them all."

She gave Raphael's hand a squeeze, then gave him a *C'mon buddy, we've just pashed in front of a thousand cars* look.

"I suppose you've figured out by now it was a real hardship being 'lumped' in with you." Her eyes brightened with another thought. "So…when Madame Couttard asked you to do something—"

"If you mean something like *not* kiss the beautiful Australian girl even though it would have made me very happy? Yes. I obeyed. I owed them so much."

"I get it now," Maggie said, nodding as she connected the dots. "I would've done the same thing." A twinkle hit her green eyes. "Even if it left a poor Aussie girl heartbroken that she'd gone all the way to France and hadn't been kissed."

Raphael made a noise to protest, but he could tell from her relaxed demeanor that she wasn't chastising him. The past was in the past.

It was a powerfully healing thought—leaving the past where it was and doing everything he could for his future. And he wanted his future to be with Maggie.

"Well, you know…" His voice dropped an octave. "I didn't fly halfway across the world to stand outside a neon lit motel and talk about the past."

"Oh, no?" Maggie's lips curled into a flirtatious smile as her lids dropped to half-mast over those green eyes of hers. "Why *did* you come?"

"I came for you."

If someone had thrown a lightning bolt straight into her heart it would have had less of an effect.

"Me?"

Raphael nodded. "It's taken me a while to figure it out." He shot her a sheepish look. "Sorry for all the glowering and thunderous looks back in Sydney."

She waved off his concerns, her insides still recovering from the glitter storm of emotion swirling in her chest. "You were fine. You were just really…"

"French?" he filled in for her, and they both laughed.

Raphael took a step closer towards her. The air grew taut with expectation. With promise.

Monster barked. He wanted his tea.

"What do you say we check in? Get this guy fed and then…bed?"

Yes, yes—yes, please. If I don't die of anticipation first.

She nodded as nonchalantly as she could. "Good idea."

A few minutes later they'd met the owners and reassessed their dodgy motel as a quirky work in progress.

The owners were a young couple who offered them the "spa room" before showing them a fenced outdoor area complete with dog house where Monster could stay the night.

"Alors." Raphael held up the large room key, a mischievous twinkle in his eye. "Shall we?"

"No time like the present!" Maggie chirped too loudly, and she grabbed her bag and smiled, just a little impressed that she could even walk. Her legs were wobbling like jelly.

The second the door to their room clicked shut behind them all Maggie's nervous energy disappeared.

She barely saw the dated bedcover. The art that looked as though someone's grandmother had won it in a tombola with poor pickings. The lampshades she was certain she'd seen at a car boot sale flanking either side of a queen-sized bed that already seemed too far away even though it couldn't have been more than a few footsteps away.

Raphael clearly felt the same way. He backed her against the door, dropped their overnight bags where they stood and cupped her face with his hands, his lips descending to hers for the most beautifully intimate kiss she'd ever known.

Not five minutes later she realized her entire body had shape-shifted into molten lava.

They'd managed to kick their shoes off, but not much more. Her blouse seemed to have lost a couple of buttons. So had that chambray shirt of Raphael's, she noted with a wicked grin as she gave the sweet spot at the base of his throat an entirely out of character lick.

Each moment in Raphael's arms—touching him, being held by him, caressed by him—was lifting her to another level of sexual revelation. Her body responded to his every touch as if she had never known a man before. And, in his arms, she knew there would never be another.

His fingers slid along her sides as he dropped heated kiss after heated kiss onto her neck. The tips of his fingers dipped in at her waist, eliciting a shiver of response along her belly. Her hands sought his, weaving their fingers together, and as one they turned toward the bed.

"Es-tu sûr?" he murmured, his thumb skimming along one of her cheekbones and shifting a stray strand of hair behind her ear.

"I've never been more certain of anything."

And she meant it. It was as if her whole life had been leading to this point. To Raphael.

When they had checked in to the motel they had giggled like the teenagers they had once been.

All that giddy effervescence was gone now.

In its place was electricity. Fire. The building blocks of desire that had begun to form so long ago leading them to this one erotically charged night of discovery.

Before she could sit on the bed Raphael held her at arm's length, looking at her as a man who'd not drunk water in a hundred days might view a clear running mountain brook.

He wanted her. Knowing that in her heart emboldened Maggie.

Where she had once felt timorous and incredibly body-shy with the two or three other boyfriends she'd had, with Raphael she felt…*beautiful*. Powerful, even. Sensual.

It was surprising, considering just how filthy she must be from the day's hard work.

Which gave her an idea…

"Would you like to take a shower?"

A gleam of heated expectation hit Raphael's eyes. It was a look that said, *Yes*. And, *Why aren't we there already?*

Again he took her hand, and they practically raced to the next room.

Much to their surprise, the bathroom *wasn't* a relic of the previous century. It had been updated into a large wet room, with beautiful earth-tone tiles on one wall, thick slabs of hardwood on the controls wall, a gorgeous cobalt-blue-tiled floor and a huge waterfall shower head. A long olive tree plank held an invitingly pristine pile of thick bath towels.

It was perfect.

"Why wait?" Raphael asked, reaching across to the controls, and then pulling her close to him, still completely clothed, he turned on the water.

Maggie lifted her head to the cascade of water, closed her eyes and let it pour down over her. When she opened her eyes she met Raphael's blue gaze, and in that moment she gave her heart to him completely.

Slowly, assuredly, he undid the remaining buttons of Maggie's blouse, dropping kisses on her bare salty skin as he peeled the cotton away first from her shoulders, then her breasts. Her fingers flew to his hair, clutching thick handfuls of the rich chestnut curls as he took one of her nipples into his mouth, slowly swirling his tongue round and round before sucking and caressing her breast as if time were no factor.

And it wasn't. Not anymore.

All that existed was Raphael.

Her second nipple tightened in anticipation of his kiss. A soft moan vibrated the length of her throat when his lips gained purchase. Her entire body responded—lifting, swelling and aching in feverish suspense, waiting for his touch.

Her knee-length skirt suddenly felt too tight. Her knickers too constricting. Every thread of cotton on Raphael's body was in the way of what she really wanted. Skin to skin contact.

She surprised herself by pushing him back against the wooden wall of the wet room, water still pouring over them, taking each side of his shirt in her hands and tearing it in two.

Raphael laughed.

Shock? Surprise, maybe?

Their eyes met and meshed.

No.

Desire.

Up until this point their movements had been slow, sensuous. Each touch, kiss and caress had carried with it a note of precaution, speaking of a wish to ensure they were pleasing the other.

But now a switch had been flicked.

Now their movements became assured, laden with sexual intent. Down went his jeans. One of them kicked them in a heap to one side. Who knew where his boxers went? Not Maggie. Her skirt hit the far wall. A blink of an eye later her lace-just-in-case knickers were history. And her brassiere...? *What* brassiere?

Raphael pulled her against him and as one they groaned with the pleasure of skin-on-skin connection. Hot. Wet. Insatiable.

They soaped one another with beautifully aromatic body wash, teasing, playing as they did so. Her hands swirled through chest hair. His fingers teased along the soft curves of breasts.

When Raphael parted Maggie's legs with one of his own and trailed his hand up and along Maggie's inner thigh she thought she'd scream with pent-up frustration. When his fingers slipped inside her she did scream. Her thighs instinctively clamped tight onto his hand as she begged him to stop. She wanted to reach her peak with him inside her. She wanted to share the exaltation of that ultimate intimacy as one united soul.

A moment later he took her hand in his and filled it with shower gel, lifting his eyebrows, taunting her to have as wicked a way with him as she could imagine.

Maggie didn't have to imagine. Having the real Raphael here and now was all the inspiration she needed.

Bathed in soft light, warm water and the gentle gaze of the man she loved, Maggie enjoyed the slick sensation of shifting a soapy hip along one of Raphael's solid thighs, her soft belly against his well-defined stomach, then moving lower…to the hard, taut, evidence of his desire.

The temptation to wrap her hands round his neck, lift her legs to his hips and lower herself onto the solid, velvety thickness of his erection nearly blinded her to any other option.

The scenario played itself out as they moved from the drenched wall behind them to the beautiful rich blue tiles beneath their feet. The need for protection shifted the immediacy of her desire into the tantalizing prospect of toweling him off and starting all over again on the bed.

As if reading her mind, Raphael turned off the water

and reached for the pile of thick bath towels. He unfurled one of the towels, wrapped her in it, and swiftly secured one around his own trim hips.

Just two seconds of being hidden from him and already Maggie felt deprived of all six foot two inches of Raphael's beautifully toned body.

Depraved, more like.

But not indecently so. More as if she'd found the key to a special door—*une porte magique*. A portal that gave her access to the richness of carnal desire with someone who was safe, someone who cared, someone who loved her as much as she loved him.

A few long-strided steps later and Raphael was ripping the covers off the bed. He was right. They didn't need anything to hide from each other.

She ran towards the bed and launched herself at it, laughing with sheer delight.

Raphael turned back from his overnight bag and held up an easily recognizable foil packet.

"You came prepared?" She feigned shock.

"I came with hope," he parried, a naughty choirboy expression playing across his features.

"Good answer." She crooked her finger and beckoned for him to join her.

Once he'd stretched out to his full length on the bed and begun reaching for her she shook that finger—no.

Plucking the packet from his hand, she straddled him, saying, "Now it's my turn to drive *you* wild."

Raphael was astonished at Maggie's transformation.

Temptress. Tactician. *Femme fatale*. All wrapped into one flame-haired package of feminine beauty.

She smiled above him, her feline eyes weighted with desire as she lowered herself just enough to give him luxurious kiss after luxurious kiss. Then, slowly, she began to work her way down.

Her lips grazed his nipples, her tongue darting out for hot, quick licks as she ran her fingers along his chest as if it were clay she was about to mold into a thing of beauty.

"You're beautiful," he whispered.

"You're all I've ever wanted." She lifted herself so that her lips shifted across his own as she spoke.

"Je t'aime."

Maggie's eyes glassed over and a single tear dropped onto his cheek.

"Je t'aime aussi."

He loved her.

At long last he'd found her, and he would never let her go.

Maggie shifted so that she was straddling one of his legs.

She looked like a goddess. Her damp hair tumbled down in waves and curls along her shoulders. Little drips of water were wending their careless way along the curves and dips of her breasts. When he tried to reach out and touch them she tsked at him and wagged a finger—no.

She lifted up the condom and smiled.

It was time.

Mieux vaut tard que jamais.

He might be thirteen years too late for the kiss he should've given her as a teen, but something told him the timing was exactly right for making love to this woman he'd always held in his heart.

Maggie's hands shook as she unwrapped the small packet. When she touched him, he met her hands with his own, helping her guide the protection along the length of his erection.

And then he couldn't wait anymore.

"*Maintenant.*"

"Now?" She smiled, lifting herself up from his leg as she did.

"*Oui. Mais doucement.*"

Taunt me. That was what he was saying. Fast. Slow. She could do what she wanted, but he needed to be inside her. *Now.*

Teasingly at first, hinting at the warm depths that would surround him, she lowered herself in excruciatingly slow increments, occasionally raising herself up again so that the cool night air hit him, until he couldn't bear it anymore.

He placed his hands on her hips and teased her down the length of him until she covered him completely. Together they moaned as she began to rock her hips back and forth, back and forth, until he thought he would go mad. Pressing his fingertips onto her hips, he encouraged her to set herself free. To abandon herself to the desire they felt for each other.

He lifted his hips, pressed them towards her with a drive and desire he'd never known before. Again and again their bodies met and sparked, sending waves of pleasure through him in such heated blasts that he couldn't restrain his longing for her anymore.

"Be with me!" he cried, his eyes connecting with hers more powerfully than they had ever done before.

It was impossible to tell if she'd heard him or not. Maggie glowed with exertion and desire.

He lifted himself up, wrapped an arm around her waist and flipped her over so that he was on top.

Her smile spoke volumes. *Take me,* it said. *I'm all yours.*

He thrust into her with renewed vigor. Hips meeting hips. Maggie's legs wrapping around him and pulling him in closer. Her thighs, breasts, belly—every touch was hypnotic and energizing. When her fingernails dug into his shoulders and scored the length of his back he knew he couldn't hold back any longer.

He met her green eyes and as if by mutual agreement they allowed themselves the luxury of the ultimate mutual release.

The detonation of pleasure was initially so powerful that he couldn't even see.

Pulling her close to him, he rolled to one side, still inside her, feeling their breath intermingling as they each floated back to earth.

"Well, that was nice," Maggie said eventually, her full grin making it obvious she had just made the understatement of the year.

"Comme-ci, comme-ca."

He played along, tipping his hand back and forth between them, letting it come to a rest atop her rapidly beating heart. He placed her free hand on his own chest, proof that his heart was pounding in time with hers.

They both knew there was nothing so-so about what had just happened between them.

They lay together in silence, wrapped in one another's arms. Gathering their breath, their thoughts, enjoying the simple pleasure of gazing into each other's eyes until eventually Maggie asked, "Do you fancy room service?" before dissolving into another fit of giggles.

CHAPTER NINE

"WELCOME TO BROKEN HILL!"

Maggie used her best tour guide voice, hoping the anxiety building in her chest wasn't bleeding through.

The morning had been magical. Of course. How could it not have been when she'd woken up to sweet kisses being dropped onto her lips by Raphael as he held her close to him?

Leaving the motel room had proved tough, so they'd opted for a late check-out and made the most of it.

Eventually—reluctantly—Maggie had answered her brothers' building number of texts and said they'd be there by teatime.

The closer they got to home, the harder the Cinderella syndrome struck.

Cinderella the morning after the ball.

The further away from the roadhouse they drove, the less she believed it had really happened.

No glass slippers anywhere. Just a girl and a guy in a car on the way to her childhood madhouse.

Raphael had gone very quiet over the last few hours of their journey. Rather than ask him what he was thinking, she had let the all too familiar fingers of doubt begin niggling away at her confidence.

Did he regret telling her he loved her?

Was making love to her and meeting her family in a twenty-four-hour period too much, too soon?

Perhaps the whole thing had simply been a release after the accident.

He'd never attended a huge pile-up like that. And it had to have unleashed some pretty dark memories.

He'd told her he *loved* her. That wasn't something that just slipped out.

"It's not as big as I expected," Raphael said as the town came into view.

His tone was hard to read—not a hint of anything other than general surprise in his voice. No disdain. No, *Have mercy upon me—I just had sex with a girl from the Woop Woop.*

Not yet, anyway.

"Well, you're probably going to see a lot of things you didn't expect over the next couple of days."

She offered him an apologetic smile, then returned her gaze to the road, chiding herself as she did.

Just because she'd entered the town's limits it didn't mean she was submitting herself to a life of servitude. All she'd have to do was unearth the kitchen counters from who knew how many weeks of washing up, scrub the floors, air the place...

Raphael would understand if she had to do fifteen loads of laundry before they headed back to Sydney, right?

To buy a bit more time she took "the scenic route", pointing out an enormous red bench someone had built eons earlier near one of the old mine sites.

"What is it for?" Raphael asked.

It was a reasonable question, considering there wasn't

really anything else near it. It was just a giant bench in the middle of the desert.

"No idea," she admitted. "Aussies like big things. If you had enough time on your hands you could visit them all. The country is full of them. A ginormous banana, a guitar, a sundial…"

She forced herself to stop, surprised at how long she could have prattled on. As if her country's super-sized objects were part of her. Which, of course, they weren't. But the culture was—the landscape, the air. They were *all* part of who she was. Who she would become.

Would Raphael stay and become a part of that too?

He peered out of the window and made one of those French noises that meant, *Peculiar, but I like it*.

It made her smile. But it made her a little sad, too. This was probably the first and last time he'd ever be here.

"We used to come out here all the time. To see the bench."

Why she'd loved it so much was beyond her. But she had begged her parents and her brothers to help her clamber up onto it countless times. They'd done so gladly, climbing up themselves after they'd hoisted her up, and then they'd all sat and watched the world go by—excepting the time a dust storm had blown in and they'd high-tailed it home so her mother's asthma didn't kick up.

Little had they known her coughing was actually lung cancer.

Raphael refocused his gaze on her, his smile shifting into a concerned frown. "Are you happy to be home?"

Maggie shot Raphael a quick smile she knew looked more nervous than chirpy.

Excited?

Not really.

Nervous?

Completely.

"Sure…" she said finally.

It wasn't much of an answer, but it would have to do. Although hightailing it back to Sydney had a certain appeal. There was so much she still hadn't told Raphael—so many reasons he might begin to regret last night.

She bit down on her lower lip and trapped it tight.

Why was coming home so painful?

It didn't take a surgeon—or indeed a paramedic—to figure that one out.

Coming home reminded her of all the dreams she hadn't realized. And having Raphael next to her was a double reminder. *He'd* gone and done it—he'd fulfilled those teenage dreams of becoming a surgeon.

She glanced at her road trip companion, unsurprised to see him looking bemused as they passed the mismatched series of houses that made up Broken Hill's eclectic aesthetic.

Wood. Cinderblock. Corrugated metal sheets rusted the same color as the iron-red earth they sat upon—and, of course, the centerpieces of the ever-shrinking town's main street: two traditionally built brick and stone hotels. Glorious yesteryear structures that sang of a golden era when precious metals had all but sprung from the earth.

Now the town was doing its best to reinvent itself as a tourist destination, but with water in short supply and not much to do if you weren't into collecting Outback art or looking at solar panels…

The place was about as far a cry from Paris as you could get, short of a village made of igloos.

Sitting at a traffic light, Maggie stared at the grand old structures. When she was little she'd thought they were the most beautiful buildings she'd ever seen. When she'd returned from Paris…well, a lot of things had changed after she'd returned from Paris.

Maggie's knuckles emptied of blood, her grip tightening on the steering wheel as she drove on a few more minutes and eventually pulled the car into the familiar covered carport.

It had been haphazardly tacked onto the family property years ago, when her brothers had flirted with the idea of becoming construction workers before finally settling upon becoming auto mechanics and setting up their own garage. The fact the carport roof was listing indicated they'd chosen wisely.

There were few signs of life in front of the wooden house, but that wasn't unusual. With their house situated only a couple of streets away from the main street, her brothers often shifted from their auto repair business to the hotel a couple of doors down for a few drinks—and, she imagined, since she was no longer there to cook for them, some dinner.

She stared at the entryway to the house, surprised to see that the trim had been repainted from a mysterious orange to a rich blue that matched the sky. In fact the whole house had been repainted.

The façade of the four-bedroom bungalow had been peeling under the desert-strength heat of the Australian sun for as long as she could remember.

So what?

A paint job didn't mean anything. It was just the same thing as if she'd taken herself out for a manicure. Superficial changes—nothing more. Hardly proof her family had changed after all these years. She stared down at her unpainted nails.

"Are you all right?"

"Yeah, sure." Maggie smiled at Raphael, almost surprised to see him there. He looked so out of context here. "Just…adjusting."

She made a fuss over tidying up a couple of serviettes left over from their trip and finishing off her water as Raphael unclipped Monster's harness and put him on a lead.

She squinted against the afternoon sun as the pair of them walked toward the house, with Monster bimbling around, sniffing this and that, as Raphael soaked in the atmosphere.

Would he stay in Australia? Make Monster a permanent part of his life? Make *her* a permanent part of his life?

She pulled her fingers through her hair and teased it into a loose plait. This wasn't the time to be asking herself questions like that.

"Maggie?" Raphael gave her a questioning look. *"C'est ta maison, n'est-ce pas?"*

"Oui, oui." Maggie confirmed on automatic pilot, then checked herself.

This wasn't Paris. Or Sydney. This was the Woop Woop and the only way to fit in was to go back to being the girl who hadn't known the difference between the Louvre and the loo.

"Prepare yourself," she said to Raphael.

"For what?"

The meaty revving of a quad bike drowned out anything she was about to say, followed by some very familiar whoops and hollers. She rolled her eyes. Sounded like another Louis Brothers experiment.

"You'll see."

Very little could have prepared Raphael for the scene unfolding in front of them as they walked through the carport and around to the back of Maggie's childhood home. Instead of the postage-stamp-sized garden he had been expecting there was a huge open sprawl of land that at one point might have been destined for another row of houses.

Two men were on the back of an all-terrain vehicle, pulling something attached to two enormous elastic bands which were, in turn, attached to two unused telephone poles. Just off to the left another man was holding up a video camera, feet propped on an Esky, a broad smile on his face.

Only when the men on the ATV released the "object" did Raphael realize it was another man. As he flew through the air and bounced back and forth against the rubbery pull of the super-sized slingshot the group collectively dissolved into fits of hysterical laughter and self-congratulation.

So this was Maggie's family.

"I told you Aussies like big toys," Maggie said dryly, her eyes rolling as if this was an everyday sight in the Louis backyard. She put a hand to the side of her mouth and called above the roar of laughter, "Get Dad down from there, you lot! Are you trying to get yourselves a Darwin Award? No prizes for proving you are idiots by vaulting father into the strastophere!"

"Daggie!" As one, the two men on the ATV turned

around, leapt off the vehicle, ran to Maggie and picked her up and squished her into a big brother sandwich.

Une baguette de Maggie, Raphael thought, a smile hitting his face as Maggie laughed and protested in equal turns. Her protests gathered strength when the other two men joined them and followed suit with a second, more rigorous hug and a proper knuckleduster.

This boisterous homecoming was a far cry from anything he could have expected. A hit of emotion gripped his heart and squeezed. It wasn't envy he was feeling… *Longing.* That was what it was. Longing to be part of a family. The sensation hit him hard.

She was part of a family. He didn't have anyone to offer her. Two years ago he would've had the Couttards…

"Let me down, you oafs!" Maggie finally shouted.

"Where's your girlfriend, Dags?"

"I didn't bring a girlfriend." She looked across at Raphael. "I brought…um… I brought Raphael."

The men—all tall, strongly built alpha males—turned to him with narrowed eyes and flexing hands. Maggie looked like a china doll next to the four of them. A china doll with a killer left hook.

"But…" One of the men shot her a bewildered look. "He's a *bloke*."

"Yeah, glad you figured that one out on your lonesome." Maggie's expression was decidedly…*mixed.* Annoyed. Embarrassed. Hopeful. Anxious.

"But…" One of the other brothers took a step forward. "You didn't say anything about bringing a *bloke*."

"I didn't say anything about bringing a girlfriend either. What does it matter?"

Hmm… Not a straightforward case of "meet my new lover", then.

"Well, it doesn't, Dags." The final brother stepped even closer and said, "Except…"

"Except what?" Maggie snapped back. "Except you've forgotten your manners and how to say, *G'day, nice to meet you, Raphael. Can I offer you a cold drink after your long journey?*"

"We've got plans tonight."

"So? We include him in them. What's the big deal?" Maggie glanced across at Raphael and gave him a *See? I told you they were a pain* look.

"Who are you, anyway?" asked the younger brother, lifting his chin as he gave Raphael a sidelong glare then moved his eyes to his sister. "We thought you were bringing one of your girlie friends from the big city to show her how real Australians get on."

Raphael was certain he saw the man's biceps twitch in anticipation.

"Raphael is…" She drew out the word, obviously struggling to find the best way to describe him.

There were a number of options she could choose from.

Colleague?

Friend with benefits?

Love of her life who couldn't make any promises?

"Raphael. Dr. Raphael Bouchon. He's testing the waters over here in Oz for a bit. We're on an ambo together. He was sort of my host-brother-type-of-thing when I lived in France." She shot him another apologetic smile.

Or that.

Her description stung. But what else was she meant to say?

He hadn't even told her whether he was staying in Australia.

He didn't know himself.

The part of him that knew he loved Maggie wanted to.

The other part—the part that couldn't keep at bay the memories of the day Jean-Luc had told him to leave his family's home, that all he did was take—that part still wasn't at peace with his past.

"Well, then, welcome, Frenchie." One of her brothers kept his gaze solidly on Raphael as he spoke. "So, Dags…what sort of sleeping arrangements are you after for your friend?"

All eyes turned to Raphael.

Though the sun had long passed over the yardarm, it still burnt down on them with a fierceness completely unlike the summer heat in Sydney. Or perhaps it was the family's heated glares that had Raphael pulling himself up to his full height.

With their Wild West demeanor, he would not have been the tiniest bit surprised to see each of the Louis men shift aside their jackets—if they'd been wearing them—to reveal sheriff's badges and holstered pistols in preparation for running him out of town if he so much as suggested he would very much approve of sharing a bed with Maggie.

It looked as if he was back to being a teenager. Looked as if he was back to being judged.

"For heaven's sake, Ed." Maggie punched one brother in the arm. "Could you not call me that anymore?"

The tension lessened as Ed relaxed his pistols-at-dawn pose and looked at the rest of his family and Raphael in disbelief. "What's this I hear? My kid sister doesn't like being the Dagster anymore? What's wrong with being our little Digga-dagga-doo?"

He cooed and gave her a little tickle under the chin, all the while calling her Dags. Whatever that was.

"I know this might sound completely mental to you lot…" Maggie crossed her arms defensively over her chest, a smile twitching at the corner of her lips "…but now that I'm a big girl, I think I might actually like to be called by my *real* name in front of our guest." She ground out the last part of her sentence and flicked her eyes in Raphael's direction.

"Oh, I doooo beg your pahhhdon." Ed put on a faux, hoity-toity English accent and bowed. "Did you bring *royalty* from the big city, Princess Margaret?"

Ed received another punch from his sister without so much as a blink.

Through gritted teeth Maggie turned and grimaced. "Raphael, I have the very obvious *dis*pleasure of introducing you to my feral family. Boys, this is Raphael. He was my best friend when I was in Paris and is a proper badass on the ambo. Not to mention a surgeon who is completely capable of removing all of your internal organs. Come along, then. Line up."

She clapped her hands together and in a well-practiced maneuver they lined up alongside her.

"This is my father, Joseph."

"Any friend of Maggie's is welcome here, mate." Her father reached forward to give Raphael a bone-crushing handshake before giving him a quick wink. "And Daddo or Joe'll do just fine."

"This is Edward," Maggie continued, pretending not to listen to the correction.

"Eddie, Ed or Big Fella work for me."

Raphael braced himself for another über-macho hand-shake, only to receive an abbreviated military salute instead, followed by a display of dark-stained hands the size of pie pans.

"Sorry, mate. My mitts are covered in grease. Wouldn't want to get your city slicker clothes all mucky straight off the bat, would we?"

Maggie gave an exasperated sigh and quickly introduced her other two brothers—Nate and Billy—both of whom seemed to be quite happy to be called Nate and Billy and to shake hands with Raphael in a straightforward, if slightly suspicious fashion.

"You made good time from—where was it you stayed last night?" asked Billy.

Maggie flushed bright red and muttered something about the roadhouse and the accident scene.

Billy nodded, clocking his sister's pinkening cheeks, then cocked his head to the side and crossed his arms over his gym-toned chest. He looked as if he was deciding whether or not to give Raphael a black eye.

Raphael pressed his heels into the ground. He'd take a shiner for Maggie. It was the least he could do, considering he had no answers to give her about a future together.

"Be honest with me, mate," Billy began, "did Daggie tell you we were a bunch of half-witted losers or did we get better billing?"

Raphael looked to Maggie, hoping for some sort of cue on how to respond to the question. Another eye-roll answered his raised brows.

"What is a Daggie?" he asked instead.

Her brothers fell about laughing so hard they were near enough swiping tears from their eyes.

"Please." Maggie drew in a deep breath and shook

her head. "Do not pay attention to the cave people in my life. A 'dag', if you must know, is an Aussie term for a person who is a bit…" Her green eyes flicked up to the sky as she sought the right definition. "Someone who is a bit like we were in high school."

"She's trying to say an A-Grade nerd," Nate jumped in, giving his sister another friendly knuckleduster.

"Aw, mate! So you were a *nerd*?" Billy's friendliness shot up a notch. "Got it. One of the book squad. Makes sense."

Maggie flushed a bit. "No, boys. *I* was a nerd. But Raphael…he was…" For an infinitesimal moment their eyes caught and then her brothers started gabbling away again.

What had she been about to say? The flush on her cheeks suggested she was glad she hadn't said it. The cinch in his heart wished she had.

"Who's this little creature, eh?" Ed knelt down and called Monster to him.

Raphael unclipped the lead, surprised to see Monster run to Ed, tail wagging, virtually jumping up and down with anticipation of getting scratched behind the ears.

"His name's Monster. He's looking for a home."

Ed sent him a sharp look. "What? This little guy's not yours? What'd you do? Kidnap him?"

"He adopted Raphael back in Sydney," Maggie jumped in giving Raphael a curious look.

Monster lay on his back and wiggled his paws in the air, easily wooing Ed into giving his furry belly a good old scrub.

The dog was obviously drawn to him. And Raphael couldn't blame him. By all appearances Ed was a settled, happy, solid guy. A man content with life and his place in it.

The type of man *he* needed to be before he took the next step in loving Maggie. And he wanted to take that step. But with one foot still firmly cemented in the past he didn't know how.

"It looks like Monster's affections have changed..." Raphael lifted up his hands, as if to add, *He's yours if you want him,* but instantly he felt the loss of his little four-legged companion.

Now it was Maggie's turn to shoot daggers at him. He swallowed.

What was he *doing*? Giving away Monster was akin to saying *au revoir* to Maggie in the crudest way possible. Bidding her farewell by proxy.

"Hey, Mags..." Nate sidled over to his sister's side and gave her a poke in the ribs. "I don't know if Frenchie is going to like our plans for dinner."

"Why?" Maggie shot an alarmed look between her brothers, then leveled her gaze at her father. "Dad...what have you let these larrikins dream up? Wait a minute!" She held up her hands, her jaw dropping. "You're not actually telling me you've made dinner all by yourselves."

They all laughed uproariously.

Raphael guessed that was a "no" on the homemade supper, then.

Maggie's father smiled mischievously and stroked his stubbled chin. "I think I'd better let your brothers explain about your birthday pressie."

"Birthday?" Raphael sent her a questioning look. "You didn't say it was your birthday."

Ed, or maybe it was Billy, slung a congenial arm across his shoulder. "She's a sly one, our Dags. Doesn't say half of what goes on in that big ol' brain of hers. That's why we thought she deserved a bit of TLC from her big brothers."

"What? TLC in the form of letting me clean your house, do your laundry and make my own cake?" Maggie's hands flew to her hips and an indignant expression that ought to have elicited steam from her ears hit her face. "Yeah. You guys *really* know how to treat a girl."

Nate guffawed. "Laundry's all done, Mags. All you have to do is get yourself scrubbed up for a night on the town. And…" he flicked a thumb at Raphael "…your mate here can tag along if he wants, but I don't know if it'll really float his *bateau*."

Raphael smiled. Not as much of a country bumpkin as he let on, then. He'd have to be careful. He'd have to win her brothers over. Without their approval he didn't stand a chance.

Maggie eyed the lot of them skeptically. The lot of her family, that was. Her eyes failed to connect with Raphael's.

If he'd known it was her birthday…

He would've what? Bought her a diamond ring and asked her to marry him?

"What have you boys planned?" Maggie's eyes crackled with impatience.

Some of that ire had to have been fuelled by him. Surprise parties were usually met with a smile.

"It's a secret," Billy said, tapping the side of his nose and then giving his sister a scan. "Got anything a bit more girlie than what you're wearing right now?"

Maggie's lids lowered as she evil-eyed her brothers, who collectively started kicking at the dirt and looking at the sky as if they weren't hearing a word of the conversation.

"Again, I ask you. *What* have you planned?"

"Perhaps you should head on down to the hotel and get changed. For tonight."

"Hotel? What happened to my room?"

"Aw, yeah…about that."

"Yeah, *that*."

Maggie's heart was thumping so hard in her chest she wouldn't have been surprised if it had started ricocheting around under her blouse. What on earth was going on? This morning Raphael had been the picture of an adoring…what? Boyfriend? Lover? And now that he'd met her family he was giving them his dog and looking as if he'd rather be anywhere but here.

Terrific.

Just as she'd predicted. Who would want to take on a family as mad as hers?

No one. That was who.

And, to make matters worse, she didn't even have her childhood bed to throw herself on and sob away her loss.

"It's been a while since you've lived here, Mags…" Nate scrubbed his hands through his short strawberry-blond hair. "We reckoned you weren't coming back so we sort of made it into a storeroom."

A level of hurt she hadn't expected to feel filled her gut.

"A storeroom?"

"Yeah. You know—extra parts for cars and suchlike. Billy put in some shelves. It looks good." There was a note of apology in his voice, but not enough to say, *Welcome home, sis.*

Maggie knew she didn't have the right to protest. She'd been gone a long time. Years. And had given no indication that she would ever be moving back.

"Don't pull a face like that, Mags. As I said, there's no need to throw your swag blanket under the stars or anything. We got you a room at the hotel."

Ed picked up the "no worries" mantle and gave a carefree shrug. "Ralph can stay here."

"Raphael," she ground out. "It's Raphael." Her eyes widened. "Wait. Why would he stay here?"

"Well, there was only one room left at the hotel." Her brother gave her a no-brainer face. "And that's yours."

"Yeah, well, I—"

I'd rather stay with Raphael?

She shot him a *Help me out, here,* look, not a little worried about his response. Or lack of one. Was he going to stand up for her, as he had with the knickers and the policeman at the crash site? Throw an arm around her shoulder with a she's-with-me attitude emanating from his every pore?

A hit of regret that she hadn't put on her Super Girl knickers that morning jagged through her. This morning she'd felt so *sure*! So certain of herself. Of Raphael.

Before she had a moment to process the expression developing on Raphael's face Billy was elbowing past Ed while pulling something out of his back pocket.

He presented her with a pink envelope with tiny little strawberries laced around the edges. All of the breath left Maggie's lungs in an instant. When she saw her name written in her mother's delicate script tears blurred her vision.

"Here, Mags. We found this when we cleaned out your room."

"What is it?"

He shrugged and stared at it, as if seeing it for the first time. "Well, I dunno, do I? It's addressed to you.

We found it behind your headboard." His voice turned a bit gruff as he continued, "Mum must've put it under your pillow, or something, before she—you know. She must've left it for you."

He held the envelope out and shook it in a gesture for her to take it. With trembling fingers she reached out, took the envelope in her hand and pressed it to her heart.

"Right." Billy clapped his hands together and shook the obvious swell of memories from his expression. "Since no one seems particularly keen on changing into their fancy duds, whaddya think about heading into town and getting this show on the road?"

CHAPTER TEN

AFTER AGREEING TO leave Monster at the family home while they headed into town, Raphael and Maggie climbed into the car. As he clicked the door shut Raphael felt the confines of the vehicle make Maggie's mood significantly more pronounced.

Whether it was the unopened letter, his insensitive behavior, her brothers or all three was difficult to divine. The least he could do was start setting the record straight in *his* corner. He did love her. He did want her. But he needed to put some things right in his own house before he could offer her full access to his heart.

The wheels screeched as she turned a corner.

"Thank you for inviting me here. It's wonderful to see where you grew up and meet your family."

"Well, it's not over yet," Maggie grumbled, her eyes flicking to her rearview mirror to see where her brothers were following in a Louis men convoy.

"Your family seem to love you very much," he tried.

"If treating me like a twelve-year-old virgin is the definition of *love* then—" She stopped herself. "Well, yeah, they do love me, but…" Her tone suggested familial love wasn't the problem.

If only she knew what it felt like to have the people

you loved most—the people you saw as family—withdraw their affections, she would understand what he
was going through. But until he had it completely figured out he didn't want to muddle things more than he
already had, so he lumbered ahead, trying to make a
light joke of things.

"You don't like surprises?"

The look on her face indicated that he shouldn't be
looking to start a career in stand-up comedy anytime
soon.

"Not when I've just opened my heart to someone
and they go and offer to give their bloody dog away because they don't even know if they're sticking around,
I don't," she snapped.

"I shouldn't have done that. With Monster…" he admitted. "And nothing's set in stone."

"So." She clapped a hand against the center com-
ponent of the steering wheel. "What exactly does this
mean? Will you be coming back to Sydney with me or
will you be flying back to Paris straight out of Broken
Hill?"

"You can *do* that?"

The second the words left his mouth he knew it was
the worst thing he could have said. And the one thing
he needed to do.

The ominous mood around Maggie grew and multiplied until it all but developed into a force field around
her.

"Maggie, please."

"Maggie, please…what?"

Maggie's emotion was barely contained. Her eyes
were glassed with obvious frustration as her foot be-

came a bit heavier on the pedal. Not exactly the ideal mood for driving.

"Please pull over the car. Let's talk about this."

"We're here anyway," she snapped, abruptly yanking the car into a space in front of one of the traditional hotels that dominated the main street.

"Maggie—" Raphael reached out to touch her arm and she pulled it away.

"Don't." She turned in her seat to face him. "Don't do that if all you want to do is to leave. I've missed enough in my life because of you!"

She covered her mouth and gasped, tears immediately cascading down her cheeks.

"I'm sorry," she sobbed. "I shouldn't have said that. It wasn't your fault. That was a horrible thing to say. It wasn't your fault at all."

"*What* wasn't?"

The over-familiar sensation of dread—of guilt—began creeping into his bloodstream.

"Missing my mum. Not seeing her before she died."

A buzzing began in his ears as he struggled to make the connections. Maggie had never told him the whole story. Though she rarely alluded to it, he knew her mother was no longer alive, but he hadn't pressed, well aware that his own ghosts were hard enough to contain without forcing someone else to release theirs.

He pulled a fresh handkerchief from his pocket and handed it to her. It was one of the few lessons he'd learned from his own mother before she'd succumbed to the temptations of drink—*"Il ne faut rien laisser au hazard,"* she would say, pressing a single, freshly ironed square of cloth into his hand each morning.

Leave nothing to chance.

It had been their one moment of true connection each day. The last thing she'd said to him before she'd passed away. And Maggie had missed that own moment with her mother.

Leave nothing to chance.

The words lodged in his heart.

They spoke of action. Risk.

Was opening his heart to more rejection a risk he was prepared to take?

Maggie steadied her breath and began to speak. "We'd planned... Well... I'd been dreaming of a trip to France ever since I read *Beauty and the Beast* when I was little."

She went on to detail how she and her mother had planned the trip in meticulous detail. How her mother had been secretly scrimping and saving ever since they'd first read the fairy tale and Maggie had become transfixed. A dreamy-eyed country girl going to the most magical place in the world...

"Going to Paris was a dream come true."

"And your mother? What happened while you were away?"

Maggie swiped a few more tears away and sniffed, unable to meet his eyes. "I didn't know it, but she had lung cancer."

Conflicting emotions threatened to split him in two.

Half of him ached to reach out and touch her, hold her in his arms and tell her how sorry he was for her loss. The other half respected the determined look on Maggie's face, her need to tell the story once and never again. He nodded for her to continue. He'd hear her out and then he'd leave. He'd face his own demons head-on, as she was doing here in Broken Hill.

"She was pretty far along when I left, but we all

thought it was something else. Something curable. She told us her cough was asthma-related." Anguish filled her voice as she continued, "We didn't *know*! *I* didn't know. My brothers eventually made her tell them the truth, and she started to get treatment while I was away, but she swore them to secrecy."

A sob escaped her throat.

"She told them they weren't to do or say anything that would interrupt my year. I finally figured it out the day I was flying home."

"How?"

"She hadn't come to the phone in over a fortnight. She'd sent emails and little notes, but her handwriting had changed. Had become weak and scratchy. When she wouldn't come to the phone to wish me a good flight I finally demanded that my brothers tell me. I wasn't getting on that plane until I knew what was going on. They said she'd just been admitted to the local hospice."

Her green eyes shone with streams of tears but her voice sounded dull when she finally spoke.

"I presume I don't need to spell out why she was there."

He shook his head, no, grateful that her mother had been given appropriate palliative care. He was astonished at the strength of a mother's love.

"That plane couldn't move fast enough," Maggie said. "It was the longest journey of my life."

"And when you arrived?" He already knew the answer, but he had to hear it from her.

"She passed away three hours before I got here." Maggie stared at him, strangely dry-eyed, as if something inside her had died all over again. "My brothers and my father had been with her the whole time. I was the only

one who wasn't there for the one person who had sacri-
ficed so much for me to reach my dreams."

A sharp series of knocks sounded on the side of the
car.

"Dags! Let's get a move on. Time to celebrate, birthday girl!"

Maggie swooshed her sleeve across her eyes and
rolled down her window with a huff. "Quit rushing me,
you big drongo."

She gave her hair a bit of a princess shake and shooed
her brother away with her fingers. A little-sister-in-
charge-of-her-big-brother move that would have made
him laugh if Raphael hadn't known she was hurting so
much inside.

"It's my birthday, I'll come in when I'm ready."

"You all right, Maggie?"

Raphael clocked Eddie's use of his sister's real name.
Genuine concern. Family love.

"Yeah. Fine. Just…you know…getting myself prepared to enter the hotel after who knows how long. I'll
be there in a minute."

"Raph? Are you not coming in to celebrate Maggie's
big three-oh?"

This one was up to Maggie. He wasn't going to pro-
long the torture if she didn't want him there.

"I don't know." She looked across at him, with nothing but questions and defiance written across her features. "*Are* you coming in?"

This wasn't a win-win situation. It was lose all the
way. But leaving was the coward's option and he didn't
want to be *that* guy anymore. The one who walked away
when the going got tough.

Don't leave anything to chance.

This time he'd see it through.

"Of course, Maggie."

She held out the handkerchief towards him, then pulled it back. "I'll wash it first."

"Keep it." He gave her hand a squeeze, doing his best to ignore the flinch that followed in its wake. "I want you to have it."

"Terrific." She gave the handkerchief a wry smile, and as her brother opened the car door for her she muttered, "Something to remind me of the best and worst birthday I've ever had."

"Why are we going in the back way? Where's Dad? You haven't put him in your slingshot to get him here, have you?"

Maggie knew she was being irritable because things were being yanked out of her control again now that she was back home.

Little sister mode.

Doing what she was told.

Correction.

Doing what was expected of her.

Which was following in her nutty big brothers' wake and then, most likely, cleaning up the inevitable mess.

Despite her determination to stay grouchy, her heart softened as she followed her brothers into the hotel. There were the usual shout-outs to the lads, all of whom played locally for an Aussie Rules footie team. Of course. The "When in the blue blazes are you going to get my car fixed?" questions were followed by a friendly laugh and a promise to buy them a drink if they went to the bar.

And there were a few other comments Maggie didn't quite understand.

"When do you want us to have the bits and pieces in place?"

"Are you sure you got the right music?"

And, the most disconcerting of all, "I've told the wife to bring her camera. This is going to be legendary."

That one she *couldn't* let go.

She skipped-ran to catch up to Nate, aiming for casual but landing on high-pitched panic. "Nate, my dear big brother, if this is some strange thing like being hit by thirty cream pies in front of the whole of Broken Hill, I am *out*."

Raphael caught up with them, but met no one's eye. He had reverted straight back to being the brooding, mysteriously enigmatic man who had met her at the Sydney Botanical Gardens all those weeks ago. The one she wasn't entirely sure she knew anymore.

Well, now she knew a lot more than she'd bargained for.

Yes, he was an incredible doctor. And he had suffered a deep loss. It seemed to have made a permanent mark on him—one that wouldn't allow full access to his heart. Unless he was able to forgive himself...

She tried to swallow the frustration building in her throat.

Why hadn't she been enough?

This was buyer's remorse at its cruelest.

He might have made sweet, intimate love to her. He might have whispered his innermost feelings. But there hadn't been any promises. Only some ridiculously unsubtle back-pedaling the second he'd got an eyeful of the real Maggie Louis.

Just what a girl needed on her thirtieth. Not that she'd forewarned him of that. Becoming an official spinster was traumatizing enough. She'd thought she'd cracked it on the eve of her birthday… Cinderella Syndrome, indeed. Only this time the handsome Prince had figured out that Cinders wasn't really all that and was going to hightail it back to his castle. Sooner rather than later if the expression on his face was anything to go by.

"All right, Mags." Billy turned around when they reached one of the lounges that were usually used for private parties. "Can you just wait here with Raphael for a minute?"

She nodded.

Billy threw a couple of looks between the pair of them, then leaned in and whispered, "He's not the jealous type, right? You're just mates?"

Less than twelve hours ago she knew her smile would have been from ear to ear. She would have told her brother that she was off the market, that her heart was Raphael's and his was hers.

What a difference a road trip could make.

She nodded her head and reluctantly whispered back, "Just mates."

"Good. Hey, mate…" He dug into his pocket, pulled out a couple of notes and handed them to Raphael. "You wouldn't mind going to the bar and getting a round, would you?"

Raphael said of course he wouldn't mind, but refused the money saying this one was on him. He was polite and sophisticated and perfect. He asked them all what they wanted, told Maggie he'd find her something with bubbles in it, then disappeared around the corner.

Would he even bother coming back?

Eddie rejoined them and gave his brother a discreet nod. Not so subtle that she didn't catch it. And, even though she felt her guts launch into Kid Sister Attack Mode, there was a comforting familiarity about it. They all knew their roles. They all played their parts. It was an upside to coming home that she hadn't really considered before. Even if it *did* most likely mean she'd be back in her pinafore and acting the spinster sister and house-keeper until she was an old, shriveled, apple-faced lady. Wrinkled. Hunch-backed, no doubt. Miserable. Alone.

"Cheer up, Dags. It's your party!"

Eddie tried to tickle her and she batted at his hands, reluctantly succumbing to the giggles until he stopped.

"What are you boys cooking up? You haven't got Dad jumping out of a birthday cake or anything, have you?"

Nate shook his head and laughed. "Nah. But I wish we had thought of that." He crossed his arms, swayed back on his heels and gave her a cheeky grin. "I think you're going to like what we've got planned for you. It's one of our best ideas *ever.*"

She gave him a wary look. "You mean like slingshot-ting our father across a vacant lot? Yes. What a terrific idea *that* was. Making us orphans on my birthday."

"Easy, there, little bear cub." Nate gave her shoulder a gentle rub. "Your brothers are looking out for you as you launch into womanhood."

"What, precisely, do you think I have been in these last ten years?"

They laughed. "Mags! Your twenties are just a warm-up for the big stuff. Trust us."

"Not ruddy likely," she grumbled, but they told her to stay put, wait for her drink and they'd come and get her in a few minutes.

She peeked round the corner and saw Raphael, waiting politely for his turn at the bar. Looking completely gorgeous. Of course.

She dug around in her handbag for some lip gloss. Might as well at least remind him of what he was missing.

Her fingers made contact with some paper.

The envelope.

Her heart cinched tight.

Sinking into a nearby chair, she decided to take advantage of the few minutes she had alone and read the note her mother had written to her all those years ago.

The back of her throat grew scratchy at the sight of the handwriting. When she lifted the letter to her nose to smell it hot tears fell in splatters on her skirt.

Forcing herself to take a deep breath and focus, she opened the letter and read.

My darling Maggie-moo,
By the time you get this letter I will have been unable to say goodbye in person. Don't let a single solitary second pass with you thinking I didn't love you with every cell in my body. You are my beautiful green-eyed, red-haired dream come true, and it was my mission in life to help you reach your goals. Or at least give you a nudge in the right direction.

Dry your eyes, love. I know it was a selfish decision not to tell you, but as well as being a dreamer you're also a realist. If you'd known... Well, it was time for your brothers to help out around the house a bit, and for you to go out there and see the world. A bit of it, at least. The bit that I hoped would inspire you the most.

Your letters were like a window to Paris. Through you I was able to go to the Louvre. Have ice-cream by the Seine. Climb the Eiffel Tower. Especially the Eiffel Tower! I felt as if I was right there beside you. The icing on my cake.

Your father once even made us crêpes based on the recipe you sent. They were awful. But he tried. And that's what I am going to ask you to do.

Please try and let those moments—the "icing" moments—be your lasting memories of our time together. An adventure. And never let anything stand in the way of following your beautiful heart. Wherever it wants to take you, near or far, your family will always be with you, no matter how many kilometers lie between you.

I love you so very much, my little Maggie-moo.

Always think of me as being with you, in your heart, for you will always live in mine.

Don't let your brothers boss you around too much. They're protective. They love you, even if they lack the ability to buy socks. Keeping you near to them is the only way they know how to keep you safe. But I know you're strong. You'll do just fine on your own.

Bisous, *my darling.*
Love, Mum

Maggie's hands dropped to her lap and she looked up to the ceiling, physically opening herself up to the waves of emotion hitting her.

Bittersweet relief at having the letter, seeing her mother's writing again, being able to cherish her scent.

This letter was the link—the farewell she'd never had.

Most of all she felt love—unconditional love—for her brothers. Sure, they lacked finesse, but they tried. Their campaign to get her to move home had never abated. Not once…until now.

That thought unleashed sorrow. All the frustration and sadness that had gone with the initial loss. Dreams unfulfilled, ambitions unrealized. Had she lost or gained more in the years following her mother's death?

It was something she'd never know.

She looked up, sensing someone approaching.

"Maggie, are you all right?"

Raphael quickly slid the tray of drinks onto a nearby table, tugged a small pile of serviettes from the tray and sat beside her, his hand halfway to wiping away her tears when she stopped him.

He was an unrealized dream. She needed to take this letter as a sign that it was time to move on. Some dreams came true—some didn't.

Her brothers appeared at the end of the corridor, bursting with excitement.

She grabbed the serviettes and scrubbed them across her face, almost relishing the scratchy pain that accompanied them. It was a marked contrast to Raphael's soft handkerchief and the love she had thought she had felt.

Well, she wouldn't rely on him anymore. Or on his love. It was her birthday, and she was going to ruddy well enjoy herself. She had her brothers here. *Family*— who, despite everything, had been there for her all along.

"C'mon." She spoke in a low voice so her approaching brothers couldn't hear. "They've gone to a lot of effort. We should at least try to look happy."

* * *

Against his better judgment, Raphael picked up the tray of drinks and pasted on what he hoped passed as a smile.

When Maggie's brothers led them down the corridor and flung open the double doors of a private lounge any hint of happiness dropped from his lips.

In front of him was a huge banner.

Broken Hill Bachelors Got Talent! Who Will Win Our Maggie's Heart?

Her brothers kept looking at the banner, at the pre-lit stage area, and back to Maggie for signs of delight.

She laughed. Punched them in the arm. Then threw Raphael a look that said, *It could've been you*, grabbed her glass of Aussie fizz from his tray and followed her brothers to the throne-like chair they had set up in front of the stage.

What followed was the most painful hour of Raphael's life.

And not just because of the ample talents of the men of Broken Hill.

The Maggie who had opened herself up to him less than twenty-four hours earlier had all but disappeared.

Whether she was the real one or the one protecting herself from the world's most idiotic Frenchman was tough to tell at this point. He'd lost his perspective.

The one thing he *was* certain of, he decided, between a live chainsaw juggling act and a fairly impressive bit of "condiment art", inspiration courtesy of legendary local artist Pro Hart, was that until he went home and made peace with his own "family" he would never settle. Never be able to offer Maggie everything she so richly deserved.

"Mate!" Nate appeared beside him, tickled pink with the evening's showcase. "Isn't this brilliant? I don't think I've ever seen Maggie have more fun."

Together they looked across at her. She was accepting a vividly decorated rain stick from a suitor who had just performed a rain dance in the hopes of "growing a life together" with Maggie.

She looked completely delighted. If not a little unconvinced.

"We should've asked you, but as Mags said you were just mates we didn't bother. Do you want to go up and do a jig or something? You're looking a little bit as if the green-eyed monster has come to life inside of you." Nate's voice was genuinely concerned and then his eyes widened. "Wait a minute. You're not in *love* with her or anything, are you?"

Raphael just stared at him. Was he that transparent? Luckily Nate wasn't waiting for an answer.

"It's unrequited love, isn't it? Poor bloke. You flew all the way Down Under to get our Mags, only to have her turn you down?"

Again he didn't wait for a response, just blew out a low, *Sorry, pal* whistle and shook his head.

"Rough. She's a bit of a treasure, though. Worth fighting for. You *sure* you don't have a little tune or something you could sing *a capella*? Dad plays the accordion if you need a bit of back-up."

Maggie *was* worth fighting for. But a song wouldn't cover what he needed to do to win her heart.

At the very least, he knew she would be surrounded

by people who loved her if he didn't get the answers he was hoping for in Paris.

"I think Maggie looks very happy here."

Nate looked across at his sister. Her green eyes were glistening, her hair lit by the bright stage lights as yet another suitor pulled her up onto the stage only to perform a traditional Maypole jig around her—Maggie as the Maypole.

He did want her.

He didn't yet deserve her.

But he was going to do everything in his power to do just that.

There was only one way to be worthy of the love she so openly gave him.

Go back to Paris and prove he was the man she had once believed him to be.

Though she was doing her best to look entertained by the dance, Maggie's eyes kept darting towards the dark-haired, blue-eyed man who, despite everything, still drew her like a magnet.

Halfway through the courtship dance that felt more like an endurance contest she saw Raphael whisper something to her brother, then get up and leave.

Her mouth went dry as tingles of fear whispered across her skin.

History was repeating itself.

Why did the people she loved most in life refuse to say goodbye to her face to face?

The thought didn't settle properly.

Her mother had done her best. The letter had been there. It had just... Maybe it had been waiting for the perfect time to surface—to serve as a reminder of the girl she had once been. The woman she had hoped to become.

Raphael stopped at the doorway and turned to look back at her. Every cell in her body ached to run after him, to demand an explanation, to ask why her love wasn't enough. Why *she* wasn't enough.

Steadfastly, she held her ground. She had her mother's faith living in her heart again. She had the knowledge that at least one person in her life had believed she was strong enough to make a go of things alone, to pursue her dreams—at least some of them—until she achieved them.

Medical school wasn't out of the question.

Nor was international travel.

It simply wouldn't be with Raphael.

Defiance and strength replaced fear. She didn't need anyone by her side to confront the future. She just needed to believe in herself.

She was thirty, single, and ready to dream again.

She forced a smile back to her lips as Darren O'Toole and his steel-toed work boots continued circling around her in a proud display of peacocking. Pounding. Thumping. Clomping round her like an elephant aspiring to be a ballerina. Okay, perhaps her future wouldn't be linked to Darren O'Toole. But there'd be someone out there.

One day.

She looked toward the back of the room. Her eyes connected with Raphael's like an electric shock. There was fire in his gaze. But it was impossible to tell if the flames burnt for *her.*

When he turned and walked away she knew she had her answer.

She'd be facing the future on her own.

CHAPTER ELEVEN

RAPHAEL HAD STOOD in front of this door so many times and never once hesitated. Not like this.

He blew on his hands, chiding himself for not remembering how cold it would be in Paris. Chiding himself for even caring. There was so much more at stake than chafed skin if he didn't take this chance.

A family.

A future.

A heart that would never break again.

He gave the door a sound knock.

When it opened he was face to face with Jean-Luc.

His friend's eyes widened with disbelief as he took a half-step back…then opened his arms and pulled Raphael into a tight embrace…

An hour later, Raphael's only regret was not having come sooner.

Jean-Luc had apologized for flinging blame in Raphael's direction. He'd been angry with the world. Now he knew, no matter how painful, that his daughter's death had been simply an awful truth he'd had to absorb and live with. Whether Raphael had stayed or left, the end result would very likely have been the same. He saw now that Raphael had been put into an impossible scenario and he no longer felt it necessary to blame anyone.

It had been no one's fault.

Just a cruel turn of events.

"I should have stayed." Raphael shook his head at his own folly. "Stayed with Amalie. Stayed with you. Given you a human punching bag. I just felt so responsible. When your parents said I had to give it time, give you some space—"

"They said that?" Jean-Luc cut in. "Give me some *space*?" He laughed drily. "You took that a bit literally, didn't you? Africa? Australia? You couldn't get much further than that."

"They aren't yet sending commercial passengers to the moon," Raphael riposted, grateful to be engaging once again in the banter that had once fuelled their friendship. "No free clinics to volunteer at in outer space. Yet."

Jean-Luc laughed again. "Well, perhaps they were right. Perhaps we both needed some space, eh, my friend?"

Raphael nodded. He knew now that living as he had been—in the eye of the storm—had been painful and scarring. Now that it had passed he thanked the heavens above for showing him how strong his friendship with Jean-Luc truly was.

"Hang on a minute," Jean-Luc said, slipping the pair of coffee cups off the table and setting them beside the sink. "Would you be able to stay for supper? There is some extra news you should know, but I would like Marianne to be here when I share it."

"*Bien sûr.* I would be delighted."

"Excellent." Jean-Luc crossed to him and gave him a

solid hug. "My parents would love to catch up as well. Shall I call them? Make it a proper family meal?"

Emotion caught at Raphael's throat.

A proper family meal.

There was only one person who would be missing—one person who would make the evening perfect.

Twenty-four hours earlier...

"Wait. You *what*?" Maggie stared at her brothers in disbelief.

"We banded together and bought you a ticket to Paris." Billy pressed it into her hand. "Go on. Get out of here."

"I don't understand."

Eddie fuzzed his lips. "C'mon, Dags. Anyone could see that the Broken Hill bachelor brigade didn't hold a single iota of interest for you. You only had eyes for one man in that room, and he was *not* a Broken Hill man."

Maggie laughed at her brother's affronted tone.

"You can't help who you love." Her shoulders hunched up round her ears and she sheepishly scanned them all.

"Love?" Her father gave a pointed look at the wall clock, distractedly scratching a curious Monster behind the ears. "If you don't begin to get a move-on you're going to miss the connecting flight. If I have to get the chief of police to put you in the back of a van to get you there on time, I will."

Tears sprang to her eyes for the millionth time that day. Well, they'd hardly been dry since she'd insisted on going back home with her brothers after Darren O'Toole had finally finished dancing.

She'd made a mistake. She'd let pride stand in the way

of her heart and that was the last lesson she was meant to have learnt from her mother's letter.

Her mother had told her to follow her heart. Not her cerebral hemispheres. Or her hurt feelings.

She loved Raphael, and when he'd got up to leave—

Her thoughts froze. Before he'd left he'd spoken to Nate.

She fixed her brother with her sternest gaze.

"What was it Raphael said to you before he left?"

Nate scuffed his work boots along the ground. "Aw, it was nothing, Dags. Just go get your plane, wouldja?"

"Nathaniel Louis! Your mother did *not* raise you to obfuscate."

"Margaret Louis," her brother countered solidly, "your mother raised you to follow your dreams, and it might have taken us a while to figure it out, but we're pretty bloody sure they're not here in Broken Hill."

He grabbed her keys from the kitchen counter and put them in her hand, then pointed to the carport.

"Now, go out there and get your man. Or become a surgeon. Or both. Otherwise the lot of us are going to have to gaffer tape you up, put you in the boot and get you on the plane ourselves."

Hands on hips, ready to give back as good as she'd got, she suddenly burst into laughter.

She had the *best* family.

She opened her arms wide and pulled them all into a group hug, in which *she* ended up getting squished. Amidst the sprawl of arms and chests and poorly shaved chins she finally managed to elbow enough room for herself to shout, "I love you lot!"

"We love you too, Margaret," her father said, opening a pathway for her to get to her car. "Now, go make

us proud and make some dreams come true. And if they
don't go the way you thought they would, we'll be right
here waiting for you. Monster included. With enough
laundry to keep you busy until you're ready to joust
again."

Keep on trying.

That should be her family's motto.

And today she was emblazoning that motto straight
onto her heart.

"Puis-je...?"

Maggie didn't even have to look up to recognize the
man asking if it was all right to sit on the patch of grass
next to her.

Her entire nervous system knew his voice.

Her memory banks were covered in images of the
two of them in this exact spot.

It was next to her favorite bench. Which was situated
at her favorite angle to tip her head back and...

She watched as his legs bent at the knee, then his
waist came into view, and his long fingers, pressing into
the grass alongside her.

"How did you know I was here?"

Maggie could barely look up, her heart was thumping so rapidly. When she did, the Raphael she'd seen
that night in the motel met her eyes. Blue irises, pure
as the uncharacteristically clear spring sky. Lips parted
in a half-smile that all but invited her to jump into his
arms and kiss him.

He pulled his phone from his pocket and shook it.
"Your brothers. I believe you just sent them a picture
message of yourself at the Eiffel Tower."

Maggie frowned. She had, but... "How did they

know—?" She stopped. "Is *that* what you told Nate. You gave him your phone number?"

"Non." He looked a bit confused himself before crossing his legs and sitting beside her on the ground. "I said if you hadn't heard from me in three days to hold another talent show. And another. Until you found someone who deserved you."

"Why would you have said that?" The note of defensiveness she'd hoped to keep from her voice leapt to the fore.

"Because I wasn't sure I would ever have anything to offer you."

"What? I don't want things. I want *you!*"

The words were out before she stood any chance of preserving her dignity. She stood up and gave the ground beneath her a stomp, reminding herself she hadn't flown halfway round the world to make idle chitchat.

Raphael stood up and met her gaze straight on.

"Good," he said, a glint of anticipation lighting up his eyes.

"Good?" she parroted.

"Oui. Good. But I have two questions before I tell you why."

Maggie tilted her chin to the side and gave him her best suspicious look. The one that said, *If you are messing with me I am turning around and flying back to Australia whilst ensuring every single person on that plane, and perhaps the whole of Australia, knows just how much of a jerk I think you are. Even if you're gorgeous. And I love you.*

"I love you," Raphael said.

"I just said that!"

"What? No, you didn't. You haven't said anything."

"I did. I said I loved you." She pointed to herself. "In my *head*. Which means we're connected. And that means you should stop running away from things, and stop jumping onto planes when people shout or yell. Or when you are forced to watch your girl be the guest of honor at incredibly ridiculous talent shows."

"Maggie." Raphael lifted a finger to her lips. "Will you just listen for a minute so I can explain? A bit of clog hopping is not going to keep me from loving you."

She tried her best not to give his finger a kiss. She was still supposed to be angry. Defiant, even. But she couldn't resist. Not when his touch unleashed a wash of glittery fireworks inside her that would have lit up the Eiffel Tower if it hadn't been broad daylight.

She kissed his finger. "See?" She grinned. "Proof I love you."

"And I wanted to get *you* proof."

"What? Why would you have to—?" She stopped herself. "You've been to see Jean-Luc?"

Raphael nodded. "And, if you would care to join me, you and I are invited to dine with them tonight."

Maggie's heart exploded with relief for him. "That's amazing, Raphael. I am so happy for you. *All* of you."

He nodded, his smile truly lighting up his face. "And, even better, his wife is pregnant. They are expecting twins!"

A wash of pure gold heat warmed her body. "That's incredible news. I'm so happy for them. For you."

"And perhaps for us?"

A tiny part of her wanted to play the coquette. To make him suffer just a tiny bit for all the nail-biting her poor fingers had endured during the long flight over. But he'd been through the wringer these past couple of years. And besides, if she'd learned anything at all in the past forty-eight hours it was that life was too short to dither. She'd flown here to get answers.

"What exactly are you saying?"

"I am saying, or rather I am asking, Margaret Louis, if you would accompany me to dinner with the Couttards as my fiancée. And then, perhaps another time, as my wife?"

"Perhaps?" she yelped. "Perhaps! You mean definitely."

Raphael's smile was unfettered. "Is that a yes?"

"You bet it is."

She could barely speak, she was so happy. And then the questions flooded in.

"Where are we going to live? Do you still want to work on the ambos? Do you hate Australia? Love it? How would you feel if I went to medical school?"

"Right now I have no idea. All I know is wherever I am, I want it to be with you." Raphael pulled her close to him and her hands naturally slipped up and around his neck. "Now, my beautiful Maggie, would you allow me the pleasure of kissing my fiancée?"

"I think that is a most excellent idea."

Maggie rose up on tiptoe and, with a fully open heart, accepted the very first kiss from her future husband.

EPILOGUE

"ARE YOU SURE it looks all right?" Maggie squinted at her reflection and shifted the white lab coat collar to the left.

"You look perfect, Dr. Bouchon. What time is the flight going to leave?"

Maggie glanced at her watch. "Probably in an hour." She laughed, her eyes connecting with Raphael's in the mirror. "I still can't get used to this."

"What? The flying doctor part or the Dr. Bouchon part?" Raphael slipped his hands round his wife's waist and dropped a kiss onto her neck.

"Either." Maggie turned and gave her husband a kiss. A hit of emotion clouded her eyes for a moment. "I wish my mum could see this. I wish she could know I've finally become a doctor."

Raphael smiled at his wife's reflection in the mirror. "She does. Because she's living—"

"In my heart," Maggie finished, knowing full well that it was true. "I wonder what she would think of our lives now."

"What? Living in Broken Hill and taking our winter holidays in France?"

"Yeah." Maggie giggled. "Part of me thinks she would tell us we're absolutely bonkers…"

She looked out of the window to where her brothers were building a super-sized swing set for their toddlers.

"The other part thinks she might've known this would happen."

"As long as you are happy, *mon amour*. That's all that matters."

She turned around in her husband's arms and embraced him tightly. "I have everything I have ever dreamed of here and now."

"Très bien." He dropped a kiss onto her cheek and took her hand in his. "Shall we make sure your brothers aren't planning to trebuchet our children over to the next-door neighbors?"

"How well you know them." She gave him a wink and, hand in hand, they headed out to be with the rest of their family.

* * * * *

MILLS & BOON

Coming soon

THE DOCTORS' BABY MIRACLE
Tina Beckett

"Tucker, are you okay?"

Kady's soft voice called him back from the depths. "I'm fine. Just didn't expect to have to hold her, that's all."

"I could tell." She linked her arm through his for a moment as they stood there on the curb, the noise of traffic and voices outside very different from the canned silence inside the hospital. "You were a good father to her. Don't ever forget that."

A sudden wash of emotion spurted from behind the wall, stabbing at the backs of his eyes and clogging his throat. Oh, hell. Not now.

He pulled his arm from hers, afraid if they stood there any longer, she would see.

"We did everything we could for her. So did her doctors." His cool businesslike tone had to be a slap in the face after what she'd just said. But it was all he could manage without the past pouring out in a very real way.

She gripped his arm again. "Hey, don't do that. Don't you *dare* do that."

"Do what?"

"Act like she was nothing more to you than one of your patients. She was our *daughter*, dammit."

"You think I don't know that? That I don't have to deal with what happened every single hour of every single day?" The dam broke and he turned, yanking her against him. "I remember the second she was born, the second she smiled. The second she . . ."

Then his lips were on hers, hand going to the back of her head and clutching her to him. Grief and want and need all melded together into a huge tangled ball that was impossible to unravel.

Kady seemed to understand exactly what he was feeling, arms wrapping around his neck, giving back every bit as good as she got.

And it *was* good—too good—the heat and pressure of her mouth changing the tone in an instant. He deepened the kiss, and a familiar stirring took place, reminding him that he could indeed do things. *Wanted* to do them.

With Kady and no one else.

Continue reading
THE DOCTORS' BABY MIRACLE
Tina Beckett

Available next month
www.millsandboon.co.uk

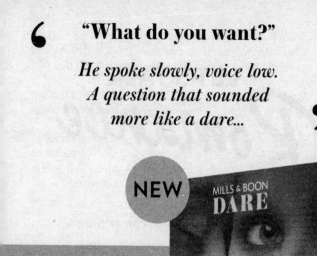

LET'S TALK
Romance

For exclusive extracts, competitions
and special offers, find us online: